D.
ADV.
(R.
**PULSE-POUNDING NOVELS OF
DEPARTMENT THIRTY**

The Black Jack Conspiracy

"A rollicking read. Page-turning action and riveting suspense
are David Kent's stock in trade."

—Ed McBain, *New York Times* bestselling author of *Fiddlers*

"Kent grounds his tale in a true historical event and provides
some nice twists and turns."

—*Publishers Weekly*

"Mysteries, twists, and turns galore. . . . . This is action adven-
ture with a real punch. . . . Fans of Tom Clancy, Larry Bond,
and even the *X-Files* will find *The Black Jack Conspiracy* a rare
novel. If you're looking for a book that reads like a summer
blockbuster, pick up *The Black Jack Conspiracy*. Good work,
Mr. Kent!"

—Roundtable Reviews.com

The Triangle Conspiracy is also available as an eBook

The Mesa Conspiracy

"After reading *The Mesa Conspiracy*, you will definitely need oxygen. It will leave you breathless. . . . You will cheer for the absolutely astounding and surprising ending. . . . If you only read one book this winter, *The Mesa Conspiracy* should be it!"

—Roundtable Reviews.com

Department Thirty
Also a bestselling eBook!

"*Department Thirty* has it all—nail-biting suspense, political intrigue, and a rich plot full of surprises—written in a smooth style that makes it almost impossible to put down. This modern-day *Manchurian Candidate* will leave its readers breathless and anxious for more. David Kent's first novel is a winner!"

—William Bernhardt

"A truly great read . . . hard to put down."

—*The Oklahoma Gazette*

"Nonstop action. . . . Kent continues to ratchet up suspense."

—*Sunday Oklahoman*

"A thrill-a-minute ride . . . a classic man-on-the-run thriller."

—*Mystery Scene*

DAVID KENT

THE TRIANGLE CONSPIRACY

POCKET STAR BOOKS

New York   London   Toronto   Sydney

An *Original* Publication of POCKET BOOKS

 A Pocket Star Book published by
POCKET BOOKS, a division of Simon & Schuster, Inc.
1230 Avenue of the Americas, New York, NY 10020

This book is a work of fiction. Names, characters, places and
incidents are products of the author's imagination or are used
fictitiously. Any resemblance to actual events or locales or persons,
living or dead, is entirely coincidental.

Copyright © 2006 by Kent Anderson

ISBN-13: 978-0-7434-9752-7
ISBN-10:   0-7434-9752-X

This Pocket Star Books paperback edition November 2006

10 9 8 7 6 5 4 3 2 1

POCKET STAR BOOKS and colophon are registered
trademarks of Simon & Schuster, Inc.

Cover design by Jae Song

Manufactured in the United States of America

For information regarding special discounts for bulk purchases,
please contact Simon & Schuster Special Sales at 1-800-456-6798
or business@simonandschuster.com.

ACKNOWLEDGMENTS

I would like to express my grateful appreciation to the following:

The usual suspects: Mike Miller, **Sami** Nepa, Dave Stanton, and Judy Tillinghast, for **insi**ghtful critique and unflagging moral support;

Police officer and fellow author **Ba**rry Ozeroff, for firearms advice;

Physicians and authors Jeff Anderson, MD, and Allen Wyler, MD, for the neurology consult;

The women who shared perspectives on their lives as escorts, and who understandably wished to remain anonymous;

Brooke H. and Charles N., my favorite friends of Bill W., for letting me pick their brains and allowing me to sit in on an AA meeting; and Art Christie, for additional information on the physiology and psychology of alcoholism;

All the friends and family members who were there for me during a difficult year, particularly Jeanette Atwood, Terry Clark, Brooke Harry, Barb Hendrickson, JoLynda Hennigh, Nancy Moore, Charles Newcomb, Ryan Pfeiffer, all my soccer kids, and everyone else who responded to my out-of-the-blue phone calls, e-mails, and visits;

My team in the publishing industry: beginning with my agent John Talbot; at Pocket Books, my outstanding editor Kevin Smith, publicist Melissa Gramstad, copyeditor Justine Valenti, and the rest of the Pocket crew. They are the best, bar none.

Mystery Writers of America and International Thriller Writers, for creating communities that allow writers to grow and thrive;

KCSC, NWCC, and the Oklahoma City Philharmonic, for transitions;

Booksellers, librarians, and book groups everywhere;

My parents, Bill and Audrey Anderson;

My sister, Teresa Anderson;

Eugene and Imogene Wood, who provided a second set of parents when I needed them;

My sons Sam, Will, and Ben, who make everything worthwhile.

David Kent
Oklahoma City, Oklahoma

THE TRIANGLE CONSPIRACY

PROLOGUE

WHEN LEE MORGAN FIRST SAW THE WOMAN HANG-
ing in the tree, he thought she was a drunk, or maybe a
homeless person who'd found a clever way to spend
the night.

As a security guard for the Oklahoma City National
Memorial, most of his job consisted of making sure
drunks didn't pee in the reflecting pool and the homeless didn't try to set up housekeeping among the 168
empty chairs. The memorial was open-air, and tourists
came at all hours of the day and night. Every now and
again Morgan would come across someone praying at
the fence at midnight, or staring at the lighted chairs at
three a.m., and would shake his head at how terrorism
had turned into tourism.

He'd just done the leg along the west side of the
memorial and was circling back to the Survivor Tree,
the big old elm that overlooked the site where the
Murrah Building had actually stood. It was about a
half-hour circuit if he did it at a deliberate pace without stopping, which he rarely did. He would occasionally stop to read the newspaper under the lights on the
Harvey Avenue side, and now and then he would sit
down on a bench and call his girlfriend. She was an
overnighter as well, an ER nurse at Mercy Hospital.

At first he actually laughed at the woman in the tree. These people were nothing if not creative. "Hey!" he called. "Hey up there! Time to wake up!"

He took a few more steps, his boots echoing on the flagstone walk that led to the tree. As he drew closer, the shape began to define itself more and more, even in the weak predawn light.

"Hello!" he called, then stopped as if he'd run into an invisible barrier.

The way the woman was situated . . . it wasn't natural. At first he'd thought she was sitting on one of the low branches and dangling her feet.

"Oh, shit," Morgan whispered.

The first thing was her shoe. One of her sandals had slipped off and fallen to the ground. Morgan's eyes trailed upward. She was wearing jeans and a light-colored polo-type shirt, except there was a dark splash of a stain beside her left breast.

Morgan stumbled backward.

The woman was young and attractive and had a rope around her neck, the other end of it securely wrapped several times around the thick tree branch.

Morgan tripped on the flagstones and tumbled over the low chain-link fence that lined the sidewalk. He fell into the dewy grass, breathing hard. Somewhere nearby, he heard a car.

Hands shaking, he fumbled his cell phone out of its harness on his belt, then stopped. Who did he call? He started to simply punch in 911, then remembered that the local cops wouldn't have jurisdiction here. *Federal,* he thought. *This is a federal reservation.* Who, then? The FBI? The National Park Service, for God's sake?

In the end, he called his supervisor at ITB Security. The boss would know what to do. After the call, Morgan got back to his feet, but he couldn't make himself go any closer to the tree.

Morgan said a silent prayer, something he hadn't done in years. Then he settled in to wait, his eyes still drawn to the pretty young woman who had been both shot and hanged.

It had all happened so fast.

That was Sean's only thought as he sat in the car in the early June predawn, in a McDonald's parking lot not far from the Oklahoma City National Memorial.

Everything had happened too fast, and now he didn't know what to do. His hands shook a little, and he rubbed them together. They felt dirty.

The light was beginning to glow off to his left, beyond the state capitol building. He hadn't grown up in this city, and didn't even live here—you couldn't call what he'd been doing here living—but he'd come to appreciate it for what it was: a medium-size prairie city with clean air and nice people. A good place to settle down. His sister thought so.

Settle down, he thought. *Not now. Not after today. Not anywhere.*

Sean swallowed. His throat felt raw, as if he'd swallowed shards of broken glass. His stomach lurched again. Once they knew who the dead woman in the tree was, it would be a short leap to him . . . to his cover, and then to his real identity. For a moment he wasn't even sure who he was supposed to be, or why.

God, I wish I had a drink.

His hands shook a little more, and he felt again how dirty they were. The McDonald's behind him was finally open, and he went inside. In the bathroom, he washed blood off his hand, scrubbing far too long, before buying a cup of coffee at the counter and going back outside.

No, no booze this morning. His sister would be proud of that. He allowed himself a bitter smile.

His sister.

She had influence, she knew things, she knew people. She could help him, if he would let her.

No.

No, she couldn't. No one could help him.

Sean put the gold Miata into gear, listening to the engine. He had to try to think, to stay one step ahead. It shouldn't be too hard, he told himself. Not long ago he'd been a man who figured things out, who linked facts together . . . who could *find people.* That's how he'd gotten into all this, after all.

He pulled out of the parking lot, back onto Twenty-third Street, then swung up the ramp to Interstate 235. His sister would be really pissed off at him now. She loved this car.

"Sorry, Faith," Sean said, and merged into the early morning traffic.

Part One:
Sean

1

WHEN THE AX FELL, SEAN KELLY WAS READY FOR it. He'd known it was coming ever since he woke up in his car yesterday, somewhere in far north Tucson, with a pounding headache and no idea how he got there.

He'd already cleaned most of his things out of his desk, in his cubicle of the United States Immigration and Customs Enforcement (ICE), Tucson field office. Once upon a time, it had been the plain old Customs Service, back in the days before the Department of Homeland Security, back when the mission had been a lot clearer. He'd put all his stuff in a trash bag and it was lumped at the edge of the cubicle.

Appropriate, he thought, *since my career has turned to garbage.*

People had been staring at him all day, mostly silent. One of the veteran agents, a big ex-military guy named Dunn, had leaned in, shaken his hand, and said, "Really fucked up big time, didn't you, Irish?" But most of the others just looked at him. He couldn't tell what the looks meant, but settled on a mixture of pity and contempt.

His phone rang at one minute after nine a.m., summoning him to the office of the special agent in charge of the Tucson office. Sean walked unsteadily to the corner office of Sonny Weller, who looked nothing like a "Sonny." Weller was another big guy. Sean was six three, and Weller had a good four inches and sixty pounds on him, none of it fat. His head was shaved bald, but he sported a wheat-colored walrus mustache. His real first name was something like Devon or Emerson or Winslow, but no one in the office dared call him that. No one screwed around with Sonny Weller.

"Sit," Weller said. Sean could tell he was barely keeping his voice under control.

Sean sat. Weller made no move to close the office door. So he wanted the whole office to know what was about to happen. He had Sean's file centered on the desk in front of him.

"Six months ago," Weller said, "you sat right there in that same chair and promised me this shit was through."

No niceties, Sean thought. It was just as well. It would be over more quickly that way. He nodded.

"You were going to get straightened out. You were going to be back on track, like you were when you first came to this office."

"Let's get it over with," Sean finally said.

Weller barked out something that might have been a laugh. "Over with? Oh, it's over with, all right." He opened the file so violently that papers flew around the desk and he had to bend over to retrieve them. "Starts simple, doesn't it, Irish? Eighteen months ago, falling asleep in a briefing. Helms was sitting next to you and said you smelled like you'd gone swimming in Jack Daniel's. A few weeks later, you missed the briefing altogether. We had to reschedule an operation just to bring you up to speed. Your paper went steadily downhill. You conveniently *forgot* to do your paper on the Meléndez operation, and he walked. The SOB had been smuggling tons of illegal assault rifles across the border for two years. We spent a year and a half building the case with ATF. And he fucking walked, Kelly! Because you 'forgot' to fill out the proper forms."

"Sorry," Sean mumbled.

"Yeah, well. January of this year. You decided to party hearty and go get shit-faced before the op at Naco. Remember that one? The sixty illegals in the back of the cattle truck? We missed them, because you weren't where you were supposed to be. You were so out of it you drove down the wrong road and were twenty fucking miles away!" His voice continued to rise.

"Sonny—"

"No, don't 'Sonny' me. I gave you more chances than you deserved. As for yesterday, you totally skipped the operation. Arivaca is the middle of a fucking war, Irish. It's the drug runners versus us versus the locals. Here we were, with this joint task force—us, the Bureau, DEA—doing what we're supposed to do, namely keeping this country's borders safe. DEA's been undercover with Ray Acosta in Arivaca for six months. We're ready for the raid, but see, our office's forward observer isn't there. You were supposed to be on the road to Acosta's place. You were to keep us aware of his movements. But no, you were drunk off your butt, in your car—nearly a hundred miles away!" Weller took the file folder and threw it across the desk at Sean.

"There's no need—" Sean began, picking up papers.

Weller crashed his fist down on the desk. Outside the open door, people were staring. "By not providing that support, you endangered the lives of other officers, Kelly. We're damn lucky no one got killed. Never mind that Acosta got across the border. And you know what? They're all screaming at me. Everyone from the local U.S. attorney all the way up the line to D.C. War on drugs, war on terror, interagency cooperation . . . all that shit. They want my head, and I'm handing them yours."

Weller leaned back and was silent a moment.

"How bad?" Sean finally asked.

"Administrative suspension without pay, pending a termination hearing," Weller said. "The hearing is in thirty days, but you're done. There's no way you won't be canned at this point." He leaned forward and dropped his voice. "And you know what's really shitty about all this? You're a smart kid, you have good instincts, and you're good at putting things together with only a little to go on. Most of the guys in this office aren't half as smart as you are." He leaned back again, chair squeaking. "We all like a drink now and then, Irish. Most of us have even been rip-roaring drunk a time or three in our lives. But by God, you put people's lives at stake. You put *other officers'* lives in jeopardy because of your . . . problem. You promised me you'd see the damn counselor, even go to AA."

"I did," Sean said.

"What, once?"

"Twice."

Weller nodded. "Right. Now get going. You'll get a certified letter with a notice of the personnel action and the hearing date. I can't support you anymore, not when you put lives at stake."

Sean nodded. He stood up and numbly offered his hand to Weller. Weller stared at the hand for a moment, then shook it.

"Your weapon and your creds," Weller said.

Sean nodded again. He didn't normally wear the gun around the office—in fact, he only carried it during actual operations—but he'd known what was coming, so he'd brought it with him this morning. He handed the SIG Sauer nine-millimeter, holstered, to Weller, then passed him the leather case with his Department of Homeland Security credentials.

Sean walked out of the office into silence. Halfway back to his cubicle, someone said, "Hey, Irish, want to hit happy hour?" He didn't recognize the voice and didn't care. He just felt tired.

Sean said nothing. He picked up the black trash bag with the stuff from his desk. He stopped in to say good-bye to Dunn, and to A. J. Helms, who'd become his closest friend in the office. Helms just looked stricken. He'd been the one who arranged for Sean to go to AA, had driven him to the meeting. Sean felt a twinge of guilt—he'd even deceived his best friend. Instead of going to the meeting, Sean had sneaked out the back door, then came out the front when Helms picked him up an hour later, without having ever gone into the actual meeting.

His grandfather Seamus Kelly, who'd been a beat cop in Chicago, was fond of saying, "There's no good Irish cop worth his salt who didn't like a good drink now and again."

Right, Sean thought. *Now and again.*

He hoisted the garbage bag onto his shoulder and walked out into the high desert air of southern Arizona. He had no idea where he was going.

2

SEAN DROVE AIMLESSLY AROUND TUCSON BEFORE finally being drawn away from the city, south and west. By midday he was in Arivaca.

Arivaca was a tiny town twenty miles or so northeast of the border. It was a strange combination of cultures. Its heritage was cattle ranching, and there was open rangeland all around it. But he'd been told it had once been an artist's colony as well, that various hippies and bohemians and artisans made it a home base during the winter. Some of that character still showed through—now and then roadside stands were set up with various arts and crafts for sale. Sean had once bought a tiger's-eye gem from an old hippie couple that came right out of Central Casting, all the way down to the VW bus. He'd sent the gem to his sister.

Then there were the drug runners, the most notorious of which was Ray Acosta. An American citizen, he'd built a hugely ostentatious ranch-style house—all sleek modern lines, brick and glass—right in the middle of Arivaca, among the trailer homes and wooden frame houses. It stood out like a diamond surrounded by broken glass.

And now he was gone, over the border, leaving his palace behind. After the blown op yesterday, officers from three federal agencies had descended on the house. They found cash and they found guns, but no cocaine. Acosta was too smart for that, and now he was in Mexico.

Thanks to me, Sean thought, rubbing his forehead.

He pulled his Jeep Cherokee back onto the road, then crossed to the other side and parked under a tree. Just driving through, no one would know that Arivaca was the center of a war zone twenty miles from the border. The town's single business, a little general store, seemed to do a brisk trade. A couple of arts and crafts tables were set up across the road from the store, and each had a few customers. Sean watched as a weary-looking man with a salt and pepper beard explained to the three young boys surrounding him that they could each have only *one* souvenir.

Sean smiled, then it faded quickly as he was aware of the jackhammers working behind his eyes. He dry-swallowed a couple of extra-strength Tylenol, then started the Jeep again.

"I never liked Arizona anyway," he muttered, which wasn't true. He recognized what he was doing, the process of rationalization. Like a child who didn't get what he wanted, then insisted he'd never wanted it in the first place. He glanced at the man with the three boys again. Same principle.

The truth was, Sean loved the desert Southwest. He'd had a choice of assignments when he joined Customs seven years ago—Detroit, Seattle, or Tucson. Having grown up in the upper Midwest, Detroit held no allure for him. He didn't care for rain, so Seattle was out. But the Southwest was exoticism and mystery and excitement, so he'd come to Tucson. And the work had been good. Confusing since September 11 and the creation of Homeland Security, but good work. Important. Even his old man, Detective Captain Joe Kelly, who was never pleased with anything, seemed to approve.

"Fuck," Sean whispered. "Fuck it all."

He pulled back onto the highway, heading west out of Arivaca. He could go anywhere. The trash bag full of stuff from his desk at ICE was in the backseat. So were his laptop and a small duffel bag with a few clothes and personal items. His career was over—he knew that. Thirty years old in a few weeks and his career was done.

"Fuck," he said again, without much enthusiasm.

He drove through the rough country, some of it open range, some of it fenced as part of the Buenos Aires National Wildlife Refuge. It was a wild and beautiful terrain, mountains rising in hazy distance from the high desert floor. Sean drove on until the road dead-ended at the junction to State Highway 286, one of the loneliest stretches of two-lane highway he'd ever seen. A right turn would take him north, back toward Tucson. Toward "civilization," whatever that meant.

A left turn meant Sasabe and the Mexican border. The town of Sasabe—though "town" was a generous description—squatted right on the border and was one of the two most isolated ports of entry along the southern boundary of the United States. One of Sean's

ICE colleagues—*former* colleagues, he corrected himself—was a woman agent, a fellow midwestern expatriate. She'd once told Sean that if "they" decided to cross the border at Sasabe, the authorities on the U.S. side wouldn't have a chance. It was that isolated. She didn't have to say who "they" were—drug runners, arms dealers, terrorists.

Sean's own take on Sasabe was that it was really a Mexican village. It didn't matter that it was on the Arizona side of the border. The flat-top houses, the adobe, the strings of peppers and onions hanging beside front doors, the gritty poverty. Sean thought a mistake had been made somewhere along the line, that the border had been moved half a mile or so too far south. It should have been redrawn so that Sasabe would be a Mexican border town, not an Arizona border town.

He turned left. Maybe he could start over in Mexico himself. His Spanish was good after seven years down here. He could live cheap in Mexico. Whiskey was inexpensive and easy to find. Maybe he could pick up Ray Acosta's trail. Maybe, maybe, *maybe* . . .

He slowed the Cherokee to a crawl as he came into Sasabe. A little copper-skinned boy, maybe four or five years old, wearing only a pair of denim shorts, darted across the road as if he were playing chicken with Sean. A woman with three other kids surrounding her and a baby on her hip yelled in rapid-fire Spanish from a front porch. Sean nodded toward her. She stared at Sean unblinking.

Barely crawling at twenty miles an hour, Sean took the Cherokee around a sharp S curve. Ragged laundry hung on clotheslines on both sides of the road. More half-naked kids scampered. Sean wondered where they went to school, if at all. Ahead and to the left, looking like a well-dressed stranger that had wandered into the midst of all this, was the port of entry. A sign unnecessarily read MEXICO, with an arrow pointing the way.

The port of entry was all brick and stone and glass, a modernistic complex that straddled the road. There was no southbound stop sign. It was so simple to drive into another country. You just passed slowly through the port and then were in Mexico. Northbound out of Mexico was only slightly different. All an American citizen had to do was stop at the booth and declare his citizenship.

But Sasabe was different from other crossings along the border, places like El Paso or even Nogales, just a bit east of here. Traffic snarled in both directions in those places, Mexicans and Americans each seeing what the other had to offer. As for Sasabe, Sean had never seen more than one vehicle at a time come through this port.

Without even realizing it, he had pulled the Cherokee to the shoulder of the road, a hundred yards or so from the border. A green-and-white Border Patrol van drove past him, the driver staring out. Sean thought he knew the guy—he knew most of the BP officers and most of those who worked the ports of entry from Nogales to Naco to Sasabe.

He rubbed his head, waiting for the Tylenol to kick in. So far it hadn't. If he crossed the border he'd have to pass by a booth where someone he knew would see him. *Shit.* More humiliation. By now every employee of ICE in Arizona would know how Sean "Irish" Kelly had screwed up and let Ray Acosta run. He didn't know who was working down here today, but he knew them all. He'd even dated one of the women who worked the booth.

Very slowly, his jaw grinding, he wheeled the Cherokee back onto the road and turned it around, back to the north. He maneuvered the S curve again and again the little boy did his dance across the road in front of him. Again the mother screamed ineffectually and glared at Sean.

The only functioning business in Sasabe was a little nameless cantina on the north side. He'd been in it multiple times and had never heard a word of English spoken there. But it was a bar, it was cheap, and Sean didn't care anymore.

The door was wide open at a little before noon. Another thing Sean appreciated about the desert—bars opened early. He left the Cherokee in the gravel parking lot and went in. It was dark, lit by a few swag lamps here and there. Tables were wooden and chipped, chairs likewise, often mismatched. Two old men sat at the bar smoking hand-rolled cigarettes. One of them wore a greasy Los Angeles Dodgers baseball cap. The bartender was a burly guy a little older than Sean, with a wispy black mustache. It was perfectly in character for Sasabe.

Sean sat at the bar at the opposite end from the two old smokers. Blinking in the dim light, he started ordering straight shots of Wild Turkey, with Dos Equis on draft to chase it.

"Leave the bottle," he said in Spanish to the bartender.

An hour passed, and the only sound in the bar was that of the old men scratching matches as they lit fresh cigarettes—Sean never heard them utter a word—and Sean putting his glasses back down on the bar after each drink. Sean had smelled bread baking from somewhere, and without being asked, the bartender wordlessly put a basket of fresh, hot flour tortillas down in front of Sean.

Another good thing about the Southwest, Sean thought. *You sure as hell don't get tortillas like this in Illinois.*

The thought made him laugh a little. *I can still laugh, so I must be all right.* He poured himself another shot.

A shadow appeared in the doorway. "You're a hard man to find, Mr. Kelly," said a voice in English.

All heads turned toward the door. Sean, a little woozy but not as drunk as he wanted to be, looked past the shadow. A black Lexus, as out of place in Sasabe as the gleaming port of entry was, sat beside his dusty Cherokee in the parking lot.

"Who are you?" Sean said.

The man came fully into the bar and sat on the stool beside Sean's. He placed a business card next to Sean's shot glass.

Tobias Owens, Attorney and Counselor at Law, with an address in Phoenix.

Sean swiveled to look at him. He was in his thirties, a few years older than Sean, overweight but not obese, pale complexion. If he was like any of the other thirty-something lawyers Sean had met, he probably worked a hundred hours a week. No time for exercise, no time for sun, no time for anything but billable hours. Owens wore stylish round glasses and a suit that probably cost as much as the entire yearly income of every single person in Sasabe, Arizona.

"What do you want?"

"I'd like to talk to you," Owens said.

"Want a drink?" Sean said. The bartender was hovering warily.

"Oh," Owens said. "Just some water."

The bartender looked at Sean.

"*Agua,*" Sean said.

The bartender made a little snorting sound and disappeared from sight, pausing to whisper to the two old smokers. In a moment he returned and put down a beer mug with water and two ice cubes floating in it.

"Let's go to a booth, shall we?" Owens said.

Did he just say "shall we," Sean thought. "Suit yourself."

Sean picked up his whiskey bottle by the neck, along with the shot glass, and ambled to a table on the far side of the room. Someone had scribbled Spanish obscenities on the wall beside the table in red marker.

"Nice place," Owens said, settling in across from Sean.

Sean noticed the brown leather briefcase in the

man's hand for the first time. He shrugged. "It serves a purpose," he said, not rising to the lawyer's sarcasm.

Owens thumped his water glass onto the table, frowning at the Spanish graffiti on the wall. "You always drink this early in the day?"

"What the fuck do you want?" Sean said, his voice rising.

Owens put up a hand. "We can help each other."

Sean thought he was going to say more, but Owens just sat there with his hand in the air, looking ridiculous.

"I doubt it," Sean said, downing another shot. He shuddered as the bourbon went through him. He was vaguely irritated at this stranger's interruption of his little Sasabe interlude, but not so much so that he was going to quit drinking long enough to show his irritation.

"You've had a rough day, haven't you, Mr. Kelly?"

Sean considered several replies, then just said, "Yep."

"News travels fast," Owens said. He glanced toward the bar. The two old men were staring in their direction. He lowered his voice. "Your career as a federal law enforcement officer has taken quite a hit, wouldn't you say?"

"Oh, please," Sean said. "I don't need a damn lawyer. Get in your car and go back to Phoenix, shyster. I'm not suing anyone."

Owens shook his head. "No, no, don't misunderstand me. I don't want to represent you. I already have a client. That's why I'm here."

Sean wished he had another tortilla, but he'd left the basket on the bar and didn't feel like expending the energy it would take to go get it. "Start making some sense, if you can."

"I'm the Arizona counsel for Senator Edward McDermott."

Owens waited for a response. Sean simply stared at him.

"You *are* familiar with the senator?" Owens said finally.

Sean sighed. "Senior U.S. senator for Arizona. Multimillionaire corporate lawyer from a long line of multimillionaire corporate lawyers. Guardian of America's morals and traditional values. Friend of big business. Goes through wives like dirty laundry. Believes government is generally incompetent. You ever wonder, counselor, how silly it is to elect people to government who don't even like government?"

Owens had stiffened noticeably. "You sound as if you don't care for the senator."

Sean thumped his empty shot glass on the wooden table. "I don't care for politicians in general. My grandfather, who was one of the best cops I ever knew before he retired, used to say that the politician was a lot more dangerous than the street thug. At least with the thug you knew where they stood and what they wanted."

Owens was silent for a long moment. "Mr. Kelly, do you think your grandfather is proud of you today?"

Even an hour into a bottle of bourbon, Sean's reflexes hadn't dimmed much. He was taller than Owens by several inches, with a long reach, and he only had to stand up halfway to grab the lawyer by the hair and slam his face into the surface of the wooden table.

Owens screeched. Sean sat back down. The whiskey bottle had been jarred by the motion, but thankfully it hadn't tipped over. Sean poured himself another drink. One of the old men at the bar, the one in the Dodgers cap, laughed. The other one growled out a few words in a low voice. Sean heard him say something about "whining like a woman." Neither of them moved. The bartender folded his arms and watched in silence. Owens howled again.

Sean said nothing.

He drank and listened to Owens trying to breathe through his nose. Sean didn't think it was broken—he hadn't slammed the guy that hard. But there was a fair amount of blood, and Sean figured it was the most physical activity Tobias Owens had felt in a long time. He smiled at the thought.

Owens raised his head and saw Sean smiling. "You think . . ." the lawyer sputtered. "You think that's funny?"

Sean's smile faded. "State your business."

Owens was digging in his pocket. He came out with a white handkerchief—*is that silk?* Sean wondered—and pressed it to his nose. "Assault," Owens muttered. "I could file assault charges on you, Kelly. There are three witnesses."

Sean laughed outright. "Don't bet on it." He raised his voice in the direction of the bar and switched to Spanish. "You see anything happen here?"

Both of the old smokers laughed. "*Nada*," one said.

The bartender turned his back.

"So much for your witnesses," Sean said in English. "I'm not feeling patient today. State your business."

Owens pressed the bloody handkerchief against his nose. With his other hand, he fumbled open his brief-case and took out a thick manila envelope. He tossed it onto the table between them.

"The senator wants to hire you," Owens said.

3

"WHAT?" SEAN SAID.

Owens tilted his head back. The blood from his nose had stopped flowing. "Hire you," Owens said. "Senator McDermott wants you to do some work for him. You have a reputation." He swiped at his nose again.

"Do I, now?"

"*Shit.*" Owens tilted his head back again. "Damn, that hurts."

"Well, you should watch what you say. Don't worry, it's not broken. I didn't hit you that hard, counselor."

"Feels broken." Owens felt along the ridge of his nose, wincing.

"It's not. You wouldn't be talking so well if it was broken. I have a reputation?"

Owens blinked at him. "For finding things. For finding people with not much of a trail to follow."

Sean remembered Sonny Weller's words this morning. It had seemed like a long time ago. *You're good at putting things together with only a little to go on. Most of the guys in this office aren't half as smart as you are.*

"So?" Sean said, but with less vehemence.

"Whether you like him or not, Senator McDermott has kept up with the work law enforcement is doing here on the border." He breathed through his nose, a wet, rattling sound. He winced again. "Your career has just taken a nosedive. You have a skill that can help the senator, and maybe you'll get a chance to . . . what's the best way to put it? . . . to redeem yourself."

"News doesn't travel *that* fast. I just got suspended this morning."

"You have a friend in the office, a Mr. Helms?"

"AJ? What about him?"

"It seems he is currently dating a young woman whose sister works in Senator McDermott's Tucson office."

Sean shook his head. "You'd think Tucson was some little town, not a major city, the way things go around."

"The way of the West, Mr. Kelly. Are you interested?"

"What's the deal?"

Owens pointed at the envelope. Sean undid the clasp and shook out the contents. Papers, newspaper and magazine articles, long narratives, and several photos, all of which included pictures of a striking young woman with dark hair and eyes.

"Daryn McDermott," Owens said. "The senator's daughter, age twenty-four."

"What about her?"

"She's missing."

Sean looked up sharply. "I haven't seen or heard anything about this."

Owens sighed. "Senator McDermott has kept it out of the media. Daryn is . . . well, Daryn is . . . difficult."

"Difficult?"

"The girl is . . . how should I say this? . . . she's out of control. She doesn't feel that the rules of society apply to her. She's done things and said things that have been politically very . . . difficult for the senator."

Sean blinked, thinking through the bourbon. He'd seen something on TV a while back.

"She's the one," he said, "that was arrested for public nudity in front of the U.S. Capitol."

Owens nodded. "Protesting her father's stand on allowing the government to access records of what people check out of libraries. Her point was that the government had no business knowing if someone read a book or a magazine that, say, had nudity or sexual references in it."

Sean stared at him.

"You're in law enforcement. Surely you understand the power of having the right information."

"Don't assume anything about me," Sean said. "She did other things, too, didn't she? Even more radical things."

Owens nodded again, touching his nose gingerly. "She went on a cross-country tour, trying to raise support for legalizing and regulating prostitution. She would go into a city and get an army of prostitutes together and they would descend on the city hall or state capitol, generating all kinds of media coverage. She wants drugs legalized and regulated too."

"So her father," Sean said, "the keeper of morals and traditional values, is embarrassed, personally and politically."

Owens's voice rose slightly. "He's given her everything! Put her through Georgetown, even allowed her to get a worthless degree in sociology, of all things. He pays for apartments in D.C. and in Phoenix for her, and she repays him by embarrassing him."

"You think she's just a spoiled princess acting out, trying to piss off her father, or is it a real issue for her?"

Owens's voice softened. "A bit of both, I'd say. Daryn actually does believe all these ridiculous things she spouts. But just because she has money and influence and a name, she gets a more public arena to speak out on all this drivel."

"And now she's missing."

"For nearly a month now. It's not like her to take off and not be heard from. I mean, in the past when she's taken off, she turns up in the media in places like West Virginia and Oklahoma and South Dakota. But now she's gone without a trace."

"And the senator didn't contact the FBI? I would think they'd pull out all the stops to find a U.S. senator's daughter."

Owens shook his head emphatically. "The senator wants this handled discreetly. He first hired private investigators in Washington and in Phoenix. All the traditional methods were dead ends. She hasn't used her credit cards, hasn't accessed her bank accounts. Her car is in its garage in D.C. None of her friends know anything. She's simply . . . gone."

"You think she's just run off again, or something else? Something criminal?"

"We don't know. There's been no kind of ransom demand, nothing like that. So the senator's presumption is that she's on her own somewhere. And he wants her back."

"The loving father?"

Owens picked up the sarcasm. "Look, they aren't close, as you might imagine. Daryn, the ungrateful little brat that she is, calls her father part of 'the ruling class,' as if we were living in some kind of aristocracy. It's one thing for a child to disagree with their parents' values. We all go through that, to a point. It's another for her to criticize and vilify everything her father stands for, and to do it as publicly as she can. He just wants her found before she . . ." Owens looked uncomfortable. He glanced toward the bar, then looked quickly away. The old smokers were still staring.

"Go ahead, say it," Sean said.

"Before she does something either stupid or embarrassing," Owens said.

"What makes you think I can find her?" Sean said. "I'm a Customs agent on suspension for screwing up an operation. There are those in this world who believe I have a drinking problem."

"As I said before—"

"Yeah, I know, I have a reputation." Sean tossed back another shot. He felt himself giving, bending, like power lines in high wind. And the painful truth was, he had nothing else to do, nowhere to go. If a United States senator wanted to pay him to look for his wayward daughter, who was he to question that?

"How much?" he asked.

Owens looked relieved. He withdrew another envelope from the briefcase. "Here's twenty thousand dollars cash."

Sean leaned forward. "I'm sorry. Say that again?"

"Mr. Kelly, the senator is hiring you based on your reputation, but he's counting on your discretion. It's a delicate situation. You can't just track down Daryn, pick her up under your arm, and bring her home to her father. Do that and she'll go straight to the media as soon as she's back in Washington, and it'll be an even worse nightmare. Not only do you have to find her, you have to gain her trust. Make her believe it's her choice to go with you. All this will take time. Also, the investigation is off the books. The senator wants it all done quietly. No one should ever know Daryn was missing in the first place."

"And all this because he's afraid she'll embarrass him politically?"

"I'm only Senator McDermott's lawyer, not his conscience, Mr. Kelly. He pays me well." Owens gestured at the envelope full of money. "Another amount equal to that will be paid when Daryn is safely, discreetly returned. Don't try to get in touch with me or with the senator before that time. Once she's home at her apartment in Washington, the senator will know."

"What, does he have his own daughter's apartment bugged?"

Owens spread his hands. "I won't comment on that."

"Nice guy." Sean fingered the envelope full of cash. "And if I do this, the senator does what he can to get me reinstated in ICE?"

"The senator will use whatever influence he may have to make sure you're able to continue in federal law enforcement."

"Typical lawyer's response," Sean said. He rubbed his forehead. He was buzzing right along now, his headache gone. "I'll look into it."

"Good," Owens said, sounding relieved. "Everything you need to know about Daryn is in that first packet. Except for one item."

Sean looked up at him.

"The girl is, quite frankly, very promiscuous," Owens said.

Sean folded his hands together on the table.

"Her sexuality is very . . . open," Owens said. "Men, women . . . it doesn't matter. This has presented problems in the past as well. Maybe she's taken up the cause of legalizing prostitution as a vicarious sort of thing. Perhaps she secretly wishes she was a prostitute herself, so she could indulge herself and be paid for it."

"Are you a psychiatrist too?"

"No, but I did fall under her spell myself once," Owens said. "All I can say to you is to be careful. Remember what your job is."

"I think I can take care of myself. Even around a politically radical, oversexed sociology major."

Owens didn't smile. He snapped his briefcase closed. "This is a nasty place," he said.

"Yeah, but it serves its purpose," Sean said.

"So it does."

"Sorry about your nose."

Owens shrugged. "The pain's going away already."

"Told you it wasn't broken."

Owens nodded and left the cantina. Sean sat for a long moment and looked at the two envelopes. Then he downed one more shot, stood a bit unsteadily, and left a wad of cash on the table. He took the envelopes, and before he left the building, pulled another tortilla out of the basket on the bar. He saluted the bartender and the old smokers with it, then headed out into the bright desert sun.

Tobias Owens drove the Lexus steadily north on 286 until it merged with Highway 86, which headed east back toward Tucson. Twenty miles outside the city, Owens pulled onto an unmarked gravel road that snaked north for several miles. He parked in a stand of cactus, right beside another car, a nondescript four-door, the kind typically used by rental agencies.

Another man got out of the rental car and looked at him. The other man was as nondescript as the car, around Owens's age, with average features. Modestly handsome, but not memorable. His clothes were khaki pants and a blue polo shirt. Unremarkable.

"He took the job," Owens said, placing his briefcase on the ground between the two cars. "But the drunken SOB nearly broke my nose."

The other man's neutral expression didn't change. "I'm sorry to hear that. You told him everything?"

"Followed the script exactly," Owens said. "Now about my fee . . ."

The other man had kept the car between the two of them, his hands shielded from Owens's view. He quickly raised his right hand, which held a pistol, and shot Owens point-blank three times in the chest. The lawyer lunged backward across the hood of his Lexus, then rolled to the ground.

The other man had no worries about the sound of gunshots. This was the Arizona desert, and gunfire was often heard as ranchers chased off various vermin, both of the two-legged and four-legged varieties. He went through Owens's pockets, removing the man's business cards and wallet. After a moment's consideration, he took the bloody handkerchief as well. He removed the license plates, registration, and insurance cards from the Lexus and placed them all in Owens's briefcase. He left Owens's body where it had fallen.

The man got back into his rental car and drove away without looking back. He had much to do, and far to go. The game had only just begun.

4

FAITH KELLY DOUBTED SHE WOULD EVER HAVE grandchildren, but if she did, she could imagine telling them the story:

Once upon a time, I was a deputy United States Marshal. But then I got caught up in a secret unit of the Justice Department called Department Thirty, and it helped to protect some bad people. See, we thought that these bad people could help us catch other bad people and keep them from doing bad things, so instead of punishing these bad people, we protected them and gave them new names and new jobs and made them promise to stay out of trouble. We did things like protecting the two most notorious assassins in the world. And there was this one time that I was forced to shoot a man. He'd worked for years and years to become very powerful and wanted to topple the president. And how about this one—I found out that the chief justice of the U.S. Supreme Court was actually a murderer.

Oh, grandma, the kids would say, *you're just making all that up.*

And she would smile. *Of course I am. You caught me. Now go to bed.*

Faith had learned a few things in the last year, ever since she'd been given her first Department Thirty recruit. Aside from that first one—where the recruit actually turned out to be innocent, a pawn in a scheme that brought down the chief justice—she'd learned that there were two types of recruits: those who were guilty and had been caught red-handed, yet continued to protest their innocence; and those who cheerfully and arrogantly admitted their guilt, almost proud of their crimes, even proud to a point of getting caught, of being asked to tell their story.

Leon Bankston fell into the latter category. He sat at the kitchen table of the safe house in the Oklahoma City suburb of Yukon, crossing and uncrossing his legs and smiling at Faith. Faith had wanted to smash his face in several times, but she forced herself to keep her mind on the job.

"You know, Leon," she said, "I understand you. I can see your perspective on this. It's the whole 'honor among thieves' thing. You haven't disputed for a second that you smuggled those guns onto that truck, or that the truck was headed to Galveston to transfer the load to a ship, or that the ship was bound for Iraq. You know what you did."

"That's right," Bankston said. He was a small man in his forties, bald except for a few tufts around his ears, with quick eyes that darted all around the room at every sound. "I did what I did. That's my living. I'll do my couple of years in a federal country club, then I'll be back in business and there's nothing you can do about it."

Faith stood up and stretched. At five ten, she was a good four inches taller than Bankston, her body slim and toned. She wasn't quite in the shape she'd been in when she ran the New York and Boston Marathons, but she still ran. It was her only obsession, other than trying to stay above the mud and muck of her job. She passed a hand through her hair, still not used to its new short cut. Her Irish-red hair had fallen to the middle of her back for most of her life, but she'd finally had it cut into a short shag a couple of months ago, the kind of haircut that magazines liked to describe as "sassy." Faith had laughed at that—she was sassy enough without a haircut, but she had to admit it was low maintenance.

"There's just one problem, Leon," she said, leaning over the table.

"What's that, beautiful?"

She smiled. "First thing is: if you call me 'beautiful' or 'sexy' or 'doll' one more time, I'm liable to kick you in a place where it would really, really hurt." She leaned in close to him, her face inches from his. "You believe I could do that, don't you?"

Bankston's smug look faltered. "Ah . . . yes. Yes, I believe that. Yes."

"Very good." She stood up again to her full height, rolling the kinks out of her back. She badly needed a run. "Second thing is, you really don't know what you did. I mean, you know you smuggled a bunch of illegal weapons. We agree on that part."

Bankston nodded.

"But see, the world is a lot more complicated now than it used to be. What used to just be considered smuggling might now be considered aiding and abetting terrorists."

"Hey, you can't blame me for whatever someone else does with guns that I just happened to move."

"Oh, actually I can blame you for that. You may have heard of the Patriot Act."

"Oh, shit," the man said.

"Uh-huh. You see, Leon, if the United States government has even an inkling that you've done anything that would lead to those weapons getting into the hands of, say, Iraqi insurgents, then that means you can be held under the Patriot Act. That means you don't get to hire a slick lawyer. You can actually be held without being charged. And it won't be in a federal country club either, Leon. I can make a phone call and see that you're escorted to Guantánamo Bay. Trust me, that's no country club."

"But—"

"I know, I know, you're just a smuggler. You've been doing business for twenty-five years. You already did one stretch in federal custody in the eighties. This isn't the eighties, Leon." She leaned in again. "Frankly, you're in deep, deep shit. But we already know that you're not at the top of the food chain, that you're part of a larger network doing business with these various terror groups." Faith began to tick items off on her fingers. "You give me names, dates, places, bank accounts. You're afraid the others involved will come after you. But see, you won't exist anymore. Your trail goes cold right here, right now. I have a new name for you—Benjamin Williams. Ben Williams can start a new job, and I've picked out a nice town for him to live in. Manhattan, Kansas—it's a pleasant college town, not far from

Kansas City. Since you're so good with supply and demand, Ben Williams will get a job as an inventory control manager for the warehouse operations of a major retailer."

"What about college? Could I have a degree? I never got to finish mine, you know."

And in that instant, Faith knew she had him. Once they became a part of the fantasy in any way, the deal was closed. She smiled. "We can give Mr. Williams a degree in business management from the University of Colorado."

"I like Colorado."

"There you go. Leon, you have to work with us. You have to come in. You don't have a choice. You don't want to be screwing around with the Patriot Act. Your partners or bosses will never know what's happened to you. And before too long, they'll be the ones headed to Guantánamo, not you. You'll be in Kansas, with a rock-solid new identity."

Leon Bankston looked at her for a moment. For a few seconds he looked pensive, almost repentant. Then the small-time crook was back. "Ah, those bastards," he finally said. "They never paid me what they should have, anyway."

"Welcome to Department Thirty," Faith said.

Bankston talked for four hours. It was nearly six p.m. before Faith packed up her tape recorder and her notes. She summoned her field officer, a big soft-spoken man named Hal Simon, to babysit Bankston. As case officer, Faith's job was to bring in the recruits, create the identities and manage their placement in the community, then manage the cases while the protectees adjusted to their new lives. But she didn't do protective duty during the period between. Leon Bankston had already ceased to exist, and Benjamin Williams had yet to be fully brought into existence. Being Irish Catholic, Faith thought of it as limbo, and her job on this case did not extend to sitting with the man.

She left the house, promising Simon and Bankston that she would be in touch during the next step of the process. Now she had to create a report that would be sent up the line to the director of Department Thirty, a man named Richard Conway, but whom Faith thought of as Dean Yorkton, the name he'd been using when she first met him nearly four years ago. From Yorkton the report—Bankston's statements about his activities and those of his associates—would then go directly to the attorney general of the United States for final approval. When the AG signed off on it, she would complete the paper trail that created Benjamin Williams, and would send him off to Kansas.

She drove away from the suburban safe house, which was on a street with the absurdly suburban name of Hyacinth Hollow Road. In five minutes her gold Mazda Miata was on Interstate 40, headed east toward Oklahoma City proper.

She picked up her cell phone and speed-dialed Scott Hendler's number. When she heard his drawling "Hello," Faith smiled. What did that mean, she wondered, when the way the man answered the phone actually made her smile?

"Hey, you," she said.

"Hey, yourself," Hendler said. "How goes the . . . you know?"

Even though Scott Hendler was a special agent in the Oklahoma City field office of the FBI, she couldn't discuss cases with him. Department Thirty was an open secret in the Justice Department, but the other agencies within DOJ treated it like a relative no one wanted to claim. Outside DOJ, Thirty was completely shrouded in shadows.

"I'm done for today and moving right along," Faith said. "And now . . ." She lowered her voice sexily. "I'm up for something . . . hot."

Hendler's voice lowered as well. "Well, you know, you can always count on me for something . . . hot."

They both laughed. "Chili at Different Roads?" Faith said in a normal voice. "I think Alex Bridge is playing there tonight."

"Meet you there," Hendler said.

There was an awkward moment's silence, the same as with every phone conversation they had. Dry humor aside, Faith always sensed that Hendler wanted to say something more, something about love, at the end of every phone call. But she hadn't used the l-word with him so far, and didn't know if she would. She came from a family that didn't just throw terms of endearment and public displays of affection around. Hendler evidently wanted such things from her, but then, he was patient with her. They'd gone in the space of two years from being professional acquaintances to friends to outright lovers, but Faith was still conscious of always holding part of herself back. She knew she got the very best part of Scott Hendler, and she treasured it. But she still couldn't give him everything. There were parts of herself that even she couldn't find, much less open them up to someone else.

"Down the road," she said, and clicked the phone off.

Just enjoy it, she reminded herself. Things were good for now. She was finally learning how to do the job, and to keep the moral ambiguities of it at bay. Her own demons, and the parts of herself that she'd walled off, stayed hidden for the most part. Scott Hendler was a good man, and they enjoyed each other's company.

Why borrow trouble? Faith thought, just as she passed the city limits sign for Oklahoma City.

5

WHEN SEAN HAD LEFT TUCSON AND POINTED HIS
Jeep southwest toward Arivaca and, ultimately, Sasabe,
he'd actually thought he would never see his apartment again. He would just drive away from it all—his
furniture, his stereo, his hundreds of compact discs,
even his own personal gun, a forty-caliber semiautomatic Glock 23.

But here he sat, at the wooden dining room table
he'd scavenged from an antique shop in Oro Valley
two years ago. He'd refinished it with great care, then
worked on the four chairs, one by one, over the
course of six months. The apartment was always a
surprise to people—they didn't expect a young single
guy to be as neat and tidy as he was. It always amused
Sean that his sister, Faith, was such a slob. Because
she was female, it was expected that she would be
into cleaning, yet he knew Faith could rarely be troubled to even pick up her dirty laundry. So they had
both confounded what was expected of them, in
more ways than one.

Sean was no longer buzzed by all the whiskey he'd
drunk in the Sasabe cantina. He'd left the little bar with
a renewed sense of purpose. Even if the purpose was
skulking around in the life of Senator McDermott's

promiscuous, politically radical daughter, it was a chance, and it held possibilities.

He made himself a bologna sandwich, opened a bottle of Dos Equis, and spread out the papers from the packet Tobias Owens had given him. There was something that looked like a briefing paper, probably prepared by Owens, as it was written in thick legalese—six words when two would suffice. He leafed through it, muddling through the dense prose.

Daryn Anisa McDermott was twenty-four years old and had been born in Washington to Senator Edward McDermott and his first wife, Regina Statham McDermott. The two divorced when Daryn was seven, and thus began the senator's experiments in finding the perfect political trophy wife. He'd tried three more thus far.

Daryn only spent vacations, the occasional holiday, and most campaign seasons in Arizona, having been raised primarily in Washington. Owens was right— she'd received a sociology degree from Georgetown, and to Sean's surprise, he saw that she'd graduated third in her class. Impressive. So Daryn McDermott was no bubbleheaded political princess.

She'd first begun moving in radical political directions during college, naturally. With the conservative ascendancy in American politics, Daryn practically ran in the other direction, especially on social, "moral" issues. Sean read a snippet of a paper she'd written her senior year, in which young Daryn called for the "overthrow" of traditional values and "dismantling" of old ways of thinking, to scrap the social order and begin again, to let the "ruling classes" know that the "real" people of America were "in revolt."

Strong language, Sean thought. The birth of a radical. But then, how much of Daryn McDermott's radicalism was true conviction, and how much was sticking it to her father, the father who dumped her mother and then had little to do with his daughter except as a campaign prop? The father who was firmly in the "family values" political camp, and who was a part of the ruling class his daughter railed against.

He put aside the bio and started looking through the newspaper and magazine clippings of Daryn's various demonstrations. There was a copy of the famous picture from the Associated Press, of Daryn marching naked in front of the U.S. Capitol, a black strip superimposed across her breasts and pubic area. There were a couple of photos that seemed like more conventional protests: outside the gates to a coal mine in West Virginia, a factory in Ohio. But most were taken with Daryn standing shoulder to shoulder with groups of other women, sometimes street prostitutes, sometimes call girls or "escorts."

Sean tried to follow Daryn's arguments in an article clipped from *Newsweek*, which included photos from a march she'd led—the "hookers' march," a local paper had called it—in downtown St. Louis. Daryn never tried to talk women out of a life of prostitution. She campaigned for them to choose the life, and if they so chose, to do it safely and legally, without fear of either disease or the police.

Sean read her quote: *"Some women are forced here*

because of circumstances. Some women are forced here to feed their children. Some women are forced here to feed their own habits. And some women, regardless of what polite society may think, aren't forced here at all! They choose to be here! Women should be free to make that choice, right or wrong!"

He sifted through more photos. Another one from the Associated Press caught his eye. Daryn was a small woman, only five two or so, and she may have been all of 110 pounds. But she wore her hair long, often twisted into intricate braids, and her brown eyes blazed with intensity, intelligence, and fury. She wasn't conventionally beautiful, but was an arresting physical presence.

I did fall under her spell myself once, Tobias Owens had said.

Sean was beginning to see how that would be the appropriate term. He could understand how a woman like Daryn McDermott would indeed cast a spell.

Sean scrutinized the photo, holding it up under the light. In it, Daryn was wearing a button-down shirt with several buttons undone, showing a great deal of cleavage. That was exactly the point, Sean quickly surmised. She wanted the photographer to see the tattoo at the top of her left breast. In swirling Old English lettering was tattooed the word *justice*.

"Jesus please us," Sean muttered.

The photo, of course, mainly captured Daryn. Sean read the caption: *Daryn McDermott, 23, daughter of U.S. Senator Edward McDermott of Arizona, at a rally to legalize prostituion, on the steps of the State Capitol, Oklahoma City.*

Just off-center from the camera shot, though, was another woman, with dark straight hair and hollowed cheeks. She was wearing a denim miniskirt and white pullover. Large hoop earrings dangled from her ears. One of her eyebrows was pierced as well. She was young, barely into her twenties, Sean guessed. Her face was half-turned, gazing at Daryn with something like awe. The other woman's arm was linked through Daryn's.

They didn't even bother to identify her, Sean thought. Just some anonymous hooker, lost in Daryn McDermott's wake.

Sean took another pull of Dos Equis, then felt the apartment grow very still.

He saw the way the other woman was looking at Daryn, the way her arm was hooked through Daryn's, her own fingers curling lightly over Daryn's wrist.

On the steps of the state capitol, Oklahoma City.

Oklahoma City.

"Well, I'll be damned," Sean said.

He traced a finger over the prostitute's face. "I'll bet you've talked to her," Sean said to the photo. "I bet you know where she is. Because you love her, don't you, honey?"

He put the photo down and opened his laptop. In his e-mail program, he found his sister's address and entered it in the address box. Then he sat for a moment. He didn't call Faith very often. He sent her an e-mail now and then, usually when he was toasted, and couldn't remember later what he wrote. Her own e-mails to him consisted mainly of asking what the hell his last e-mail to her had meant.

Sean smiled at the thought of his baby sister, eighteen months younger than he. His best friend, his worst nightmare. She wasn't in the Marshals Service anymore. She'd told their father that she was doing "special projects" for DOJ. She'd been interested in WITSEC—the Witness Security Program—when she was with the Marshals, so Sean thought he knew what Faith was doing now. He'd never spoken or written the words *Department Thirty* to her, but that had to be what she was doing. *No one* in the federal law enforcement community talked about Thirty if they could help it. Even talking casually about Thirty was asking for trouble.

But his sister still lived in Oklahoma City, and she liked it there. That much Sean knew. He believed in fate. The fact that he'd found a lead to Daryn McDermott in the same city where his sister lived meant he was on the right trail. He was doing the right thing. He knew it.

Sean drained the last of his beer and typed a message to his sister:

Here comes trouble, Sister. See you soon.

6

FAITH AND HENDLER GENERALLY SPENT THE NIGHT at each other's homes once or twice a week. It was impromptu, rarely planned, and just depended on where they were and what they'd been doing when it began to get late. Sometimes there was sex, sometimes there wasn't. They'd grown comfortable enough in the last year to just want to *be* together.

They'd stayed out until after ten at Different Roads, a small folk club on Classen Boulevard, where Faith's friend Alex Bridge played fiddle and flute with a Celtic band. Though Faith wasn't much into folk music, preferring contemporary jazz, she always tried to catch Alex when she played locally. They'd lived through a nightmare together a year ago, and the bond between them had grown strong.

When it had approached ten thirty last night, Faith and Hendler decided by an almost silent mutual assent to go to her house. Hendler lived in the northern suburb of Edmond, and Faith's home in The Village area was a good ten miles or so closer in. So they slept together in her queen-size bed, and both were up shortly after five a.m. to run. Faith knew Hendler preferred to sleep later, and she also knew he preferred more "organized" exercise to running, but when he stayed with her, he rose with her and ran with her with no complaints.

They'd done three-plus miles on an overcast spring morning that promised rain later in the day, when they rounded the corner of Faith's block. Her modest brick home, built in the fifties as most homes in The Village had been, was in the middle of the block, north side of the street. The garage was full of junk, so she always parked her Miata in the driveway. Hendler's sensible Toyota was parked behind her. In front of the house, on the street, sat a dirty dark green Jeep Cherokee with a man sitting behind the wheel.

"Hmm," Faith said, slowing.

Hendler pulled up beside her. "What?"

"In front of my house."

Hendler frowned, stopping beside her, stretching out his legs. "I don't have my gun. It's in the house."

"I have mine." Faith had learned the hard way about keeping her weapon with her, even on the run, so she now always wore a large fanny pack in which she kept her gun. The Glock that she'd had for so long had been washed away into the waters of Galveston Bay a year ago, and she'd bought a SIG Sauer nine-millimeter, the "Cadillac of pistols," not long thereafter.

She unzipped the fanny pack halfway.

"Maybe your paper boy, here to collect?" Hendler said.

"Maybe," Faith said. But she'd gone to that unreachable place where everything clicked off except instinct.

Her long vision wasn't that great, but the man in the Jeep had started moving. He was making no attempt to be furtive, movements smooth and natural. Of course, that meant nothing. In the world where Faith lived, people and places and things were often nothing like what they appeared to be.

The man's head popped out of the Jeep. "Holy shit," Faith said.

"Hey, that's my line," Hendler said.

"It's my brother."

"Your *what?*"

"My brother."

They were two houses away from hers now, from the Jeep and Sean. In a movie, Faith supposed they would have run toward each other and embraced madly. Brother and sister hadn't seen each other in nearly three years, not since the last time they were both at the famous Kelly Memorial Day picnic in Chicago. But this was no movie, and they weren't hugging people.

The sight of Sean did elicit a smile, though. Aside from the red hair of the Kellys, she and her brother had inherited the height and slender build of their mother's family, the O'Connells. Their father's people were all short and round, but she and Sean were five ten and six three, respectively, big boned and well built. Faith realized with a pleasant rush how happy she was to see him.

She jogged the last few feet, Hendler trailing discreetly behind, and leaned over the hood of the Jeep. "I hadn't seen your new wheels," Faith said. "I was ready to shoot on sight. Can't be too careful with all the riffraff about."

Sean smiled through a day's growth of beard. "Well, I'm the riffraff of the family, that's for sure. Still obsessively running while normal people are in bed, I see. And now you're dragging innocent bystanders along with you."

Faith smiled. "This is my friend Scott Hendler."

Hendler extended a hand and Sean shook it.

"Sean Kelly," Sean said. "I think Faith mentioned you in an e-mail at one time or other. Aren't you with the Bureau?"

"That's the one," Hendler said. "It's good to finally meet you, Sean." Hendler did a few stretches. "You two have a lot of catching up to do." He squeezed Faith's shoulder. "I'll get my stuff. I'll go shower at my place, then I've got to get to work."

He jogged up the driveway and let himself in the house. Sean watched with interest, then looked back at Faith.

"Don't start," Faith warned. "He's a good guy."

Sean shrugged. "A little on the geeky side. Bald spot the size of Rhode Island up there. Kind of short. You never went for that type before."

Faith shrugged to mimic him. "What can I say? When it's there, it's there."

They walked up the front steps together. "I never thought I'd see the day when Faith Siobhan Kelly would cut off all her hair, though."

"It's comfortable."

Sean laughed. "I guess if the Bureau likes it—"

"Sean Micheal Kelly." She gave the middle name the Gaelic pronunciation of *MEE-hall*. "I've never changed any aspect of myself for a man, and I'm not about to start. I did it for me. And yes, he does like it, incidentally. Where the hell did you come from?"

"Tucson, remember?"

"I remember Tucson. What are you doing here?"

"Don't you read your e-mail anymore?"

"I've had a very busy couple of days this week. I had a . . ." She swallowed back the words. She couldn't talk about Department Thirty and Leon Bankston to her brother. ". . . project to work on," she finished.

"Ah." Sean made quotation marks with his fingers. " 'Special projects' for DOJ."

"Yes, sir. That's me. I'm all about special projects." She mimicked his finger quotes.

"Smart-ass."

"Learned from the best." She elbowed him in the ribs. That was as good as a hug for the two of them.

"Well, anyway, I e-mailed you yesterday and told you I was coming to town."

"What brings you this way?" Faith asked. "Homeland Security in the heartland?"

They reached the front door, and as Faith opened it, Hendler came out, dressed in yesterday's clothes, carrying his briefcase. "See you two later," he said, pecked Faith quickly on the cheek, and jogged to the Toyota. A minute later he was gone.

Faith and Sean walked into the house. Sean took a look at the newspapers on the floor, a few stray items of clothing here and there, cups and glasses still on the table. The place smelled musty.

"Man, sister, you never learn," Sean said. "Still can't pick up after yourself."

"Don't start, you. I have a lot more interesting things to do than worry about whether there's a place for everything and everything in its place."

"I believe you." Sean sat down on Faith's paisley-patterned couch. "I drove straight through. I'm sort of on leave from ICE, and I picked up a little freelance job."

Faith pulled off her green headband and tossed it onto the dining room table. She wiped her sweaty face with a towel. "On leave? What, you mean on vacation?"

"Sort of."

"That's twice you've said 'sort of.' "

"Don't worry about it." He looked at her, his blue-green eyes finding her darker green ones. "It's good to see you, Faith."

Faith nodded. "Yeah." She wiped her face again. "Look at us. One or two-line e-mails now and then, a call on Thanksgiving, not seeing each other for three years. Once upon a time, neither of us could get rid of the other."

Sean looked surprised. "Boy, that's deep. I guess hanging out with the Bureau has made you sensitive or something."

Faith threw the towel at him. "You are so full of shit."

"Always have been." Sean kicked off his shoes.

"I'm going to take a shower," Faith said. "You want some breakfast?"

"No, I still don't like to eat in the mornings."

"Good, because neither do I."

"You got anything to drink around here, though?"

"I made coffee already," Faith said, her voice trailing down the hall. "If you want juice, I think there's some in the fridge. Check the expiration date on the bottle before you drink it."

Sean was already on his feet, working his way to the kitchen. "Not quite what I had in mind," he muttered. He heard the bathroom door close and the shower start as he opened the refrigerator.

"Here we go," he said, and pulled out a bottle of Harp ale. "Good Irish beer. Way to go, baby sister."

Half an hour later, Faith came back into the living room, fully dressed in jeans, a polo shirt, and tennis shoes. Since she no longer had a supervisor to report to locally, she dressed how she wanted for each workday. Today was mainly going to be a day spent in front of her computer working on Leon Bankston's details, so she'd dressed down.

She found Sean fast asleep on the couch. She smiled. He did say he'd driven straight through from Tucson, after all. The smile faltered a bit when she saw the three empty bottles of Harp on the coffee table.

She looked pensively at him for a moment. *Don't jump to conclusions*, she thought. He'd just come off a long, long drive, and his body's clock was probably mixed up.

She scribbled him a note, tucked it under the edge of one of the Harp bottles, and headed for the door. She stopped with her hand on the knob and looked back at her brother.

She remembered that line her grandfather had always used, the one about any Irish cop worth his salt liking a good drink now and again. Faith looked at the empty beer bottles. Even her grandfather and father had never drunk three bottles of beer in less than half an hour, before seven o'clock in the morning, to her knowledge.

Faith never drank hard liquor herself, only beer or wine, and never more than three drinks at one sitting. She hadn't been what she considered drunk since her junior year in college, when she woke up in a strange bed with a strange guy beside her. Given her family history, Faith became a "lightweight" in a profession where social drinking was common and expected.

She'd never thought of Sean as having a problem with it. But then, she and Sean hadn't been around each other much as adults.

Benefit of the doubt, Faith, she told herself. *He's your brother. Talk about it later.*

She closed the door quietly behind her and headed out into a light mist.

7

SEAN SLEPT UNTIL THE MIDDLE OF THE AFTERNOON, while a plains thunderstorm raged outside, thunder cracking like a whip and rain pounding the house like a demon begging to be let inside. Getting up, he read Faith's note, blinking at the three Harp bottles. He very carefully took them to the kitchen trash and put them in, taking care not to shatter them.

He retrieved his duffel and laptop from the Jeep, getting soaked in the process. Then he showered, shaved, and put on clean clothes. His sister didn't seem to have a laundry basket or hamper, just a large pile in the corner of her bedroom. Grimacing at the mess, he took his clothes and some of hers, dark colors mostly, to the washing machine and started a load. Then he went to the wooden kitchen table—not as nice as his, but a good piece of work nonetheless—and powered up his laptop.

He was still online when Faith came home at a little after five. He saw her eyes fall on the coffee table first, then on him. "Hey," Faith said.

"Hey," Sean said. "Busy day?"

"Special projects," she reminded him.

"Aha. Do you have plans for tonight? Are you seeing the Bureau?"

"He has a name, Sean."

"What is it again?"

"Scott. His name is Scott."

"Right. So are you?"

Faith dropped her purse and briefcase on the couch. "Hadn't planned on it. What would you like to do while you're here?"

"I need to find a hooker."

Faith stopped in her tracks, staring at him. He wasn't smiling.

"A hooker," Faith said.

"You know what that means?" Sean said.

"I know what it means. They don't have hookers in Arizona? Besides, you were always the guy who got all the dates."

"Very funny. Not for me, thank you. The freelance job I mentioned? I need to talk to this woman, who I believe is a hooker in Oklahoma City."

"You must be kidding."

"Nope." He turned back to his laptop. "You know where Shields Boulevard is?"

"Southeast part of the city. Why?"

"That's where I'll start. That seems to be a starting point for a lot of the working girls."

"How did you find that out? You're in this town less than twelve hours and you know where to find a prostitute?"

Sean tapped the computer. "The Internet, sister. If you're patient, you could find almost anything." *Almost,* he thought.

"You want me to go with you?" Faith said.

"No," Sean said. "This is a low-profile job. I looked it up on Mapquest, so it shouldn't be too hard to find. It's sort of a 'special project.' "

Faith, heading down the hall, flipped him off without turning around. Sean grinned.

Sean waited until after dark to set out. He stopped by a copy shop and made an enlarged copy of the photo of Daryn and the taller woman with the stringy hair. Then he carefully cropped Daryn out of the picture as much as he could, until all that could be seen of her was her arm where the other woman's was linked through it.

Following Mapquest, he made his way to Interstate 44, then to Interstate 40 just south of downtown Oklahoma City. He took the downtown exit, but instead of turning north toward the skyline, he went south. He crossed a long bridge, then slowed as the street became Shields Boulevard.

Sean had read online that Oklahoma City's prostitution district had once been along Lincoln Boulevard, just north of the state capitol. Then it was cleaned up in the eighties, most of the ratty pay-by-the-hour motels being bulldozed, replaced by new state government buildings and legitimate businesses, parks, and landscaping. A great triumph of urban renewal, especially since the location in the shadow of the state capitol had been a major civic embarrassment for years.

But, as with any city of size, the scene searched for a new location and was reborn on the south side, along a strip of motels on Shields Boulevard, with additional street corners being worked a mile or so away on South Robinson Avenue.

It was still raining lightly, the streets slick, as Sean drove the Jeep slowly south on Shields. He'd never seen the area during the day, but at night it looked dreary: the cheap motels, the liquor stores, convenience stores with bars on the doors and windows, even the chain fast-food places looked depressed. Sean could almost smell the despair. Every city had its own answer to this, Sean knew, but it didn't make him feel better about it.

And this leads me to the wealthy, educated daughter of a powerful U.S. senator?

Stranger things had happened. Sean swallowed. He hadn't had a drink since the beer this morning at Faith's house, and he was feeling a bit shaky. *Just need to settle my nerves a bit,* he thought. He pulled into a liquor store, grabbed his wallet and the photocopied Associated Press picture, and bought a pint of Jack Black.

The liquor store clerk was a young Latino man who looked barely old enough to legally work in such a place. Sean paid for his bourbon, then put the picture on the counter.

"You know this girl?" he said in Spanish.

The clerk looked at him, surprised at hearing the *bolillo* speak perfect Spanish. "Don't know her," he responded in kind.

"Look again. Maybe you've seen her around the neighborhood. I think she works around here."

The clerk gave him a long look. "*Dinero, señor.*"

Sean was prepared for this. He'd already transferred some of Owens's cash to his wallet. He peeled off three twenties and gave them to the clerk.

"Britt," the clerk said. "She works the other side of Shields. Check the parking lots of the three motels. She's usually in one of them."

"*Gracias.*"

"*De nada.*"

Sean pulled out of the parking lot as the rain increased. He heard thunder cracking in the distance. Was this Oklahoma City or Seattle? He made a mental note to ask Faith if the weather was always like this here. He pulled the Jeep back onto Shields, crossed Southeast Forty-fourth Street, and drove a few blocks. Then he pulled a U-turn on the wide boulevard and headed back toward the strip of three motels.

Each of the motels was laid out in the same way, shaped like a rectangle with one open end facing the street. He couldn't find a name anywhere for the first one. Its sign only read *Vacancy HBO Free calls.*

I wonder how many people who rent rooms here watch HBO, Sean thought wryly. None of the motel's doors was open, but he knew that by itself didn't mean anything. ICE had busted a huge ring two years ago, in which young Mexican girls—many of them underage and all of them illegal—were brought across the border to Nogales and Tucson and basically sold into indentured servitude. Since the *I* in ICE now stood for Immigration, Sean had been on the team that raided several motels much like this one. It had been a good operation, and Sean liked to think the lives of several of those girls had been saved by what the team had done.

He blinked. That was back when his career still mattered, when he could still make things work.

"Cut that shit out," he said aloud, watching the doors to the motel rooms.

After a few minutes, one of them opened. A skinny young white guy with fuzzy stubble on his face came out, red-faced, still tucking in his shirt. He got into a rusty Ford pickup and drove away. A black woman, older than Sean, in leather shorts and a black halter top, came to the doorway, scanning the parking lot. Sean inched the Jeep toward her.

He rolled down the window. Before he could speak, she leaned down and said, "I'm Monica. Fifty for BJ in the car, one-twenty for half-and-half inside. I'm bad and I'm good, baby."

Sean held up the photo and turned on his dome light. "You know this girl?"

"Turn that light off! Are you crazy? Shit! Turn that off!" The woman backed away from the Jeep.

Sean shook his head. *Must be slipping.* He'd bought the Jack Black to settle his nerves, but hadn't opened it yet. "Sorry," he said, and flicked the light off.

Monica snatched the picture from his hand and took it back to the light of the motel room. She was back in only a few seconds. "Where'd you get this?"

"Does it matter?"

"You a preacher?"

"No."

"You a cop?"

He hesitated slightly. "No."

"Yes, you are. Shit, what are you, federal? OKC cops don't get Jeeps with Arizona plates."

So she was more observant than Sean had thought. That was good. "It's complicated."

"Good-bye, Arizona. I gotta earn a living."

Sean kept his voice even. "Come here, Monica. It'll be worth your while."

She turned expertly on her spike heels. "Show me."

He peeled off ten twenties. "This is as much as you'll get from your next three tricks put together, and just to talk."

"You're a dumb fuck if you pay me that much just to talk. Give it here." He passed her the money. "Okay, so you ain't a cop. That picture was taken at that stupid little march we had here last year."

"You didn't like it?"

"Stupid shit. Some big-shot governor's daughter comes in here with a megaphone, wantin' all the girls to 'organize,' like she's the United Fucking Mine Workers or some shit like that. Talkin' 'bout choice. I told her, 'Honey, I didn't choose shit. This body's all I got to earn my pay. I got three kids and I got expenses and this is what I do.' "

The rain had slacked off, but Monica had seemed oblivious to it anyway. Sean decided not to correct her on who Daryn's father was. "So what happened?"

"Some of the girls went with her. Like Britt, the one in that picture. She was so proud of gettin' her picture took like that. She fell hard for all those lines, 'bout

making a political statement." She drew out the word
political.

"Where is Britt now?"

"She mainly works the Oasis. I used to, but the
rooms are cleaner here. Don't smell as bad."

"Thanks, Monica. Why don't you take a break? Go
get some coffee or something, get out of the rain."

"Shit, Arizona, if I ain't on my back or my knees, I
ain't making a living. I got no time for coffee."

Sean nodded to her and pulled out of the parking
lot. The third motel in the strip was the Oasis, or at
least Sean assumed it was. The sign had an *O* and an *s*,
but the rest of the letters were gone. He parked in a
corner and waited.

A door opened. A heavyset Latina came to the Jeep.
"You want to party?" she said in heavily accented English.

"Waiting for Britt," Sean said.

"Well, piss on you, then," she said, and wobbled
around the parking lot on absurdly high heels.

Ten minutes passed. Another door opened. Another
man got into another pickup truck and drove off. Sean
recognized Britt's hair before anything else—long,
dark, and straight, almost stringy. She was taller than
he'd thought, probably almost as tall as his sister. Her
body was well proportioned, and she looked strong.
He made eye contact with her, and she started toward
him.

She leaned in the window—they all leaned in the
window, Sean thought. "What's your pleasure, honey?"
Her accent sounded upper midwestern.

He took a wild leap. "You from Chicago?" he said.

"Rockford," Britt said. "You?"

"Evanston."

"Oh well, Evanston. Do Evanston boys pay to fuck girls from Rockford in Oklahoma City?"

"Not tonight, Britt."

He watched her reaction to his knowing her name. "Do I know you?" she said.

"No." He showed her the photo.

"Hey, you cut—" Britt stopped herself. "Who are you?"

"I want to talk to you, Britt. About Daryn."

"What about—" Britt backed a step away from the Jeep. "I don't want to talk to you. Who told you where I was?" She straightened up and looked out into the street. "I bet it was that goddamn Monica." She raised her voice into the rain. "Fuck you, Monica, you bitch!"

"Britt, I want to help Daryn." Sean took a deep breath. "I know you care about her. When I saw this picture, the *whole* picture, I knew. I knew you cared about Daryn."

Britt's posture softened. "What's it to you one way or the other?"

"You've seen her, haven't you? Haven't you talked to her in the last month?"

Britt shook her head very slowly. "She was here last year. We did the march."

"I know. But since then. She came here, didn't she? She came back to Oklahoma City. Not for the march. For something else. For some*one* else." Sean ached for a pull of the bourbon, but he couldn't look away from Britt. Not now.

Britt waited a long moment. "Why should I talk to you? I don't know who you are."

Sean breathed out very carefully. On the road last night, he'd come to the conclusion that he might need a new set of ID to complete this project. As an ICE agent for seven years, he'd learned a few tricks outside the book, as most law enforcement officers did. The country's best ID forger was in El Paso, and Sean had taken a detour and stopped there late last night. For two thousand of Tobias Owens's dollars, he had a new ID showing that he lived in Oklahoma City and that his name was Michael Sullivan.

"I'm Michael," he said. "I just want to make sure she's all right. I'm not here to tie her up and take her back to her father, if that's what you're wondering. You can trust me, Britt. Do you want to get in?"

"I don't trust anyone," Britt said. "Anyone except—" She wiped a hand across her face and pulled the strings of her hair back. Rain dripped off her chin, but she made no move to get in the Jeep. "She wanted to get off the road. She wanted to be someone else, something else. She didn't want to be the senator's daughter anymore. And me and her, we kind of hit it off when she was here. She liked the city, not too big, not too small."

"So where is she now?"

"It's not that easy. She's—you have to get it, you know? Dar—she's not like other people. She's, like, brilliant. I mean, she has this vision, she calls it. Justice for all. Not like that stupid shit that kids say in the flag salute. No, real justice for all people. She's so smart and she's so *good*. And she wants to know what other people are like. I mean, look at her. She's this rich senator's daughter, but she doesn't touch her trust fund and she cut up all her credit cards and she left behind her car. The girl's got a Porsche and she left it. She wants to feel what we feel." Britt dropped her voice down. "She wants to feel what *I* feel."

Sean remembered what Owens had said: *Perhaps she secretly wishes she was a prostitute herself, so she could indulge herself and be paid for it.*

Well, I'll be damned, he thought.

"Britt," he said slowly, "is Daryn working the streets herself? Right here in Oklahoma City?"

Britt gazed out toward the street. "Not the streets." She swept an arm back toward the Oasis Motel. "Not this scene. She wanted to, but I thought—you know, no one would believe it. You meet her, and she's just different, you know? The guys, the tricks, wouldn't believe it. They'd think she was a female cop or something, trying to trap them. I mean, you know her, right? Could you see her in a place like this?"

"No," Sean said. "No, I couldn't."

"So I told her she should—"

Much to Sean's surprise, the girl started to cry.

Sean opened the car door and started to get out. Britt scrambled away from him with sudden vehemence. "Stay away! Don't fucking touch me! Just don't!"

Sean held up both hands and backed away. "I'm sorry."

"Sorry," Britt whispered, wiping her nose with the back of her hand. "You fucking men. You're all sorry. You say you're sorry and think you've got to take care of us. I've been taking care of myself since I was fourteen." She sniffled again. "Shit, I told her she should set herself up as a, you know, a high-dollar call girl. Like an escort service."

Sean drew in a breath.

"That sounds more like her, doesn't it? Those escorts . . . they make big money, and the guys they see expect a woman to talk to them, to give them massages and stuff. They want to talk about . . . I don't know what . . . like Shakespeare and stuff. Because they want it to be like they're not paying a whore for sex. They have, like, two-hour minimums and some of them make a thousand bucks for the two hours. And they get to go in really nice hotel rooms, not dumps like this."

"So you told Daryn McDermott to set herself up as an escort. Here in Oklahoma City."

Britt nodded, sniffling again. "Yeah."

"And did she?"

Britt nodded again.

"How do I find her?"

Britt smiled crookedly. She pulled her hair back from her face again, shaking the rain out of it. "Those girls that do escort gigs: They put up websites and everything. That's how they get their tricks. She told me www.katpurrs.com. That's Kat with a K. That's her name now. She wanted to be totally new, so she's Katherine—Kat." Britt looked at the ground, almost shyly. "I helped her pick out the name."

"It's a good name."

They looked at each other. After a long moment, Sean said, "Here, let me pay you for your time."

Britt shook her head. "I only get paid for fucking, not for talking." She spun around and walked toward a wine-colored minivan that had just pulled into the parking lot.

"So you do," Sean said, dropped the Jeep into gear, and drove north.

Britt had two more tricks right in a row before she got a break. The guy in the minivan paid her for half-and-half, but he couldn't finish inside her, kept losing his hard-on. She wound up wasting nearly half an hour and three condoms on him. Then, right after that, a big black guy named Elvin, a semiregular customer, wanted a BJ in his car before he headed home to his wife.

After Elvin was gone, she went into her motel room, closed the door, and went to the bathroom. She took a quick shower, then gargled with Listerine. Feeling better, a little cleaner, she made the call.

The other woman's voice was soft and low on the phone. "Hello, this is Kat."

"Hi, it's me. I mean, Britt. It's me."

"Hey, sweetie. I know your voice by now. What's up?"

"There was a guy here," Britt said.

There was a short silence. "Go on."

"Tall, red hair, driving a Jeep, Arizona plates. Who is he? He acted like he knew you."

"Hmm."

"What?"

"Nothing. It was bound to happen. It just happened sooner rather than later."

"What? What do you mean by that?"

"Don't worry. It's fine. It's just as well that he came now."

Britt thought for a moment. "Have you been okay?"

"Fine, sweetie. A little tired tonight. I had a bad headache yesterday, but it went away. I'm doing just great."

"Daryn? Daryn, when can I see you?"

There was a slight clucking noise. "Remember, I'm Kat now. I'm always Kat."

"I know. I just . . . I like the sound of your name. Your real name."

"I know you do. Soon, Britt. We'll see each other soon."

"Okay."

"Okay, honey."

"I love you," Britt said, but the line was already dead.

8

FAITH WAS SITTING ON THE COUCH READING, WITH Joe Sample's new solo piano CD on the stereo, when Sean returned to the house at a little after nine o'clock. She looked up from her paperback copy of *Blood Will Tell*, about the famous Cullen Davis murder trials in Texas in the seventies, to see her brother, dripping wet, standing there with a mostly empty Jack Daniel's bottle clutched in one hand.

"Hey, baby sister," he said, shaking the rain off himself. "Is the weather always like this here?"

Faith put down her book. "Just in the spring, mainly. That's the stormy season. Looks like you've been out in it."

"Yep." He sat beside her, placing the whiskey bottle very carefully on the table. Her eyes followed the bottle. "You and your books and your jazz," Sean said. "Don't you ever watch TV or anything?"

"Most TV is crap," Faith said. "I catch C-SPAN sometimes."

"Oh, that's exciting."

Faith shrugged. "Find your hooker?"

"I did."

"Get what you wanted?"

"She pointed me in the right direction."

Sean pulled the bottle to him and swigged from it. "Want a drink?" he offered.

"No, thanks."

"More for me."

"I could get you a glass," Faith said, looking at him.

"I don't want to dirty any of your glasses. I put in a load of laundry this morning, by the way."

"So I saw. Thanks."

They sat in silence for a few seconds.

"Have you told Mom and Dad that you're here?" Faith said after a while.

"Nope. None of their business. If I did, you know how it would go. Dad would just try to find out what the two of us talked about. Always being the captain, trying to control us the way he controls his department."

Faith said nothing.

"Come on, admit it. I bet you five thousand dollars that every time you talk to the old man on the phone and mention that you've talked to me or e-mailed me he wants to know what it was about. We live in three separate states, and he still wants to control the way you and I talk to each other."

"No bet," Faith said.

Sean nodded. "I knew I was right." He leaned back against the couch and closed his eyes. The bourbon had taken the edge off, and he was in the gray in-between area. He'd been a bit shaky through the whole encounter on Shields Boulevard with Monica and Britt, but he'd started on the bottle as he drove back here, feeling flushed with knowing how he'd unearthed

Daryn McDermott. Now he wasn't quite totally shit-faced either. He might get shaky again if he had any more, but for now he was somewhere between the two. Having a little more might be nice, but he'd drunk all of Faith's beer this morning and he didn't think she had anything else in the house.

Faith was looking at him again. She tucked one of her long legs up under her—the same way she'd also sat on the couch at home when they were kids—and turned to face him fully. Her eyes, solid green and just as angry at times as their father's, locked onto him. "You drank those three bottles of Harp I had in the fridge this morning."

Sean twirled the whiskey bottle in his hand. "Yeah. It was a long drive in from Tucson."

"You finish off that whole bottle right there, straight, by yourself?"

Sean thumped the bottle on the coffee table, then checked to make sure he hadn't scratched it. It was good wood, and he didn't want to nick it. "You got something to say, sister, say it."

"How did you get to be 'on leave' from ICE? How could you just pick up and leave and come to Oklahoma to do a freelance job?"

Sean blinked. So his sister had shifted into full interrogation mode. "Hey, two can play that game. What's your job? 'Special projects'? Come on, you can do better than that."

They stared at each other for a long moment.

"So we both have our little secrets," Sean finally said. "Big deal."

Faith leaned over and tapped the whiskey bottle with a fingernail. "Your secrets have anything to do with this?"

"What?"

"You having any trouble with this, Sean?"

Sean made a snorting sound. " 'Any good Irish cop worth his salt likes a good drink now and again,' " he quoted.

"Yeah, and you see where it got Seamus, too."

Sean shifted on the couch. "He was due to retire anyway."

"Bullshit," Faith said. "He could have worked another ten years. They let him retire so he could keep his pension and it wouldn't tarnish all the commendations he got while he was on the force."

"What's your point, Faith?"

Faith folded her hands together and squeezed. Sean saw her knuckles turn white. This was what she had done since she was a teenager when she was talking about something intense. She'd stopped biting her fingernails at sixteen, but then started doing this trick of squeezing her hands together so hard that they hurt.

"Say it," Sean said.

"We have a family history," Faith said. "And you've been in a really stressful job situation, with the switch to DHS these last couple of years. I guess . . . I guess I just want to know you're not losing control."

Shit, Sean thought. *Shit, shit, shit. We don't see each other for three years, but still she reads me like a cheap paperback, just like when we were kids. Faith could always close herself up, but me . . . I'm an open book to her.*

Sean flexed his own hands, just to make sure they weren't shaking. Then he very carefully took Faith's smaller hands in his, and pried her fingers apart. "You should quit doing that," he said. "One of these days you'll break your own fingers."

Faith didn't smile.

Sean cleared his throat. "Don't worry about me. Yeah, I've been through a lot. Yeah, I like a good drink now and again. It helps smooth out the hard edges. I've seen some stuff down along the border . . ."

Faith nodded. "I know. I've seen some stuff these last couple of years myself."

Sean let go of her hands. Suddenly it felt awkward, the old Kelly family reluctance toward physical affection. "I bet you have."

Faith stood up. "What next? You want to do some sightseeing tomorrow, or what?"

"Maybe," Sean said. "You set your own hours or what?"

"More or less. Right now I'm just finishing up paperwork on this latest project. Sometimes I have to pick up and go at a moment's notice, so when I'm just hanging out in town doing office work, I'm pretty laid-back on the hours."

"And your boss likes this?"

"My boss is in another time zone. As long as things go the way they're supposed to, and as long as he can reach me at any time, he doesn't care if I'm not in the office nine-to-five."

"Nice work if you can get it," Sean said with a smile.

"Sometimes," Faith said, not smiling.

Sean's smile faded. He thought of something that had happened when he and Faith were nine and eight, respectively. Sean had wanted a new bicycle desperately, but their father was still just making a patrol officer's salary and they couldn't afford it. So Sean—who never believed anything his father said about money—put his old bicycle under the wheels of his dad's car, and the next morning his father backed over it, destroying the bike and the tire of the car as well. Sean blamed it on one of the neighborhood kids. Joe Kelly, in his wrath—he never believed anything Sean said either—had turned to Faith, as he often did. Sean had teased Faith mercilessly in those days, daring her to tell even the tiniest of white lies, saying she was physically incapable of lying. He had begged her with his eyes not to tell the old man, but she looked straight at Sean and said, "He did it, Dad. I saw him. Sean did it."

Joe Kelly had beaten Sean's butt so hard that Sean was sore for ten days. Faith had watched the beating in silence, tears streaming down her face. And Sean never got another bicycle, ever. Sean hated Faith for a long time, with the kind of hate only adolescents are capable of managing. But then some things happened with Faith and she was away from the rest of the family for a while, and when she came back, Sean didn't hate her so much anymore. The incident haunted him for years, and when they were both in college, he'd called her one night and brought it up again.

"I never should have put that bike there, Faith. I put you in the position of wanting you to lie to protect me, and the

old man put you in the position of having to rat on me. We were both wrong, Dad and I. You held on to the truth, as much as it hurt."

Sean looked at his sister now, framed in the lamplight of the messy living room. They were both a long way from what they used to be. Looking at her, thinking of how she evaded any specifics about her job, Sean thought that Faith had probably finally learned how to lie, and that it was tearing her up inside. The thought saddened him.

He nodded at her. "Yeah, we'll sightsee tomorrow," he finally said. "I've got some more work to do on this thing, but it'll be tomorrow night."

"Okay," Faith said. "I'm going to go to bed, I think. There's a bunch of junk in the spare bedroom, but that couch folds out. There are pillows and sheets and stuff in the hall closet."

"I'll find it," Sean said.

She looked at him again. Her eyes flickered over the empty whiskey bottle. "Good night," she said.

Sean puttered around the living room for an hour or so after Faith went to bed. He straightened a few things, then stopped himself, realizing Faith would probably be annoyed with him for doing it. He stopped at her bookshelf, reading spines. Mostly nonfiction volumes on unsolved crimes—same old Faith. But there was one hardcover, something called *The Secret Six*. Curious, Sean pulled it out. It seemed to be about John Brown and the Civil War. When did Faith get interested in Civil War history?

Sean thumbed a few pages. The book was by a man named Edward J. Renehan Jr., and appeared to be about wealthy Northern abolitionists who helped John Brown, who went so far as to bankroll his operation leading up to the raid on Harper's Ferry. *Boring*, Sean thought. He'd never been one for history books. Just before he put it back, his eye caught some handwriting on the title page.

My dear Officer Kelly, Until we meet again, I leave you this reminder of our time together. The note was signed: *Isaac Smith.* Who the hell was Isaac Smith? Sean shook his head. His baby sister had her secrets, all right. Of course, if she really was in Department Thirty, as he suspected, secrets were her business. The idea depressed him even further. He wished he had another pint of Jack, but didn't want to go back out in the rain. He put the book back on the shelf.

He went into the kitchen and rummaged in the refrigerator, finding several takeout containers and microwave dishes.

"Don't you ever cook?" he muttered.

He inspected half of a leftover chicken burrito with refried beans and Mexican rice, then found a microwave plate and heated it. It turned out to be surprisingly good, and it was the most he'd eaten all day. He ate it in front of the TV, watching the ten o'clock news. News was as depressing in Oklahoma City as it was in Tucson, he decided, despite the anchors' attempts to be happy-go-lucky. He turned it off after a few minutes.

After eating, he washed his plate and put it carefully

back in the cabinet where he'd found it. Then Sean returned to the living room and powered up his laptop on the coffee table. He turned off the lamp so that the only light in the room came from the glow of the computer screen.

He logged onto the Internet, waited a moment, and typed in www.katpurrs.com.

An image in soft pastel colors settled onto the screen. Sean adjusted the computer so he could see the screen better. He leaned forward.

There were several shadowy pictures of a young woman, mostly in profile, the photographs having been taken in subdued lighting. None of the photos showed a full shot of her face—they all were cropped just above her mouth.

In one photo, the woman straddled a chair, wearing a white bra, matching panties, garter belt, and stockings. In another she wore a black version of the same outfit.

Still, Sean couldn't be sure. This young woman, though she looked to be Daryn McDermott's size and build, had honey-blond, shoulder-length hair. All of Daryn's photos had shown a young woman with much longer, braided, dark hair.

But then, Sean thought, if she wanted to become someone else—some*thing* else, as Britt had said—she could cut and dye her hair, couldn't she? It even made a sort of sense.

He entered the website. Another shadowy image, this one in black lingerie, was on the left side of the page. He began to read the text that ran beside it:

Hello, and welcome to my personal website. I am Kat Hall, and I am a professionl, independent escort serving gentlemen in the Oklahoma City area. I am very exclusive and selective about my companions, but I am well worth it for those who do spend time with me. I am educated and intelligent, thoughtful and passionate. I can fulfill any fantasies you may entertain. Role playing is welcomed. I will provide the ultimate GFE (Girl Friend Experience) to those who spend time with me.

I appreciate getting to know my companions, so I strongly suggest that you book at least a two-hour appointment. Yes, my rates are higher than most. But I repeat—I am worth it. I am available for incall at my location, or outcall at select downtown Oklahoma City hotels. For those who desire the best and who are willing and able to pay, I await your call.

"Jesus," Sean muttered.

He clicked over to a page marked "donations."

My gift is $600 for one hour, $1000 for two hours, $2000 for a four-hour dinner date, $3500 for overnights. My rates are all inclusive, cash only. Please keep in mind that any contribution is for my time and personal services only. Anything else that may transpire is a matter of personal choice between two consenting adults of legal age, and is not contracted for, or compensated for, in any other manner.

A disclaimer, Sean thought. *This is how escorts can openly advertise on the Internet and not get busted.*

He went to the contact page. A phone number and e-mail link were listed. The photo on this page, still shrouded in subdued lighting and still not showing the woman's face, did feature a close-up of her cleavage inside a pink bra.

The word *justice* was tattooed across the woman's left breast.

"Daryn," Sean whispered. "It is you. I'll be damned."

He sat back. Senator McDermott's radical activist daughter, living a secret life away from the prying eyes of Washington, as an escort, a high-priced call girl.

He thought for a moment. Daryn had only been missing for a little over a month, according to Tobias Owens. But this website was well done and very elaborate, not something hurriedly thrown together. Plus the domain name was her own, not some free web hosting service. It had taken time, effort, and money to develop this.

How long had Daryn McDermott been planning her new life as Kat Hall? Sean wondered.

Sean realized his heart was beating wildly, and he gradually became aware that he was sexually aroused as well.

"My God," he whispered.

He slowly pulled out his cell phone and punched in the numbers on the screen.

"Hello, this is Kat," said the voice a moment later.

Sean was silent a moment, his heart pounding. He felt sweat ringing his forehead. "Hello, Kat," he finally said. "This is Michael. I'd like to make a date with you."

9

FAITH LEFT SEAN SLEEPING ON THE COUCH AND was in her office in Oklahoma City's U.S. Courthouse downtown by seven thirty in the morning. There wasn't much to the office. It was small, the door unmarked. Official occupancy records for the building showed that the small second-floor room was vacant and being used as storage for the U.S. Marshals Service, whose main office suite was down the hall.

The desk was standard issue, metal with a faux wood top. There was a single filing cabinet, one phone line, a computer. There were two "guest" chairs that Faith had scavenged from a used office furniture store, paying for them herself so she didn't have to go through the General Services Administration paperwork. Director Yorkton had appreciated her initiative on that purchase.

She'd added a couple of plants in the last year. Faith was generally no good with plants, but one was an ivy, which was notoriously hard to kill. The other commanding feature of the office continued to be a wooden plaque with a stuffed fish on it. It had belonged to her mentor, the previous occupant of the office, Art Dorian. There was a dent in the fish's body now, though, since she'd ripped the plaque off the wall and flung it across the room in a fit of frustration last summer.

And that, really, was all. Faith didn't keep any photographs on her desk, nothing that said anything personal about her. *This office is not my life,* she reminded herself constantly, *so it shouldn't look like my life.* Still, in unguarded moments—sometimes alone, sometimes with Scott Hendler—she wondered if it wasn't becoming her life after all, her own protestations to the contrary notwithstanding.

She raised the blinds behind the desk, which looked out on the Oklahoma City National Memorial, across Northwest Fourth Street. She only looked for a moment, though—she had mixed feelings about the place. Even though she hadn't lived in Oklahoma City on April 19, 1995, when the Murrah Building was destroyed, she'd felt the sadness and outrage of the rest of the country when watching the news reports. Then she'd wound up living here, assigned to Oklahoma when she joined the Marshals Service. She understood what the memorial meant, but for her, it also stirred up personal feelings. It was there, standing under the Survivor Tree, that she'd been recruited—*forced*, she often thought—to join Department Thirty by now-director Yorkton.

Faith turned to her computer and booted it up, then waited a moment. She took a few minutes, as she did every day, to mentally review the cases under her jurisdiction as a regional Department Thirty case officer. She now had seven in her region, which encompassed New Mexico, Texas, Oklahoma, Kansas, Missouri, and Arkansas. She currently had two cases living in Texas, one in Oklahoma, one in Kansas, three in Missouri, and none in Arkansas. She'd inherited all but two from her predecessor. She'd processed two new ones in the past year, one of them going to St. Charles, Missouri, one to Enid, Oklahoma. Leon Bankston would make eight, which was a pretty good case load. Case officers weren't privy to the cases of other regional officers—Yorkton often trumpeted the virtues of compartmentalization—but she thought one of the other regions had a dozen cases, and one of the others had only three. It was a strange and surreal program, and some aspect confounded her nearly every day.

But then, she thought, maybe the very fact that she hadn't figured out all the angles yet kept her alert. Yorkton seemed to be pleased with her. Her field assistant, Simon, gave her wary respect, though Faith was still leery of him.

All of her cases were fairly self-sustaining right now, and there was no major administrative work to be done. She'd have to begin annual reviews in another couple of months, but for now, her little corner of the shadow world was running smoothly.

Back to Leon Bankston, gun runner extraordinaire. Faith smiled. Actually, Bankston was an idiot, which explained why he wasn't further along in the underworld. The truck into which he'd smuggled the weaponry had an expired license plate, just waiting for an alert Oklahoma Highway Patrol trooper to pull it over.

First she called the safe house and talked to Simon. Bankston, soon to be Benjamin Williams, was doing fine. He was obsessing about various details of the house and getting on Simon's nerves, but was otherwise all right.

"Just get him out of here soon," Simon said, "or I may have to kill him."

She had a couple of steps left in completing the Williams identity. The attorney general still had to give his go-ahead, but the AG always followed the department's recommendation without fail. She had the documents creating his background—birth certificate, Social Security card, school records, college degree, work history, references. She just had to make the final arrangements for someplace for him to live, and iron out the details of his employment. Employers of Department Thirty protectees never knew their employees' real identities or what they had done, only that they were being guaranteed a job through a federal placement program. Sometimes Faith used a Department of Labor cover, sometimes Department of Education, when dealing with the employers.

She spent two hours on the phone working out the details, still awaiting the official go-ahead. Then she sat back, having caught up everything she needed to do today. She was about to call Sean and tell him to meet her downtown for lunch, when Hendler called on her cell.

"Hey, gorgeous," Hendler said.

"Hey, gorgeous," Faith repeated, and smiled.

"Lunch?"

She thought for a moment. "What about a threesome?"

Hendler started laughing.

"You know what I mean," Faith said. "For lunch."

"Ah, dammit," Hendler said. "Just when I thought—"

"Watch it, pal. You never know who's listening."

"Right, right. Your brother joining us for lunch?"

"And smart too," Faith said. "Yep. I was just getting ready to call him."

"I'll meet you in front of the courthouse at eleven thirty."

"It's a date," Faith said, and clicked off before the awkward end-of-call silence could come.

She started to call Sean, then put the phone down again. It would only take a quick e-mail, and she could find out about Sean being "on leave" from ICE. Department Thirty had access to every database the United States Government possessed, through The Basement, which was the entity that did the actual creation of the new identities for protectees. Faith had no idea how many people worked in The Basement, or its physical location. It was alleged to literally be in the basement of one of Washington's myriad government buildings. The Basement had access to *everything*, and Faith had access to The Basement.

"Sean," she said aloud, without even realizing it.

Her big brother. Something wasn't right about him now. She didn't know if it was booze or the stress of the job. He'd been married briefly—less than a year— right after he moved to Arizona, and he never talked about it. He'd never mentioned his wife's name to Faith in the five-plus years since the divorce. Neither of their lives, brother's or sister's, had quite turned out the way they'd always envisioned.

"Sean," she said again.

She typed a message to The Basement.

The Basement returned her e-mail in less than half an hour. She skipped over the details of Sean's background—she knew *that* well enough.

She quickly learned that his career with the Customs Service, later ICE, had been a twisting carnival ride. In the first couple of years, before Customs was absorbed into Homeland Security and reorganized into Immigration and Customs Enforcement, he had no fewer than six commendations. Most were garden-variety bureaucratic notes, but one talked about his outstanding service in helping to break up a ring that was importing young Mexican girls into Arizona and selling them as sex slaves. Things had deteriorated quickly thereafter. She began to read vaguely worded reprimands, just the sort of thing a supervisor would write when an underling had screwed up but the supervisor still thought highly of him overall.

The reprimands became more specific as time went by, and they began to reference a growing problem with alcohol. At one point, an ICE-appointed counselor had referred Sean to undergo outpatient alcohol treatment and to attend meetings of Alcoholics Anonymous.

The final entry in the file, dated two days ago, written by Special Agent in Charge Weller, noted that Special Agent Sean M. Kelly had been placed on administrative suspension without pay, pending a termination hearing. The reason: severe dereliction of duty, related to uncontrolled consumption of alcohol.

"Oh, shit, Sean," Faith said. "Why couldn't you—"
She choked off the words.

Her big brother. Her only sibling. No wonder he
didn't want their father to know he was here. All the
talk about Joe Kelly trying to control their relationship
aside, Faith knew that the old man would see right
through any talk about Sean being "on leave," and
would demand to know why.

A long time ago, Faith would have called her father
and told him everything she knew about what was
going on with Sean.

But Faith was a different person now. She'd learned
how to walk in the shadows, and she saw things outside the shades of black and white and right and
wrong that had been so clear to her a long time ago.

There were other ways.

She picked up her cell phone and called Cara Dunaway. Dunaway was an FBI agent in the local field office, a colleague of Hendler's. She was one of Faith's
few female friends in Oklahoma, a petite blonde of
around forty, with two teenage kids. She was also a re-
covering alcoholic and had been sober for twelve years.

"Hi, Cara," Faith said. "It's Faith Kelly."

"Well hello, Faith Kelly," her friend said. "What's up
in your world? Don't answer that, I'm being rhetorical."

Faith forced a chuckle. "Hey, Cara, I need your
help."

"What do you need?" Dunaway said.

Faith told her.

10

SEAN ENDURED THE LUNCH WITH HIS SISTER AND her geeky boyfriend the FBI agent. He quickly surmised that Scott Hendler was far further along in the relationship than Faith was, but he kept silent about it. He wasn't one to lecture his sister on her personal life.

They'd done the tour of the memorial, which Sean found to be powerful beyond words. They visited the nearby Oklahoma City Museum of Art, which turned out to be a world-class facility. Sean had always been more interested in visual arts than Faith was, and he'd become quite fond of art museums over the last few years.

By midafternoon, Sean begged off, saying he wanted a nap before going to "work" tonight. He went to a little bar he'd passed earlier on Pennsylvania Avenue, spent an hour with Jack Daniel, then proceeded to Faith's house. She'd given him a key, and he slept for three hours.

Just after eight o'clock, using the directions that "Kat" had given him on the phone last night, he drove up Northwest Fiftieth Street, west of Interstate 44, west of Portland Avenue. Her "incall" location was actually a small gated apartment complex. It was a single building of two-story apartments, one row facing east, one row facing west. There were probably no more than a dozen units altogether. It was a relatively quiet, middle-class neighborhood. Unobtrusive.

Hide in plain sight, Sean thought.

"The gate code is 218," she had told him. *"Go in the east gate. It's unit number five. Ring the bell. When I answer, you will initiate a hug. Anything you have to give me should be in a plain white envelope and you'll give it to me then without any comment about what's in it. After that's out of the way, it's just the two of us."*

Fascinating, Sean thought. *The business of escorting has its own culture, its own language and lingo.* He'd done some more research online after setting the appointment. There were entire websites devoted to "reviews" of escorts, who were referred to as "providers." There was all kinds of shorthand about various sexual activities, and the customers—what Britt or Monica would have called "tricks"—were referred to as "hobbyists," with prostitution known as "The Hobby."

Fascinating, he thought again. Sean himself had never paid for sex in his life. He'd never had to, he thought with a touch of . . . what? Arrogance? Pride? He had a feeling he was about to descend into a very strange netherworld.

He'd talked Faith into swapping cars for the evening, as he'd been afraid that if Daryn saw the Arizona plates, she might get spooked. He was supposed to be Michael Sullivan of Oklahoma City, after all. So he'd driven Faith's little two-seater Miata instead.

Sean rang the bell at apartment number five. He heard movement inside, and the door opened.

Daryn McDermott was simply a breathtaking

woman. She wasn't classically beautiful, but Sean couldn't take his eyes from her. She was petite, almost fragile in appearance, but the woman radiated sensuality and intelligence and passion. Her hair was indeed dyed blond—Sean caught sight of a few dark roots, as well as her dark eyebrows—and cut shorter than in the photos Owens had given him. But it framed her face beautifully, with its high cheekbones, gently upturned nose, and sensuous lips. She wasn't wearing much makeup—a touch of eye shadow, very light blush, a subtle shade of lipstick. She didn't need much else.

She was wearing a short skirt that came midthigh, and it fit her as if it had been tailored. Women like Monica and Britt could only dream of looking so good in such a skirt, Sean decided. Her blouse was white and simple and showing just enough cleavage to tantalize. He couldn't quite see the tattoo on her left breast.

"Hello, Michael," she said.

"Hello, Kat."

Remembering her instructions, he opened his arms and they embraced. He had to bend down, his six three to her five one. Her touch was electric. Simply putting her arms around him and rubbing his back for a moment had made him more aroused than he would have thought possible.

Easy, he told himself. *Just take it easy.*

He handed her the white envelope without speaking. She took it without looking at it and put it on a wooden stand beside the door.

"Come in," she said. "Please, come in."

She led the way down a short hall. The apartment

was clean and tidy. Sean suspected it had come furnished, as the furniture was all strictly middle of the line, neutral colors, nothing personal about it.

"You'll have to forgive the décor," Daryn said.

Or should I think of her as Kat? Sean wondered. *I have to gain her trust, to develop a relationship with her. Can't just take her to her father at gunpoint.*

"I'm new to the city and haven't had time to settle in yet," she said.

Who are you? Sean felt like shouting. *Daryn or Kat? Or someone else altogether?*

"So am I," he said slowly. "Just moved here."

"Oh?" she said. "Where are you from?"

"Chicago, originally. You?"

"I've lived lots of places. Come, have a seat."

They sat near to each other, but not too near, on a couch upholstered in soft earth tones. Sean heard music from somewhere, a solo acoustic guitar with a new age feel to it. He could feel the heat from Daryn. She positively *radiated* passion. He inhaled a bit of her scent, something musky and understated, but powerful, like the woman herself.

"What do you do, Michael?" Daryn draped her arm along the back of the couch. It reached far enough that she could almost touch his shoulder with her fingertips. He wished she would.

Sean had already decided on his cover story, and it wasn't even a total lie. "I work with wood," he said. "I design and build furniture."

"With your own hands?"

Sean nodded.

"Let me see," Daryn said.

The senator's daughter took both his hands and turned them over, palms up. She traced the lines on his hands with her fingers. Sean shivered.

"Are you all right?" she asked.

"Yes. I'm fine."

She touched his fingertips with her own. "They're good hands. I love men's hands."

She put one of his hands on top of one of hers, then reached up with her thumb and began kneading his palm, then worked her way up, massaging each of his fingers.

"That's wonderful," Sean whispered. "You have such a . . ."

"Yes?"

"An amazing touch. Firm and gentle at the same time."

Daryn laughed lightly. "That's a good description of me."

Sean closed his eyes. On one level, he was aware that he'd accomplished at least part of what he had been hired to do—find Senator McDermott's daughter. But in a more visceral place, he felt only the things she was stirring in him, right here, right now. And she'd barely even touched him.

"You like?" Daryn said softly.

"Very much. You have pretty good hands yourself."

"Thank you. Shall we explore further? Come upstairs with me."

Would he do it? Sean thought dimly. Would he actually have sex with this girl as part of this job?

Without breaking the hand contact, Daryn rose from the couch, lightly pulling Sean with her. She led him to the stairs, which opened just off the front door.

The lighting upstairs was more subdued, one bedside lamp and three votive candles. Sean smelled a hint of vanilla from one of them. Daryn sat on the edge of the full-size bed, but made no move to undress.

"You want to talk?" Daryn said. "My instinct tells me, Michael, that you haven't been with a woman in a while and you'd just like to talk, for now."

Jesus Christ, she could read him as easily as Faith could. Was he that transparent to all women?

Sean nodded. "Like I said, I'm new in town." He cleared his throat.

They talked. More accurately, Sean talked and Daryn—as Kat—listened. He embellished his cover story, made up a fictional family on the fly, talked about how much he loved designing classic American furniture and building it with his own hands. That much, at least, was true.

Daryn listened, asking a question here and there, never giving up anything of herself. Sean let it go and didn't pry. This was about him gaining her trust, and he had to dance very carefully with her or he might lose sight of who was leading and who was following.

Three-quarters of an hour passed. They gradually became a bit more physical. Daryn opened her shirt all the way. He felt her breasts. She rubbed his crotch through his pants. She kissed his neck a couple of times. Sean thought he would explode, but he kept it under control.

He was fondling her left breast—the one with the *jus-*

tice tattoo—and was moving his head toward it, as if being guided by an unseen hand. Daryn's head was back, her arms gripping the headboard of the bed, her legs parted ever so slightly. The tension was almost unbearable, cracking in the air like prairie thunder. The world of street hookers like Monica and Britt was light-years away from the sensuality of this moment, of this woman.

His lips were inches from her breast when Sean heard a faint sound. He couldn't quite place it—he thought it came from downstairs. Something familiar, an ordinary sound, but somehow out of place right here, right now.

A second later, the apartment door exploded inward.

Daryn screamed, pulling her shirt closed around her breasts. Sean rolled off the bed and came up in a crouch.

"Where the fuck is she?" a male voice growled from downstairs.

"Search the back," said a second voice.

So there were at least two of them. Sean crawled toward the chair at the foot of the bed. He'd carefully draped his windbreaker over it when they came upstairs. His Glock was in it—he hadn't anticipated trouble, at least not this kind, but he knew better than to walk into any kind of volatile situation unarmed. Seven years on the border had taught him that.

He raised his eyebrows at Daryn. She shook her head violently. *I don't know!*

Shit!

They'd certainly heard Daryn's scream, and it wouldn't take them long to figure out that the sound had come from upstairs. The apartment wasn't that large.

"Upstairs," said the first voice.

Sean mimed blowing out the candles, which Daryn did, and she also turned off the lamp. The room went black.

Sean silently took his Glock from the pocket of the windbreaker. He looked over his shoulder. He could barely see Daryn, just the outline of the white shirt she wore. She was beside the bed, squatting on the balls of her feet. At least she hadn't screamed again.

A host of possibilities ran through Sean's mind. *Who were they?*

Maybe Tobias Owens and Senator McDermott had covered their bases in a different way. Maybe they'd had Sean followed, and all the talk about gaining her trust and convincing her to come home of her own accord was just that—talk. Let Sean find the girl, then send in the commandos.

Maybe they were political enemies, someone else who had been searching for Daryn McDermott because of her radical ideas. Maybe Sean had led them to her.

Maybe they were psycho former customers of the escort they knew as Kat Hall. Maybe they were common thieves.

Maybe, maybe . . .

Sean heard a heavy step turn toward the stairs. The other set of footsteps was still farther back in the apartment, perhaps in the living room or kitchen.

"It's fuckin' dark," said the voice at the foot of the

stairs. Then, louder: "You up there, girl? Come on now, you can't hide."

Daryn expelled a breath. Sean saw her move slightly in the darkness, and willed her to be still. He very carefully angled his body around so that he was facing the place where the stairs reached the bedroom.

The heavy steps started up the stairs. One stair, two, three . . .

Who were they?

Sean tried to remember how many steps there were. He'd been so consumed by Daryn's touch that he hadn't really noticed. Were there eleven, was that right? Or was it twelve?

Four steps up, five . . .

Weren't all stairways built with an *odd* number of steps? Hadn't he read that somewhere? Maybe it was eleven. Eleven steps up to the bedroom.

Six, seven, eight.

He couldn't shoot up here, not in the dark. No one in their right mind got into a gun battle in the dark. Did they even have guns? He couldn't tell, but they sure as hell weren't friendly.

He put the Glock down, looking wildly around the darkened room. On some level it registered with him that there was still music playing, that flowing, soft acoustic guitar, and that the source of it was very near. An arm's length from him was a wooden stand, just like the one downstairs by the door. On it sat a small portable CD player. Its tiny digital readout, the only light in the room, told him it was playing track number ten.

The intruder on the stairs took two more steps.

Sean moved. He swiveled and grabbed the little stereo, the cord ripping out of the wall socket. He angled back around as the man hit the eleventh step. Holding the stereo in one hand, like a baseball pitcher going into his windup, Sean drew back with all his strength and flung it around the corner.

"What the—" muttered the man on the stairs.

Sean really didn't think the little stereo would hurt the man, but if he was lucky, it would make him lose his balance. Sean leaped to his feet and rounded the corner. The man, who was shorter and older than Sean, though with a muscular build, had taken the blow right in his knee. A perfect shot. He was teetering on the top step. Sean reached out with his long arms. He could smell the man's breath, stale with cigarettes. He shoved him in the chest and the man tumbled backward down the stairs.

He watched as the man's head thumped against the wood floor. "Let's go!" he yelled at Daryn.

She obeyed him with no hesitation. He grabbed the Glock and they ran down the stairs. Their attacker was still dazed and Sean stepped over him easily, but Daryn, with her shorter legs, had to actually go *around* him, and his hand reached out and closed over her bare ankle.

"Michael!" she screamed.

Even though the man's eyes were still closed, he had a firm hold on Daryn's leg, shaking her, trying to make her lose her own balance, just as Sean had done to him. Her arms flailed.

Sean had the Glock out in an instant, turning it

around, butt first, bringing it down with all his force on the man's wrist. Sean heard a sick cracking sound and the man's hand went limp, releasing Daryn's leg.

Sean reached out a hand to Daryn. She stepped past the groaning man and came toward him.

"Hey!" shouted the second man, from the entryway to the living room.

Sean half-turned. He saw the pistol in the man's hand, saw it being raised, saw the barrel glint.

He whipped up the Glock and was thankful there was no safety on this gun. He hated guns with safeties—he would never have been able to learn to fire the damn things under stress if they had. He squeezed the trigger.

Marksmanship had never been Sean's strong point, but the shot went right where he wanted it to go, into the shoulder of the second man's gun arm. The gun flew out of the man's hand and he stumbled backward, bouncing off the wood cabinet of the television set in the living room.

"Let's go," Sean said again.

He took Daryn's hand and they ducked through what was left of the front door. For a moment Sean was confused when he stepped outside, looking for his Cherokee. Then he had it—Faith's little Miata. He pointed to it. He and Daryn ran.

In less than five minutes Sean had the Miata on Interstate 44, driving south as it looped around the west side of Oklahoma City.

"Do you know who they were?" he asked.

Daryn sat in the passenger seat, trembling, hugging herself, each hand on the opposite shoulder. She shook her head.

"Do you have someplace you want me to take you?" He decided to do a little gentle probing, to see what, if anything, she might reveal. "Any family here in town?"

"No," she whispered. "No family."

"What about friends?" He thought of Britt, standing in the rain outside the Oasis Motel.

Another head shake. "I'm new here. I just got set up in town a little while ago. I haven't . . . no, there's no one. Help me. Please, Michael. Can you help me? You said you're new here too."

Christ Almighty, Sean thought. He had to be very careful, to try to remember what was real and what wasn't. Kat Hall wasn't real. Daryn McDermott was. Michael Sullivan wasn't real. Sean Kelly was. And until he could break through Kat and get to Daryn, he would have to remember that everything was a lie. And by the same token, Michael would have to tell lies that Sean would have to deal with later. He shook his head, catching his reflection in the windshield.

What have I gotten into? Sean wondered.

"Let's get you somewhere safe," he said. "Then we'll try to sort all this out."

Daryn was still hugging herself. "You'll stay with me?"

"I'll stay with you."

"Good," she said, and Sean saw her face in the windshield as well.

11

SEAN WOUND UP DRIVING WEST ON INTERSTATE 40 until they reached El Reno, a midsize town half an hour's drive outside the Oklahoma City metro. He got them a motel room, though for a moment he'd hesitated when the clerk asked if he wanted one bed or two.

We were about to have sex, he thought. *But that was business, wasn't it? And if so, what is it now?*

He finally opted for one bed, thinking it would arouse more suspicion if a man and a woman checked into a single room with two beds. He paid cash and steered Daryn to an upstairs room. He sat her down on the bed, then went to the sink and ran cold water onto a white motel washcloth.

"Run this over your face," he said, handing her the cloth. He noticed that his own hands were shaking ever so slightly.

She looked at his hands, then at the cloth, then into his eyes. She slowly took the cloth and wiped her face and neck.

Sean pulled the hard plastic motel chair near the bed and sat down. "Did you recognize them at all?" he asked.

Daryn shook her head.

Sean waited a moment, choosing his words. "Do you think they might have been former . . . clients?"

Daryn managed a smile. "I'm a professional escort, not a street hooker, Michael."

Sean's eyebrows knitted.

"The girls on the street try hard to forget the men they're with. For most of the girls, the guys don't even have faces. Why do you think I recommend my clients book two full hours? It's not just sex." She handed the damp cloth back to him. "I remember the men I spend time with. Neither of those guys looked the least bit familiar."

"Is there any other . . ." Sean let the sentence hang.

Daryn stared at him. She was calm now, and Sean realized how striking her dark eyes were under the dyed blond hair.

"There is a possibility," she said.

Sean leaned forward until his knees were almost touching hers.

"I have some . . . unusual . . . views," she said.

"Go on."

"Political, social views. I've had some clients that were powerful men, and it's in their best interest to keep the status quo. Maybe I mouthed off about my views to the wrong person."

"And they sent someone around to scare you?" Sean said. "That sounds—"

"Farfetched?" Daryn said. "Have you ever heard the term 'gun thugs'?"

Sean nodded. "It's kind of an old term."

"Read your American history. In the early twentieth century, in the early years of the labor movement in this country, it was pretty common. Especially in the coal fields in Appalachia, where the miners were trying to organize. The coal companies would hire these guys as freelancers to come and shoot up the miners' camps, to send them warnings. There were several pretty notorious massacres when things got out of hand."

Sean nodded again. "It's a pretty bloody history."

"Maybe these guys were modern-day gun thugs, sending me a warning to be careful about my pillow talk."

Sean smiled. "Unusual political and social views, huh?"

Daryn met his gaze head-on. "Yes."

"Can you tell me? I'm just a woodworker, no one with powerful interests in keeping the status quo." Sean breathed deeply. He was starting to dance along the tightrope.

Gain her trust.

How better to gain her trust? Even as Kat the professional escort, Daryn's politics would shine through. He was certain of it. When a human being was as passionate about something as Daryn McDermott was about her issues, they wouldn't ever leave those issues totally behind, even when descending into a different person's life.

Gain her trust. Make her want to tell you. Make her want to strip Kat away and become Daryn again with you, for you.

"Please," he said. "Please, I want to know."

She looked at him squarely. "You saved my life," she said, almost in a whisper.

Sean shrugged.

"No, don't shrug it away. *You saved my life.*" She stood up and began unbuttoning the white blouse.

Sean started to hold out his hands, but he realized they were shaking again.

"This first," Daryn said. She peeled off the blouse and stood there, braless, before him. "Then talk."

She came to him, leaned over him, straddled him, her legs on either side of him. Her lips found his.

God help me, Sean thought.

When they were finished, Sean felt as sated as he ever had. She had moved with him as if they'd known each other forever, as if they'd already made intimate explorations of each other's bodies. She took him places he had scarcely imagined. Her responses to him were raw and passionate and utterly breathtaking.

He lay bathed in perspiration on the motel bed. He stole a glance at the bedside clock, surprised to see that it was after eleven.

Sean had never been with a woman who so reveled in her own nakedness. All of the women he'd been with before had wanted to get dressed immediately, or at least slip under the sheets. But Daryn/Kat was absolutely unself-conscious about her body. She wore her nudity proudly, sitting cross-legged beside him.

"You're quite a man," she said softly.

Sean smiled at her.

She stroked his leg. "Let's talk now," she said.

Sean propped himself on one elbow.

His cell phone rang. They looked at each other.

"Do you need to get that?" Daryn asked.

Sean waited a long moment before answering. "No," he said. "Let it go."

Daryn smiled.

They talked for three hours, and Sean began to see how brilliant Daryn McDermott really was. She laid out all her arguments, the ones he'd already read about in the papers Owens had given him. She was like a lawyer arguing before the Supreme Court—passionate and articulate, with facts and figures to back her up. Her ideas were wild, radical, some would say dangerous. She even envisioned a sort of salary-control socialism, where CEOs of major corporations would have their salaries capped by the federal government. Then what she called the "overage"—the amount the CEOs would have earned above their salary cap—would be put into a federal fund that would then be used to raise the salaries of professions like teachers, nurses, and social workers. Sean could certainly see how politicians like her father and those of like mind would feel threatened.

When the conversation waned, Sean realized that all she'd told him about were her ideas, her opinions . . . nothing about herself. Not even anything about the fictitious Katherine Hall.

He stretched out on the bed. "How long have you been doing the escort gig?"

"Long enough to know not to answer that question."

They both laughed.

"And now," she said, "the next thing you're going to ask is how a smart girl like me becomes an escort."

Sean shrugged. "I guess we've kind of gone past our original, uh, professional relationship. I'd like to know more about you."

Daryn was silent for a long moment, studying him. "The obvious answer is that I like sex."

Sean smiled.

"But that's not all of it," Daryn added quickly. "I like people. I like getting to know people. I like touching. I *love* touching." She traced a finger along Sean's forearm. "There's such power in touch. On some level I'm probably overcompensating."

"What do you mean?"

She smiled, letting it touch her eyes, and Sean thought for a second that he had seen the first glimpse past the veneer of Kat Hall, and into the soul of Daryn McDermott. "My family didn't touch. Not at all."

"It's just who we were," Daryn said. "My mother . . . well, I don't remember much of her anyway. She was gone when I was little." A little tone of bitterness crept into her voice. "And my father . . . I remember going to hug him, and he would just go all stiff. He wouldn't actually push me away, but he wouldn't return the hug, and after a while I quit trying."

Sean was silent. *Let her talk*, he thought.

"None of my stepmothers paid much attention to me either," Daryn said. "They were there for my father, the 'great man,' and I was just part of the scenery."

Sean sat up. "Your father, the 'great man'?"

Daryn backed off. "Forget it. It's just me being bitter, and I recognize it for what it is. You don't really want to hear a bunch of crazy stuff about me, after all."

Yes, I do, Sean thought, but said nothing.

Daryn smiled wickedly, and it seemed Kat Hall was back, the invisible mask having been put on again. "Speaking of touching . . ." She leaned toward him.

They coupled again—briefly, intensely—then drifted off to sleep, naked beside each other, sometime after three a.m. Just before sleep claimed him, Sean wondered, *So who were the gun thugs? Really, who were they?*

Sean woke to the sound of his phone ringing. He looked at the clock: just past seven a.m.

"Faith," he muttered, digging the phone out of his pants pocket.

"Where the hell are you?" his sister said.

Sean sat up. Daryn stirred but stayed asleep. "I ran into a little trouble last night," he said.

"Why didn't you call me?"

"Sorry, Dad, just stupid, I guess."

"Don't bullshit me. Are you all right?"

"Fine, fine. At least there aren't any bullet holes in your car."

"What?"

"Nothing, I'm kidding." He glanced at Daryn. The sheet had fallen away from her breasts. The word *justice* stared up at him. He thought about all the things she'd told him. She'd presented her views with as much passion as she presented her body. But when talking about herself, even as she thought she was carefully preserving the fiction that was Kat Hall, it was like she was another person, one who'd been wounded deeply. One who wasn't nearly as sure of herself as she was of her politics.

"Faith, I need your help," Sean said.

Faith recognized the tone. "I'm listening."

"Not on the phone. Let me meet you."

"I'm leaving for the office now, driving that god-awful monster truck of yours."

"Sorry," Sean said. He began to fumble for his clothes. "I'm in a town called El Reno."

"El Reno! How did you get way out there?"

"Never mind. I'll be in front of the building where your office is in one hour."

There was a long silence. Sean listened to his sister's breathing. She would be turning over in her mind the reason he hadn't just said "the courthouse." "You're not alone?" she finally said.

"No, I'm not. I will be when I meet you, but I'll need to . . ." *I'll need to what?* He squeezed his eyes open and closed. *God, I need a drink right about now.* "I'll need to come back."

"Sean—"

"Trust me, sister. I need you to just trust me."

"Okay, okay. I'll see you in an hour."

Sean clicked off. He looked back at Daryn. Her eyes were wide open and staring at him. "Who was that?" she said, her voice husky with sleep.

"Maybe someone who can help keep us safe," Sean said. "I have to go out for a while."

"But you'll be back?"

"Oh, yes, I'll be back," Sean said, and started to get dressed.

12

IT WAS A GORGEOUS SPRING MORNING. THE LATEST round of storms had moved out of Oklahoma City and left moderately cool morning temperatures under blazing clear blue skies. Faith waited for Sean on the sidewalk in front of the federal courthouse. When she saw her Miata turn onto Fourth, she waved Sean to a parking place around the corner and started up the sidewalk.

He parked at a meter on the Harvey Avenue side of the courthouse and they met each other at the corner. "You're late," Faith said. "You said an hour. It's been nearly two."

"Good morning to you, too," Sean said.

She looked at him. His clothes were rumpled, his hair sticking up in back. He was unshaven, and she could smell the liquor from three feet away.

Faith clenched a fist, then slowly let it out. "What happened?"

Sean rubbed a finger under his nose. "Let's take a walk. At least that damn rain's stopped."

They walked west, passing the front door of the courthouse. Sean was silent, and Faith suppressed her natural urge to pump him for details. They crossed the street, passing Saint Joseph Old Cathedral, the oldest

Catholic church in Oklahoma City, dating from years before statehood.

"You go to mass much?" Sean asked as they walked past the beautifully restored brick cathedral.

"Not too often," Faith said.

"Me either. I'm sure Mom's disappointed. Kind of a curse to have the name Faith, huh?"

Faith shrugged. "It's my name. What can I say?"

"Yeah, I suppose." Sean stuffed both hands in the pockets of his khakis.

Faith flexed and unflexed her hands. "What happened, Sean?"

"Did you see or hear any news this morning?"

"A little bit on the radio driving in. Why?"

"Anything about shots fired at an apartment complex?"

Faith glanced at him. "Yeah, on the northwest side. Neighbors heard a big ruckus in the apartment next door. By the time the cops got there, the girl who lives there was missing."

Sean covered his eyes with the back of his hand, as if the sun were too bright.

"Sean?" Faith said. "Hello?"

"What did they say about the girl who lived there?"

"What's this about? Do you know something about this?" Faith tugged his sleeve, making him stop. "Were you there?"

Sean jerked away from her touch. "The girl who lived there! What did they say about her?"

Faith stared at him for a long moment, then dropped her hand. They continued walking, leaving the cathedral behind. "I don't remember her name. It was something fairly common-sounding, I think. Just that she was young and hadn't lived there very long." They reached the corner at Hudson Avenue. Diagonally across the street was the new Metro Transit bus terminal.

"Shit," Sean whispered.

"Tell me," Faith said, as they started to cross Hudson.

Sean gathered in a shaky breath. "It's part of this job I'm doing. Yes, I was there." They reached the other side of the street. Faith motioned to a bench outside the main part of the bus terminal, and they sat down. Sean put a hand on his sister's shoulder. "Faith, I need your help. I need to keep this girl safe and out of sight for a while."

Faith was silent for a while. Behind them, a bus pulled into the terminal, bringing noise and fumes and only half a dozen passengers. "Who is she?" Faith finally said.

"Sorry, I can't," Sean said. "If I start talking about it, then the whole thing's blown."

"And you think I have a way to help you keep her safe and out of sight?"

"I need a safe house," Sean said abruptly.

Faith half-turned on the bench. "You need a *what?*"

Sean tilted his head back, looked at the sky, then looked at the ground. "Let's cut the bullshit, sister. If you're working for Department Thirty, you've got access to safe houses."

At the words *Department Thirty* coming from her

brother's mouth, Faith leaned back as if she'd been slapped.

"Don't do that," Sean said. "Come on, you're working for Thirty. 'Special projects' in DOJ? That only means one thing. Federal law enforcement is like a small town, Faith. Even if we don't all know each other, we've all heard of each other, and we all have an opinion of each other. You were always interested in WITSEC when you joined the Marshals anyway. Thirty is just one step through the looking glass from WITSEC."

"You're quite the philosopher."

Sean slammed a hand down on the metal bus bench. "Goddammit, Faith! I need your help!" He lowered his voice. "You do work for Department Thirty, don't you?"

Faith was silent.

"Jesus Christ," Sean said. "What do I have to do? Remember in the eighties? People started to hear rumors about this federal department called the National Security Agency—NSA. The joke was that it really stood for No Such Agency, and you didn't talk about it. You just *didn't*. Now the NSA's got a website. A *website*, for Christ's sake, Faith! Thirty is now what NSA was then. I understand that. I don't agree with what it does, but I guess that's not for me to say, either. Maybe all of what I know is myth and rumor. Doesn't matter. I . . . need . . . your . . . help."

"You're putting me in an impossible position," Faith said. "You know that, don't you?"

Sean got out, looking around. A few people were milling around the parking lot, some smoking cigarettes. There were a few older, well-dressed men and women, a few guys who looked like laborers, a couple of twentysomething girls who looked like punk rockers, complete with flaming pink hair and multiple tattoos. They all seemed to be waiting for something.

"What is this?" Sean said.

"Come on," Faith said.

"Sister, what the hell is this?"

Faith led him through a glass door and into a small waiting room. The décor was neutral, with a couple of outdated but clean office-type chairs, a potted ivy, a couple of neutral pictures on the walls.

A tiny blond woman was walking toward them. "Hi, there you are!" she said.

"Hi, Cara," Faith said. "Cara Dunaway, this is my brother, Sean Kelly. Sean, my friend Cara."

Dunaway extended a hand. "Hi, Sean. Glad you're here."

Sean shook her hand. "Where exactly is 'here'?"

Dunaway slid a glance to Faith, who only shrugged.

"Why don't you come on back?" Dunaway said. "We're about ready to start."

Sean made more questioning sounds, but followed the two women down a short hallway, which then opened into a large meeting room. Rows and rows of folding chairs were set up, facing a slightly raised platform and podium. In one back corner of the room was what looked like a bar area, except no liquor bottles were visible. Faith and Sean smelled strong coffee brewing.

At the front of the room, next to the platform, was a series of framed photographs. On each side of the platform was a huge framed plaque. They came a bit closer, and Dunaway motioned them to seats. Others were filing in a few at a time. A couple of people spoke to Dunaway. One older woman hugged her.

As they grew closer, Sean read the first few lines of the plaque that commanded the wall at the front of the room.

We admitted we were powerless over alcohol—that our lives had become unmanageable.

"Oh, for shit's sake," Sean said in a stage whisper. He jabbed Faith in the ribs. "You brought me to an Alcoholics Fucking Anonymous meeting."

Faith glared. "Keep your voice down, Sean."

"No, I won't keep my voice down. How could you drag me here? To this?" He swept a hand around the room.

"Because, dammit, you're an alcoholic."

"And you're full of shit, sister." Sean abruptly stood and worked his way along the row of chairs and toward the exit.

Faith was right behind him. She caught his sleeve just before he turned into the hallway. Behind them, a man in his fifties, in a flannel shirt and jeans, had ascended the podium. He introduced himself—*Hello, I'm Ed, and I'm an alcoholic*—offered words of welcome, then said something about a prayer.

"You must be kidding," Sean breathed.

The assembled group, with no prompting, spoke in unison:

God grant me the serenity to accept the things I cannot change, to change the things I can, and the wisdom to know the difference.

"This is a fucking cult," Sean said in full voice.

"Shut your damn mouth," Faith hissed at him. "Sean, you have a problem. You were an hour late to meet me this morning, even for something you say is vitally important, because you had to stop off somewhere and drink. Did you think I wouldn't know? Do you think I can't tell?"

Now the meeting progressed around the room, with each person—every single one of them, more than a hundred strong—introducing to the gathering at large, to which the gathering responded in turn.

I'm Jack, and I'm an alcoholic.

Hi, Jack!

I'm Denise, and I'm an alcoholic.

Hi, Denise!

Henry, alcoholic.

Hi, Henry!

Melissa, alcoholic and addict.

Hi, Melissa!

"I'm getting out of here," Sean said. "This gives me the creeps. I can't believe you brought me here."

Faith looked back toward the group. Cara Dunaway was staring back with a concerned look on her face. Faith spread her hands.

"He may not be ready," Dunaway mouthed.

Faith dropped her hands in exasperation and followed Sean down the hall, out the door, and onto the sidewalk. He spun abruptly, almost losing his balance, and grabbed Faith by both shoulders. "That was a shitty trick, Faith. I come to you for help and you bring me to some preaching, praying, AA group. If I wanted praying in unison, I'd just go to mass. What's the matter with you?"

"It's not what's the matter with me, you fool," Faith growled. "Don't you get it? It's not just recreational anymore. It's not just getting plastered at a party anymore. It's not even 'taking the edge off' anymore. The bottle's holding you instead of the other way around. It's going to destroy your life, piece by piece, until you don't have *anything*."

"I just wanted your help." Sean turned his back on her and started toward the parking lot.

"What do you think I'm trying to do?" Faith screamed at the top of her lungs.

Sean stopped. He had never heard Faith shout like that. Never. She was always the one who was tightly controlled, able to wall off the emotions, able to hide behind intellect or ambition.

"My God, but you've changed," Sean said in a low voice.

"And do you think you haven't?"

"Not really, no. Maybe I drink a little more than I used to. So what? I'm a little older than I used to be."

Faith's voice rose again. "What the hell is the matter with you? You're not a kid, you're not stupid. Can't you see it? It's already destroyed your career. What's next?"

Sean went still. Faith felt a coldness descend between them, as if a freakish winter wind had wandered into this May morning.

"I never said anything to you about my career," Sean said, in a very soft, dangerous voice.

Faith raised both hands, then dropped them to her sides again.

"Now you're checking up on me?" Sean said. His own hands balled into fists. "You're in Department Thirty and you've got access to anything and everything, so you thought you'd check up on me?"

"Sean, I just—"

"No! No, you don't 'just.' You're not any better than Dad, the way he likes to control us. You're just like him . . . better check up on ol' Sean, make sure he doesn't fuck up again. Is that it? Huh, is that it, Faith? Oh, Jesus, you're good. You're really good at that, aren't you? You have your life of digging around in secrets and rolling around in mud and muck, and look at you now, Faith! You're covered in it yourself. Jesus Christ, and you have the fucking *nerve* to talk about trying to *help* me. Man, that takes real balls, sister." He threw her a mock salute, and began stalking away from the parking lot toward the street.

Faith's heart was pounding wildly. "Where are you going? What about the . . . the house?"

"Forget it. Forget I asked. I'll handle it myself. Just forget I came to town. Go back to your mud and your muck."

"Sean . . ." Faith jogged a few steps toward him. "Sean, you don't know your way around this city. Here, let me drive you back to your car. Come on, we can—"

"I'll find a bus, a cab, something. You leave me the hell alone."

He crossed Western on foot and began working his way south. Faith watched him go, riveted to the ground. In a few minutes he was only a speck in the distance.

Faith felt a hand in the small of her back. "Where's your brother?" Cara Dunaway said.

"He's gone," Faith said.

13

IT TOOK SEAN OVER HALF AN HOUR, VIA OKLAHOMA
City's convoluted bus system, to reach the Metro Transit terminal downtown. The city was a lot like Tucson,
and very *un*like his hometown of Chicago, in that very
few people used public transportation here. The farther
west you went, the more people were wedded to their
cars, he mused.

He and three others got off the bus, and Sean started
across the street toward Saint Joseph Old Cathedral
and, beyond it, the federal courthouse. *The nerve!* he
raged to himself. *Of all the nerve . . . I went to her for
help, for protection, and she takes me to A-fucking-A!*

So I've screwed up a few times.

That doesn't make me an alcoholic.

That doesn't make me an alcoholic, dammit!

He shook away the conflicting stew of feelings that
swirled around him, almost jogging now. *If I run faster,
will I outrun all this?* Sean wanted to shout.

He had no idea where Faith had parked his Jeep. He
circled around the block several times before spotting
it in a parking lot on the west side of the building. As
he dug in his pocket for his keys, his hand brushed
something else.

Faith had figured out that he'd stopped and had a

few drinks. But he was even later meeting her because he'd also stopped off at a hardware store. His hand closed on the additional key in his pocket—a key to Faith's car that he'd had copied this morning.

Just in case, Sean told himself. *Just in case of emergency.*

He needed to go to a bad part of the city. Remembering Monica and Britt, he headed south from downtown. After a couple of wrong turns, he located Shields Boulevard again. He drove up and down a few side streets until he found what he was looking for—a deserted-looking block with a few cars parked on the street.

The houses were generally in poor repair, with peeling paint and sagging foundations. *Rent houses,* Sean thought. He felt sorry for the people who had to rent places like these just to have a roof over their heads.

Halfway down the block, he found a perfect target, an old pea-green Chevy Monte Carlo. Its back end was parked on the gravel driveway in front of a sad white frame house, and its front end was angled onto the thin grass of the front yard. Both front tires were gone, the proverbial concrete blocks propped under the wheels.

But it had a current Oklahoma license plate. Sean stopped one house down and withdrew a screwdriver from the Jeep's glove compartment. He got out and moved quickly down the sidewalk, stepping around a broken tricycle and an empty Smirnoff vodka bottle.

It took him less than half a minute to get the Monte Carlo's plate off. He'd noticed, while driving around this city, that Oklahoma did not require a front license plate, only the rear. That made his job much easier.

He had the plate under his arm and was halfway back to the Jeep when he heard a screen door slam.

"Hey!" a woman shouted.

He didn't look back, but lengthened his stride back to the Jeep. He slid behind the wheel and started the Cherokee in one smooth motion. From the porch of the house, the woman yelled again.

"*Alto!*" Stop!

She was young, Hispanic, and tired-looking, with a baby on her hip. She reminded him eerily of the woman back in Sasabe who had glared at him as her little boy darted across the road in front of him.

"*Alto!*"

He gunned the Cherokee down the street, made a quick turn, and was out of sight. In a few minutes he was back on the interstate, heading west toward El Reno. Toward Daryn.

Forty-five minutes later, Sean exited Interstate 40 and pulled into the parking lot of the Super 8 Motel in El Reno. He circled to the back of the motel, away from the highway, and put the stolen Oklahoma plate on the Cherokee. He tucked his own Arizona plates under the rear seat, then drove around to the front again.

As he got out of the Jeep, with two bags of hastily purchased clothes and supplies in his arms, he looked up at Room 213. He saw a shadowy face in the window, and then the curtains fell back into place.

"Here I am," he said as he entered the room a moment later. "I bought you some clothes. I sort of guessed at the sizes. Plus some water and sandwich stuff. Kat?"

He realized the room was very dark, none of the lights on, the thick curtains completely covering the window.

"Kat? It's me, Michael. Are you here?"

I know she's here. I saw the curtains move. She was watching for me.

"I'm here, Michael," she said.

Sean's eyes slowly adjusted to the darkness. Kat's form took shape in the chair on the far side of the bed, sitting very still.

"Are you all right?" Sean asked.

"Yes. I'm glad you're back. I was beginning to wonder."

She'd been just sitting there, in a dark room, no TV on, no radio on, nothing to read . . . just waiting for him. Sean blinked into the darkness. She was a woman of extremes, he thought, contrasting the unbridled lust she brought to her lovemaking with the incredible stillness of being able to sit in a room for hours, simply waiting. Sean shuddered, and it wasn't just because he wanted a drink.

"Why don't you turn on a light?" he said.

"I had a migraine. When I get one of those, it's better in the dark."

Sounds like having a bad hangover, Sean thought, but said nothing as he dropped the bags on the floor.

"Did you get the help?"

"What?" Sean said.

"The person who was going to help you. Did it work out?"

Sean sighed. "No. But look, I'll stay with you and help you keep safe. I bought some food."

"What about your business?"

Sean cocked his head. "What?"

"Your woodworking business. What will you do about it?"

Sean stuffed his hands in his pockets, suddenly thankful for the dark, that Kat couldn't see his hands trembling. "I set my own hours. I work for myself, so I can do that. Might get behind on a couple of custom orders, but I'll get caught up eventually."

"Good. I hoped you'd want to stay with me, Michael."

Sean nodded.

"You saved my life," Daryn said.

"You don't have to . . ."

Daryn reached over and flicked on the bedside lamp. It took a moment for Sean to focus in on her face, like watching an old television set warm up before the picture fully settled on the screen. In the harsh lamplight, her forehead was lined. It was quite striking on such a young, beautiful face.

"Migraines can really be painful," Sean said. "I have a friend who gets them."

Daryn nodded. "Very painful. But I feel better now. The dark and the quiet helped, and now you're back. I was worried that you wouldn't come back. You have your own life . . . I'm just an escort."

Sean said nothing. She was leading the conversation, trying to take it somewhere, and he couldn't tell where yet. He'd learned by now that whether it was in sex or in conversation, it was better to let her lead and see where she was going before committing.

She opened her dark eyes wide and looked straight at him. *Into* him. Deep into him.

Jesus, Sean thought. He'd stared down drug dealers and arms smugglers and child stealers and professional assassins, people with no regard whatsoever for human life, and he'd never seen a gaze as sharp as the one Daryn McDermott was giving him now. Sean was *never* one to look away, but he finally dropped his eyes from hers. He couldn't take that gaze any longer.

"You *do* want to stay with me?" Daryn said, and her voice was very soft. "Michael," she added, saying the name as if it were the *amen* at the end of a prayer.

Sean rubbed the back of his neck. He felt a growing heat there, and in some unfathomable way he felt powerless to control, he felt himself becoming rapidly aroused.

"Yes, Kat," he whispered. "I do."

A smile touched her face for a moment; then she stood and came toward him, stepping out of her clothes as she moved. Naked, she put her arms around him and held him very tightly.

"Take me, Michael," she said. "Please, I want you to take me now."

He looked down at her. This woman was so strange, he thought. She was equal parts power and yearning, strength and vulnerability, all in the same moment.

He kissed her, and both their mouths opened in

hunger. Their tongues met. Sean felt as if his body was one giant nerve ending, and that Daryn knew how to tap into every part of it. Her mouth, her hands, her body . . . she was everywhere.

She was so petite that he could pick her up in his arms and she felt no heavier than a child. He turned around and sat her on the edge of the bed. She opened her legs for him, and within moments Sean had found her center.

Over the next two hours, Sean spent himself three times, something he'd *never* done before. Daryn drained him, physically and emotionally, until he felt he could scarcely move. They lay spooned together on the bed, the torn and tangled sheets surrounding them, the scent of their lust all around.

"Michael," Daryn said softly.

Stroking her back very gently, Sean stirred a bit from his stupor. "Hmm?"

"If you really want to stay with me, I know a place we can go."

"Oh?"

"Do you remember last night, when we talked about my ideas? The social and political changes I want to see?"

Sean blinked, becoming more alert. "Yes."

"What did you think of what I said?"

Sean let out a long, slow breath. *Tread carefully. Tread very, very carefully.* "Your ideas are . . ."

"Yes?"

Sean stepped off the edge and into nothingness.

"Amazing. They would change the way our whole society functions."

Daryn rolled over to face him. Her dark eyes were wide. "Yes. Yes, they would."

"But I don't see," Sean said, "how any of those things will get done."

"Michael . . . I know some people."

Sean met her eyes.

"I know people," she said. "We're starting a movement. It's called the Coalition for Social Justice. We're going to try to make these things happen. Will you join us? Will you go with me, Michael?"

"Where?"

"We have a house. It's in a little town called Mulhall. Do you know where that is?"

Sean shook his head. "No. I'm too new to the area. I haven't explored many of the small towns."

"It's north of Oklahoma City. I know where it is. It's out of the way. We can stay there. We'll be safe."

"What about those goons who came to your apartment?"

Daryn shook her head for emphasis. "They'll never find us. Whoever they were, we'll be safe with the Coalition. Come with me, Michael. We can make things happen. The leader of the Coalition is a man named Franklin Sanborn. He's a visionary, and he and I agree on these things. We're gathering more people all the time."

Sean nodded slowly. He remembered something Faith had said, standing outside the AA building, something about how the bottle was holding him instead of the other way around. Now, he wondered, who was in control? Was he holding Daryn, or was she holding him?

He pushed the thoughts roughly away, as if trying to get away from something dead and rotting, something vile.

"I'll go," he said.

Daryn smiled.

Part Two:
Daryn

14

SEAN COULDN'T STOP LOOKING AT DARYN.

She was that kind of woman. She drew his eyes—and the rest of his senses as well. If "sensual" truly meant to open the senses, then Daryn McDermott was the most sensual creature Sean had ever met. Not only her look, but the sound of her voice, her scent, the way her skin had tasted . . . and her touch. *God, her touch.*

But now he'd begun to get into her mind. She'd shown him a few glimpses into her life. Even masked as Kat Hall, she'd been telling him of Daryn McDermott's life. The "wealthy, powerful" father, the mother cast aside, the father's hypocrisy, the search that eventually led her to become an escort . . . both sensual and complex. A rare breed.

He kept the Jeep pointed north on Interstate 35, letting Daryn give the directions. He glanced at her again, then at her left hand, which extended behind her seat. Britt, in the back, was tugging on Daryn's hand again.

Sean had been suspicious when Daryn told him they needed to pick up a friend. Then he'd had to struggle to keep his poker face when the friend turned out to be Britt. He said nothing, and neither did Britt, but their eyes had met for a short moment as she got into the Jeep and Daryn "introduced" them.

Britt looked at Daryn with absolute love and devotion. For all her time on the streets, for everything she'd done and seen, Britt still seemed like a child, easily led. Sean had known from the time he saw the photo of the Oklahoma City march that Britt had fallen in love with her, or at least into whatever form of infatuation Britt could view as love. She would do anything Daryn asked.

Daryn directed Sean to exit the interstate at the town of Guthrie, thirty miles or so north of Oklahoma City. Guthrie had in fact been the first capital of Oklahoma Territory after the famous land run of 1889 opened the previously "unassigned" lands. Now it was a pleasant town of Victorian homes and a beautifully restored downtown area, capitalizing on its history to draw in a healthy tourism industry.

Daryn showed Sean where to turn, and he headed north out of Guthrie on U.S. 77. A mile outside the city limits, he said, "We're being followed."

"What?" Britt said.

Daryn dropped Britt's hand. "How do you know?"

"Big blue SUV back there, two guys in the front. It's been with us since before we left the highway." Sean thumped the steering wheel. "I'm not sure how long. I wasn't looking for a tail."

Daryn looked at him strangely, and Sean thought, *Be careful! I'm a woodworker, not a law enforcement officer trained to spot surveillance.*

"Just kind of spooked after the other night," he added quickly.

"How could they have followed us?" Daryn said.

"They may have tracked us from the motel," Sean said. "Hell, I don't know. You seem to have pissed off some pretty persistent people."

Daryn said nothing.

Sean let it go. This wasn't the time to push it, not with a tail right behind them on a lonely stretch of rural highway.

He nudged the Jeep forward, the speedometer moving past seventy. He saw a bridge ahead.

"Shit," he muttered.

A green-and-white sign took shape, announcing that the bridge crossed the Cimarron River. The Jeep rolled onto the bridge. The blue SUV moved to overtake them, swinging out into the opposite lane.

"What are they doing?" Britt said. Her voice rose. "What's going on?"

Neither Sean nor Daryn spoke. Sean punched the accelerator and listened to the Jeep's engine growl in overdrive. The SUV's driver kept pace, the right front fender of the bigger vehicle moving toward the Jeep's left rear.

"Oh no, you don't," Sean whispered. He wasn't about to let the other driver tap him on a bridge at nearly eighty miles an hour. "Hold on," he said to Daryn and Britt.

He floored the accelerator and jerked the wheel to the left, cutting in front of the other driver. Now they were both speeding north in the bridge's southbound lane. Sean imagined the other driver's surprise at the maneuver.

Just as quickly, he saw in the mirror that the other

driver was starting to slide over into the northbound lane, and Sean thought: *amateurs*. Then: *but I'm supposed to be an amateur, too*. Nevertheless, he repeated the maneuver in reverse, cutting off the SUV's angle of attack again and putting both vehicles back in the right lane.

Five seconds later, a car entered the bridge from the other direction, a white compact sedan. The SUV nudged into the other lane. The white sedan's driver leaned on the horn. The SUV ducked backed behind Sean. Ahead, Sean saw the point where the bridge ended.

"Hold on," he said again. "This is really going to piss them off."

Beside him, Daryn's eyes were wide. He couldn't see Britt. As soon as the Jeep's front wheels left the bridge and Sean saw the land to the side, he slammed on the brakes and spun the wheel hard to the right. The Jeep skidded into the gravel by the side of the road. The SUV's driver, caught by surprise, slammed on his own brakes and turned hard the other direction. Sean heard tires squealing, whether his or the other vehicle's he didn't know.

The Jeep came to rest pointing east toward the river, in a loose gravel area beside the road. As soon as he'd stopped, Sean was out of the driver's seat. Almost mirroring the Jeep, the SUV was in a similar position on the opposite side of the highway, its nose pointing west.

It was empty.

Sean turned back toward the Jeep, and for a moment his mind wavered. *Who am I? What am I doing here?*

He blinked. Daryn. Daryn McDermott. Kat Hall. He was trying to immerse himself in her world, and he'd been slowly descending into it, as Michael Sullivan. And now, twice since he'd met her, there had been an attack. Tobias Owens hadn't told him this part, back in the Sasabe cantina.

Who was after her? Were they after Daryn, the senator's daughter and radical? Or were they after Kat, the mysterious professional escort? The political princess or the call girl?

Sean took a step toward the highway, then stopped again. He couldn't just leave Daryn and Britt here unprotected. What if the guys from the SUV circled back around? What if they had another team approaching from the other direction?

But there might be answers out there in the brush by the river.

Sean's mind clouded again.

Dammit, I can't think!

I need a drink. Just one, so I can . . .

He shook his head. He jogged back to the Jeep. Daryn and Britt were both staring at him, Daryn in terror, Britt with a strange curiosity on her face.

"Do you know how to use a gun?" Sean asked Daryn.

Daryn's eyes grew impossibly wide. She shook her head slowly. "I never—"

"I do," Britt said.

Sean looked at her slowly. Something passed between them, a subtle understanding, a *knowing*. "In my duffel bag," Sean said. "If anyone comes near the car, shoot them."

"Michael—" Daryn said.

"I'll be back," Sean said.

He ran across the road. The SUV was totally empty, both the driver's and passenger's doors standing open. He looked back toward the river. A barbed wire fence snaked away toward the west. The ground—green grass and red dirt—sloped downward to the south, toward the Cimarron River itself. Sean saw movement below, a flash of blue, underneath one of the bridge supports.

Every fiber of his training rebelled—he was going into an unknown situation, unarmed, with no real backup.

But this wasn't about training anymore. He wasn't an ICE agent now. He was a civilian, an ordinary woodworker, and this was about the woman he knew as both Kat and Daryn.

His head pounding, Sean took a step toward the river, then another. He stepped into the tall grass. The ground sloped sharply away ahead of him. He saw the movement again, an outline of a man moving behind the bridge support.

Sean took another step. His foot came down on loose red dirt, and the ground sloughed away under him. He went down, tumbling through grass and dirt and rocks before coming to rest on concrete, at least fifty feet below where he had been, lying on his side with his cheek scraping gravel.

At first he heard, saw, felt nothing, though he tasted grass in his mouth. Then there was sound—the river, birds, a car going by on the bridge above his head. Finally, his vision cleared. He saw graffiti scrawled on the bridge—*I Love Tina, GHS Sr. '05, Tony & Marie 4-ever, Rachel gives hot BJ.*

The man stood over him. A few years older than he, tall, sandy hair, a few days' growth of beard, blue jeans and a denim shirt, cowboy boots.

Sean coughed grass out of his mouth. "What . . ." He spat. "What do you want with her?"

"Who the hell are you?" the man said. "Why do you care about her?"

"She's . . . do you know who she is?" Sean said.

"Do you?" the man said.

Sean started to sit up, then the man's boot connected with his ribs. Sean grunted and rolled over, and the man kicked him again. Before he landed a third kick, Sean tried to grab his leg, but the man backed off.

He heard another voice, not the booted man: *"Leave him. We're done."*

The booted man grunted in reply, but sent one more sharp kick to Sean's abdomen. Then he moved away quickly, footsteps receding toward the river. Sean rolled over and retched into the grass, tasting all the whiskey he'd drunk.

He lay there for a long time, listening to the river and all the damned birds singing on all sides of him. He heard a car door slam, an engine start.

He raised himself up, his ribs stinging. He felt up and down his chest. Probably bruised but not broken.

He took a few deep breaths—hard, but not too painful. Encouraging.

Sean slowly got to his feet, remembering the man's words.

Do you?

What the hell did that mean? What kind of game were these people playing?

Leave him. We're done.

By that time, they hadn't seemed interested in Daryn. They'd been dealing with him, with Sean.

Leave him. We're done.

Slowly, painfully, Sean began the climb back up toward the highway.

15

THE TOWN OF MULHALL, OKLAHOMA, EMBODIED history in a rougher, harder-edged way than Guthrie. If Guthrie was a shining example of urban renewal, Mulhall was a slice of rural America at its most real. Poverty coexisted with strong community ties; resilience took a seat right next to the despair that pervaded so many of America's small towns. Not all of Mulhall's history was over a century old, either—on May 3, 1999, most of the town had been wiped out by one of the more than sixty tornadoes that struck the state in a single day.

Now, more than half a decade later, Daryn could still see evidence of what had happened here—dead trees and mangled brush by the side of the road. She'd only been to the Coalition house once before, and Franklin Sanborn, who was a history buff, had explained Mulhall's history to her. It was part of the reason he'd chosen Mulhall as the place to give birth to the Coalition.

Mulhall is the struggle of real people to survive, Sanborn had said. *Mulhall is what the ruling classes have forgotten. From the natives to the cattlemen to the laborers who have to find work in the cities, to the desperation that gave way to hope after the storms destroyed the town—Mulhall is real.*

The irony wasn't lost on Daryn. In order to get at what was real, to get the ruling classes—people like her father—to pay attention, they'd had to construct a series of elaborate lies. Daryn had read once that the road to truth was paved with lies. She'd learned the lesson many times over by now.

"Real," she muttered, without realizing she'd spoken aloud.

"What?" Sean said, half-turning to her.

Daryn shook her head. "Nothing."

"It sounded like you said 'real.' Real was those guys back at the bridge. That's twice in a very short time."

Daryn swallowed. "They're threatened. We're pushing the envelope of society, and someone up the line is threatened by that."

Sean said no more, grimacing behind the wheel. She looked at the scratches on his face. She'd already seen the bruises the man's boots had left on his abdomen. Daryn closed her eyes, trying to shut it all out.

Britt squeezed her hand inquiringly. Daryn gave her what she hoped was a reassuring glance, then turned toward the front again.

Very little moved in the streets of Mulhall. There were a couple of brick Victorian-style buildings, including an old bank that had most recently housed a restaurant, now shuttered. There were a few frame houses along the main drag. Up the hill to the right was a gleaming new school, seeming so out of place that it looked like it had been placed here by mistake. But it was part of the history, having been rebuilt after the deadly tornado.

It took all of two minutes to travel the entire length of the town. Then Daryn pointed to a gravel road just north of the city limits. Sean turned left and drove another half mile between barbed wire fences. Daryn pointed again, and Sean made another left onto a driveway that was simply two deep ruts split by a line of grass. A hundred yards back from the road was a small, unremarkable white two-story frame house. It was neither well kept nor in noticeable disrepair. There was greenery around it, but not much. A chain-link fence surrounded it. Two pickup trucks and a dark four-door—with Oklahoma, Texas, and New Mexico plates, respectively—were parked in the clearing outside the fence.

Two men appeared at the door to the house—big, burly men in jeans, boots, and button-down shirts. They flanked the door and then Franklin Sanborn strode out onto the small porch.

Daryn almost laughed, despite the tension of what had happened a few miles back down the road. Sanborn himself was almost as forgettable in appearance as the house, as the black sedan he drove: his hair that held just a few gray threads; his eyes a light chocolate brown; his complexion was medium. He was right around six feet tall, weight proportionate, not a hard body but not flabby. Sometimes he wore glasses. Sometimes he didn't. He was no one to be remembered.

Remember The Cause, he liked to say. *Don't remember me.*

That was part of the reason Daryn believed in him. He wasn't some messianic egomaniac like David Koresh, or an introverted, antisocial genius like Ted Kaczynski. He wasn't some deprived little boy trying to get the world's attention. He had a true social and political agenda, and a genius for planning.

Daryn and Britt got out of the Jeep, and Britt immediately reached for Daryn's hand again as soon as they were outside. Sean got out more slowly, gingerly feeling his ribs. He looked around, then took out his duffel bag, which held his clothes and the extras he'd bought for Daryn.

Sanborn stepped forward. "Welcome," he said. "Glad you made it out here."

Even his voice was unremarkable. No discernible accent or regionalism. His English was so perfect that Daryn had often wondered if it might not be his first language, but he'd studied it and mastered general American dialect to perfection. He was fairly soft-spoken, and Daryn had never heard him raise his voice. He'd never needed to.

The two burly men stayed where they were, but Sanborn stepped off the porch and came out to the gate. He swung it open. "Come on in."

Daryn leaned up to peck his cheek as she passed him. "Franklin, you remember my friend Britt."

"Of course I do." Sanborn turned and gave Britt his full attention. "Britt is part of the reason we exist."

Britt nodded, casting her eyes down as if unworthy. She held even more tightly to Daryn's hand.

"And this is my new friend Michael," Daryn said.

Sanborn moved toward Sean, his hand extended. They shook. "It's a pleasure to meet you, Michael,"

Sanborn said. "Welcome to the home of the Coalition. I'm Franklin Sanborn. I help to sort of facilitate things around here."

"He's much too modest," Daryn said, looking over her shoulder at Sean. "He leads us."

"We have different leaders for different things," Sanborn said with a shrug. "Kat herself is our spiritual leader, if you will, the one who always brings us back to the Cause. I focus on plans and details. Don and CJ back there are our operational leaders. They figure out how to put plans into action. We all lead each other. Unlike the ruling classes, we don't have to have anointed leaders with titles."

Sean kept his eyes fixed on Sanborn. "It's good to meet you," he finally said. "What Kat said about your . . . what do you want to call it—a movement, maybe?—made a lot of sense." He glanced at Daryn. "Some people are pretty intent on sending some sort of message to Kat, though."

Sanborn looked questioningly at Daryn.

"Twice now," Daryn said, "we've been attacked." She described both incidents in detail.

Sanborn frowned. "The ruling classes are nervous. You must be more careful, Katherine. Until the Coalition begins its actual work, you have to be careful what you say, and to whom you say it. If we lost you, I don't know what we'd do. You are our heart and soul." He looked at Sean. "Are you all right, Michael? I didn't notice at first, but you look a bit roughed up."

"I'm okay," Sean said. "I'm just glad I could be there for Kat."

Sanborn nodded. "So am I."

"So," Sean said, steering the conversation back around. "Your movement."

"I suppose you could call us a movement," Sanborn said. "Not quite what you expected, though, are we? Be honest. When you conjure up an image of a group of people living outside the mainstream, working toward radical change in society, you think of survivalist compounds where everyone carries an AK-47, or some kind of racial superiority complex, or some bunch of nutcases who babble on and on about black helicopters and computer chips implanted in their bodies by the government."

Sean smiled.

"You'll find none of that foolishness here," Sanborn said. "We're not conspiracy theorists. We don't have to be. The reality speaks for itself. Read the *Congressional Record*. That's all the evidence we need, right there in the public record. We do have a few weapons scattered around, but more to protect our privacy than anything. No one here carries them on a regular basis, though. We're not that kind of community." His brown eyes bore into Sean's. "May I ask, Michael, if you are carrying a weapon?"

"Yes," Sean said. "I own a pistol. It's in my duffel bag right now."

Sanborn nodded, the look of the genial host never leaving his face. "Of course. You didn't know what to expect from us. I understand completely. You're welcome to keep it. I'm certainly not going to ask you to give it up. It's your own personal property, after all. I'll just ask you to respect the others here and not show it around a lot. We have a couple of members who actively dislike guns and are quite afraid of them."

"Sure," Sean said, confusion evident in his voice.

Sanborn smiled again. "As I said, we're not what you expected. I take that as a compliment. Come in the house."

They went in. There was a large, open front room with a few chairs and mismatched tables that looked like yard sale refugees. A man and two women, ranging in age from early twenties to late forties, were scattered around. The two women were reading—one a newspaper, one a battered Edgar Allan Poe anthology. The man had spread out papers on a chipped coffee table and was making notes. There was a chorus of greetings, mostly directed at Daryn, all of them calling her Kat. A couple of nods went in Sean's direction when he was introduced.

"How many people are here?" Sean asked.

"We're small but mighty," Sanborn said. "There are thirteen of us right now. Eight women, five men. We range in age from twenty-one to fifty-eight. We come from all different backgrounds." He nodded toward Daryn. "Kat brought most of us together."

Sean waited a moment. "She's very passionate," he said slowly.

Sanborn laughed. So did Daryn. "Indeed," Sanborn said. "So she is. And quite persuasive."

"Quite," Sean said.

"We've converted all the rooms upstairs into bedrooms," Sanborn said. "They're not very big, but they give a small amount of privacy. Unfortunately there's only one bathroom. We make do, just as any group of people does when they live somewhat communally. There's a deck out back, and a basement off the kitchen. It has its challenges, but we get by. This place isn't permanent, but it's the perfect starting point for us."

"What about you?" Sean said. "What's your background?"

"Me?" Sanborn said. "I'm an academic. I was a professor at Indiana University in Bloomington."

"Professor of what?"

"Interpersonal communication. One of those liberal arts fields where our graduates are expected to ask, 'Do you want fries with that?' But, then, someone with a ridiculous number of degrees in communication can actually be useful in setting up a group dynamic like this. I'm an organizer. That's what I do."

One of the two big men had come back into the house. He was late twenties, blond, with cold blue eyes and a muscular build. "Let me take your bag," he said to Sean in a soft Oklahoma drawl. "I'll put it upstairs."

"Thank you, Don," Sanborn said. "Go ahead and show Michael where he'll be bunking. Then round everyone up, if you would, please. It's time for the meeting." He turned to Sean. "You're just in time for our major planning session."

"Planning for what?" Sean said.

Sanborn's expression lost a little of its hostlike veneer and grew deadly serious. He looked in Daryn's direction before answering Sean. Daryn felt his cool, steady gaze.

"Planning how the Coalition will begin to reshape American society," Sanborn said.

Sean waited a moment. Sanborn and Daryn both looked at him.

"That's why we're here, right?" Sean finally said.

"Yes, that's why we're here," Sanborn said. "There's only one rule here, Michael. We don't have a bunch of silly regimens and routines to follow. We're not a cult, we're a political organization with political and social goals. But we do require absolute loyalty. Once you've joined us, you pledge to follow the goals and objectives laid out by the Coalition for Social Justice. There will be no backing out, and no betrayals, no contacting the 'authorities' if you don't like something. If you do have a problem, we'll deal with it internally, as a group. You take your problem outside the group, then we have a *real* problem. Do you accept that, Michael?"

Sean looked at Daryn. Daryn, standing next to Sanborn and still holding hands with the much taller Britt, looked at him, *into* him, just as she had in the motel room in El Reno.

All eyes in the room focused on Sean. The two women had stopped their reading. The man with the papers stopped making his notes. Don, holding Sean's duffel bag, paused on the stairs.

"I accept that," Sean said.

Daryn let out a breath. *Anything for The Cause,* she thought. She really had a headache now and wanted to lie down, to disentangle herself from Britt and from the rampant, raging emotions of the last few hours, to just be alone in a dark, quiet room for a while. But there was much work to be done. She would rest later.

"Welcome, Michael," she said.

"Welcome, Michael," Franklin Sanborn echoed. "Let's get to work."

16

DON, WHO TOLD SEAN HIS FULL NAME WAS DONALD
Wheaton, showed Sean up the stairs to a small room at
the end of a wood-floored hallway.

"Here," Wheaton said. "Kat asked for the three of
you to share a room, and this is the last empty one."

"Wait a minute," Sean said. "The three of us?"

"You and her and the other girl. Britt." Wheaton
didn't smile, but his face lightened somewhat. "Nice
arrangement."

Sean shook his head. "Thanks. So tell me, Don.
What's your story?"

Wheaton shrugged, working his tongue around the
inside of his mouth. "No real story," he drawled. "I'm
in heavy construction. I live in Noble. Got tired of
scraping and struggling and other people getting rich
off my sweat."

Sean noticed a silver wedding band on the man's
finger. "Is your wife here with you?"

Wheaton looked embarrassed, fiddling with the ring.
"No, but she understands. I call her every other day."

He tossed Sean's duffel onto the queen-size mattress
in the little room, then backed away.

"Where will the women sleep?" Sean asked. "Kat
and Britt."

Wheaton looked amused. "Well, with you, of course. Aren't you with them?"

"Well, I . . ." Sean shut up.

"Some guys have all the luck," Wheaton said, and went off down the hall.

Sean headed downstairs, where the group was assembling. In addition to a diversity of age, there were two black men, one black woman, and a very young, college-age Asian woman. There were two middle-aged men who stayed very close to each other, and by their body language, Sean took them to be a gay couple. He shook his head. The Coalition for Social Justice was unlike any extremist group he'd ever known. But then, with Daryn McDermott as one of the driving forces behind it, that made sense. She was certainly unlike any woman he'd known.

Franklin Sanborn sat in one of the battered armchairs at the periphery of the group. "Let's get started," he said. He was still genial, with the easygoing air, but now there was something else underlying it, a let's-get-down-to-business sort of urgency.

Sean slid onto one of the couches, squeezing between Kat and one of the black men. Britt was on Kat's other side, pressed close to her. Sean tried several times to catch Britt's eye, but she never looked at him.

Partners in this deception, Sean thought, and she doesn't want to acknowledge me, doesn't want to acknowledge her own part in it.

Sanborn looked directly at Sean. "For the benefit of our newest members, I should explain that we do have one tiny little ritual that we observe at all general meetings."

Sean stiffened slightly.

"Don't worry, Michael," Sanborn said. "No ritual bloodletting. Not even a secret handshake." There were a few chuckles from around the room. "We simply reaffirm verbally our commitment to the cause." He cleared his throat. "I'll begin. I'm Franklin Sanborn, and I accept the Coalition for Social Justice's mission and objectives."

He nodded to his left. A heavyset blond woman in her thirties said, "I'm Jeannie Davis, and I accept the Coalition."

And so it went around the room. Sean was reminded eerily of the AA meeting Faith had dragged him to—*I'm Jack and I'm an alcoholic. Hi, Jack!*—but when it came to him, he said, "I'm Michael Sullivan, and I accept the Coalition." His hands were trembling a little, and he had to sit on one of them to keep Daryn from seeing. It was late afternoon, and he hadn't had a drink since morning. *Just a couple of shots to steady myself. That's all I need.*

Daryn beamed at him and said, "I'm Katherine Hall. I accept the Coalition and believe it will change America!"

There was scattered applause. After it died down, Britt said in a small voice, "I'm Brittany Ray. I believe in Kat, so I believe in the Coalition."

Sanborn nodded approvingly. "Thank you, friends." He steepled his fingers in front of his face and touched his index fingers to his lips, looking very professorial. "We've had many discussions about how to get the attention of the ruling classes in this country. They weary us with moralistic platitudes and blather on about 'family values,' as if every family in America shares the same values, as if we were all carbon copies of each other. While oil companies and brokerage houses reap record profits and their CEOs earn tens of millions of dollars for doing essentially nothing, real people struggle for their lives every day. Women like Kat and Britt have no protection, no health care. People like Jeannie, a social worker, someone who helps others on a daily basis, can barely make ends meet. It's wrong, and we know it's wrong."

Sanborn's gaze traveled the room. He made eye contact with everyone, lingering for a moment on Daryn.

What's with the two of them? Sean wondered. *Just the connection between the two leaders of the group, or something deeper?* He felt a pang of what he recognized as jealousy.

What the hell is happening to me? This is a job, an undercover operation to get Daryn McDermott to come back home willingly. Gain her trust. Bring her back. Period.

But it's not that simple anymore.

"But then, I'm preaching to the choir, right?" Sanborn said, to another round of chuckles. "What defines the ruling classes?"

"Money," one of the men said.

"Exactly," Sanborn said, clapping his hands together. "So we strike at the monetary system. Many groups with radical ideas have tried many things to get the world's attention. Just a few miles from here, in downtown Oklahoma City, is the evidence of one of them. Did the Murrah Building bombing really accomplish anything? Of course not. Timothy McVeigh was an idiot. Was one single governmental policy changed because of his strike?" Sanborn shook his head.

"It's because he didn't strike at the rulers," Daryn said, leaning forward. "In fact, the people he hurt, the people he *murdered*, were real people, low and midlevel employees who were all at the mercy of the policy makers, just like the rest of us. That should be a lesson to all of us. To bring about change, real societal change, means you strike at those who have the most to lose." She smiled. "And you hit them where it hurts."

Sanborn nodded. "The rulers derive their power from their money. We don't live in a democracy or a republic anymore. Elections are bought and sold. It's all about the money. No attempt at reforming the system from within will work, because of the enormous sums of money involved. No ruler wants to give up his kingdom, after all." He spread his hands apart. "So we strike at the money."

The man who'd been making notes earlier at the coffee table raised a hand. He had introduced himself as Alan Davenport. "We'll make surgical strikes at banks. Not to rob them, of course. That's a silly cliché. To damage them. To *destroy* them, in some cases."

Sean's pulse quickened. They were talking about terrorist acts, pure and simple. Blowing up banks. *Good God, they're a bunch of terrorists! They have a wholesome-sounding name and they're not blithering idiots, but they're planning acts of terrorism!*

He must have unconsciously made a noise, because Sanborn and Davenport were both looking at him.

"Yes, Michael?" Sanborn said. "Do you have something to offer to the discussion?"

Sean's mouth twitched. *Jesus God Almighty, I've never needed a drink like I need one right now.*

"Michael?" Daryn said.

Daryn McDermott. The reason he was here. How far would he have to go with this? How deeply into her extremist politics did he have to go to get her to trust him, to convince her to go with him? He was still technically a federal law enforcement officer, after all. How much longer could he do this? How much further could he go?

He looked at Daryn, at those deep dark eyes, that perfect face, at a silent plea that she sent to him. For a moment he thought he would do anything for her. She'd seduced him with her body and her mind, had reached into his essence like no one ever had. He understood how Britt—poor tragic Britt, naïve and worldly at the same time—could view Daryn with such utter and absolute devotion. She was intoxicating, more so than any drink he'd ever had.

But how far can I go?

"Fine," he said, and it came out a rasp. He cleared his throat. "Fine. I'm fine. Just taking it all in."

He caught a glimpse of Daryn looking at him with relief painted on her face. Britt was appraising him coolly. Sanborn nodded. "There's a lot to take in," Sanborn finally said. He sat back in his chair, then a slightly bemused look came over his face. "Perhaps you've misunderstood, Michael."

"How so?"

"We're not talking about violence here. When we use words like *damage* or *destroy* in talking about the banking industry, we don't mean a literal, physical destruction."

Sean breathed out slowly.

Sanborn exchanged a long glance with Daryn. "Kat would never allow us to devolve into terrorism. No, we mean demonstrations designed to point up the weaknesses of the ruling classes and their wealth."

Sean closed his eyes for a second, then nodded. "Thanks for clarifying that."

Sanborn chuckled. "You were looking rather pale over there." Another look toward Daryn.

What is it with those two? Sean wondered. *And how long will this go on?*

"Go ahead, Alan," Sanborn said.

Davenport nodded. "I've come up with a first target. Based on many factors, I believe we should start with the Bank of America in downtown Oklahoma City."

There were several murmurs. Sean saw Daryn nodding approvingly.

"There's the symbolic value of the location. It's literally right around the corner from the national memorial, the site of the Murrah Building. Plus, B of A is a large nationwide banking company, and very powerful in the financial world. Their downtown building faces Robinson Avenue, and there's a large open courtyard that faces the street. That will be good for media coverage."

Sanborn nodded. "A good choice, Alan. Everyone needs to spend the next few days staying on message, doing what you need to do to prepare yourself for the start of the campaign. Alan, do you have a list of the next targets and where we'll go from here?"

Davenport shuffled some papers. "I made copies for everyone."

"Good. Pass them around." Sanborn nodded toward Daryn. "Kat, anything to add?"

"The Coalition is about to go public," she said, almost breathlessly. "Be ready. They won't be able to ignore us, or our goals."

"Got an attention getter in mind?" Don Wheaton said.

Daryn grinned. She patted Britt's leg beside her, then reached up and squeezed the other woman's breast. "Maybe," she said. "Britt and I may put on an exhibition for them. That would get it going, wouldn't it?"

Sean watched the group's reactions. Some stared openly, others were noncommittal. The social worker, Jeannie Davis, looked quickly away.

"I think that means the meeting is dismissed," Sanborn laughed.

The group broke up slowly, people talking in small groups. Sean lingered on the couch for a moment, reading the list Davenport had passed around. It was a list of banks that started in Oklahoma City, then spread out across the country. There were twenty-seven in all, ending with Citibank in New York.

"Wow," Sean said. "So we're going to travel to all these places? The whole group?"

Daryn touched his arm. "That's the idea. And we'll

gather more people along the way, once the word starts spreading. We already have small cells near all these places. And it starts right here." She gestured around the living room. "Appropriate, don't you think?"

What do you mean by that? Sean thought, but just nodded.

"Come on," Daryn said. "Let's see if there's anything in the kitchen to drink."

They made their way to the kitchen, Daryn saying a few words here and there to members of the group as she passed them. Like the rest of the house, it was large and open. The linoleum floor was peeling a bit, but otherwise it seemed clean and relatively well kept.

Daryn reached into the refrigerator. "There's Coke, juice, beer."

Thank you, God. "I'd love a beer," Sean said.

"Looks like you can have Michelob or Michelob."

"I'll take the Michelob."

"Good choice," Daryn said, and handed him a can. "Britt?"

"What are you having?" Britt said.

"Oh, honey, I'm just having some juice, I think. But you can have a beer if you want."

"Sure, okay," Britt said.

Sean opened his beer and drank half of it in one swallow. "What's out there?" He gestured toward the back door.

"Come on, I'll show you," Daryn said.

The kitchen door opened onto a huge wooden deck that spanned the entire length of the house. Just like the rest of the place, it showed wear and tear in places but was still in reasonable condition. "Nice," Sean said, drinking a little more beer.

They walked to the edge of the deck. The ground behind the house sloped gently down, with an excellent view of the rolling countryside. The grass, high from spring rains, was very, very green, Sean noticed, and there were areas of brick-red clay that dotted the land. After seven years in the deserts of southern Arizona, he found the colors almost blinding.

The three of them were alone on the deck, and Daryn said softly, "What did you think, Michael?"

Sean waited a long time before answering. He finished the can of Michelob and set it carefully on the railing of the deck. He saw Britt watching him, standing in Daryn's shadow.

"I think the ideas are solid," Sean said. "I don't know about the rest. The banks, I mean. Change is a hard thing to bring about."

Daryn smiled at him. "You're right. But it can be done. If people can reinvent themselves, why can't societies, countries?"

Sean looked at her long and hard. *If people can reinvent themselves.* What was she saying to him?

"We all want to change who we are sometimes," Daryn went on. "We want to throw off the things that shackled us to our past and just become something new."

"But not many people actually get to do that," Sean said. "They stay *shackled*, to use your word. Whether it's to a job they hate, or a spouse they don't love anymore, or a city they don't like living in. Most people don't have the luxury of going out and just becoming someone new."

Daryn cocked her head. "Luxury? That's an interesting way to put it. But you're right again. If we reshape the way American society looks at people—those very people you're talking about, people who feel they don't have any choices—then there will be more freedom. Freedom to choose how they can live their lives, without fear of some moral or financial controls put in place by some out-of-touch rulers."

Sean managed a smile of his own. "I love your passion. It . . . it sort of defines you, makes you who you are."

"Oh, is *that* what makes me who I am?"

They let that hang in the air for a few seconds, then Sean said, "Do you trust me, Kat?"

"Yes. You saved my life."

Sean nodded. "But you still haven't trusted me with much about yourself."

Daryn lowered her head, then glanced toward Britt, who was still watching Sean intently. Daryn finally looked back to Sean. "What is it you want to know?"

"I don't know. Anecdotes. Stories. That sort of thing."

Sean watched her, saw her dark eyes flicker.

Daryn sighed. "My father is a wealthy, powerful man. He's part of the ruling class. I grew up as part of it before I realized what was going on. My father's values disgust me. He pushed my mother aside when I was a little girl and paraded a group of whores in and out as trophy wives. Don't worry, the word *whore* doesn't bother me. Since I am one, of course."

Britt looked at the floor. Daryn took her hand. "Oh, don't be embarrassed, sweetie. We know what we are. We know *who* we are. It's the rest of society that can't handle it." She looked back up at Sean. "When I was seventeen, my father had been away, out of the country for some meetings. And like any self-respecting rich, spoiled teenager, I threw a party while he was gone. You name it, it went on. Booze, dope, sex. All of us were stupidly wealthy, so none of us cared about anything. Our fathers could buy our way out of any trouble we got into. It was late, two or three in the morning, and most of the others had gone home. I was in my room, in bed with two of my good friends, Bryan and Jennifer. We were all so busy screwing each other's brains out that we didn't notice my father had come into the room."

Britt drew in a sharp breath. Sean was silent, watching.

"I have no idea how long he stood there watching us have sex with each other. He didn't say a word, didn't make a sound. When we were finished, Bryan happened to look up and saw him. My father only said one word. 'Go.' Bryan and Jen grabbed their clothes and left me naked in the bed. I was waiting for the storm to hit, but it didn't. My father never spoke. He simply took off his clothes, came to the bed, and climbed on top of me. It took maybe three minutes, then he got up, got dressed, and left the room. Neither of us ever spoke about it. I never told a soul." Daryn looked up at Sean. "Until now. There's your anecdote. There's your story."

"Kat, I—" Sean said.

"I'd like to go inside now," Daryn said. "I need to talk to Franklin for a minute, then I'm going up to our room. Britt, honey, I'd like you and Michael to get to know each other better. I want my two friends to know each other well."

"Whatever you want," Britt said.

"Good girl." Daryn leaned up and kissed Britt lightly on the lips, then turned and went in the house. "I'll be waiting upstairs."

She turned, and a moment later the kitchen door closed behind her. Sean leaned on the deck railing. A warm breeze came up the slope from below and tousled his hair. He felt Britt's presence behind him.

"Does anyone else here know?" Sean asked without turning around. "Who she really is, I mean."

"I don't think so," Britt said.

"Interesting."

"What does all this mean? I don't get it. I just want to be with Dar . . . Kat."

"I'm not sure," Sean said.

Britt nodded. "She gets those awful migraines. Her forehead scrunches up when she has one. I wish I could take her pain away."

Devotion bordering on obsession? Sean wondered. "I know. Did you know about . . . what she just said?"

Britt cleared her throat. "No. She said she never told a soul. I believe her. She wouldn't lie." The girl shuffled her feet. "She wants me to be with you."

Sean turned to look at her childlike face. "You don't have to. I'm not a customer."

"No, it's not like that. If she wants me to, it's not

like that. She knows what's best." She put out a hand and touched his chest.

"No, Britt. I don't think so."

She dropped her hand. A sly look came over her face. "You like a good drink, don't you? One of the other guys has some hard stuff. She told me where to find it."

Sean's mouth felt dry. He opened his mouth to say something, then his cell phone rang.

Britt frowned.

Sean pulled the phone off the clip he wore on his belt. He saw Faith's number on the caller ID.

"Do you need to get that?" Britt asked.

"No," Sean said after a long moment. When it stopped ringing, he turned off the phone.

Britt looked triumphant. "You know, even if you don't want to be with me now, you will later."

"What makes you say that?"

"Isn't it every guy's fantasy to be with two girls who are into each other, too?"

Sean gaped at her.

"We're sleeping together in the same room. In the same bed. You're like me, you know. You can't resist her either."

A shudder crawled up Sean's spine. Britt smiled crookedly at him, then turned around and started toward the house. In a moment he followed her.

17

FAITH SLEPT POORLY AND WOKE UP UNRESTED.
Even her morning run didn't help her feel better. Moving by rote, letting the inertia of routine drive her, she got dressed and drove downtown to her office. By seven thirty she was staring at the catfish, Styrofoam coffee cup in her hand.

Her brother was an alcoholic. Too many of the signs were there. It had ruined his career, and she suspected it was the underlying cause his brief marriage hadn't worked. And now, when she'd tried to help him, it had shredded their relationship as well.

"Dammit," she said aloud, then repeated it, louder.

She logged onto her computer. Still nothing from Director Yorkton on the final decision about Leon Bankston. She was sure Bankston would be green-lighted, but sometimes it took a while for the attorney general to sign off on the cases. In the meantime Bankston would sit in the safe house in identity limbo, driving Hal Simon crazy. The thought of Bankston haranguing Simon over the house's décor made Faith smile a little.

It faded quickly, though. *Sean*, she thought. What to do about Sean? She'd called him seven times from the moment he walked away from the AA meeting, up until this morning, and he never picked up. She had no idea where he was or what he was into. For all she knew, he could have gone out and gotten even drunker, then driven his Jeep off a bridge somewhere.

Aside from times in her teens, Faith had rarely felt powerless. There was always *something* that could be done. She relied on her intellect, and then took action. *At least there's one thing I have in common with my father,* she thought.

She tried to remember everything Sean had said and done since he'd shown up outside her house the other morning. He'd gone searching for a hooker, who, he'd said, had pointed him in the right direction. Then he'd stayed gone all night and had come to her for help. He'd wanted a safe house.

Faith tapped a pen on her desk, then did what she always did when deep in thought: she doodled on her legal pad.

He had talked to her about an incident at an apartment complex. Shots had been fired, and the girl who lived there was missing.

It's part of this job I'm doing. Yes, I was there, he'd said.

He'd mentioned Department Thirty for the first time, said he wanted Faith to provide a safe house.

Faith, I need your help. I need to keep this girl safe and out of sight for a while.

They'd argued. She finally agreed to let him use the department's Edmond safe house temporarily, since it wasn't currently being used for any Department Thirty recruits, with Bankston being kept at the Yukon house.

Then she'd demanded that he do something for her, and she'd dragged him to the AA meeting.

"Stupid," Faith said aloud. It had been the wrong way to approach it. Not only had it not worked, Sean had disappeared and another wedge had been driven into their relationship.

I need to keep this girl safe and out of sight for a while.

So Sean knew where the missing girl was. Or at least he had yesterday morning.

Faith knew nothing about who the girl was, or how deep Sean's involvement went.

But I'll find out what I can, she thought.

She picked up the phone.

"Hey," she said when Hendler came on the line.

"Hey, yourself, beautiful. What's up?"

"Nothing much. Do you know anything about this missing persons case, a girl who disappeared from an apartment complex? Neighbors reported a disturbance, then a shot, then the girl is gone. Ring any bells?"

"Don't beat around the bush, Faith. Tell me what you really want to know."

Faith smiled. "Sorry. You know subtlety isn't my strong suit."

"No, really? I know what case you're talking about. I don't think we're in it, though. Oklahoma City PD's handling it."

Faith doodled a few more shapes on her pad, ending with a triangle. She traced over each of the three sides of it several times with her pen. "Do you know anyone there who could tell you anything?"

"I don't know, maybe. Why?"

Faith scribbled Sean's name along one side of the triangle. "I think . . ." She stopped.

"What?"

"I think my brother might have something to do with it."

Hendler waited a moment. When he spoke again, his voice was lower. "What do you mean?"

"I'm not sure." She explained some of Sean's activities, ending with his request for a safe house, and the disastrous AA meeting.

"Holy shit," Hendler said softly when she'd finished. "I don't know which part of that is worse, the fact that your brother might have a real drinking problem, or that he might be mixed up in something with this girl, whoever she is."

Faith was touched. Leave it to Scott Hendler to think of the family aspect of any problem before the law enforcement aspect.

"Well," Hendler said, "we can't just go to the city PD and start talking about Department Thirty safe houses here in town. Number one, local cops aren't going to know what Thirty is, and number two . . ."

". . . They don't *need* to know," Faith finished.

"Exactly. We could try to find out who's working the case and see what they know. You could use your DOJ 'special projects' line if you need to tell them something."

"Okay. Do you have time to make the calls?"

"Yep. Today's a computer day for me, writing reports. I'll call you back."

Faith hung up and doodled a bit more. She scribbled her own name on the triangle's second side, then wrote *Mystery Girl* along the base, followed by several question marks.

Hendler called back in half an hour. "The lead detective is named Rob Cain. I know him. He's a pro and a nice guy. We're taking him to lunch at Barry's Grill. Meet you there at twelve thirty?"

"Got it," Faith said. "Thanks, Scott." She thumped her pen some more. "You want to come over tonight? I . . . I don't think I want to be alone tonight."

The last few words were so unlike her that Hendler waited a long, long moment on the phone.

Faith closed her eyes, gripping the phone. "Come on, say something," she said irritably. "Here I am, being all vulnerable . . . the least you can do is speak."

"I'll be there, Faith," Hendler said.

"Okay. Okay, then." The awkward silence descended. "Barry's at twelve thirty. Detective Cain. Got it." She hung up quickly.

Barry's Grill had always seemed to Faith to be a small-town diner that had been plopped down in the inner city, just off the intersection of Northwest Thirtieth Street and May Avenue. It didn't have the "retro diner" décor that so many restaurants tried for these days, with vintage Americana road signs and such. Barry's didn't need them—it was the real thing. It held the standard tables in the center, booths along the wall, old wood paneling that was cracked in a few places, a long ordering counter behind which was the grill.

Faith and Hendler arrived first, and each ordered

one of Barry's legendary cheeseburger baskets. All the burgers at Barry's were double meat and double cheese, with extras piled on, fries, and a drink, all for only about six dollars. In Chicago, Faith thought, the same meal would have cost twice as much.

Detective Rob Cain arrived a few minutes late, briefcase in tow. He raised an index finger at Hendler, dropped his briefcase at the table, and went to the counter to order before sitting down.

In movies and books, police detectives were often depicted in one of two ways: either as veterans just shy of retirement, rumpled, overweight, and wearing bad suits; or, as young hotshot studs, with three or four days' growth of beard, tight jeans, and bad attitudes. Rob Cain was neither. Faith thought he was a pleasant-looking man in his late thirties, with light brown hair and soft hazel eyes with a few worry lines. He looked trim and fit, but not overly so. Cain clearly didn't haunt the gym. His clothes were simple—clean, pressed khakis, a navy blue polo shirt, brown loafers. He wore a simple silver wedding band and a white ribbon on the breast of his shirt.

He and Hendler shook hands. "Sleepy Scott Hendler," Cain said, in a pleasant voice. "Good to hear from you. I haven't been to Barry's in ages."

Hendler nodded. "Rob, this is my friend Faith Kelly. She's in special projects for DOJ."

"Sounds ominous," Cain said easily.

"It is," Faith said with a smile.

Cain smiled back "And I really don't want to know. Not even mildly curious. Trust me, I have enough special projects on my plate these days."

"What's the ribbon?" Hendler said.

Cain fingered the little white ribbon pinned to his shirt. His smile widened. "Parental pride. Once a month my youngest daughter's preschool gives these out to parents to wear for the day, just to show you're proud of your kid. Neat idea."

Faith couldn't help but smile as well. In the space of a couple of minutes, Rob Cain had shattered every possible stereotype about urban cops. She could see why he and Hendler would like each other—they were both inherently decent human beings. In the murky world Faith had inhabited for the last few years, something as simple as a white ribbon denoting a father's pride had the power to move her enormously.

Her smile faded. If only Joe Kelly—another father, another cop—had worn a few white ribbons in his time, maybe things would be a lot different. Maybe . . .

Their names were called, one by one, and they went to the counter to get huge burgers—a chicken mushroom sandwich, equally huge, for Cain—and baskets of thick-cut French fries.

"This may kill me," Hendler said, "but I'll die happy."

Cain snorted. "Don't give me that. You haven't put on a pound in at least five years, Hendler."

Hendler shrugged and dug into his burger. They ate in silence, with both Cain and Faith adding liberal jolts of Louisiana Hot Sauce to their burgers.

"Good stuff," Hendler said after they'd eaten.

"Yup," Cain said. "Down to business?"

Hendler and Faith both nodded.

"Well, Sleepy Scott Hendler doesn't call me on cases every day," Cain said. "And even though he's Sleepy Scott, he's still a fed, so I'm required by law to pay attention."

Hendler laughed. Even though the tension between local police forces and the FBI was legendary, the Oklahoma City Police Department had a good and solid working relationship with the local FBI field office. "Right you are, Rob. Tell me about this strange little missing persons case."

"Two nights ago, just after ten o'clock, we get a 911 call of a disturbance at this apartment complex on Fiftieth near Portland. The neighbors to the apartment in question are a couple in their eighties, a Mr. and Mrs. Holzbauer. They were at home watching the ten o'clock news when Mrs. Holzbauer heard what sounded like the door being broken down next door, followed by loud voices. We had units rolling immediately, but before they got there, according to the neighbor lady, there was something of a scuffle, then a gunshot. One single shot."

"She didn't go outside?" Faith said. "Stayed in her own apartment the whole time?"

"I see where you're headed," Cain said. "The walls in these apartments are basically made of plywood and chewing gum. They're so thin you could probably hear your neighbor getting up to go to the bathroom in the middle of the night. No, she stayed put. Smart lady. Her husband is mostly deaf, by the way, and heard none of this. Just sat there watching Gary England's weather forecast like nothing was happening. Mrs.

Holzbauer hears a car start up and roar out of the parking lot. Then it's quiet for a little while. She goes to the window and peeks out in time to see two men coming out of the next-door apartment, arms around each other, sort of helping each other move. It was dark, but she swears she saw blood on one guy's shirt."

"Curiouser and curiouser," Hendler said, glancing at Faith.

"Yep," Cain said. "The two guys get into a dark four-door and drive off fast. They just pass our unit as it's turning into the parking lot."

"The girl who lived in the apartment," Faith said. "What about her?"

Cain shifted a little on his seat and took a drink of Diet Coke. "You know, I hate diet drinks. They're nasty, vile, awful stuff. Nutrasweet is evil. But my doc says I'm prediabetic, have to cut down on the calories." He took another drink and made a face. "The apartment was leased to a Katherine J. Hall, age twenty-four. She'd just lived there about a month. Mrs. Holzbauer said she was friendly enough, but she didn't see her very often. The girl, Hall, was supposedly a writer working on a book. At least that's what she told the neighbors, and that's what she put on her rental application. She paid the first three months rent in cash, in advance."

"Any other leads on her?" Hendler said.

"She's not real," Cain said.

"What?"

"She's a phantom. We couldn't reach any of her rent references. The landlord says they all checked out a month ago, but all we got were post office boxes and disconnected phones. Her Oklahoma driver's license was issued just last month, and—get this—her Social Security card was only issued two months ago. Her credit history is all bogus. She has no credit cards, no employment records, hasn't paid taxes or paid into Social Security. The girl's a ghost. A ghost who's missing. How do you find someone like that?"

They all looked at each other.

"One theory that I've floated," Cain said after a long moment, "is that she was in some sort of witness protection."

Faith shifted on her seat, bumping **her** knee against the bottom of the table.

Cain looked at her.

"Sorry," she said.

Cain appraised both of them. "Neither of you know anything about that, do you?"

"WITSEC is run by the U.S. Marshals Service," Faith said.

"I know that," Cain said quickly. "I've already talked to them. The chief deputy in the local office is a guy named Mark Raines. He checked up the line, and to his knowledge, they have no jurisdiction in the case. That's his way of telling me the girl's not theirs."

"Any lead on the two men?" Hendler said.

Cain shifted again. Faith marveled at how the man had given them every bit of information without once referring to written notes.

"Oh, this all gets better," Cain said. "Have you been watching TV and listening to the radio on this?"

"A little," Hendler said.

"The media's loving it. They've fallen in love with the neighbor lady. Refugee from Nazi Germany, she's lived in Oklahoma for sixty years but still sounds like she's just off the boat from Munich. Sweet face, probably bakes cookies for the reporters. They love her, so they love the story. Mrs. Holzbauer talks about how she viewed 'poor dear Katherine' as a surrogate granddaughter, since all her own grandkids live in California. Literally wrings her hands on camera."

Faith smiled.

"Anyway, she got a partial license plate on the dark four-door that the two guys left in. Wasn't hard to find, though. We found it in the parking lot of French Market, over at Sixty-third and May."

"That's barely a mile from the apartment complex," Faith said.

"Right. Theory was, they had another car ready and waiting for them there."

"Did you run the car?" Faith asked.

"Oh, yeah," Cain said. "The plot thickens, as they say. It was a rental, and it was rented to a Franklin Sanborn, with an address in Bloomington, Indiana. So we track him, and he's a ghost too. His address is fake, so's his phone number. You get a time and temp recording from Indiana if you call the number he left with the car rental place."

"One ghost going after another," Faith said quietly.

Sounds like Department Thirty business, she thought, then had to remind herself that not all strangeness in the world was centered on her little corner of the Department of Justice.

"There were bloodstains in the rental car," Cain said. "The lab's working on them now, along with the fingerprints." He spread his hands apart. "That's all we have. Chasing shadows while the TV stations wonder what we're doing to find 'poor, dear Katherine.' " Cain leaned back against the back of the booth. "So what's your interest here? I'll take all the help I can get, but I admit that I'm not quite sure why you called me, Scott."

Hendler nodded at Faith.

Faith sat motionless.

Franklin Sanborn.

I know that name, she thought.

"Hello?" Cain said.

Franklin Sanborn.

It was nothing to do with any of her Department Thirty cases. She knew that—all of those names, past and present, were burned into her memory by now. But she'd heard the name Franklin Sanborn, had seen it, *knew* it.

"Faith?" Hendler said. "Did you want to . . ." He tilted his head in an *are-you-going-to-tell-him* gesture.

She'd told Hendler on the way to the restaurant that she intended to give the detective her brother's name, and describe what had happened with him, carefully omitting details about his suspension from ICE. In a way, he was a missing person as well, and he wasn't a phantom.

But now . . .

Cain was looking at her intently. She thought he was seeing for the first time the white line scar that ran from alongside her nose almost to the edge of her upper lip. He didn't look away.

Faith met his eyes.

"I'm sorry," she said.

Hendler's eyebrows went up.

"I have nothing to say," she said. "Thanks for the information, Detective Cain."

But why do I know the name Franklin Sanborn? Faith thought.

She stood up. "I have to get back to my office," she said abruptly. She needed the DOJ database, and she needed it right now. Hendler had met her at the courthouse and driven them to Barry's, so he stood with her.

Hendler shook hands with Cain. "I'll be in touch, Rob," he said quietly.

Cain clasped his hand a moment too long. "What was all this about, Scott?"

Faith was already halfway out the door. "I'm not sure," Hendler said.

18

A WEEK PASSED.

The house near Mulhall was alive with activity. Two members were responsible for "media relations" and began drafting press releases. Two others—Daryn and Alan Davenport—kept the troops focused with "pep rallies" every evening, with lectures and readings ranging from de Tocqueville to Marx to Emerson.

Sean and Daryn talked and talked. She gave up more little pieces of herself to him, embellishing the portrait of her fictional father with tidbits from her real father's life and career. She never mentioned the incest again. Sean played the game with her, creating an authoritarian father and a bad marriage that mirrored his own real life. She'd also kept Sean well supplied with bourbon. She'd learned to watch his signs, knew the tremble of his hands and the furrow in his brow when he'd gone too long without a drink. It was a strange twilight existence.

Every night they unleashed physical passion with wildness and abandon. Daryn let him take her in every way possible, and she took him as well a few times. Sometimes Britt joined. Sometimes she watched. But when she joined the sex, she only touched Sean at Daryn's urging, at her direction, and only seemed to derive pleasure from Daryn herself.

At six o'clock in the morning of the seventh day since their arrival at the house, Daryn slipped out of bed and pulled on a pair of gray sweatpants and a T-shirt. She rarely slept well anymore and was always tired, but she couldn't think about herself. Not any longer.

She took three extra-strength Tylenol and went downstairs. Jeannie Davis, the unlikely revolutionary—a social worker from Edmond—was in the kitchen, making coffee.

"Morning, Jeannie," Daryn said.

Davis turned. "Good morning, Kat."

Of the Coalition members, only Britt and Franklin Sanborn knew her real identity. The others knew her name wasn't Kat Hall, and that she'd only been an "escort" long enough to establish a cover, but they hadn't been told who she really was. They would learn in time.

The whole world will know in time, Daryn thought, rubbing her forehead. *And it won't be too long, thank God.*

"Is he out there?" Daryn asked.

Davis nodded. "Every morning. You want some coffee?"

"No, thanks. Wrong chemical for me."

She reached into a kitchen drawer and took out a pack of cigarettes and lighter. She didn't smoke often, and had taken up the habit at fifteen mainly to annoy her father. No one smoked in the house, and Daryn escaped to the deck to light up a couple of times a day.

She walked out into the predawn. The humidity was up, and thick mists had formed across the lowlands downhill from the house. She could barely make out the dark ribbon of Skeleton Creek in the far distance, the mists rising off it like steam from a kettle.

Sanborn was standing at the rail of the deck, unmoving, as he did every morning. "Good morning," he said without turning around.

Daryn lit her cigarette and exhaled. "Morning."

Sanborn sniffed the air. "Should you be doing that?"

"What's the difference?" she said, taking a long drag.

She didn't really *like* Sanborn, and didn't trust him at all. But he was the organizer, the one who'd worked out all the exquisite, painstaking details of the plan. He had his own motivations—he'd never made a secret of that—but then, they all came to The Cause from different perspectives, with different ways of thinking. That was part of the beauty of it, that their diversity created unity.

"We need to move," she said, leaning against the railing a few steps away from Sanborn.

"He's really on board?"

"Just about." She stared into the mists. "Britt and I have almost literally fucked his brains out. He's totally under my control." She took another deep drag on the cigarette, holding the smoke in. The burning in her lungs helped dull the pounding in her head. "Let's move today."

"Yes," Sanborn said.

Daryn ground out the cigarette on the deck railing and left the butt sitting there. She glanced at Sanborn. He'd grown increasingly edgy over the past week, nervous and short-tempered. The open-minded academic and the easygoing host was still there, but an undercurrent to the man was rising. The closer they'd come to today, the more in evidence it was.

"I'll wake everyone," Daryn said, and went back in the house.

By eight o'clock all thirteen of them were up and dressed. Tension ran like whitewater rapids through the group.

Sanborn walked into the center of the living room and clapped his hands. "The day is here," he announced. "Today the message of the Coalition for Social Justice starts to be spread."

There were general murmurs of approval.

"Four cars should do it," Sanborn said. "Especially since Jeannie has brought her minivan for us to use." He looked directly at Sean. "Your Cherokee has some room, Michael. I'm sure Kat and Britt would like to ride with you, but could you take a couple of others?"

Sean looked at Daryn. "Sure, why not?"

"Excellent, then, it's settled. Michael's Jeep, Jeannie's minivan, my car, and one of the trucks. That should be sufficient for all of us. Let's get ready to roll."

People talked in low voices and began moving toward the front door. Sean stepped out onto the porch, squinting into the sunlight. The fog and mist had burned away, and the morning was brilliant and blinding. He blinked several times.

"A little bright for you?" Don Wheaton said as he went past him, carrying a suitcase.

"Not too much," Sean said. He'd taken two big shots of bourbon this morning, then quietly gone into the bathroom and vomited. That had been happening more and more of late, so much so that he almost began to accept it as part of his morning routine. *My own kind of morning sickness,* he'd thought at first.

Daryn came up beside him and put a hand on his arm. Her touch was both soft and electric at the same time. He thought for a long moment. Soon, very soon, he needed to talk to her about why he was here.

But why am I here?

To find Daryn McDermott, of course. To do a job, to convince her to go back home. To have Senator McDermott put in a good word for me and redeem my career. He repeated the words to himself like a mantra. But even as he did, the images of Daryn—above him, below him, inside her, the way she used her body, giving it to him as if he owned it—crowded his mind, jostling his thoughts like people standing in line for an amusement park ride.

A part of him didn't want this to end.

God help me, Sean thought.

A communal living situation in an old house outside the tiny town of Mulhall, Oklahoma. All the liquor he wanted, no demands placed on him, and imaginative, unbridled sex every night, sometimes with two women at once.

Sean felt he could just drift away on a tide of the Coalition for Social Justice, with Daryn McDermott, as Kat Hall, steering the way.

He closed his eyes against the sun again. *Don't be stupid. You have a job to do. Don't be led around by your cock.*

Then he looked at Daryn again, the big dark eyes.

The conflicting feelings careened through him. He swallowed, his mouth suddenly dry.

"Let's go," Daryn said.

Sean nodded. *Later.* Later, after they'd done the demonstration. He'd talk to her then. He'd get her away from Britt, away from Franklin Sanborn, and they would talk.

Later.

They started toward the Cherokee, two others of the group following silently. Daryn stopped, watching Don Wheaton putting the suitcase he'd been carrying carefully into the bed of one of the pickup trucks, then climbing in the bed himself. The man named CJ—Sean had never heard his last name—had an identical suitcase.

"What's in the cases, guys?" Daryn called.

Wheaton and CJ looked at each other.

"Hello?" Daryn said.

"Nothing," Wheaton said. CJ nodded. Sean hadn't heard the man speak once during the entire week.

"Nothing?" Daryn echoed. "Hey, this is me, guys. What's in the suitcases?"

Sanborn stepped between them. He'd been just about to get behind the wheel of the dark sedan. "Problem?"

"I'm just curious about what Don and CJ are carrying," Daryn said. "Those cases seem awfully bulky, and I think we have everything we need for today."

"Don't worry about it, Kat, my dear," Sanborn said. The words were meant to be reassuring, but an edge crept into Sanborn's voice.

Daryn's voice rose. "I will worry about it. You don't keep things from me around here. *What's in the cases?*"

"Leave it alone," Sanborn said, his voice low.

"Goddammit, Franklin, what's in the fucking cases?"

Sanborn faced her savagely. "C-4. Plastic explosive."

All movement had stopped, as if choreographed.

"Oh, shit," Sean said.

"*What?*" Daryn whispered.

"Come on now, Kat," Sanborn said. "Don't be foolish. You're not as naïve as your little pet over there, after all." He pointed at Britt. "You understand the world. Going and making speeches or putting on sex shows or sending out press releases will not get the attention of the rulers. Those things are components of the plan, but they will be useless, utterly pointless, unless we get their attention first!" His voice had risen steadily until he was almost shouting.

"But you said . . ." Daryn was trembling. "Franklin, what about how violence dilutes the message of the Coalition? You said—"

"This is what we're doing, Kat!" Sanborn shouted, and all resemblance to the genial, easygoing professor was gone, as if it had vanished along with the morning mists. "Does anyone want to challenge me?"

No one moved. No one spoke.

"Well?" Sanborn thundered.

Britt shuffled her feet.

"You keep quiet, young Britt," Sanborn said. "I only allowed you here so Kat could have a toy to play with. Stay in her shadow where you belong."

"Look, Sanborn . . ." Sean said.

"The same with you, you drunken fool!" He lowered his voice, then softened his posture. "Listen to me, people. The explosives are only enough to break some windows, to grab attention. Then we go through with the demonstration."

Sean swallowed. "You think you can set off an explosive at a downtown bank building, and calmly go about doing an organized demonstration? It'll never happen. It'll be pure chaos, and you'll be arrested. You stand around there to make speeches after doing that and everyone will be arrested under the Patriot Act."

"And how do you know so much about this, Michael?"

Sean tossed his duffel bag into the Jeep and slammed the door. "Drunken fool or not, I do pay attention to the world around me. It's suicide for yourselves, and for the movement, if you do it this way."

"I can do without your input," Sanborn said. "But perhaps I should clarify one thing—the demonstration won't be at the same bank as the attention getter. There are other banks downtown. Alan?"

Davenport, who'd been standing by Sanborn's car, stepped forward. "There's a Chase Bank around the corner from Bank of America Plaza, at Main and Broadway. Those of us doing the demonstration will be there instead of at B of A. We point out that while the ruling classes and their law enforcement puppets scurry to find out what happened to their banking center, *real* people everywhere have no choices. It's a fine point and counterpoint."

"You're crazy," Sean muttered.

"Wait, Michael," Daryn said.

Sean turned, his heart pounding. Daryn was looking at him strangely. She looked at him for a long moment, then slowly turned to Sanborn. "We don't want to hurt any real people."

Sanborn exhaled noisily. "Of course not. We break some glass, that's all. Don and CJ simply walk up to the door and put down the cases. They walk away. There's a small explosion. We're around the corner. We do our public demonstration. By the time anyone figures out what's going on, we're finished and on the move again. Don't you see, Kat? It has to be this way."

Daryn waited for a long moment. "We've come too far to let the Coalition fall apart."

"I know that," Sanborn said. "You have to trust me, Kat. I don't want real people to be hurt either. But if we don't first start with getting their attention, then the message itself will be lost. We're not terrorists, because the *message* is always secondary to whatever action we take to open the door to it. People will listen this way."

Daryn waited again, looking across the clearing, watching every face.

"Let's go," she said.

"Kat," Sean said.

"Shhh, let's go."

"And you should control your pets a little better, Kat," Sanborn said.

"They're not pets, Franklin. They're real people."

"Perhaps," Sanborn said, and walked to his car.

"Kat," Sean said.

"Get in the car, Michael," Daryn said.

"But—"

"Get in the car!"

The other two Coalition members who'd been assigned to ride with them approached the Jeep, but Sean said, "No, ride with someone else!" and they melted away.

Sean, Britt, and Daryn climbed into the Jeep. "I'm not a pet," Britt said. "He shouldn't have called me that."

"No, sweetie, he shouldn't have," Daryn said without looking at the other woman. "And he shouldn't have kept it from me that he was planning to use explosives."

She stared through the glass of the windshield. Sanborn's car pulled out of the clearing. Next came one of the trucks. Don Wheaton sat in the bed, staring at her as they passed. Jeannie Davis's minivan went next. CJ sat in the front passenger seat. Sean pulled the Jeep in behind them.

"You can't let this happen," Sean said as they wound toward the road.

"I know," Daryn said, "but you heard him. I didn't . . . dammit, no one stood up to him." She dropped her head into her hands. "I've been an idiot. I believed him, I trusted him, and he's taken my movement—*my* movement! I started this, not him! If we use violence, we're no better than McVeigh or bin Laden or any of the cults and the antigovernment nuts. We're better than this!"

She looked up. Her eyes burned into him. To Sean's surprise, she began to cry. Tears were not something he associated with her—for some reason, he hadn't thought she was capable of crying.

They reached the highway and the little caravan turned south toward Mulhall, toward Guthrie, the interstate, and Oklahoma City. Toward Bank of America Plaza.

"Michael," Daryn said, still crying, tears streaking her pale face.

Sean glanced at her. He still saw Britt out of the corner of his eye. She was staring at him too.

"Michael, please," Daryn said. "We have to stop this. Even if he says it'll just break windows, it might not. What if someone is standing right next to the window when it breaks? We can't . . ."

Sean pulled off the road in front an abandoned car wash just as they crossed into Mulhall. He took out his cell phone and started punching buttons.

"Who are you calling?" Britt said.

"Someone who can help."

The phone rang three times. *Look at the caller ID, Faith,* Sean urged her silently. *Come on, don't be so pissed off at me that you won't answer the phone.*

A moment later he heard his sister's voice: "Where the hell are you?"

"I don't have time to explain," Sean said. "Listen to me. Call your friend."

"What? What friend?"

"What do you mean, *what friend?* The geeky one, with the bald spot. You remember him?"

Faith was quiet for a moment. "Why?"

"He needs to get some more friends and they need to go to the Bank of America in downtown Oklahoma City. It's on . . ." He glanced at Daryn. "What's the street again?" He realized he was supposed to live in Oklahoma City, and by asking the question, his cover may have been blown. But then, he was going to blow it himself anyway, very soon.

Daryn looked at him quizzically, turning the question over in her mind. "Well, it's on Robinson."

"Robinson," Sean said into the phone. "It's right downtown, near the memorial. Your friend and his friends should get there quick if they want to stop something from happening."

"Sean," Faith said. "I can tell that you feel like you can't talk, but what's this about?"

Sean took a deep breath. "It's about preventing an act of terrorism. Please believe me. Whatever bullshit there may be between you and me, believe me on this. It's real, and it's serious."

Faith waited. "I believe you," she finally said. "I'll call Scott."

"I'll talk to you later," Sean said before she could say anything else, then clicked the End button on his phone.

"Who was that?" Daryn asked. She reached out and took Sean's free hand. His other hand was gripping the steering wheel so hard that his knuckles were the color of paste.

"Just someone I know," Sean said.

He pulled back onto Highway 77 and accelerated to catch up with the rest of the Coalition for Social Justice.

19

FORTY-FIVE MINUTES LATER SEAN EXITED THE
Centennial Expressway into downtown Oklahoma
City. He took Sixth Street west to Robinson, then
turned south toward the heart of downtown. He recognized the area now—it was very, very close to the federal courthouse and his sister's office.

With the stop he'd made to call Faith, they'd fallen a
few minutes behind the other Coalition cars. As he
slowed into the southbound flow of traffic, Sean
searched for them. Bank of America Plaza was ahead
on his right. He recognized the red, white, and blue
logo and saw the courtyard, which was commanded by
an unusual modernistic sculpture just off the street:
huge reddish orange metal cylinders, each open on
one side, all twining around each other, reaching toward the sky.

People were milling around the courtyard, up and
down the sidewalks. Men and women in FBI wind-
breakers were scattered about. A knot of people broke
behind a car that was parked illegally right in front of
the courtyard. Sean drew in his breath—it was Jeannie
Davis's van.

"My God," Daryn whispered.

Sean angled the Jeep into the far left lane, away

from the bank on the one-way street. As he drove slowly past the van and the courtyard, he could see more people. He recognized some of the Coalition members. They'd been cuffed and were standing alongside several unmarked cars. CJ was lying on the ground, his hands cuffed behind his back. Several feet away, with three officers standing next to it, was the suitcase full of explosives.

"Who did you call?" Daryn said.

"Someone who knows someone in the FBI," Sean said.

Daryn bowed her head. "It wasn't supposed to be like this. If Franklin had just told me what—"

They had just crossed Couch Drive, approaching Park Avenue, when they heard the explosion.

Daryn screamed. Britt leaned forward.

"Jesus, what was that?" Sean said.

Then it came to him—he hadn't seen Sanborn's car or the truck. The truck into which Don Wheaton had loaded the other suitcase of explosives.

"Shit," he muttered. "Where's that other bank?"

"Main and Broadway," Britt said. "The big tower. Chase Bank."

Daryn was shivering, arms wrapped around herself. Britt stared at her as if seeing her for the first time.

"He blew the other bank," Sean said. "He used this one as a diversion, sacrificed the people, and blew the other one."

"He lied to me again," Daryn whispered. "He lied again."

"But Daryn," Britt said, "what about The Cause?"

Sean jerked as if he'd been poked with something hot. Britt had just called Daryn by her real name.

Daryn seemed not to notice. She was staring forward through the windshield, eyes unmoving, as if in a waking coma.

Sean turned onto Park, a tiny downtown street that dead-ended one block later at Broadway. Directly across the way was Santa Fe Plaza and the Skirvin Hotel, the landmark three-towered hotel that was in a state of constant renovation, always seemingly on the verge of reopening, just to be sold again and again. So Faith had told him, in the early days of her life in Oklahoma City. She'd pointed it out to him during their sightseeing last week.

Was that only a week ago? Sean thought. *Seems like a hell of a lot longer than that.*

To the right was the Chase Tower.

Thick black smoke rolled out from the glass front of the ground floor. Sean could see broken glass on the concrete, but the smoke was so thick and so dark that he couldn't tell the extent of the damage.

"Jesus," he said.

On the far side of the building, along Main Street, was Franklin Sanborn's car and the other Coalition truck.

"There!" Britt pointed.

"Son of a bitch," Sean whispered. "Hang on, people."

He whipped the steering wheel to the left, climbed the median, and came back down on the other side of Broadway. Contradicting its name, the street was very narrow in this stretch of downtown. Sean kept the Jeep pointed diagonally southeast, toward Sanborn's car on the other side.

Sirens sounded. People were beginning to run, some toward the Chase Tower, some away from it. People fell to their knees, coughing from the smoke. One woman had blood on her face. But Sean could still see very little for the smoke. He drove under it and through it, across the sidewalk toward Main.

Sanborn's car pulled away from the curb.

"No you don't, you bastard," Sean said.

"Why are you chasing him?" Britt blurted. "He just tried . . . I mean, the Coalition. You didn't . . . he—"

"Britt, that's enough," Daryn said, turning to face Britt with blood in her eyes. "Don't get into things you don't know about."

"But he called the FBI. You didn't . . . you didn't go through with it." Britt's eyes filled with tears. "I don't understand."

"*Shut up!*" Daryn screamed. "Shut up, shut up, god-dammit, Britt!" She pressed her hands to her head as if she were trying to keep it from cracking in two. "Just leave it alone!"

Sanborn's car shot into the intersection and into E.K. Gaylord Boulevard, which marked the eastern edge of downtown and the beginning of the Brick-town entertainment district. It was a wider, large thoroughfare, and Sanborn went through against the light.

Sean, three car lengths behind, watched as a burgundy-colored four-door twisted to get out of San-born's way. The driver was almost successful, and wound up just clipping Sanborn's bumper. Sanborn fishtailed, but he righted the car and made it through the intersection.

The burgundy car's driver stopped, like any normal citizen involved in a fender bender, and started to get out. Sean whipped around the car and followed Sanborn across the boulevard, under a railroad bridge, and into Bricktown. Main was at the north edge of the former warehouse district that had come to redefine Oklahoma City's cultural life.

Just past the bridge, Sean blinked at what had to be an apparition: to the left, in a vacant area, dozens of buffalo. Sculptures—ceramic, papier-mâché, he had no idea, but they were all standing in a field, as if in a real buffalo herd, and all were painted with brightly colored designs.

He squeezed his eyes closed. Had to be the booze, playing tricks on his mind. He opened his eyes. The buffalo stood there serenely.

"I'm losing it," he muttered.

"Look," Daryn said.

There were brick buildings lining either side of Main, but it only ran two blocks before dead-ending at a high wire fence and several pieces of heavy construction equipment.

"No way out," Sean said.

He braked the Jeep, and it came to rest in the middle of the street. Ahead, Sanborn saw the dead end too late. He tried to turn, but the car fishtailed again, the passenger side slamming into the fence.

Sean reached over the seat of the Jeep and retrieved

his duffel bag from near Britt's feet. He felt in it, but his gun wasn't there.

"*Goddammit!*" Now he remembered—he'd taken it out of the duffel and put it in the little nightstand beside the bed, back in the Mulhall house.

He flung open the door of the Jeep, then crouched behind it.

"Sanborn!" he shouted. "They'll be coming for you, any minute now. You son of a bitch, you have no idea what you've just done! You've done more harm to your own movement than you could possibly imagine!"

To his surprise, Sean heard laughter, low and controlled. Sanborn stepped out of the black car. A tiny trickle of blood bloomed from his hairline, running down his left cheek. Behind him, in the car, Don Wheaton was slumped against the passenger door, unmoving. "You're the one who doesn't know what's going on here," he said. He took a few steps forward. Sean spotted the gun in his hand, pointed downward. "Agent Sean Kelly," Sanborn added.

Sean jerked again.

Behind him, Daryn got slowly out of the Jeep.

Sanborn made a *tsk-tsk* sound. "All that trouble with the bottle, Agent Kelly. It could make a man desperate to salvage his career. It could convince him to take a job hunting down the wayward, politically extreme daughter of a United States senator. One of the rulers himself."

"Franklin, don't," Daryn said, but she was staring at Sean.

"Don't? Don't, my dear?" Sanborn raised the gun. "I

knew someone would betray the Coalition. I didn't know it would be you, but I knew someone would. Betrayals run rampant in the world of revolutionaries. You called the authorities, and they've taken CJ and Jeannie and the others. I knew it would happen. That's why I had to be ready to strike at a second target. I'm very disappointed."

Daryn walked slowly into the middle of the street, closing the distance between them. "Franklin, let's stop while we can salvage the Coalition."

"But what about your friend?" Sanborn said, pointing at Sean with the gun. "Your little sex toy there represents the ruling classes. He came to get you, Daryn. He came to bring you back to your daddy."

Daryn stopped, closer to Sanborn now than to Sean and Britt. She turned and looked at Sean.

"This isn't what you wanted, Daryn," Sean said. It was the first time he'd called her by her real name. "All your commitment to social justice. This isn't social justice. This is terrorist bullshit, all his nonsense about getting people's attention. Terrorism doesn't work. 'Attention getters' don't work. It cuts off your message and then no one hears it."

Daryn walked a few steps farther toward Sanborn. "Franklin—"

"Daryn?" Britt said, in a small voice. "What about me?"

Daryn stopped again. She turned to look at Britt, and in a lightning move, Sanborn closed the distance between them. In one motion he had his arm around Daryn's neck, the gun at her temple.

Sean flexed his hands. Suddenly he felt nauseous,

just like he did most mornings. "You don't want to do that, Sanborn. Right now you might still be able to get out of this, but anything else and you're a dead man."

"And what about you?" Sanborn said. "Anything I've done, you've done too. It's called conspiracy. Little more than you bargained for, isn't it, Agent Kelly?" He moved then gun from Daryn's temple and shoved it under her chin.

The driver of the burgundy car, a middle-aged, well-dressed black woman, was running toward them, but stopped short when she saw the gun. She turned and began to run back toward the street.

"The cops will be all over this street in a minute or two," Sean said. "That woman's pulling out her cell phone and calling them now."

"Don't be so sure," Sanborn said. "There's just been an act of terrorism at the Chase Tower. See that smoke? That means a lot more right now than some strange little altercation on a dead-end street." He twisted the gun under Daryn's chin. "I could just fix this right now, Daryn. One shot, a blinding split-second of pain, and then no more pain at all, of any kind, ever again. But no, maybe I won't do that after all. You'd like that too much, wouldn't you?"

Sean stared at him, not understanding.

Sanborn raised his voice. "Britt! Come here, girl."

Britt didn't move.

"Now, girl. Come to me or Daryn dies right here, right now."

Britt walked slowly to him.

"Now you, Mr. Kelly. You're going to step away from

your car, over to the curb. Should have kept your weapon with you, shouldn't you? But then, I suppose whiskey and sex have your mind a bit rattled these days, yes?"

Sean very slowly moved away from the open door of the Jeep, toward the last building on the block, which was vacant. A faded sign on the building read *Billy's Candy & Nectar Co.*

He moved to the curb, holding his hands out away from his body, trying to think. But his brain felt encased in some kind of gel, something that surrounded him and wouldn't let him go, wouldn't let him think.

"Traitor," Sanborn hissed, lowered the gun and shoved her hard. She tumbled to the ground and he kicked her in the ribs. "We'll regroup in Mulhall. The Coalition isn't dead, young Miss McDermott. We're just getting started. The rulers will know that we've spoken, and one of them will be your father."

He motioned to Britt with the gun, then ran for the Jeep.

"Daryn?" Britt said.

"Come now, Britt!" Sanborn shouted. "She betrayed the Coalition. She betrayed you! You loved her and she betrayed everything we stand for! Come on!"

"Daryn?"

Daryn was curled into a fetal position, clutching her ribs. Sean moved toward her. Daryn didn't speak. She hadn't made a sound since Sanborn grabbed her. Her eyes were squeezed closed. Tears streaked her face and ran onto the asphalt.

Britt finally walked to the Jeep, never taking her eyes from Daryn.

"If you try to come back to the Coalition," Sanborn said, "I'll kill you, or I'll have you killed. And maybe . . ." He slid behind the wheel of Sean's Jeep. ". . . maybe I'll have you killed anyway."

Britt got in beside him, and Sanborn turned the Jeep around, maneuvering it out of the dead-end street.

Sean looked up. He saw a face at a window across the street. He heard more sirens, and pandemonium from down the street. Smoke billowed and streamed from the Chase Tower.

He went to Daryn, picked her up in his arms, and took her back to the curb.

"He's going to kill me," Daryn whispered. "He's going to come after me. He thinks I'm a traitor . . . but he . . . he's the traitor. It wasn't supposed to . . ." She contorted her face in pain, in anguish.

Sean's head was pounding. Everything had gotten mixed up. He didn't know who was who or what was what anymore. For a moment he could almost imagine that he was back in the cantina in Sasabe, drinking whiskey and eating tortillas half a mile from the Mexican border.

But he'd found Daryn McDermott. Her identity was in the open, as was his. Somehow Sanborn had broken his cover. But that didn't matter anymore. Nothing was the same. Sanborn was right—Daryn would be implicated in any conspiracy charges. She and Sanborn had together been the driving forces behind the Coalition's plans. Behind the plans yet to come. He remembered the list of other banks, all over the country, culminating with a "strike" on Citibank in New York City.

A little bit of the gel surrounding his mind melted. "Oh my God," he said aloud. He knew in that instant he would never see the rest of Tobias Owens's money, that Senator McDermott would probably never see his daughter again, and there was no chance at redemption for his career. But he had to make a choice. He pulled out his cell phone.

When Faith answered, he said, "Where are you right now?"

"At my office. All hell's broken loose downtown. Why didn't you—"

"Faith, we're not far away. Come and get us."

"What? What do you mean, *us?*"

Sean cradled Daryn's head in his lap. "You're in the protection business, right? I have someone who needs protection, and I think she might have some information you and your bosses would find useful."

20

FAITH HAD TO LITERALLY PLUCK THEM OUT FROM under the noses of the local cops. As soon as she hung up the phone with her brother, she knew the *us* he referred to had to be himself and the missing girl, Katherine Hall. She also knew that if she was about to become officially involved, not as Sean's sister but as a Department Thirty case officer, she needed to avoid any entanglements with the locals. All she would need was Detective Cain sniffing around what had turned into a federal matter.

Since her Miata was strictly a two-seater, she pried Hendler temporarily away from the downtown melee. The girl was to ride with Faith, and Sean with Hendler in his Toyota. Sean complained about the arrangement, but Faith silenced him with a look. He was in her territory now.

With no time to make other arrangements, she decided to use the Edmond safe house after all, and they headed north. The girl, Kat Hall, kept looking at her during the half-hour drive, kept trying to talk to her.

"Wait," Faith told her. "Just wait, then you can talk all you want."

Faith did look at her quite a bit herself, though. She looked almost frail, waiflike, but with eyes of pure steel. There was something vaguely familiar about her, though Faith couldn't place it. Just like the elusive Franklin Sanborn. She'd searched every database she had access to, and had come up empty. But she was still positive she knew the name. With any luck, she'd know why very shortly.

Department Thirty's safe house in the white-collar suburb of Edmond had once been the home of Frank and Anna Elder, the new identities assigned to James and Natalia Brickens, aka "Adam and Eve," who had once been the world's premier freelance assassins. They were still considered the biggest catches ever in the department, though both were now dead. Their case, and the turbulent search of their son to find his own real identity, had been her introduction to Department Thirty. That case had led to the death of her mentor and father figure, Art Dorian, and had brought her into his world.

The department had held on to the house, though, paying the mortgage, taxes, utilities, and insurance through a variety of accounts. It was in a quiet subdivision just off Santa Fe Avenue and Danforth Road on the north side of Edmond. The suburb had grown hugely just in the years Faith had lived in Oklahoma. The corner of Danforth and Santa Fe had once been an open field. A single convenience store had been the only business. Now all four corners were occupied by bustling shopping centers.

Faith kept a garage door opener for the house, just as she did for the Yukon safe house. She pressed the button and pulled the Miata into the two-car garage.

Hendler's Toyota pulled in behind her. Sean got out, but Hendler leaned out his window and said, "I have to get back downtown. There are a lot of . . . well, we're still not quite sure what happened."

"I'll talk to you later," Faith called. Hendler backed out. Faith lowered the garage door.

They went into the house through the garage and into the kitchen. The house was quite musty. Unlike the one in Yukon, this house had once been occupied on a long-term basis, and consequently, all its furnishings had belonged to the occupants, Frank and Anna Elder. Faith had scavenged some furniture for the place, but it wasn't much: a couple of sagging armchairs in the living room, a coffee table, an ancient TV set. Those cases who'd been housed here temporarily slept in sleeping bags on the floor.

"It's not much," Faith said, "but it'll do for now." She turned and faced Sean and the younger woman. Her eyes zeroed in on the girl's scratched face, and the way she was slightly hunched over. "Are you hurt? Do you need a doctor? I have one that I can get here if you need medical attention."

"No, I don't need a doctor," she said. Faith thought she detected a ghost of a smile on her face, and wondered what it meant.

"You hit your head when he shoved you," Sean said. "And he kicked your ribs. You might need X-rays."

"No. No X-rays. My ribs aren't broken, and my head's pretty hard." There was the strange little smile again.

"All right, then," Faith said. "I've made the offer. If

you don't think you need medical attention, I can't force you to get it." She walked into the living room and motioned them to chairs. She sat on the edge of the coffee table. She didn't even look at her brother. "Your name is Katherine Hall, is that right?"

"Yes," she said.

"No," Sean said.

Faith looked at both of them. "We're not going to get anywhere if we can't even get past the basic stuff."

"Tell her everything," Sean said. "This is the time to tell the truth, good and bad, Daryn. If you want protection from Sanborn, and if you want to save your cause from turning into just another domestic terrorist group, you have to tell everything."

"And you?" Daryn said. "Why don't you tell the truth?"

Sean shrugged. "My name is Sean Kelly. I'm an agent of Immigration and Customs Enforcement, Department of Homeland Security. At least I was."

Daryn said nothing, staring at him.

"But none of this was official," Sean added quickly. "This is a freelance job."

"My father hired you." A statement, not a question.

"He sent someone to hire me, yes."

"To bring me back before I embarrassed him?"

"Essentially, yes."

"Bastard," Daryn said.

"Who are you?" Faith asked.

Daryn looked up at her slowly. For a moment it seemed as if she wasn't focusing. Then her eyes cleared, and Faith noticed the same hard darkness she'd seen there before. "My name is Daryn McDermott. My father is Senator Edward McDermott of Arizona."

Faith waited, thinking. "Now I know why I recognized you. You're the one who was arrested for public nudity at the demonstration in front of the Capitol."

"Isn't it funny," Daryn said, "how society works? It doesn't matter what else I've done or said. But once I took off my clothes, people paid attention. The very fact that we have laws against public nudity in this country are proof of the change we need."

Faith glanced over at Sean. Sean shrugged. Faith looked back to Daryn. "So you were involved in what happened downtown today?"

Daryn squared her shoulders and looked Faith in the eye. "Yes. And now let me ask you a question."

"Go ahead."

"Who are *you?* The two of you are related, right?"

Before Faith could speak, Sean said, "I guess that's pretty obvious when you see us together. Daryn, this is my sister, Faith Kelly."

"And what exactly is it you do, sister Faith Kelly?"

Faith took note of the way Daryn McDermott had swung from quiet bemusement to anger to insolence in her tone, all in the space of a few minutes. "I work for a special unit of the Justice Department."

"Witness protection."

"Not exactly. Not witness protection, but criminal protection." As she always did, she paused for a moment to let that sink in.

Faith and Daryn locked gazes for a long moment. Daryn looked away first.

"If you were involved in what just happened downtown, you've been involved in an act of terrorism. In this country, here and now, that's taken pretty damn seriously. Now, Sean seems to think you need protection, and he also seems to think you have something to tell, something that might warrant that protection by the U.S. Government. Do you?"

Daryn looked at Sean.

"There's no other way," Sean said. "You heard what Sanborn said at the end."

"Sean," Faith said, "I'm going to advise you to keep your big Irish mouth shut, okay? This is what I do, and you stay out of it. Also, the fact that I still don't know the extent of your involvement in this makes me wonder how deep *you* are in it. I'll deal with you later."

Sean sat back. He'd never heard the cold, official Department Thirty side of Faith before. He raised his hands in a mock surrender.

"Who's older?" Daryn said suddenly.

"What?" Faith said.

"You're brother and sister. Which one of you is older?"

"He is, by eighteen months," Faith said.

Daryn nodded. "Interesting dynamic, isn't it?"

"It would be if we were talking about my family dynamics," Faith said. "But we're not. There are two questions you have to answer. Do you believe you need protection, either from prosecution or from the threat of bodily harm? And do you believe you have information vital to the national interests of the United States? Yes or no, right now."

"Yes, on both counts," Daryn said, her head high.

Faith spoke to Sean but kept looking at Daryn. "Sean, you have to leave now."

"What?" Sean said. "But I brought her in. I'm the one who—"

Faith whirled to face him. "Listen to me, dammit! The less you say the better, for her, for me, for yourself. Just for your information, most of my department's cases don't come in this way. We find them, they don't find us. There's only been one exception in the department's history. So we all have to be very, very careful here. Do you understand me? I'm not bullshitting you, Sean. This is the way it has to be done."

"But—"

"No buts. If she qualifies for the program, which we still don't know at this point, every aspect of her life will change. She will have no connection with her past life. Do you know what that means? It means you won't ever see her again. I don't know what's going on here, between the two of you, but you brought this to me, and now you have to understand the implications of what you've done. You get that, big brother?"

"Jesus, Faith, you're—"

"A coldhearted bitch, I know. I've been called everything in this job. Don't get me wrong. You're still my brother and you'll always be my brother, but by calling me in on this, you're in a whole different universe now."

"I know. At least I guess I . . ." Sean's voice died away. He looked past his sister to Daryn.

"I guess you didn't finish the job my father hired

you to do," Daryn said. Her look now was triumphant.

Sean pressed his fingertips to his head. "No. I'm not even thinking about that anymore. I . . . Kat, I mean, Daryn . . . it's different. I didn't have to call Faith. I could have let them arrest you, or I could have let you take your chances with Sanborn. You're so committed to your agenda, and Sanborn twisted it so much, that—"

"You should listen to your younger sister," Daryn said. "Just stay out of it from here on out. I'll deal with whatever happens next." She sat back in the lumpy armchair. "No last fucks for the road, Sean. Or I could call you Michael, for old times' sake. You got a lot more sex than you paid Kat Hall for, so you shouldn't complain."

Faith looked at both of them, but kept silent. Pain was scribbled on Sean's face, as if in bloody red capital letters. When she looked back at Daryn McDermott, the girl's own expression had changed again, with a softness she hadn't expected. Furrows slashed into her forehead.

"I'm sorry," Daryn said, and her voice was very gentle, almost faint. "Could I just lie down for a while?"

Faith observed the way Daryn's manner could shift so abruptly, so completely. This was, she thought, a very dangerous young woman.

"Yes," Faith said. "Down the hall, first bedroom to the right. There's a sleeping bag you can use. Be sure to shake it out. It hasn't been used in a while."

"Thank you, Faith."

Without looking back at Sean, Daryn heaved herself up from the chair, as if it were a great effort, and walked out of the room.

Faith looked at Sean. "You should stay out of sight for now," she finally said. "I still don't know what's going on here. The tip about Bank of America . . . they caught the group there."

"We didn't know about the Chase bomb," Sean said wearily. "Turns out Sanborn anticipated that we'd call someone, and he used the B of A group as a diversion, while he took the other set of explosives to Chase. Jesus Christ, Faith. How bad is it? The bombing. Could this city stand another thing like that? Could any city?"

"If any city could, this one could," Faith said. "But I don't know anything else about the extent of the damage. Scott's there, and I'll find out more from him later. For now, you go back to the house. Don't stop anywhere, don't do anything."

"You mean, don't drink," Sean said, standing up.

"Yeah, I do mean that. Take my car." She dug in her purse for keys and tossed them to him. "Yours is gone, I guess?"

A strange look came over Sean's face. "Sanborn took it. He had a gun on us, on Daryn. My gun's . . ."

"Where?"

"Never mind. It doesn't matter now. How will you get home?"

Faith shrugged. "I'm not sure when I'll get to go home. When I'm doing an intake like this, I sometimes don't get to go home for a couple of days at the very beginning. I'll either get Scott to give me a ride, or if he's too tied up, I'll have someone from the Marshals Service get me a car. I'll have to call in a couple of them to work protective detail for your friend in there."

"Faith," Sean said.

Faith waited.

"I'm sorry."

Faith nodded. "Go on back home. Try to forget about her. I don't know what's already happened, and I don't know what's going to happen next, but you have to put her out of your mind."

"She's not an easy woman to forget."

Faith glanced down the hall. "I believe you," she said.

21

FAITH WAITED UNTIL SHE HEARD THE MIATA LEAVE
the garage. Then she walked to the front window,
pulled aside the curtains, and watched her car until it
reached the corner and turned.

She walked down the hall, doing a breathing exercise as she went. When her friend Alex had had a baby,
three months premature, last year, Faith had learned
about the power of controlling one's breathing, and
now often used prenatal breathing exercises to steady
her nerves and focus her senses.

Daryn McDermott wasn't lying down when Faith
walked into the bedroom. Rather, she was sitting on
top of the sleeping bag, her back propped against the
wall. The lights were off.

"Let me turn on the light," Faith said.

"Don't, please," Daryn said. "I get these terrible
headaches, and it's better in the dark when I have
one."

"If someone shoved you to the ground, you may
have a mild concussion," Faith said. "The offer of medical attention still stands."

"No, thank you. Getting shoved to the ground
didn't cause my headache."

"All right." Faith sat down on the floor, at an angle

to where Daryn sat. Not too close, not too far away. "Can I get you anything? A glass of water? I'll do some shopping later and get some supplies in here."

"No, nothing." The sky outside had become overcast, and much of the room was in shadow. "Tell me something, Faith. Are you as good a lover as your brother?"

Faith didn't blink and didn't hesitate. "That depends on who you ask, I suppose."

Daryn chuckled lightly, yet another new emotion from her. "True. Your brother's quite good, actually."

"I wouldn't know."

"No, I guess you wouldn't. Though you never can tell in some families."

"Voice of experience?" Faith said.

Daryn was silent for a long time. "You're impressive. Usually when I make statements like I just made, people are shocked, appalled, outraged that such a pretty young *'thing'* would talk about such matters."

"Number one: you're not a thing. Number two: nothing shocks me. I am capable of outrage, though."

"I'm sure you are. So am I."

"Obviously." Faith crossed her long legs at the ankle. "What outrages you, Daryn?"

"Social injustice. Phony moralistic laws, unfair tax codes that punish real people while the ruling classes—those like my father and his cronies—gain wealth and power on the backs of others. My father's never worked an honest day in his life."

"Well, I'm no lover of politicians myself, and trust me, I've known a few." Faith wondered what Daryn would say if she knew that the newly reelected president of the United States considered Faith a personal friend. Faith didn't like the man, but that hadn't stopped them from doing "professional favors" for each other.

"Oh, it's not just politicians. I'm not just another antigovernment nutcase."

"That's refreshing."

"Yes. It's the entire fabric of society. It's corrupt and immoral, cloaked in this invisible language of 'values' and 'the American dream' and that kind of silliness."

"Okay, then," Faith said. "What led the daughter of a United States senator to be here, at this point, talking to me? Start with this guy Sanborn. He sent people to break into your apartment, you get away, and somehow you wind up connected with him afterward."

Daryn moved her head in the semidarkness, but only slightly. "I misjudged Franklin."

"You don't seem surprised to find out that he sent those guys to your apartment."

"I'm not surprised by anything I learn about Franklin Sanborn now. I trusted him, and he betrayed that trust."

"Who is he? Ever since you—or ever since Katherine Hall, I should say—became a missing person a week ago, and I found out from the local police that the guys who broke into your apartment drove a car rented by Franklin Sanborn, I've been trying to find out about him. He's a ghost, a phantom. He doesn't exist."

"He was a professor in Indiana." Daryn's voice was very soft and very even. "I think he was fired for his political views. He'd read about one of my tours last year and he found me in Washington. He had a plan, he had a vision for the cause I was already promoting. That's how we created the Coalition for Social Justice."

"Nice name. This Coalition for Social Justice? It's responsible for bombing the Chase Tower?"

Daryn sighed. "I don't know when, but somewhere Franklin lost control. Maybe it was seeing me with Michael . . . I mean Sean. I was never with Franklin sexually, yet he struck me as the kind who could have been very possessive, even without having ever done it."

Faith shook her head. "You speak a lot of different languages, Daryn. You talk to Sean about 'last fucks for the road,' like any street hooker, and here and now, you sound like a social scientist."

Daryn said nothing.

"So you and Sanborn created this Coalition. Why here? Why Oklahoma?"

"I'd been through here on my tour last year. I made a friend here, one of the girls on the street. Plus, there's the whole 'heartland' syndrome. That's about the only possible thing I could agree with that fool McVeigh on. Starting in New York or Washington or Chicago or Los Angeles would have been lost on everyone." Daryn shifted on the sleeping bag. She moved a little closer to Faith "Why don't we get down to business, Faith?"

"Okay, we'll get down to business. When I talk to my boss, he's going to want to know what information you have, and how important it is to national interests. Let's start there."

Faith thought she heard Daryn's breathing quicken.

"And so," Daryn said after a moment, "you would protect a terrorist if the information was right?"

"Are you a terrorist, Daryn?"

"You answered my question with a question."

"Yes, I did," Faith said. She didn't move, staring at the other woman with unflinching eyes.

There was a long silence.

"You're a very disarming woman," Daryn said after a full minute. "I'm rarely at a loss, and you've done it twice now."

Faith shrugged.

"It's a very attractive quality. To me, it's quite erotic." Daryn's voice was almost a whisper.

Breathe, Faith, breathe.

"Well," she said slowly, "I'm only into guys, Daryn."

Daryn moved a little closer. "No, you're not, Faith. You say that, but you're not. Let me touch you, Faith. I want to touch you everywhere." She reached toward Faith, fingers outstretched.

"Daryn," Faith said. "If you put your hand on me, I will break your wrist."

Daryn froze.

"And then I'll take you back downtown and drop you off where I found you. You'll have to face the choices you've made, whether it's with the FBI or your father or Sanborn. Your window of opportunity will close because of inappropriate behavior toward a federal officer."

"You're not just a federal officer, Faith. You're also a woman."

"Yep, and I'm a woman who's into guys. And I'm a

woman who doesn't do quickie fucks with people who might be under her official jurisdiction."

Daryn pulled away. "You're not much like your brother. And you're pretty good at speaking two languages yourself."

"Comes with the territory. And as for my brother, he's off limits to you now. Are you a terrorist, Daryn? Yes or no?"

Daryn leaned back and closed her eyes. "I didn't intend to be. It wasn't supposed to turn out the way it did."

"Were you involved in a conspiracy to bomb the Chase Tower today?"

"Yes." Eyes still closed.

"Are you involved in a conspiracy to do other similar acts with this Coalition?"

"Yes."

"Do you have information about these other acts?"

"Yes." Daryn reached into the pocket of her black jeans. She pulled out a folded piece of paper and tossed it to Faith.

"What's this?"

"It's a list of other targets, other banks we were going to strike, with the dates. It's Franklin's master plan."

Faith squinted in the dim light. The list included some of the largest banks in the country, and the dates began one week from today.

"You've made your point," Faith said. "Do you know where Sanborn is now?"

"He . . ." Daryn cleared her throat. "He took Britt—"

"Who's Britt?"

"She's my . . . friend here in town. She's a street girl. She's not very bright, and she was obsessed with me, never wanted to be far away from me. I don't know how she'll do."

"Where did he take her?"

"They took your brother's Jeep. Franklin said they were going to regroup in Mulhall."

"Mulhall? As in the town of Mulhall? North of Guthrie, that Mulhall?"

"We had a house there where we were all living together. I guess the ones who didn't get caught today went back there. They might still be there."

Faith rattled the list in her hand. "These other locations. Do you have other groups of your Coalition?"

"Small cells in towns outside the metro areas of each bank. Five or six people each. We were the main center here, because this is where we were starting. I can give you the towns where every group is."

Faith stopped a moment, studying the younger woman. When talking about the Coalition, Sanborn—anything but sex—Daryn's voice had been flat, almost without emotion. Only when she'd tried to seduce Faith had she seemed animated. Daryn McDermott was complicated, and Faith still didn't have a feel for which Daryn was the "real" one.

"Let me shift gears for a moment," Faith said. "Who was Katherine Hall? She wasn't a writer working on a book."

"No. That's what I told the landlord and the neighbors."

"Mrs. Holzbauer is quite upset about what happened to you."

"She and her husband are very sweet people. I'm sorry I had to lie to them."

Did she just use the word sweet? *Faith thought. She's even more complex than I thought.*

"More sorry than being a part of blowing up a building?"

"I'm not going to answer that."

"That's okay," Faith said. "I wouldn't answer it either, if I were you. So what about Kat?"

"I knew the Coalition was coming together, and that we'd be moving on our agenda very soon. And I knew that Daryn McDermott would have to lend her name to it." A little note of bitterness crept into her voice. "The nutty daughter of the U.S. senator. Like it or not, Daryn McDermott's name is known. She's a minor celebrity. But for a while, I didn't want to be her." She seemed on the verge of saying something else, but was silent.

"That's a fairly common feeling among people who've been in the spotlight for most of their lives."

Daryn nodded. "I was born into the ruling class, and as much as I despise what it stands for now, I can't deny being part of it. That would be hypocritical, and regardless of everything else I may be, I'm not a hypocrite. I wanted to taste the real world. I've crusaded for the rights of sex workers, and my own sexuality helps define a big part of who I am, so that's what I became."

"Sex workers? Isn't that what they call them in the European countries where prostitution is legal?"

"That's right. Very good. I spent a summer interning in Amsterdam, and that's part of what opened my eyes about this issue. But I'd never had the experiences, and I wanted the experiences. I craved a real life. So Kat Hall was born. I knew her life would be short. I designed a website, put escort ads in various places on the Internet, and just like that, I was a professional escort. I met some intriguing men and women, had some great sex, some not-so-great sex, made connections with people. I knew it wouldn't last long." Her voice grew far away. "I had even asked the people at the Mulhall house to call me Kat, at least for a while, until we went public. It kept her alive a little longer."

Faith got to her feet. "You're a very unusual person, Daryn. I've dealt with some intriguing people in the last few years, but none like you."

Daryn's tone changed, became animated again. "You could still stay here with me for a while, woman to woman. I'm still interested."

"And I'm still just into guys." Faith moved toward the door. "There are some things I have to do now, to begin processing your case. I have phone calls to make, paperwork to do."

"You're not going to leave me here alone, are you?"

"I'll call in a protective detail. There will be two deputy United States marshals here with you, a man and a woman. Do not under any circumstances try to seduce them, Daryn. If you do, I'll know about it, and you'll be on the street. Is that clear?"

"Yes."

"They will not know any details of why you're here,

or what's happening. They will not try to get information out of you. I am the only one you talk to about the case. The only things they can talk to you about are neutral subjects like what you want to eat, if you're comfortable in the house, that sort of thing. Just so you know, they will be armed. They're required to be, just in case. Don't do anything stupid."

"Do I look like I could overpower two federal marshals?"

"Stranger things have happened," Faith said. "I'll be back when I can."

"Will you be seeing your brother?"

"Not for a while. He needs a 'time out' too. I'll deal with him later."

"You know that he's an alcoholic," Daryn said, without emotion. "It controls him."

"Yes, I know that," Faith said, and left the room.

22

AT FIRST FAITH THOUGHT DARYN WOULD FOLLOW her out of the bedroom, but Daryn stayed where she was, propped against the wall in the semidarkness. Faith whipped out her cell phone. Her first call was to Chief Deputy Mark Raines in the office of the Marshals Service. She ordered a protective detail—two teams, twelve-hour shifts—and Raines got right on it, no questions asked. She also asked if they could provide her a car for the short term. Affirmative, with no questions. Such was the way of Department Thirty.

The two deputies arrived in two cars, a little less than an hour later. Faith knew both of them. The woman, Hagy, had done protection on the Alex Bridge case last year, and the man, Leneski, was one of the few Faith actually counted as personal friends. She gave them vague instructions—*vague instructions are my life,* she thought for a moment—then left to go shopping. She went to the giant supermarket on the corner of Danforth and Santa Fe and bought a variety of ready-to-eat and microwavable foods, bottled water, juice, and some Tylenol for Daryn's headaches. She took the groceries back to the safe house, then left Daryn and the two deputies.

It was a little past noon, and the brilliant skies of

morning had turned to drizzle. *You don't like the weather in Oklahoma, wait five minutes,* someone had told her shortly after she moved to the state. It was especially volatile in spring: sunshine, heat, wind, thunderstorms, even tornadoes—all in the space of a single day. She'd seen it many times by now.

She wasn't really hungry, adrenaline pumping in overdrive, but she'd learned in doing recruitments—or "intakes"—that she got so wrapped up in things that she sometimes simply forgot to eat, and would then suddenly find herself sapped of energy when her adrenaline crashed. So she drove through McDonald's, ate without tasting, and made her next call as she drove south through Edmond.

"Richard Conway," said a voice she knew well.

She had to wait a moment, as she always did. She knew the voice, the precise, occasionally pompous diction, but he wasn't Conway to her, and never would be. He was still Dean Yorkton in her mind. Ironically for the present case, he'd been a field officer, living next door to Frank and Anna Elder in the neighborhood she'd just left, for more than twenty years. Now he was the director of Department Thirty, administering the unit from a tiny unmarked office in the Shenandoah Valley of Virginia.

"Mr. Director," she said, knowing how he liked formality.

"My dear Officer Kelly," Yorkton said. "I haven't heard your voice in a while, though I was just preparing to type you a message giving you the go-ahead on the Bankston case."

Faith nodded. "Good. I'll move him as soon as I can. I'm calling about something new that's come my way."

"I'm listening," he said.

"Have you heard anything about a bombing of the Chase bank building here in Oklahoma City this morning?"

"It was on CNN. Dreadful business. I know that building well, from when I lived there. Though it wasn't Chase then . . . that was three or four bank mergers ago. From the coverage I'm seeing here, it could have been much worse than it was."

"I don't know details yet," Faith said. "What I do know is that I have one of the lead conspirators in the bombing sitting in the safe house in Edmond."

Long pause. "He came to you?"

"She. And yes, she was brought to me."

"What do you mean, she was brought to you?"

Faith slowed through a construction zone on Santa Fe. All parts of Oklahoma City were under construction these days, it seemed. "It's complicated."

"Yes?"

"I know, I know, everything we do is complicated. Actually, my brother brought her to me."

"Your *what?*"

"My brother." She explained Sean's involvement, omitting any references to his drinking. By the time she'd explained what she knew of the situation, she was out of Edmond, on the Broadway Extension crossing Interstate 44.

"Oh my," Yorkton said when she'd finished. "This is

messy, isn't it? How did your brother know about your job? Oh wait a moment . . . he's Customs, isn't he? So he knew of our existence, then put two and two together and brought the girl to you for protection. You didn't actually *tell* your brother you worked for Department Thirty, did you?"

"No, of course not."

"That would have been a severe breach of security protocols."

"Blah, blah, blah. I know that. What's your take on the girl?"

"A senator's daughter. Very, very messy. But if she's truly the force behind this coalition, she could qualify. If we can prevent any other bombings from happening . . ."

He was counting political brownie points, Faith knew. That was what he did, what she supposed he had to do. She had enough difficulty grappling with Department Thirty's mission at times, just as a case officer. She wasn't sure she could have handled the political end of it.

"You'll investigate her information, of course," Yorkton was saying.

"I'm moving on it now."

"Send me the list of targets."

"I'll do it as soon as I get to the office. Can you run this Franklin Sanborn name?"

"You sound uncomfortable about it."

"I am," Faith said. She steered around a slow-moving truck. "I know the name. I'm *positive* I know Sanborn, but I've come up totally empty so far. When the local cops were running this as a missing persons case, they looked for him, and he's a phantom. But I don't think so. I know him, I'm just not sure why."

"I have confidence in your abilities, Officer Kelly," Yorkton said. "If he's there to be found, you'll find him, I'm sure. And you have access to almost every resource that I do. But I will do some checking on this end."

"Thanks. I'll keep you updated."

She ended the call and drove on. A deep, irrational part of her didn't want to know damage estimates or the death and injury toll from the Chase Tower bombing. She couldn't make herself listen to the radio news. She was in the middle of it now, and even worse, so was Sean.

Her own brother.

Her hero.

Her handsome, intelligent, intuitive big brother. The one who kept things neat and tidy and who could cook gourmet meals and who was popular with small kids and animals. When the Kellys gathered in Chicago for the big Memorial Day reunion— dozens and dozens of relatives, from as far away as California and Vermont, and one time some distant cousins had come from County Wicklow, Ireland— the young children were drawn to Sean as if magnetized. She'd finally realized it was because he was one of them, childlike to the end. He rarely considered consequences, whether it was rolling down a hill with his little cousins or drinking whiskey for breakfast or being sexually manipulated by a vixen like Daryn Mc-

Dermott. He had an innocence that betrayed all he'd done and all he'd seen. Faith supposed she no longer had that, and the children could sense it, gravitating toward their cousin Sean instead of their cousin Faith.

Sean. If only he'd thought about the consequences.

If only were the two most useless words in any language. That sounded like something her father would say. The thought made Faith a little sad.

Downtown was cordoned off after the bombing, so Faith had to backtrack to the Tenth Street exit and drive several blocks west, before working her way back to the courthouse. She saw a handful of FBI and ATF officers she knew on the streets, talking in small groups. She thought she also caught a glimpse of Detective Rob Cain, huddled in a knot of uniformed officers a few blocks away from Bank of America Plaza.

She parked in the garage, then walked right in the front door of the federal courthouse. There was no lockdown in progress. The security guard simply nodded to her as she put her SIG Sauer in the tray and passed through the metal detector.

"Ms. Kelly," he said.

"Hey, Clayton," she said. She went through the detector without setting it off, then retrieved and holstered her SIG. "Much excitement over here?"

"Nah," Clayton said. "They locked us down for a while, but we were on top of it pretty quick."

"I had to leave," Faith said. "I've been out of the loop for a couple of hours."

Clayton looked at her but knew better than to ask questions. "Well, your friend is upstairs."

"Which friend?"

Clayton smiled. They both knew she didn't have that many friends that would visit her at the courthouse. The guard motioned to the top of his own head and drew a little circle with his index finger.

"Bald spot," he said.

Faith smiled. "Thanks, Clayton."

"He said he'd wait for you down in the Marshals' office."

She took the ornate stairs to the second floor and turned down the hallway. To her surprise, Hendler was standing in the hall across from her office door. He was wearing his dark blue FBI windbreaker over his standard white shirt and red tie, with charcoal gray suit pants. Faith, who'd once prided herself on "dressing for success," felt suddenly scruffy in her uniform of blue jeans and a polo shirt. Her only jewelry was the tiger's-eye gem Sean had sent her from Arizona, encircled by stainless steel wire and worn on a thin black string around her neck.

"Hey," she said. "Clayton said you were waiting with the Marshals."

"No one I knew was around. Seems Hagy and Leneski had to run out on a last-minute protective detail."

"Do tell." Faith unlocked the bare door to her office and they went in. Once inside, the door closed, she leaned down and kissed his cheek. "You don't look half bad, for having gone through a bombing. Who's doing what over there?"

"Dunaway's running it now. She runs the antiterrorist squad these days anyway. She lives for terror, you know."

Faith pictured petite, elegant Cara Dunaway living for terror. She smiled. "I know."

Hendler plopped into one of the guest chairs. "Man, we got off lucky this time."

"How do you mean?" Faith perched on the edge of her desk and kicked off her sneakers.

"Of course, I guess the families of the six people who died won't say we got off lucky." Hendler rubbed his face. "When you called and we mobilized to Bank of America, we were ready for the worst. Another Murrah Building. We evacuated, set up a perimeter, it was one smooth operation."

"I didn't know about Chase when I called you," Faith said. "I guess Bank of America was a diversion, and they planned to hit Chase all along."

Hendler looked at her strangely.

"What?" Faith said, growing impatient. "What's that look about?"

"The woman you drove to Edmond . . . she's the missing one, right? The one Rob Cain was working on. How much are she and your brother connected to what went down a few blocks from here?"

"Neither confirm nor deny." She'd said the same thing many, many times by now. "What kind of casualty figures do you have from Chase? Six dead. What else?"

"It could have been much, much worse. It was a relatively small cache of C-4. Six dead, twenty-nine taken to hospitals, thirteen of those treated and released, mostly glass cuts, bruises, smoke inhalation. The ones who died were people nearest the suitcase of C-4, which was placed right outside the bank's revolving door. Structurally, the building will be fine. Lots of ground-floor damage, but nothing approaching the scale of the Murrah Building. Still . . ." Hendler bowed his head. "Six dead. One was a two-year-old boy, Faith. His mom was going into the bank to make a deposit. She was one of the ones treated and released. The little boy was standing almost on top of the suitcase, right by the door. The mom was two steps ahead of him."

Faith leaned forward, steadying her hands on Hendler's knees.

"Faith, I don't know what this is," Hendler said. "And I don't know where you and Thirty are in it. But terrorism just came back to Oklahoma City."

Faith found Sean half an hour later, passed out on the couch in her living room, an empty bottle of Jack Daniel's placed carefully in the center of the coffee table.

That's Sean, Faith thought bitterly. *He might pass out dead drunk, but he'll be damn sure he doesn't spill anything or knock anything over. Wouldn't want to make a mess, after all.*

"Hey!" she called, kicking at the edge of the couch.

Sean stirred slightly, moved an arm, stayed asleep.

"Wake up!"

He didn't move.

"Shit," Faith muttered.

She slapped his leg. He rolled over, away from the edge of the couch.

Sean was wearing heavy-soled hiking boots. Faith grabbed one, unlaced it, and pulled it from his foot. She started hitting him lightly with it, working up his body.

Sean finally started moving. "Hey," he said thickly.

"Wake up! Wake up before I get to your head!"

She hit his rib cage with the boot and he rolled over defensively, finally coming up in a half-sitting position.

"What the hell, Faith," he said. "Let a guy get a nap." He squinted; then his hands went to his temples.

"Some nap. I specifically told you not to stop anywhere, not to get a drink. I wanted you to come straight here."

"What . . . well, shit, Faith." Sean pressed his hands tightly to his head. "I . . . shit, I can't think."

"Now that's a surprise." She flung the boot at him. He put up his hands in a halfhearted effort to deflect it. "Ow! What's the matter with you?"

"I told you to come straight here!"

Sean's eyes seemed to clear. "Well, you know what, baby girl, I don't take orders from you. You're getting just a little bossy for my taste."

"Can you possibly be that stupid, or that drunk, or both?" Faith kicked the air in front of her. "You're hooked up with an extremist group, you've been screwing around with a senator's daughter, and you've dragged Department Thirty and me into it. Right now you'd better damn well take orders from me."

"Can't I just sleep for a little while? I've been through a lot of shit the last week. I bought a bottle just to—"

"Don't even say it, because I don't want to hear it. I don't care what today's excuse is. Go in the bathroom, wash your face, do whatever you have to do so you can pay attention to me. We have a bit of a problem."

Sean focused on her with great effort. "Problem? Is Daryn all right?"

"She's fine for the moment."

"What do you mean, 'for the moment'?"

"Dammit, you sober up and then we'll talk."

Faith stalked down the hall to her bedroom and slammed the door behind her. In a strange mimicry of Sean, her own hands were shaking, but from rage instead of alcohol. She remembered something Cara Dunaway had told her, about an alcoholic's only three choices: *Get sobered up, get locked up, or get covered up.* Sobriety, jail, or death.

Her brother had faced a real potential of the second, with all of this mess. She worried about how dangerously close he might be skating to the third.

She stomped about the room like an enraged lioness, losing track of time. A knock sounded at her bedroom door.

"Faith, I'm here," Sean said. "Let's talk. What's going on?"

She opened the door. Water dripped off his face and

he'd smoothed out some of the wrinkles in his shirt. "Can you pay attention?" Faith snapped.

"I can always pay attention," Sean shot back. "Whether I'm shit-faced or not, I can comprehend what someone says to me."

Faith shook her head. "I can't believe you."

"You have something to say? Something about Daryn?"

They walked down the hall to the living room. "Six people died at Chase, Sean, including a toddler. Nearly thirty were hurt."

Faith lowered herself onto the couch. It was still warm from where Sean had lain. She pounded an armrest. "What the hell are you trying to pull? Be straight with me, Sean. No bullshit, I just want to know and I want to know right now."

"Trying to . . . nothing. Christ, Faith, the guy told us he felt the Coalition had to get people's attention, that speeches and demonstrations wouldn't do it alone. Ask Daryn. Ask any of the Coalition people. Let's find them—they all heard it. Thirteen people were standing there listening when he said that."

"But still nothing from your Coalition. No claims of responsibility, no speeches, no demonstration following the bomb. Nothing. Zero."

Sean came to the couch and sat down at arm's length from his sister. "I don't know . . . it's real, Faith. This isn't some bullshit fantasy, and it isn't booze either. Daryn is real, the Coalition is real. Franklin Sanborn is real. For Christ's sake, I lived at the house for a week. I didn't just imagine that. I can tell you exactly where it is, every bump in the road up to it. And believe me, there are a lot of damn bumps on that road, way back in the country. Kat and Britt and I slept in the room upstairs at the end of the hall. Jesus, Faith, I had both of those women every night."

Faith noticed he'd called her Kat, not Daryn. She looked at him carefully. "I don't need to know about that."

"No, my point is—I didn't hallucinate all this. I haven't imagined stuff like *that* since I was going through puberty, believe me."

Faith was silent for a moment. She remembered a line from the movie *Amadeus*. Mozart was trying to convince the emperor to let him write a certain opera for the court, and the emperor had said, "*Mozart, you are passionate . . . but you do not persuade.*"

"Sean," Faith said, softening her voice. "I think that girl's got you tied up in knots, so you're not even sure who you are, much less who she is."

"Oh, bullshit."

"I don't know what you'd call her. Some kind of a sexual predator, maybe? I hadn't been in the room alone with her five minutes before she was trying to hit on me, Sean."

Sean sat back.

"Isn't is just possible that you took this job to find Daryn, you found her, and she manipulated you? Instead of you convincing her to go home, back to Washington and her father and respectability, that *she* convinced *you* to find another way for her to escape her father forever? And I just happened to be close by?"

Sean shook his head. "No."

"Sean, please."

"Faith, I'm telling you, as your brother and as a law enforcement officer, for God's sake . . . maybe I'm a screwed-up officer but I've still been one for seven years. This was a real conspiracy. We need to find the other members of the Coalition. We need to find Sanborn."

Faith looked at him, at those sad blue-green eyes that had made him so popular with girls in high school. "I'm not sure what to believe," she said. "But then, that's my job, to find whatever truth is skulking around in all the lies in this world, and then decide if I have to make up a new set of lies to protect that truth."

Sean smiled for the first time since Faith had come home. "Now that *is* a tough job."

"Yeah," Faith said. She didn't return the smile. "It is."

23

FAITH DIDN'T KNOW IF DARYN MCDERMOTT WAS A Department Thirty case or not. She knew her brother *thought* Daryn qualified for the program. In observing Daryn, Faith believed she was genuinely afraid of retribution from this Franklin Sanborn. But much depended on whether the Coalition was truly growing and spreading, scheduling other similar acts against banks across the country. Just talking about who the Coalition was and what they had already done wouldn't meet the "vital national interest" criteria of the department. Preventing other acts of terrorism would.

Still, Faith knew better than to dismiss things out of hand. She sent the list of banks to Yorkton. She spent forty-eight hours questioning Daryn intensively, never leaving the Edmond house, sleeping in her own sleeping bag across the hall from Daryn's room while the two silent deputy marshals rotated in their twelve-hour shifts.

Daryn was confusing. She was indeed a chameleon, shedding one mood and putting on another as quickly as an eyeblink: the revolutionary, the academic, the seductress, the victim, and many others. Faith recorded all their conversations on microcassette, then listened to the playbacks, straining to pick up nuances and subtleties in the way Daryn responded to her.

Daryn gave her the names of towns where the other Coalition cells were supposedly waiting to strike the next targets. They were places like Franktown, Colorado, near Denver; Rosemark, Tennessee, outside Memphis; Marine City, Michigan, near Detroit, on and on. She had a memory for details, and she recited it all, everything Faith asked her. She didn't hesitate. In that respect it was one of the best sets of intake interviews Faith had ever done.

Now, she thought, *if only there's a case.*

She sent the information to Yorkton. Three days after Daryn moved into the Edmond house, Faith announced that she had to leave for a few days. She'd put off Leon Bankston long enough. His transfer was approved, and everything was ready for him to become Benjamin Williams and begin his new life. *His new life as a college graduate*, Faith thought wryly.

She and Hal Simon packed up the few things Bankston was allowed to take with him. She called Sean at her house and told him she'd be away, and was taking her car. She'd managed to convince him that it was in his best interest to stay out of sight for the time being, until she'd had time to figure out what was going on. He was strangely silent.

Keep it together, Sean, she thought. He'd taken cabs from The Village to Edmond twice already, trying to see Daryn. She or the marshals had met him at the door and kept him from setting foot in the house. Only after Faith threatened to actually have him arrested and thrown in a federal holding cell did he seem to get it. She left strict instructions with both teams of deputies that Sean Kelly was under no circumstances to be admitted to the house.

"By God, Kelly, but you're a hard-ass," Deputy Marshal Hunnicutt of the night shift had told her.

So she drove to Manhattan, Kansas. Since Simon had been babysitting Bankston for over a week, she gave him a break and let Bankston ride with her in the Miata for the six-hour drive. Bankston chattered most of the way about what a model citizen he was going to be, asking if he could join the Y and swim at their pool, how long until he was allowed to go to bars and pick up women . . . Faith understood Simon's frustration. After an hour in the car with Bankston, she wanted to shoot him just to shut him up.

Faith stayed in Kansas for two days, getting Bankston into his apartment, going over last-minute details. As was the usual procedure, field officer Simon stayed behind. He would live undercover near the new recruit for anywhere from two weeks to six months, depending on how well Bankston did in his transition to Williams.

"At least I don't have to live *with* him," Simon said to Faith as she drove away. "Thank God for small favors."

Faith drove south from Manhattan on a Friday morning under blue skies with only a few puffy cumulus clouds floating overhead. She took a back road, State Highway 177, winding lazily through the Flint Hills. The day was cool for late spring, but it felt good.

She drove with the windows down, letting the clean air wash over her like waves.

She took several detours, crossing back into Oklahoma at Newkirk and passing through the historic oil town of Ponca City before finally picking up Interstate 35 for the last leg south.

She'd avoided thinking about Daryn McDermott and Sean and Franklin Sanborn and the Coalition for Social Justice for most of the trip. Dealing with a high-maintenance individual like Leon Bankston tended to crowd out everything else. But now, with the prairieland of northern Oklahoma sliding by at seventy-five miles an hour, and only Lee Ritenour's guitar on the CD player as company, she couldn't help going back to the case.

A week had gone by. The date had passed for the Coalition's alleged attack on the National Bank of Commerce in downtown Memphis. Nothing happened. Yorkton had called her to say there was no sign of any communal radical group anywhere near the place where Daryn had said they would be.

So who was fooling whom?

Had Franklin Sanborn, phantom extraordinaire, fooled everyone? Had he angered Daryn by going against her wishes and saying he was going to use violence to achieve the Coalition's stated goals? Was it a *gotcha* on the senator's daughter? If so, was Sanborn's sole purpose to embarrass Daryn? Had he just faded into the ether?

Or was this part of Daryn's grand design anyway? She was a spoiled political princess, to be sure, but one who had a radical, revolutionary agenda of her own. Had she engineered the scheme just to escape her father's tyranny and his politics forever? To get a free ride from Department Thirty?

But there was a problem with that scenario. Department Thirty wasn't public knowledge. Most of the general public had heard of the Marshals Service's WITSEC, but not Thirty. There were even government officials, highly placed ones, who didn't know of the department's existence.

Sean.

She kept coming back to her brother. How long had he known she worked for the department? Had he really blundered into the whole situation, like he said? Or was there something deeper and darker about her brother's involvement?

Faith sighed, clutching the steering wheel hard. This is what she and Sean had become. She didn't trust her own brother.

There were too many questions, and she was getting a headache.

I'll fit right in, then, she thought. Sean was always hung over, and Daryn had her migraines.

Driving south, lulled by the mindless interstate travel, she almost missed the sign, lost as she was in her own questions.

MULHALL–ORLANDO ROAD, 1 MILE.

She'd spent nearly an hour musing on the whole situation. She'd passed the two exits for the town of Perry and hadn't even noticed them. She was around forty miles from Oklahoma City.

MULHALL–ORLANDO ROAD, 1 MILE.

Mulhall.

According to Daryn, that was where it had all started. The jumping-off point for the Coalition's nationwide activities.

But there hadn't been any nationwide activities.

The only activity had been in downtown Oklahoma City. Faith thought it said something about what American society had become when "only" six deaths were treated as a reason to be grateful.

And according to both Daryn and Sean, it had originated right here.

She punched in Sean's cell number on her phone. When he answered, she said, "Are you sober?"

"Faith?"

"I said, are you sober?"

"Well, I walked to that liquor store down the street, and they had—"

"Goddammit, Sean, are you sober enough to give me directions to that house where you said you stayed?"

There was a silence. "You mean in Mulhall?"

"Yes, in Mulhall!"

"What are you going to do?"

"Directions. Now."

MULHALL–ORLANDO ROAD. An arrow, an exit sign.

Faith left the highway and pointed the Miata toward Mulhall.

She got turned around twice. *Quite an accomplishment, considering the size of Mulhall, Oklahoma*, Faith thought.

But Sean's directions had been from the south, and her approach was from the east.

She finally righted the Miata, heading north on U.S. 77. At the north end of town was a sign made of white brick, with black letters that read YA'LL COME BACK SOON. Faith slowed the car, looking for the gravel road Sean had mentioned.

She didn't let herself think. She'd become a more instinctive person in the last few years, as opposed to someone who used to think only in terms of facts and evidence. Department Thirty had changed her that way, and it had been so subtle that she hadn't even realized it was happening.

Doing things by the book would dictate that she call the Marshals Service for backup before going into a potentially unfriendly situation. Technically, the Mulhall house could be considered a terrorist staging area. People with an extreme, revolutionary, and ultimately violent agenda had made this house their headquarters.

Let's just take a look, Faith thought, ignoring the voices that told her to follow the book. Department Thirty had no book. Department Thirty was its own book.

Stay safe and don't let any of your cases be compromised. That was Department Thirty protocol, as Yorkton had told her many times. The rest was up to the individual officer.

She found the rutted driveway and turned left. Orienting herself, Faith realized she'd turned south, back in the direction of town. Sean had told her the house sat about a hundred yards back from the road. When she estimated she'd gone about fifty yards, she pulled the car off the driveway into the grass.

She reached into the glove compartment, took out her new SIG Sauer, and double-checked its load. Then Faith got out of the car and began to move slowly forward.

She couldn't see the house yet. Sean had said it sat at the top of a small rise. For the moment she thought it worked to her advantage. Her car would be out of sight of anyone who might conceivably be in the house.

On the down side, she would be in the open as she approached. There wasn't much tree coverage here. She could see groves of trees in the distance, but in the immediate area the trees had been cleared. Evidently this had been working farmland at one point. She noticed barbed wire fencing along both sides of the driveway. Perhaps livestock had been run here as well.

She smiled to herself. *Here I am, a kid from suburban Chicago, paying attention to things like barbed wire fences way out in the country.* Just another way in which she'd come millions of miles away from the person she used to be.

She kept the SIG in her right hand, pointed at the ground, watching her path carefully, not wanting to step in a hole and twist her ankle. Something buzzed near her face. She waved away a dragonfly.

The trail began to incline slightly upward. Faith's pulse quickened. She moved a little faster, almost at a jog, as if an unseen hand were tugging on her shirt, urging her forward.

A few trees were grouped to her right now, just outside the fence. She moved toward them, hugging them closely. The trail flattened out again and she saw the house.

It was completely ordinary, neither a hovel nor a mansion. She'd seen many houses just like it as she'd driven through rural Oklahoma over the last few years.

She emerged from the trees. The first thing that caught her attention was a rusting real estate sign staked to the ground in front of the house, just outside the fence that surrounded its small front yard. That it had a fence around it was unusual. Most farm and ranch homes in this part of the country didn't have front yards per se. Perhaps a family with very young children had lived here at some point, and put in the fence to keep the little ones from wandering away.

Faith thought of a two-year-old toddler, going with his mother to the bank. Anger flared in her again.

She approached from the north side. Everything was quiet. There was no movement. No cars sat in the clearing before the fence. While the white house wasn't in obvious disrepair, it didn't look inhabited, either.

She moved closer, eyes darting everywhere, up, down, all sides, taking in everything. She passed in front of the gate. There were tire tracks in the red dirt, at a logical place where a car would have parked. Next to them was a second set of tracks.

Someone had been here, and recently. It had rained within the last couple of days, which meant the tracks were fairly new or the rain would have washed them away.

The house was listed for sale. It wasn't inconceivable that the realtor had shown it in the last day or two. That would explain the two sets of tires. A mundane, ordinary explanation. No Coalition. No potential terrorists.

Faith opened the gate—it squeaked—and started toward the house. There was no sidewalk, only a trail of bricks flush with the ground. She took slow, deliberate steps, concentrating on both her own breathing and her surroundings, achieving that eerie sense of disconnectedness she often felt when her senses were on high alert.

A strong wind gust came up from the south, to her left. Above her, something crashed.

Faith whirled, placing her SIG in the two-handed firing stance.

She slowly let out a breath. The unlatched screen door had been standing open, and it had slammed in the breeze. She carefully put the SIG into the pocket of her windbreaker and started up the steps.

The second one creaked. She felt a loose board shift under her foot. A bird called from somewhere near. A blue jay or a cardinal, she thought, though she could never keep the two straight. This part of the country was filled with them.

Faith blinked. An empty Michelob can sat on the porch railing, the lettering on the can faded as if it had been in the sun for a long time. A Tostitos bag with a few chips trailing out of it blew across the porch in front of her like some kind of latter-day tumbleweed. An open package of Trojan condoms sat on the lip of one of the front windows.

The window was dusty. She drew a line in the dust with her index finger, then rubbed a circle, feeling the grit under her palm. She peered through the circle.

The front room was totally empty.

There was no furniture whatsoever. The wood floor looked as dusty as the window.

"I'll be damned," she whispered, unaware she'd spoken aloud.

According to Daryn and Sean, thirteen people had been living in this house scarcely more than a week ago. Could the Coalition have cleared out any sign of them in that amount of time, leaving no trace?

Of course, but to clear out furniture, there would have to be a lot of coming and going, trucks filled with the items being moved. Would a group like Daryn had described want the townspeople of Mulhall to see them moving things around? She doubted it. News traveled fast in small towns, and the people of Mulhall would have had to notice such an operation.

The other answer was that Daryn and Sean were both lying.

Faith's throat tightened. She blinked as another burst of wind stirred up more of the dust on the porch.

She pulled on the screen door that had slammed a few minutes earlier. The frame door behind it was ajar. She took the SIG out of her pocket again, then pushed on the door and stepped over the threshold, her eyes immediately seeking out the trouble spots, the corners.

Nothing.

She sniffed the interior of the front room. It just smelled musty, with an underlying odor of cigarette smoke. That meant nothing—she knew smoke could linger in a room for months or even years.

She made a quick circuit of the downstairs. No appliances in the kitchen, empty cabinets and drawers. The wallpaper, which looked like it had come straight from the 1970s, was peeling. She stepped onto the back deck. Nothing.

Inside again, she decided to check the upstairs just for the sake of thoroughness. There was a single bathroom, the mirrored door to the medicine cabinet standing open. A nickel and a dime sat on the dirty sink.

She poked through bedrooms. There were several small ones and an empty linen closet. One of the windows in the front bedroom was broken. A good-size rock sat on the floor underneath the the window, surrounded by glass.

Faith shook her head. It was all too surreal. She didn't understand the power this woman Daryn had over her brother, but somehow she convinced him to lie to Faith about all of this.

Sean wasn't stupid. Troubled, maybe, but not stupid. He should have known Faith would investigate, that she wouldn't just open her arms give Daryn Mc-Dermott a new life in Department Thirty because he asked her to. Two criteria had to be met to gain serious consideration for protection: that the person had committed a crime serious enough to warrant either prosecution and or retribution from others involved in the crime; and that the person possessed information deemed to be of vital national interest.

Daryn McDermott's crime seemed to be conspiracy to commit an act of terror. But her "information"—the list of banks the Coalition was allegedly going to strike—hadn't panned out. Daryn certainly seemed frightened of Franklin Sanborn, but other than Faith's vague sense of knowing the name, there was no evidence that there *was* a Franklin Sanborn.

She'd come to the end of the hall, to the last little bedroom. Sean had said he and Daryn and the girl Britt had slept together in this room. There was a large gash in the wood of the door. The doorknob was missing.

Faith ducked her head inside. There was a large pile of blankets in the corner farthest from the window.

"Hmm," she said, and took a couple of steps into the room.

With the toe of her sneaker, she pulled off the top blanket, SIG at the ready. More blankets, all ripped, the lining coming out of them. One was a quilt done in a beautiful Dutch-doll pattern that looked like someone's grandmother had made it by hand. But it was filthy and the edges were torn. Three layers down, she found a few bottles of water, some packages of cheese and crackers, some stiff French fries in a yellow Wendy's carton. A threadbare paperback copy of the Gospel of John, with a stain of something that smelled like excrement, was at the bottom.

"Don't touch that!"

Faith wheeled around at the voice, snapping up her gun arm. Her gun settled with a chest-high aim at a man in the doorway.

"Hey!" he said. "Don't point that at me. Leave me alone. I'm not hurting nobody."

Faith couldn't really tell his age, but she guessed mid-to late forties. He was mostly bald on top, with more than week's scruffy growth of grayish beard on his face. His eyes were gray and wary. His body odor was overpowering, even from several feet away. His clothing consisted of ripped, baggy jeans, a filthy once-white dress shirt, a gray cardigan covered in grass stains, and mismatched shoes—one hiking boot, one tennis shoe with toes gaping out.

"I got squatter's rights," the man drawled. "Door was unlocked. I can stay here as long as I want. You can't shoot me. If you shoot me it's murder."

Faith lowered the gun. "Who are you?"

"You first."

"Doesn't matter."

"Neither do I," the man said. "So there."

"Mind if I ask you a couple of questions?"

"I got squatter's rights. You can't make me leave. This is my room. It's my whole house. I moved out to the country, you know, for my health."

Faith shook her head. "How long have you been here?"

"A while. I don't know." He scurried around Faith, giving her a wide berth, heading to his corner. "You didn't tear up none of my stuff, did you? This is all my stuff."

"Just looked at it, that's all. This place looks pretty deserted except for this room."

"Yeah, well," the man said. "So what?"

"You just live in the one room, I guess?"

"Well, I go outside to take a dump. The plumbing ain't on. But sometimes I like to pee out the window."

Faith put the gun back in her jacket. "You see anyone else around here?"

"Anyone else who?"

"Like some sort of commune, bunch of people all living together like one big family." Faith realized how ridiculous it sounded even as she said it.

"Nope," the man said in a matter-of-fact tone. "I been here a long time."

"No furniture?"

"You see any furniture?"

"No," Faith said. "Any cars ever come out here?"

A shadow crossed the man's face. "Couple of times. Kids in those cars with the noisy mufflers. They think they're hotshots, come out here and throw rocks through the windows, drink beer, smoke dope. Shouldn't drink or do drugs. That's bad."

Faith smiled. "So I hear."

"I stay out of sight when they come around. But I still got the squatter's rights. Not you and not the kids in the cars."

Faith tapped her foot on the wood floor. "You think you've been here longer than a week?"

"I been here a long time. Prob'ly a month. It's nice out here in the country. Quiet. I like quiet."

"So do I. And no one else has lived here?"

The man sat down on top of the pile of blankets. "Just me. It's my room and my house."

Faith reached into the pocket of her jeans. The man tensed and flattened himself against the wall. "Don't shoot me!"

Faith pulled out a twenty-dollar bill and handed it to him. He looked at it as if he'd never seen one before, then held it up by the window. "That's one of them new ones. Jackson's head is bigger."

"Sure is," Faith said.

"Not counterfeit, is it? You didn't make it, did you? That's illegal."

"It's real. I'm going now. You take care."

"That's right, you better go. You can't make me leave. Not even with your gun. I know my rights."

Faith quietly stepped out of the room and retreated to the stairs. She took them slowly, then let herself out of the house. The front porch step creaked under her feet again. The screen door banged behind her.

She took one look back. It was as if she'd never been there. The place looked the same.

In a moment she was over the rise. Ten minutes later the Miata was back on Interstate 35 heading south.

Alan Davenport watched her go. He craned his neck and watched the car. From the second floor of the house he could see the little gold sports car until it left the driveway and turned back onto the road.

When it was out of sight, he dug in the pocket of the filthy cardigan and pulled out a new cell phone.

He made his call. When it was answered, he said, "Contact."

"Understood," said the voice on the other end.

Davenport broke the connection. Then, just as he'd been instructed, he left the house by the back door and took the steps down from the deck. He checked underneath the wooden floor of the deck, looking at all the furniture where they'd shoved it, far back from the edge, wedged into the corner where the deck met the foundation of the house. Most of it was junk anyway, not worth stowing, but the object—so Sanborn had said—had been to ensure that the house did not look lived in, and not to attract attention by moving the stuff out onto the road. So under the deck it went.

Davenport had even embellished the look of the house, by transporting dirt from the field near the creek and scattering it around. He'd earned his money.

He had no clue who the woman was, although he could tell she resembled the man that Kat—or whatever Kat's real name was—had brought to the house for that crazy week. All Sanborn had said was that he was sure a tall young woman with long red hair would come around. She hadn't had long hair, but other than that, Sanborn was right.

He walked through the tall grass in the field behind the house until he came to the banks of Skeleton Creek. He took out the new cell phone—the one call was all that had ever been made on it—and threw it into the middle of the creek. Then he started walking, not back to the house, but cross-country toward the spot where he'd hidden his car, nearly a mile away.

Davenport had no clue what it all meant. He'd played a part and played it well. Sanborn had told him so. Now it was finished and he was ready to go home. If he drove straight through, he'd be home in Dallas by nightfall, where he could take a bath, have a good meal, throw away these filthy clothes, and sleep in his own bed.

Davenport gave no further thought to the woman with the red hair.

24

"DO YOU KNOW WHO I AM?" DARYN ASKED THE heavyset deputy marshal with the curly hair.

"No," Leneski said.

"My father is a United States senator."

"I don't care."

"I'm also a whore. What do you think of that?"

"I don't care," Leneski said again, and left the living room of the safe house for the kitchen.

Daryn sat back in the uncomfortable armchair. None of the deputies assigned to her would talk about anything other than her immediate needs—did she want to eat, was she going to bed, did she need any Tylenol for her headache? It was a strange existence. She knew why she was here, she knew what she was doing, and still believed it would advance The Cause.

But she couldn't talk to anyone. She'd been able to make people pay attention to her for her entire life, through her intellect and her looks and later, through her sexuality. This entire plan had been about getting people to pay attention.

But now, in this anonymous house with its sparse garage-sale furnishings, she sat in a bubble of nothingness, not quite Daryn but not Kat anymore, either.

She lit a cigarette, which was guaranteed to give her

even more privacy. Neither Hagy nor Leneski smoked, and they both tended to move away from her when she lit up. Daryn found herself actually wanting the Kelly woman to come back. She was tired of this waiting.

Faith Kelly wouldn't even let her brother come around. That had disappointed Daryn. She'd enjoyed playing with Sean Kelly, lived for the manipulation, but in another place, she actually *liked* the poor guy. She'd had a few moments, drifting outside herself in moments when she had a bad headache, when she fantasized about running away with him. Both of them would be new people. They'd hide in a cabin somewhere in the mountains where no one knew either of them. He would escape the bottle and his bitchy sister. She would forever escape her father's name and his hypocrisy and the stupidity of everyday society. There would be no further need for The Cause, because they would simply rise above all the petty foolishness that made The Cause necessary.

Britt even wandered her way into Daryn's fantasy. She missed the girl's absolute, unwavering devotion, and in the fantasy she let the girl serve Sean and her, and she would happily fulfill anything they asked of her.

Oh, stop it, she would tell herself. *It would never happen.*

It never could happen, for more reasons than Daryn could count. She would simply put a cold wet cloth on her face and lie still in the dark, and the fantasy would break apart until she was left with nothing but darkness and silence.

Come on, Faith Kelly, she would say in her mind. *Let's get this over with.*

Faith arrived in the early evening, carrying a black soft-sided briefcase. She looked harried, her short hair tangled and windblown. The deputies' shifts had just changed, and Daryn and Deputy Carson of the night shift were watching *Antiques Roadshow* on PBS. There was no cable service to the safe house, and the local PBS affiliate had the strongest signal of any of the over-the-air TV stations.

Faith came in the front door and nodded to Carson. Hunnicutt came in from the back of the house. "Hi, guys," Faith said. "You're relieved. The detail's over. Go on home."

"Tired?" Hunnicutt said.

"Busy, busy," Faith said, nodding.

The two deputy marshals gathered their things and left. Faith snapped off the TV set, dropped the briefcase, and lowered herself heavily into the armchair across from Daryn.

"I was beginning to wonder," Daryn said, "if you were coming back, or if I was cursed to a life of watching TV and eating microwave dinners with those deputies."

"You can send out for food," Faith said. "I told you that before I left."

Daryn shrugged.

Faith unzipped the side pocket of the briefcase, took out a few papers, shuffled them, and looked directly at Daryn.

Daryn felt uncomfortable. She was always the one who gazed directly at someone else, daring them to drop their eyes from hers. But Faith Kelly's green eyes blazed at her, never wavering, never moving.

"I guess two women like us shouldn't get into a staring contest," Daryn finally said, and blinked.

" 'Two women like us?' " Faith echoed.

Daryn shrugged again. "We do what needs to be done." She thought about saying more, but let it go at that.

"Do we?" Faith said.

They stared at each other again, and this time Faith looked away first, to the papers in her lap.

"You have something to say to me?" Daryn said.

Faith cleared her throat. "Daryn, I've already told you the criteria for entry into Department Thirty protection. I won't go over that again. But I've been investigating the things you . . . and Sean . . . told me. The Coalition for Social Justice, this Franklin Sanborn character, all of it."

"And the list of targets?"

"Yes, the targets. I sent that list on up the line, so we could try to prevent anything else from happening."

Daryn nodded.

"Do you have any other evidence?" Faith asked.

Daryn cocked her head slightly. "Excuse me?"

"Anything else that could prove what you've told me? About your fear of Sanborn, about the Coalition's future plans, that sort of thing."

"No, I've given you everything there is. Why?"

Faith thumped the papers against her leg. Her face

took on a resigned look. "I haven't been able to find one single bit of corroborating evidence for anything you told me. Franklin Sanborn is a phantom. There's no evidence he exists."

"But—"

Faith held up a hand. "There were no Coalition cells in any of the towns you mentioned. The dates for the next two 'strikes' on your list have passed. Nothing has happened in either Memphis or Denver."

Daryn stared at her.

"I even went to Mulhall. Sean gave me directions to the house you said you lived in for that week. Except for a homeless man who's been squatting there for several weeks, it's empty. No furniture, nothing. It looks like no one has lived there for a long time."

Daryn shook her head.

"Aside from what you did in Oklahoma City, there is no evidence of the Coalition for Social Justice ever existing, nor this Sanborn."

Daryn went totally still. She'd been headache-free for more than twenty-four hours, and could feel her heart beating, faster and faster. "I don't understand," she said, very slowly.

Faith dropped the papers on the floor and leaned forward, elbows on knees. "I don't know who's lying, whether it's you and my brother, or someone else. And right now, I just don't care anymore. None of the information you provided me checked out." She leaned back again. "We can't protect you. I can't give you a new identity and a new life. You can go."

Daryn's heart raced. She felt sweat beading on her

lip. "Go? Go where? What do you mean, *go*? What about Sanborn? What about . . . what about the FBI?"

"What about Sanborn? I can't find any evidence of him. As for the FBI, I'm obligated to turn you over to them at least as a material witness in the bombing. For what it's worth, I believe you when you say you didn't know the group was planning to use violence. But you still have to understand that six people died at Chase Tower."

"But Sanborn sent those guys to my apartment! They chased us on the highway! There's your evidence!"

"All I know is that someone using the name of Franklin Sanborn sent two thugs to your apartment. I don't know why. I do know that you and my brother got away from them. I admit that the name of Franklin Sanborn sounds familiar to me, but I don't know why, and my boss and *his* boss aren't going to admit you to the department because you know my brother and I think I recognize a name. It just doesn't work that way."

Daryn closed her eyes, squeezing them shut until they hurt. "You . . ." She almost choked on the words. "You fucking bitch. You sorry, worthless Irish bitch." She picked up the lamp from the end table beside her, and with a strength betrayed by her small frame, ripped the plug out of the wall and heaved it at Faith.

Faith dodged it easily and the lamp bounced off the arm of her chair. It crashed to the ground, lightbulb and lamp base shattering simultaneously. Faith stayed where she was.

"Don't you get it?" Daryn screamed, on her feet, between her chair and Faith's. "Don't you fucking get it, you stupid wench? It's Sanborn . . . he's trying to make you think I'm crazy, make you think I'm lying. You let me go and he'll come after me. He'll kill me, and the Coalition—everything I've fought for—will die. How can you be that stupid, Kelly? You're smarter than your brother, you should know . . ."

Faith stood up slowly, towering over her. "You leave Sean out of it. I'll deal with him. And once you leave here, you stay away from my brother. He's sick, and all you've done is feed his sickness."

"I haven't lied to you, and your brother hasn't lied to you! It's like a big circle. We lied to each other about who we were, but not to you, not about the Coalition. What about Sanborn? When he comes after me, what then? If he kills me, what do you do then?"

Faith winced. Daryn felt flushed—she'd just poked a hole in Faith Kelly's armor.

"Yeah, you've thought about that," Daryn said, starting to circle around the room. She maneuvered around the broken glass from the lamp. "You have your doubts, you're not one hundred percent sure about this, and deep down, you're afraid to let me walk out of here, because there's a little tiny voice that says I'm not lying, and your brother's not lying, and you know it could happen. You know Sanborn could get to me, and you know he could go on and blow up all those banks."

Faith stayed in place, but followed Daryn around the room with her eyes, never letting the smaller woman get behind her. "I have no evidence—"

"Fuck the evidence!" Daryn screamed. "What do your insides tell you? Way down, under all the pompous federal nonsense they've been feeding you, way down past all your own pathetic defenses, what do you see there?"

Daryn put her hands to both sides of her head and wailed at the top of her lungs. "I've done so much, I've come so far." Her eyes zeroed in on Faith's again. "I've used others and I've been used, Faith. And when I try to do right, when I try to throw off the world of the ruling classes and save the lives of innocent people, *real* people, *you* say you have no evidence."

"I think—"

"What if he kills me?"

The words rippled off the walls and toppled over each other. Then the silence came, a living, breathing thing, larger than both women in the room.

Daryn was breathing hard, gripping the back of the chair she'd been sitting in before she threw the lamp. Her head was splitting, but it wasn't her usual headache. For the first time in all this—the first time since she'd met Sanborn, since they'd conceived the plan and created the Coalition—she was afraid. Fear rolled over her like a cloud across the sun.

"I think," Faith said, "that you're troubled. You're brilliant and passionate and troubled, and I'm sorry. But I can't offer you protection. I have no basis to do that." She folded her hands together.

Daryn looked at her, at the way her hands gripped each other. She looked at her face, at the white line scar beside her nose. Daryn blinked at her and sagged against the chair. She blinked again, several times in rapid succession. Even without the light of the lamp, it suddenly seemed very bright in the living room.

"Your brother believed me," Daryn said.

Faith nodded. "I know."

They were both silent a while longer.

"I can drop you off somewhere," Faith said. "I don't have the authority to arrest you, or to hold you as a material witness."

"I want to see Sean."

"I told you, leave my brother alone."

"Are you his keeper?"

"Maybe I should be."

Daryn nodded. She actually smiled a little. Faith Kelly looked confused.

"My apartment," Daryn said. "Could you take me there?"

"You mean the one you lived in as Kat Hall?"

"I suppose I'm Kat again. And I have nowhere else to go."

Faith looked at her for a long moment. "I'll drop you off a couple of blocks from there. Close enough?"

"Of course. I understand."

Faith turned off all the lights and locked the house. The evening was cool and clear. It was the first time Daryn had been outside in nearly a week. She stood for a moment and breathed in the air. A grackle called from one of the nearby trees.

Faith appeared to shudder.

Daryn smiled in the dark.

They got in the Miata. "He'll kill me, you know," Daryn said as Faith started the car.

Faith was silent. She pulled the car out of the drive-way and pointed it south. She didn't speak to Daryn for the entire trip.

25

Margaret Holzbauer hadn't been sleeping well, ever since poor Katherine was kidnapped.

She knew the police weren't necessarily calling it a kidnapping, just a standard missing persons case, but Holzbauer knew. She'd known it the same way she knew what was happening when her Jewish neighbors began disappearing sixty-five years ago in Munich. She'd known they were dead, and she'd known that her beloved Deutschland was in the grip of a madman, and that she and Ernst and their babies would have to leave.

These days Ernst sat watching television, trying to read the lips of the news reporters and the actors. He caught a few words now and then, but the old fool missed almost everything. Refused to wear his hearing aids because they were for "old people."

We are old, you fool! She'd shouted at him.

What? He said back.

So she walked the floor, watching the windows. A police car came by now and then to check on things, and sometimes reporters still showed up. She always talked to them, anything to keep alive the search for the poor girl.

It was a little past nine o'clock and it had been fifteen minutes since she'd last looked outside. She raised the curtains, and her heart almost stopped.

Katherine walked into the parking lot from the direction of the street. She was alone, her clothes were dirty . . . she had nothing but the clothes on her back.

"Ernst!" she shouted. "She's back!"

"What?" her husband bellowed.

She ignored him, grabbed the phone, and called 911.

The door to her apartment had been repaired, and Daryn had to wonder for a moment if they'd put a new lock on it. But no, her key still worked. She let herself in and walked down the hall to where it opened onto the small living room. Things didn't look much amiss. There was still a tiny bloodstain on the TV from where Sean Kelly had shot one of the guys who broke in.

She sat on the couch, closed her eyes, and waited.

She didn't have to wait long. She knew she could count on Mrs. Holzbauer, and within ten minutes the cops were at her door. There were two uniformed officers, a detective, and Mrs. Holzbauer, ever-present, hovering in the background.

The detective introduced himself as Rob Cain. He was a handsome man, very alert, wearing a white ribbon on his wine-colored shirt. Daryn felt a deep stirring, and resisted the urge to reach for his crotch.

"Ms. Hall," he said. "Are you all right?"

"I'm fine, thank you." She smiled.

"May I ask where you've been the last two weeks?"

"I had to go away."

"Did that going away have anything to do with the two men who broke into your apartment?"

Daryn looked at him but said nothing.

"Did you leave voluntarily?" he asked.

"Yes," Daryn said.

Cain seemed to think for a moment. "Did you return voluntarily?"

"Yes."

"You understand that you've been listed as a missing person?"

Daryn crossed her legs at the knee, just wanting the police to be gone. She knew this was necessary, but she had other things to do, other tasks yet to perform. "I'm sorry for any inconvenience I've caused anyone."

Cain tapped a legal pad against his knee. "Inconvenience." He leaned forward. "Ms. Hall, where were you?"

Daryn folded her hands in her lap. "I was pretty shaken up when those men broke in here. I needed some time away."

"Have you ever heard the name Franklin Sanborn?"

"I don't think so. Why?"

Cain acted as if he hadn't heard her. "Did you falsify your references on your rental application for this apartment?"

"Detective, am I under suspicion of something? If so, please tell me now so I can contact a lawyer."

"What do you think I might suspect you of?" Cain asked.

"You tell me."

"What about those references?"

"I paid cash in advance for my lease. The apartment

manager didn't seem to mind. Maybe you should check with him."

"I have," Cain said. "Are you running from someone, Ms. Hall?"

If only you knew, Daryn thought. She made herself fidget on the couch. "Yes."

"An abusive husband or boyfriend, maybe?"

Daryn closed her eyes. "Yes."

"Franklin Sanborn."

Daryn nodded, eyes still closed.

"From Indiana," Cain said, looking at his notes.

"Yes. He's a professor." She opened her eyes and looked directly at Cain. "But it's all right now. He won't bother me anymore. He understands now."

Cain met her gaze, then slowly dropped his eyes. He was really a very good-looking man.

"Your neighbor was very worried about you," he said. He waved toward Margaret Holzbauer, who stood near the doorway.

"I'm sorry," Daryn said.

Cain was quiet for a long moment. "You're back safe, and that's the important thing." He stood up and handed her a card. "If you think of anything we might need to know, please call me."

"Anything you might need to know? Like what, Detective Cain?"

"You tell me."

They exchanged wary smiles. "I can't think of anything," Daryn said. "But I'll keep your card."

Cain nodded to her, beckoned to the two uniforms, and they left the apartment. Mrs. Holzbauer stayed for a few minutes, fluttering over her. Daryn talked to her mindlessly, not remembering what she'd said only seconds after saying it. It was shortly after ten before the old woman left and Daryn was alone. She breathed out quietly and sat motionless on the couch. Her head was pounding.

Rob Cain had been at his ten-year-old son's baseball game at Woodson Park in south Oklahoma City when dispatch called him. Dylan wasn't a particularly athletic kid, but he loved the game of baseball, and Cain was proud to bursting that the boy kept trying, regardless of what he did on the field during the games.

He called his wife's cell. "Game over?" he said.

"Yep," she said. "Nearly half an hour ago."

"Damn," Cain said. "Sorry."

He pictured his wife's shrug. She was the wife of a detective, after all.

"Was it her?" his wife asked. "The missing girl."

"It was."

"She's okay?"

"Physically she's fine. She's also lying to me through her teeth."

"What?"

"Never mind. It may be a while before I get home."

After he hung up, he headed toward his office downtown. Inside the Detective Division of the Oklahoma City Police Department, he found his desk and started sifting through piles of paper. After a moment he had the phone number he wanted. He didn't look at the time before he called.

"Scott Hendler," said a voice a moment later.

"Scott, it's Rob Cain," he said. "Sorry to call so late. But I think you and I need to talk."

Daryn sat in silence for a few minutes, then took her cell and made a call.

Sean Kelly answered after four rings. "Yeah?"

"Hello, Sean."

There was a long silence. "Where are you?"

"I'm at home. I mean, at Kat's apartment. She cut me loose, Sean. Your sister turned me away."

"But Sanborn—"

"No evidence, she said. I—I'm not quite sure what to do right now." She lowered her voice. "But I know I don't want to be alone."

"I—"

"Please, Sean. *Please.* I need you. I need you beside me, I need to see you and hear your voice and taste you and smell you. I need you *inside* me, Sean. Please."

"But I can't—"

"I'll be waiting for you."

She broke the connection. Then she went upstairs, stepping around the little boombox Sean had thrown at one of the attackers. In the bedroom, she lit a couple of candles, took off her clothes, and lay down on the bed to wait.

Sean was electrified by Daryn's words. It was too much to digest. He didn't understand how Faith could have turned her loose. Faith had come home about an hour before, saw that he was drunk, and stalked down the hall to her room. She'd come out a few minutes later in fresh clothes, carrying her little overnight bag.

"Sober up, Sean," she said. "We need to talk."

Then she'd gone out again, slamming the front door behind her. She paced the front yard for fifteen minutes while he watched from the window. He wasn't going to run after her, that was for sure. He wouldn't give her the satisfaction.

Just who the hell did she think she was?

Scott Hendler's Toyota appeared in a few minutes and Faith got in, casting one look back at the house. Sean let the curtains fall back over the window.

Sean got up and wandered around the house, gripping the neck of his bottle, even though it was empty. He thought about Daryn's words. He hadn't been able to stop thinking about her, whether sober, drunk, or somewhere between. Her touch, her body, her acute sensuality, her outrage, her raw and powerful lust. They beckoned to him, and in sober moments over the last week he'd wondered if this was how the sailors in the old folk tales felt when they heard the mermaid singing to them.

He kept gripping the bottle, even using it to brace himself against the wall a couple of times. He was more drunk than he'd been the entire week, and hadn't much cared before Daryn called.

She wanted him. She wanted him now.

And he wanted her.

But I'm so shit-faced I probably can't even get it up, he thought, which then struck him as funny. He laughed uncontrollably, then blinked it away, wondering why he was laughing.

He thumbed through Faith's bookshelves again. Books on the Zodiac killer, Jack the Ripper . . . how could his sister read this crap? Then there was the strange one, something about the Civil War. More crap. He paged through it, then it suddenly felt slippery and fell from his fingers.

Screw it, he thought. *If Faith is going to be a bitch, then she can pick up her own goddamn book from the floor.*

He jammed a hand, not the one holding the bottle, into his pants pocket. He felt his keys—fat lot of good they did him, since his Jeep was long gone—some coins, and . . .

Another key.

By itself. Not on his key ring.

His hand closed on it, and he remembered. The morning he'd asked Faith to provide a safe house for Daryn, he'd had her car. He'd stopped and had a copy made of her car key.

Just in case, he'd thought at the time.

Just in case had just arrived, he thought now.

He dropped the bottle. It shattered on the wood floor.

You can clean that up too, Faith.

He found his wallet, though he stumbled on the coffee table to get to it, and almost went sprawling. But he had to have it. Wouldn't want to drive without a license. The thought cracked him up, and he laughed again.

He thought of Daryn's body, of her warmth, her wetness, her lust . . . just for him.

So what if there was no fucking evidence of Franklin Sanborn or the Coalition or of anything else?

He made it to the door, then outside. He slammed it behind him. The gold Miata was in the driveway.

Sean smiled.

26

WHAT THE HELL WAS TAKING HIM SO LONG?

Daryn's patience wore thin, and she had to remind herself that Sean was probably drunk, and probably hadn't climbed very far out of the bottle for the entire week. She knew that he had come to the safe house in Edmond twice, and that the marshals had turned him away at the door. She'd heard him shouting her name.

All of which would only inflame him further, make him desire her more. He would do *anything* to be next to her.

It took him nearly half an hour. *Goddamn fool's probably so drunk he got lost,* she thought. But he pounded on her door at ten minutes before eleven o'clock. She didn't get out of bed to see if it was him, but she called "Come in!" at the top of her lungs, hoping he was coherent enough to hear her.

She heard the door open. "Daryn?" he whispered.

"In the bedroom," she said. "Come up here, now."

She heard his steps on the stairs. She positioned herself on the bed and opened her legs. She moved her hands to her breasts and began massaging her nipples. Her breathing grew heavy.

He entered the room.

"Daryn," he breathed. "My God, Daryn."

"Come to me, Sean," she whispered.

He fumbled with his clothes, almost falling over twice. She continued putting on a show for him until he joined her on the bed. He thrust his tongue into her mouth. She tasted the whiskey, tasted the danger. But sex was *life*.

She snaked a hand between his legs, found him, held him, manipulated him.

"Roll over," she ordered.

He rolled onto his back. She positioned herself over him.

"But I didn't . . ." he slurred. "No condoms."

She had always provided condoms every time before, and with all the other men she'd seen as Kat Hall. She smiled at him, straddling him, lowering herself inch by inch.

"No," she said. "I want to feel *you*. Nothing else, just you, Sean. I'm not an escort anymore. This is just the two of us."

She engulfed him. He moaned. They moved together.

She rode him for a few minutes. He clutched the sheets. Then she felt him begin to lose his erection inside her.

"Oh, shit," he said. "Daryn, I—"

"Goddammit," she whispered. "I *need* you. I need you all the way, Sean."

"Maybe I'm too shit-faced. Maybe we could just—"

"No, we won't *just!*" She slid off him, worked her way down, used her mouth.

It took nearly an hour, and before they were finished, he'd lost his erection twice more. But each time she brought him back. By the time he climaxed inside her, his grunt of release sounded almost like relief instead of pleasure.

She'd been on top of him again, and she rolled away. His eyes were closed, his body bathed in sweat. The sheets were as wet as if they'd been left on a clothesline in the rain.

"My God," Sean said. "My God, Daryn."

She rolled on her side and slapped his face.

"What the fuck . . ." he grunted.

She curled her lip savagely. "Guess you got what you wanted, didn't you?"

"Daryn? What . . . I don't understand."

"No, you don't fucking understand, Sean. Get your clothes on and get out of here."

"But I didn't—"

"We're done! We had a last tumble and now we're done! You can tell your bitch sister all about it." Her voice rose steadily. "Get out! Get out, get out, do you hear me? Get out of here!"

She rolled off the bed, picked up a clump of his clothing, and threw it at him. Much to her own surprise, tears began rolling down her cheeks. She couldn't think, couldn't focus. Raw emotion built behind her eyes like floodwaters behind a cracking dam. Everything she had said and done in her life, in her entire miserable existence, had led to this moment, standing naked in a room that wasn't really hers, screaming at a man who wasn't really hers, either.

"Shhh!" Sean said. He put out a hand.

"Go!" she screamed.

He gathered his clothes and clumsily began dressing himself. "Daryn, I—"

All of her pain, all of her grief, all of her outrage, was right there, right then. Later, after he was gone, she would be calm again, she would accept everything and do what had to be done. But now . . .

She rushed him, beating his chest with both fists. She raked his chest with her nails. She slapped both sides of his face. She screamed like an animal descending onto its prey.

Sean pulled up his pants, staggering away from her. He got his shirt on, but didn't button it. He kept his shoes in his hand and made for the stairs. He turned one last time.

"Who *are* you?" he said in a raw, wounded voice.

She wailed again, beyond words. Daryn vaguely remembered the fantasy, she and Sean escaping the world, moving to the mountains, to be completely different people. She would be neither Daryn nor Kat, and he would be neither Sean nor Michael. They would emerge anew with each other.

"No," she whispered. The fantasy wouldn't come all the way into focus, and then it was gone altogether.

She met Sean's eyes; then he turned the corner and was gone. She heard him shambling down the stairs. She heard the door open and close. In a little while she heard a car engine start, then fade away.

Daryn collapsed onto the bed and wept bitterly.

Very gradually, over the course of the last year, Faith had come to feel comfortable in Scott Hendler's Edmond condo. It was just off Danforth Road, not far from the safe house. It had a lived-in feel to it, but was still neat and tidy, like Hendler himself. He had a thing for windmills and old train stations, and there were numerous photos and paintings of both throughout the place, even over the bed.

She was propped up under the sheets, wearing only a long blue T-shirt and reading yesterday's newspaper. She'd listened to Hendler's end of the brief phone call, and realized with resignation that she still wasn't finished dealing with Daryn McDermott. Even though Department Thirty had officially rejected her, there was still going to be cleanup duty. The call from Rob Cain confirmed it.

After Hendler hung up, she said, "He talked to her, is pretty sure she's lying, and he wants to know what the hell is going on."

Hendler settled back into the bed. "Not in those words, but that's pretty much it." He looked at her. "Faith, what the hell *is* going on?"

She put down the newspaper. "I'm not really sure, and that's the truth. I just know Thirty couldn't work with the girl." It was as close as she ever came to giving him actual details of one of her cases. "None of her information was right."

"And Sean?"

"I don't know what to think about Sean. When I got home, he was so drunk he could barely move. I was so pissed off at him, that's when I called you." She tilted her head back until it was touching the frame. "I don't know what to do with him."

"I'm sorry, Faith," Hendler said. "All the weirdness with your case aside, I know this business with your brother has been tearing you up."

She leaned toward him. "Yeah," she said.

They held each other. Faith savored the unspoken connection between them. They could just *be* together, nothing else required. For a few moments she felt safe, the last two weeks falling away. It was a frail feeling, and Faith was afraid that if she dwelled on it too much, it would be gone, and so would Scott.

Hendler turned off the light, keeping one arm around her. "He wants to see us in the morning," he said sleepily.

"Who?" Faith said. She'd been far away from the FBI and Department Thirty and her brother and the bizarre events of the last two weeks.

"Cain," Hendler said. "He wants to talk to us about the case. He specifically mentioned he wanted me to bring you."

Faith nodded. "In the morning," she said.

It took Daryn more than two hours to find the calm she needed for what came next. The whole gamut of emotions, some real and some imagined, had drained her. The exhaustion had been gaining on her, but she had more to do before she could rest.

It was nearly one thirty a.m. when she opened the dresser drawer that had come with the furnished apartment, and began to get dressed. She chose plain blue jeans, a pastel-pink T-shirt, and open-toed sandals with low heels. She stepped back and looked at herself in the mirror. It wasn't Daryn McDermott, or even Kat Hall. The look was nothing like her. It appeared like something Faith Kelly would wear. Daryn smiled at that irony, but it faded quickly. She touched her short blond hair, wishing for a moment she could take time to wash the dye out and have her natural dark color back. But there was no time. She also missed the long braid she'd worn for most of her life—it was part of her.

It occurred to her that this was a strange way to be thinking now. She'd wanted to become someone else, and had actually done it for a while. Yet here she was, feeling nostalgic for something that had physically defined her as Daryn McDermott. She blinked, feeling sudden tears welling. The tears were decidedly different from those that she'd wept upon throwing Sean Kelly out of the apartment. Now she cried silently, letting the tears run straight down while she looked at the image in the mirror.

She stood there for a long time, until the tears ran dry and her mind began to clear. She applied some light makeup, took one last glance at the mirror, and went downstairs.

She booted up her laptop on the cheap coffee table, then logged in to her Web-based e-mail account on the Hubopag server. She turned off all the lights, letting the only light in the apartment come from the glow of the computer screen.

In some ways, this was the most difficult part of the plan, yet ultimately would be the most satisfactory. She loathed everything her father stood for, hated what he had done to her mother, hated the unspeakable atrocity he had committed on *her*. Her father had used her as a prop for all her life. Now she would do the same with him.

She typed in the address: mcdermott@senate.gov.

She typed *Dear Dad*, then stopped.

Daryn closed her eyes.

Anything for The Cause. Anything for The Cause. Anything.

She swallowed hard, and this time she warded away the tears before they came. The time for crying was past now.

I know I've been out of touch, she wrote. Daryn smiled.

You know me. I've been busy, traveling a lot. I have to tell you something now. Even though you and I don't talk much, something tells me I need to reach out to you now.

I'm scared, Daddy. I'm really, really afraid.

She thought the use of *Daddy* would really get to him. Daryn kept typing.

Sean had no clue where he was, nor how he got there. He knew he was still in Faith's car, and that it was damnably uncomfortable. *How could Faith have bought a car this small?* he wondered.

Light played across his face as he slowly awoke. He blinked fiercely, trying to orient himself. It was still dark outside, but the car was parked at the periphery of a lot of bright lights. His hearing started to awaken. He heard traffic sounds. The picture came into focus: gas pumps, a high canopy overhead, bright blazing fluorescence. In the distance was a straight line of black, broken by occasional headlights.

A truck stop, somewhere along an interstate highway.

He remembered the sex, and he remembered that by the time he climaxed, he'd just wanted it to be over with. It had become work, and he'd just wanted to finish and go to sleep. But Daryn had been maniacal, doing everything to stimulate him, oblivious to herself, determined beyond reason that he should finish inside her.

He remembered her screaming, her rage as she hit him and scratched him. He'd stumbled out into the night until he found the car where he'd parked it around the corner.

That was all.

He didn't recall driving, certainly didn't remember getting on a major highway and coming to this truck stop.

His neck was sore from the contorted position he'd slept in behind the wheel, slumped slightly to the side. The gearshift of the Miata had poked into his ribs, and they were sore as well. He held up his arm to the light that spilled through the window. His watch read 3:56.

Nearly four o'clock in the morning, and he had no idea where he was.

He blinked again. He remembered snippets of other things. Faith had been angry at him . . . so what else was new? He'd dropped something or knocked something over in his house, but hadn't cleaned it up. He felt vaguely ashamed about that.

Daryn . . . Daryn wasn't going into Department Thirty protection.

He sat up straight. Faith hadn't protected Daryn. Now Daryn was back in Kat's apartment.

Sean closed his eyes again. It all seemed to be spinning around him. Daryn, Faith, Kat, Sanborn, Britt, Tobias Owens . . .

He wrenched open the car door and vomited onto the pavement, heaving until he had nothing left.

Even after he'd emptied his stomach, he still hung out the door, feeling the cool night air. After nearly five minutes, he swung his legs out and stood unsteadily. He slammed the car door, wincing at the sound, and went into the truck stop. He went to the bathroom, emptied his bladder, washed his face. He bought a bottle of water. The clerk, a young Middle Eastern man with a scraggly beard, eyed him strangely as he walked back out into the night.

He turned the corner at the edge of the building, back to where the Miata was parked haphazardly, taking up parts of two spaces.

Franklin Sanborn was leaning against it.

"Hello, Sean," Sanborn said, in the same genial, easygoing voice he'd used the day Sean and Daryn first arrived at the Mulhall house. "At least I can call you by your real name now."

Sean lengthened his strides.

"Don't do anything stupid," Sanborn said. "You've done quite enough of that already, don't you think? It's all quite complicated, really, and you don't know anything. Think twice about anything you may think you know, because chances are it's not true."

"What . . ." Sean's mouth felt like he'd been chewing rocks, and his stomach was still queasy. "What do you want? Why are you here?"

Sanborn looked at his watch. "Well, it's too late to save Daryn, but maybe if you hurry, you can catch the real killer."

Sean dropped the bottle of water. It rolled away from him until it smacked into one of the Miata's tires. Even as his stomach threatened to revolt again, he grabbed Sanborn by the throat and slammed him into the car.

"Go ahead," Sanborn breathed. "Beat me to a pulp, Sean. You could even kill me and it wouldn't matter. You're too late. Way too late."

"What have you done with her? What the fuck have you done with Daryn?"

"Weren't you just with her? You probably should have stayed with her, Sean. Maybe she'd still be alive now if you had."

Sean couldn't mistake the taunt in his voice, a school bully picking on a weaker child. With all his strength, Sean took both hands and shoved Sanborn to the side. He rolled off the Miata's hood and stumbled into the ice machine that stood on the sidewalk. Sean was on top of him in an instant, crashing his fist into Sanborn's face.

"Where is she?" he panted.

"They'll find her soon," Sanborn said, his cheek

starting to swell. "And then they'll find you. In death, she'll be Kat for a little while, but then she'll be Daryn. She'll die as the senator's daughter. That's rather ironic. Don't you think that's ironic?"

Sean grabbed his shoulders and slammed him repeatedly against the ground. "Tell me, you piece of shit! Tell me what you've done!"

"It wasn't hard to follow you from her apartment, you know. The way you were driving, it was an easy trail. You're just lucky you escaped the Oklahoma Highway Patrol. Now that might have been unpleasant."

Sean slammed him to the pavement again.

Sanborn grunted in pain, but he didn't stop. "They'll find you, Sean. See, they'll find your Jeep—remember it?—and it'll have Daryn's blood in it. And in the glove box, they'll find your gun. You shouldn't have left it at the Mulhall house. That was very unprofessional. In a day or two, when they do the ballistics tests, they'll find that the gun that killed the senator's daughter was registered to Sean Michael Kelly of Tucson, late of Immigration and Customs Enforcement."

Sean toppled to the side, his head spinning. "I don't—"

"Then after the autopsy, they'll find your semen inside her. As a federal law enforcement officer, your DNA is on file and it won't take long for them to match it up." Sanborn shook his head, blood trickling down one side of it, just as it had when his car crashed in Bricktown. For a moment Sean thought he was seeing things, time caught in an endless loop.

"Where is she?" Sean muttered, but the vehemence was draining out of his voice.

"She probably had sex with five hundred men in the last few years," Sanborn said, "and almost as many women, for that matter. But she was careful. Remember how she always had condoms handy for you? What made her decide not to use them tonight?"

"Who *are* you?" Sean whispered, and then he remembered that those were the exact words he'd said to Daryn as he left her apartment a few hours ago.

"Why, I'm Franklin Sanborn. At least I am to you. Now that was a pointless question, Sean. You know, you might still catch the killer if you hurry. There's a place in this city where people go to remember, where time stands still. You'll find it, I think."

The two men looked at each other. Sean couldn't feel, couldn't think. Daryn could not be dead. Sanborn was messing with his mind—that was what Sanborn did. He used that nice, easygoing, let's-all-be-friends voice, but it was pure manipulation.

"You should go to her, Sean," Sanborn said. "I think it's the least you owe her."

"If you . . ." Sean pulled himself up, holding to the hood of the car. "If she's . . . I'll find you. If she's hurt or dead or . . . Jesus Christ, Sanborn, I will find you and I will kill you. You know that, don't you?"

"Yes, Sean," Sanborn said, and his voice took on an eerie chill. "I know that."

27

*A PLACE WHERE PEOPLE GO TO REMEMBER. A PLACE
where time stands still.*

Sean knew.

He had visited the memorial with Faith and Scott
Hendler, on a sunny day when sightseeing seemed a
perfectly normal thing to do. Back then, he'd been able
to imagine that he was in town on vacation, visiting his
sister, and they could go for a few hours and act like
normal people, doing the things normal people do.

He first had to orient himself as to where he was.
Blinking against the alcohol that was still in his system, along with the emotions raging through him, he
figured out that the highway was Interstate 35, and
that the truck stop was situated just off Northeast
122nd Street in far north Oklahoma City.

He roared onto the access road, then crossed the
highway and merged onto the southbound interstate.
He nudged the Miata up past eighty. He turned on the
stereo. He knew his sister was into "smooth jazz,"
whatever that meant, while he preferred old-time rock
and roll, the Doobies, the Eagles, Kansas. He expected
soft and flowing jazz on the CD, but to his surprise, it
was a rock-jazz fusion led by an electric guitar. He
turned it up as loud as he could. His head didn't hurt

anymore, and while his stomach still churned and he had moments of dizziness, his head was clearing. He let the guitar pound into him, absorbing the bass beats as if they were blows raining down on him.

"Daryn, I'm coming," he said.

Some of Oklahoma City's downtown streets were one-way, and he had to double back a couple of times before he found himself on Robinson Avenue, approaching the National Memorial from the north, on its east side.

The dashboard clock said the time was 4:43. There were few cars in the predawn downtown area. He could see traffic lights stretching all the way through downtown, past Bank of America Plaza and on toward the south side of the city.

He was unsure of parking around the memorial itself, so he swung into the lot of a church across the street. An open-air structure, rough-hewn with wooden pews, stood at the corner of Sixth and Robinson. A sign proclaimed it as Heartland Chapel. Sean stumbled through it, then across the street.

He entered from the east, through the "wall of time" that was stamped *9:01*. Its counterpart at the far end read *9:03*.

A place where time stands still, Sanborn had said.

"Daryn," he whispered.

He saw movement on the far side, outside the wall, along the sidewalk. A single uniformed security man passed under a streetlight.

Directly before him was the reflecting pool. To the

left was the knoll where the 168 empty chairs sat, each lighted from within at night. It was an eerie tableau, much different from the daytime one. To the right was the plaza where the Survivor Tree stood, above all else. Behind it was the old Journal Record Building, which now housed the memorial's indoor museum.

Sean walked to the right, down one walkway and up another, toward the big old elm tree. When he turned the corner, he saw her.

"Holy Mother of God," Sean whispered.

She was hanging in the tree, a rope looped around both her neck and a low branch. Her light-colored T-shirt was stained.

Sean's knees buckled. He collapsed onto the flagstone walkway.

He forced himself to look up again. He scrabbled along the stones, then pulled himself to his feet.

"I'll get you down, Daryn," he said. "I'll—"

He grabbed hold of her legs and lifted them up, trying to relieve the pressure around her neck.

"Come on," he whispered.

He glanced out toward the west side. The security man had left the street and walked back onto the memorial grounds, heading this way, up past the children's area.

"Daryn, please." Still whispering.

She wasn't heavy, barely a hundred pounds, and Sean had lifted his share of weights, but there was no "give" in Daryn's body.

Dead weight.

He almost screamed. He put out a hand, touched her shirt. The blood was fresh and warm.

"Oh God. Oh dear God. *Please.*"

He looked up at her face. Her neck was twisted grotesquely by the rope, her eyes closed, lips slightly parted.

No breath.

Sean backed away as if burned. The watchman was closer, coming toward the edge of the building. When he came around it, he would be able to see Sean.

He remembered what Sanborn had said. They'd set him up for Daryn's murder. Somehow . . .

The intensity of the sex—had that only been a few hours ago?—replayed itself in his mind. Daryn's insistence that he not use a condom this time, her overwhelming desire to have him climax inside her, followed by her violent reaction to him after he had done so.

What the hell is going on here?

The watchman had disappeared behind the corner of the building. Sean estimated he had less than a minute.

He wrapped his arms around Daryn's legs again. One of her sandals came off and fell to the pavement.

"I'm sorry," he said.

Sean turned and ran. He fled across the street, back toward the church parking lot. He didn't look back. He made it to the Miata and pointed the little car east on Sixth. He came out on Broadway and turned north.

He came to a McDonald's at Twenty-third and Broadway and pulled in. His hands were shaking so badly he could barely keep them on the wheel. His right hand was covered in Daryn's blood from where he'd touched her chest.

His mind functioning on automatic, he got out of the car, jamming the bloody hand in his pocket. He went to the door of the McDonald's, but it was locked. He peered at the hours listed on the sign—it didn't open until six o'clock. He looked at his watch. Nearly an hour.

He went back to the Miata and got in, sitting in the car. His hands felt dirty, but his mouth could still taste Kat.

Kat. He wanted to think of her that way, rather than as Daryn. As Kat, his time with her had been uncomplicated and free. Her passion, her anger, her lust—they were *real*. Even though he knew intellectually that they weren't real, that he really knew very little about the woman hanging in the tree back there, Daryn McDermott or Kat Hall or whoever she was.

When she'd been Kat, he'd been Michael Sullivan, a guy who lived here in this city and made furniture for a living.

All in all, if not for everything that had happened, that might not have been a bad life. Set up a woodworking shop and custom-design and build furniture. Live in this pleasant prairie city, with its distinct seasons and friendly people. Hang out with his sister now and then—get to know her again. As adults, they were pretty much strangers.

But no, he was about to be a fugitive, wanted for the murder of a woman that everyone would soon know was Senator Edward McDermott's daughter.

God, I wish I had a drink.

Not now, he told himself. Maybe later, when he could stop. He would have to be far from here before that could happen.

He fidgeted in the car, watching the faint glow in the east. The Oklahoma State Capitol was only a few blocks away and he could see its dome from where he sat. The predawn light behind it was postcard-perfect. He looked at his watch and was surprised to see that more than an hour had passed.

Sean wanted to scream.

He turned on the radio, found the news station, listened. The early morning editions were already feasting on the "grisly discovery" at the National Memorial, reporting that "details were sketchy this morning," but reporting details anyway. It wouldn't be long before the missing girl Katherine Hall, who'd come home only last night, was identified as Daryn McDermott. And then the coverage would be national.

He put the bloody hand in his pocket again, went into McDonald's, and used the restroom. He washed his hands and stuffed the bloody paper towel into his pocket. He bought a cup of coffee at the counter, then headed back out into the dawn.

"Sorry, Faith," he said, starting his sister's car. He swung onto the highway onramp that ran next to the McDonald's, and then Sean was gone.

Part Three:
Faith

28

FAITH HADN'T SLEPT, OTHER THAN DOZING FOR AN hour here and there, since the call came.

An early riser, even when she spent the night with Hendler, she'd walked into the condo's kitchen and started coffee. She knew Hendler would probably stay in bed for another hour and a half or so, and Faith rather enjoyed the quiet time before the day began. She would probably wait until she got home to take her run. She had her own route, and it helped to organize her life by sticking to it.

She was sitting at Hendler's kitchen table, wearing only the long T-shirt, drinking her coffee, lost in thoughts of Sean and Daryn McDermott and what she could possibly do to straighten out her brother, when Hendler appeared in the doorway.

One look at his face told her something was wrong.

"What is it?"

"Rob Cain called. They found the girl."

"He said that last night," Faith said. "Doesn't he—" She broke off, staring at Hendler's normally placid face.

"No, I mean they found her this morning. We'd better get dressed."

By the time they'd reached the memorial, the crime scene unit was already there. So was Cain. So were other FBI agents. So was a swarm of the media.

When Faith had first seen the body hanging in the tree, she'd remembered Daryn, back at the safe house. At first there had been hysteria—*What if he kills me?*—and later, driving away from the house, a resigned air, almost a quiet acceptance—*He'll kill me, you know.*

And then, when Hendler had finally taken her home, both Sean and her car were gone. She tried calling Sean's cell every two hours, then every hour, with no answer. Not even voice mail.

She rented a car, a Ford Focus hatchback, and shuttled back and forth between her office and the house. She talked to Yorkton once.

"Even the most brilliant surgeon loses a patient now and then," he'd told her, then proceeded to ask questions about departmental security.

She'd snapped at him that it should be fine, and quickly hung up.

No one understood, and she could talk to no one.

She'd found no evidence to support any of Daryn McDermott's claims.

Or Sean's, she reminded herself.

There had been no solid footing on which to build a Department Thirty case with Daryn. There was no independent confirmation that the Coalition for Social Justice was planning anything. Franklin Sanborn was a nobody. There was no evidence to suggest he even existed, much less that he would come after Daryn.

He'll kill me, you know.

So she held it all in. Hendler knew her brother was gone, but he knew nothing else. He didn't know how deep Sean's involvement with "Katherine Hall" ran. He knew only that "Kat" had been a potential Department Thirty case, but had been rejected. That was as far as Faith could go. Even for a fellow Department of Justice agent—and her lover, she mused—she could go no further. Yorkton had cautioned her more than once about her involvement with Hendler, and she'd assured him she could manage it, could keep all the balls in the air.

And now it was crashing down around her, and there was no one in the world she could talk to about it.

Since the body was found on the grounds of a federal reservation, the investigation of the murder fell to the FBI. Rob Cain had worked the missing persons case of Katherine Hall, though, so he and Hendler were working closely together. They'd jointly assured the media that local and federal turf battles would not get in the way of solving this bizarre case.

If they only knew, Faith thought. *If they only knew that I am withholding information from a murder investigation.* That would strain, and might even end, her relationship with Hendler.

As the sun rose on the second day after Katherine Hall's body was found, Faith finished her run. The run gave her no pleasure—her body was exhausted, and she hadn't eaten much the last two days. When she rounded the bend and entered her block, she saw Hendler's Toyota and an Oklahoma City police cruiser sitting in front of her house.

Hendler was waiting on her porch. Rob Cain got out of the passenger side of the patrol car, said a few words to the uniformed officer behind the wheel, and the car drove away. Then he turned to watch Faith as she jogged up to the door.

"How far do you run?" Cain asked her.

Faith shrugged. "It varies. Some days three miles, some days five or six."

"Ever do any real long-distance running?"

"I've done marathons." She saw no need to give the man details.

"So have I," Cain said. "Back before the kids came along."

Faith nodded. She unlocked the door and held it open. Hendler didn't look at her as he went in.

"Coffee?" Faith said. "Scott? Detective Cain?"

Hendler shook his head, still not looking at her.

"Cream and sugar, please," Cain said. "And call me Rob. We're all professionals here, right? I think we can dispense with the titles."

They all looked at each other. Cain glanced around the room, taking in the clutter. "What happened here?" he said, waving a hand toward her bookshelf.

Faith looked over her shoulder, saw where he was pointing. She still hadn't picked up the dropped book or the shattered whiskey bottle.

"Sorry about the mess," she said.

He looked back at her, knowing she'd evaded his question. In a minute she brought coffee into the dining room.

"What's going on?" she asked, looking first at Hendler.

Hendler looked up at her with those soft eyes of his. They weren't striking eyes, always looking vaguely tired. Hence the "Sleepy Scott" nickname. But they were open and they were faithful, and right now, they were troubled.

"Faith," Hendler said, "Katherine Hall has just been identified as Daryn Anisa McDermott. She's the only child of U.S. Senator Edward McDermott of Arizona."

"Which explains, at least partially," Cain said, "why her paper trail was so short."

They all looked at each other for a long moment.

"Did you know about this?" Hendler finally asked.

Faith sipped her coffee, not really tasting it, weighing her options.

He'll kill me, you know.

She pulled at her lower lip with her teeth. "Yes," she said finally.

Cain leaned forward across the table. "What exactly do you for DOJ, Faith?"

"Special projects," she said by rote.

"Uh-huh. And what exactly does that entail, and how is it connected to McDermott?"

Faith said nothing.

Cain shifted in his seat. "I've known Scott for three or four years now, and I trust him. He's never tried to pull any jurisdictional nonsense on me, and has always bent over backwards to be helpful on the cases where we have a mutual interest."

Hendler looked uncomfortable.

"But," Cain said, "I'm beginning to get a feeling that some of the children in the federal sandbox don't all like to play nice with others."

"I suppose that's true of any organization," Faith said mildly.

"Did you spend some time with Daryn McDermott?" Cain asked.

"What difference does it make?"

"Did you kill Daryn McDermott?"

Hendler nearly came out of his chair. "What the hell was that all about? Holy shit, Rob, have you lost your mind?"

"We're still waiting on the autopsy and ballistics," Cain said. "The final reports should be in soon, maybe by this afternoon. But you know, that poor woman was killed twice. She was shot in the heart, and then someone tied that rope around her neck and lifted her into the tree, where they then tied the other end of the rope around a tree branch. That would need to be someone fairly tall, fairly strong, in good physical condition."

"Rob, you're out of line," Hendler said.

"Am I?" He locked eyes with Faith. "Did you kill Daryn McDermott?"

"No," Faith said without breaking eye contact.

"She was with me," Hendler said. "From a little after nine o'clock that night, until you called me in the morning. She was never away from my side."

Cain swiveled to look at Hendler. "So you're closer than friends."

No one spoke for a moment. Then Hendler said, "Yes, we are."

Cain looked at Faith again.

"It's not a secret," Faith said. "We don't broadcast it, but we don't keep it a secret either. We don't have any kind of formal professional relationship, so there are no protocol violations."

"That's good to know," Cain said. "Okay, so you didn't kill her. Let's just assume that's the truth. But I'm also assuming you know more about her than you're telling."

Faith hesitated, then nodded.

"Do you know who did kill her?"

Faith hesitated longer. "I'm not sure."

"Tell me about Franklin Sanborn."

"Haven't we covered this?" Hendler said. "Sanborn's a ghost."

"So was Katherine Hall," Cain said. "Kind of strange to be talking about a dead ghost, isn't it? When I talked to her a few hours before her death, she said she was running from Sanborn, had had an abusive relationship with him, but that now he understood, now he wasn't going to bother her anymore."

Faith rubbed her cheek, touched her scar. "Franklin Sanborn's not an abusive boyfriend. I can tell you that."

Cain nodded. "When I first met you, that day at Barry's, I thought you recognized the name. Our nice little lunch ended pretty quickly after his name came up. So if Sanborn's not the abusive boyfriend, two questions come up." He raised his index finger. "One:

why did she say he was?" His middle finger went up beside the other one. "Two: who is he?"

Faith swallowed. Facts and feelings and shifting loyalties collided. Faith had declined to protect Daryn. Now Daryn was dead. Within a few hours after Faith cut her loose, the young woman was dead, shot and hanged from a tree.

Faith hadn't thought anything about Department Thirty could make her feel guilt. Generally, everyone she dealt with was guilty of *something*. But now, the guilt had turned around. The girl had pleaded for protection and Faith hadn't protected her. It was that simple. There must have been some kind of evidence, something Faith hadn't seen. Maybe if Sean hadn't been so twisted up in the middle of it, she would have seen what she needed to see to protect Daryn. And maybe Daryn would still be alive today.

Or maybe not, the cold, pragmatic professional voice told her.

It's about the people, Art Dorian had told her when she first learned of Department Thirty's existence. *If we lose sight of the people, the rest of it doesn't matter a whit.*

Strange words to come from a Department Thirty case officer. Department Thirty's first case officer, in fact. The words didn't seem to jibe with the whole idea of the department. It was about information, wasn't it? Not people. It had certainly seemed that way to Faith since she joined Thirty.

But she thought back, to some of the people she'd met in the last three years. There were the "ordinary" cases, people like Leon Bankston who were criminals, had been caught, and a straight exchange of information was made with them. But there were also people like Ryan Elder, and Eric Anthony and his beautiful deaf son, Patrick. And Alex Bridge, whom she now considered a close friend. All people that had butted up against the Department Thirty apparatus for one reason or another. And with them, the information had served the people, not the other way around.

But no amount of information had been there to save Daryn McDermott.

Or her brother. God only knew what had happened to Sean, what had been done to him.

Or what he'd done, she thought for the first time.

"Faith?" Hendler said.

And here was Scott Hendler, a good man, arguably a great one, who somehow saw things in Faith that she didn't see in herself.

Faith shook her head. What would happen if she told enough of the truth to put aside some of the lies? Could she walk the tightrope? What would Yorkton say?

To hell with Yorkton.

A woman was dead, a woman Faith could have protected.

"I think," she said to Cain, "that she told you Sanborn was an abusive boyfriend just to get you to back off."

Cain looked surprised.

"We all empathize with a woman who's been in an abusive relationship," Faith said. "She'd been gone without a trace for two weeks, now she's back with no explanation. If she's hiding something, she wants to get rid of you as quickly as she can."

"So she tells him a story that she thinks will get him to back off the questions," Hendler said.

"She was lying from the get-go," Cain said. "But she wasn't trying very hard at it. I could see that right away. That's why I decided to cut it short. That's why I called you and wanted to meet with you in the morning." He turned his coffee cup around a couple of times. "I just didn't think the circumstances would be what they were."

"Faith," Hendler said, "who is Sanborn?"

Faith took a deep breath and swam out into treacherous waters. "I don't know, but I can tell you who Daryn told me he was."

Cain took out a small spiral notebook and a pen.

"We know Sanborn's not real," Faith said. "At least not by that name. Just like we know Katherine Hall wasn't real by that name."

"At least we know that now," Hendler said.

Faith glanced at him. They would have a long, private talk sometime soon.

"Point taken," Faith said. "Daryn told me that Franklin Sanborn was one of the leaders of a radical political group called the Coalition for Social Justice."

She went on to give a carefully sanitized account of what Daryn had told her—the Coalition's goals, its involvement with the terrorist attack downtown, the "target" list that turned out to be a fantasy. She omitted Sean's role altogether, and never mentioned the fact that Daryn had requested any kind of protection.

When she finished, Hendler gave her a long look. By now he expected her to dance around the issue of Department Thirty with "outsiders," namely anyone outside the DOJ structure. But Faith suspected he was dismayed that she'd left out her brother completely.

"And what's your role in all this?" Cain asked her directly, barely waiting a breath after she'd finished. "Why would this girl, this senator's daughter who has strange ideas of social justice and likes to stick it to her father, be telling you all this? Don't insult my intelligence by telling me 'special projects,' either."

"I can't answer that," Faith said.

"Can't or won't?"

"Can't. And won't. I'm not trying to hold up your investigation, Rob. I hope you believe me on that. I want to know who killed Daryn McDermott just as much as you do, and probably more so."

"You know," Hendler said, "that probably within a few hours there's going to be a shit storm over this. The fact that she's the daughter of a U.S. senator."

"I know," Faith said.

Cain looked at both of them, then stood up. "For the record, Faith, I've never seriously considered you a suspect. But I had to bring it up. I wanted to see how you'd react. You're a pro. I'm sure you understand."

"Yes, I do."

"Also for the record, I'm royally pissed off that you know more than you're telling me. Pardon my language."

Faith shrugged.

"Under normal circumstances," Cain said, "I could

hold you as a material witness, charge you with obstruction, all that good stuff. But if I did that, I'm guessing that my bosses would get calls from somewhere east of here. And that's never good."

Faith said nothing.

"Of course, we're all going to be getting some of those calls pretty soon, from Senator McDermott." Cain leaned against the table. "Daryn McDermott's address is listed as a condo in the Georgetown area of D.C. Her father, being a senator from Arizona, has a place outside of Phoenix. I wonder what this girl who had no ties at all to Oklahoma was doing here, why she wound up dead in downtown Oklahoma City. She was a long way from either Phoenix or Washington. Food for thought, isn't it?"

Hendler stood up. "I'll drive you back downtown, Rob. Would you head on out to the car and wait for me?"

Cain nodded to both of them and left the house. Faith walked Hendler to the door.

"Answer me this," Hendler said. "When you called me over to Bricktown on the morning the shit hit the fan downtown, did you know then who she was? Please tell me the truth. When I drove your brother, and you drove that girl, to the Edmond house, did you know then? I need to know."

Faith put a hand on his shoulder, then slid it over to the back of his neck. She touched him lightly there. "I found out just after that," she said. "After we got to the house."

"That's the truth?"

"That's the truth, Scott."

Relief swept across Hendler's face. "I believe you. We've been down this road enough times that I know you wouldn't tell me an outright lie, that you'd just say you couldn't answer."

Faith nodded. "I do the best I can. I worry that it's not enough sometimes, but I guess once you do the best you can, you can't do anything else."

"That's a fact. Anything from Sean?"

"No, and I don't know what to think."

"Faith . . ."

Faith recognized the tone and saw what was coming next. "I don't think he's capable of murder, Scott. I think he's an alcoholic, and I think because of that he's easily led sometimes. Daryn McDermott certainly manipulated him. But I don't think he's capable of doing what was done to her."

"But you've said you really don't know him anymore," Hendler said gently.

"That's true, but . . . we both saw the body. If Sean had killed her, it would have had to be a crime of passion. That was no crime of passion. That was someone making a point, someone delivering a message. The gunshot, the hanging, the location of the body."

Hendler smiled a little. "See, I knew there was still a cop lurking under all that Department Thirty secret-agent stuff." The smile faded. "It would make things a lot easier if we could talk to Sean, though."

It took Faith a minute to catch his meaning. "I don't know where he is, Scott. He even took my car, for God's sake. I'm not hiding him."

"Okay, then. I hope you're right about him. It's

just . . . this is a murder investigation. Even if you didn't mention it to Rob, I have to consider it. I have to think about it. You understand that, don't you?"

She stroked his cheek. "You're such a good man, Sleepy Scott. Yes, I understand that."

"Maybe you should lie low for a few more days. I'm sure your boss has already told you that. Departmental security and all that."

"And all that," Faith echoed.

"Dinner tonight?"

"Dinner sounds great," Faith said. "Maybe we can grab onto a little something normal in the midst of all this."

"Maybe so," Hendler said. But he sounded doubtful.

Hendler dropped Cain off at the Investigations Division downtown, and each promised they'd be in touch later in the day.

For once, Cain didn't mind that the Bureau was the lead jurisdictional agency on the case. Scott Hendler was faced with the unpleasant task of contacting Senator Edward McDermott.

At his own desk, Cain listened to his voice mail messages. Most were from the media, all of which he deleted. They could contact Public Information if they wanted a statement. One was from his wife, wondering if he would be able to take their older daughter to her choir rehearsal that evening.

Absolutely, he thought. *It might get me away from this madness for a while, get me back to what's real and where people are just who they're supposed to be.*

The last message was from the medical examiner's office. There would be a short delay in processing the report on the autopsy of Katherine Hall. Cain made a mental note to let the ME's office know the deceased's real identity. He wondered what the holdup was in getting the report.

He hung up the phone and logged onto his computer. He didn't have access to quite as many databases as the U.S. Department of Justice did, but he could still go a lot of places and peek into a lot of dark corners.

He thought for a long moment, then began clicking his mouse and working his keyboard, seeing what he could find out about one Faith Kelly.

29

FAITH AND HENDLER HAD CHILI AND BEER AT DIF-
ferent Roads, where they listened to Faith's friend Alex
Bridge and her band, The Cove of Cork, play Celtic
and American folk music until nearly midnight. They
didn't talk about the case. They were two normal people who cared about each other, out for a low-key
evening on the town, two normal people de-stressing
after a normal week.

For a while Faith even believed it.

She'd muted her phone while listening to the
music, but she checked it every fifteen minutes or so,
hoping against hope for a message from Sean. She
tried to be furtive, but caught Hendler looking at her a
couple of times when she was checking the phone.

"Relax," he mouthed to her.

They'd gone back to her house to spend the night.
They made love gently, tenderly. There was nothing
frenzied or hurried about it. It wasn't even about passion, Faith thought. It was *connection*, two people who
needed to be with each other, and to express what
they meant to each other. It felt good, and for a while
Faith really could believe they were just two normal
lovers.

She woke early, ran, showered, and dressed. Hendler

was in the shower when she left. She pulled the curtain aside, leaned in, and kissed him.

"You'll get your hair all wet again," he said, wiping shampoo out of his eyes.

"So what?" she said.

"See you later," Hendler said.

She was in her office by seven thirty, and at five minutes after eight her phone rang. It was Yorkton, and he was uncharacteristically blunt and straightforward.

"Do you have a televison?" he said without identifying himself.

"Not here in the office."

"Find one, quickly."

"What channel?"

"Pick one," Yorkton said, and hung up.

Yorkton had sounded genuinely alarmed, and Yorkton *never* sounded alarmed. Faith jogged down the hall to the Marshals Service office. Several of the deputies were gathered around a TV set in one corner of the "bullpen" area. They looked up when she came into the room. Someone said, "Oh, no." Several stared openly.

The group parted as Faith came closer. Chief Deputy Mark Raines, looking as always more like a banker than a U.S. marshal in his charcoal gray suit and his gold-rimmed glasses, stepped aside.

"Faith, you need to see this," he said.

Faith stepped in front of the screen. The set was tuned to CNN. The graphic at the bottom of the screen read: *The Capitol, Washington. News conference of Senator Edward McDermott (AZ).*

"Oh, no," Faith said.

"Didn't I already say that?" someone said behind her. She thought it sounded like Leneski.

Senator Edward McDermott was a large, florid-looking man in his late fifties. His hair was completely silver, his eyes a dark brown—*Daryn's eyes*, Faith thought. He wore a perfectly tailored suit that fashionably hid much of his bulk. He wore glasses, but kept taking them off and putting them on again, using them as pointers, waving them around. Faith wondered if he really needed them to see, or if they were just props.

He was holding a few sheets of paper in one hand, and he was speaking directly to the camera. By his side stood a perfectly groomed blond woman in her thirties. The current wife, Faith guessed.

"I'm not speaking just as a senator from Arizona," he said. His voice was deep and resonant, no doubt honed by many courtrooms and campaign speeches. "I'm speaking as a father, as a family man whose job just happens to be in elective office."

"Oh, give me a break," Leneski said, behind Faith.

"You know by now that my daughter—my beloved Daryn, only twenty-four, with her entire life ahead of her—was murdered three days ago. It was brutal beyond words, a senseless act of depraved individuals with no respect for human life. But it goes deeper than that, much deeper."

"What was she doing in Oklahoma?" shouted a reporter on the screen.

McDermott shook his head. "I don't have any answers. But I have many, many questions. Suzanne and I—" he nodded toward the blond woman, "—will be flying to Oklahoma City in a few hours to claim Daryn's body, to take her back home to Arizona for burial in our family plot. That's what she wanted."

Liar, Faith thought. *Daryn never felt at home in Arizona, and only went there when you went back to campaign.*

"But my friends," he went on, "something startling came to my attention the night Daryn was killed." His posture seemed to soften. "You know that she and I disagreed about many things politically. She had some ideas that were, frankly, outside the mainstream. She's done some things of which I do not approve, could never approve. I don't know how much of that was youthful rebellion, but as wrong as many of her ideas were, she was passionate about them and believed in principle." He held up the papers. "She'd been traveling. We hadn't talked or seen each other in . . . well, in quite a while. But the night she died—only hours before her life was so violently ended—she wrote to me. She sent me this e-mail."

Faith felt stones descend into the pit of her stomach.

"I won't read all of it to you, because some of it is intensely personal. But there are parts of it that should concern all of us. Every American who believes in openness of government and the rule of law should hear what my daughter wrote a few hours before she was killed."

Sounds like a campaign speech, Faith thought.

McDermott took off his glasses. His wife laid her hand on his forearm. "She wrote:

> *I'm scared, Daddy. Really, really scared. You know I've always had an agenda to promote, and I met some other people that felt the same way I do. We formed a group, and we were planning to travel around the country, doing demonstrations and helping people understand our agenda. I was out here in Oklahoma when I met them, so that's been our headquarters. But Dad, after I was around these people for a few weeks, I realized they didn't want the same things I did. These people are violent! They want to destroy banks to show how money corrupts our political and social system. I agree with the idea, but they're talking about terrorism, Dad!*

McDermott stopped. His voice had cracked the last time he read the word *Dad*.

He waited a moment. Faith stared at the screen. She thought the veneer of the politician had just melted a little, and she was finally seeing the Edward McDermott who'd lost his daughter. He may have been a terrible father, but in the final analysis, he was still a father and his daughter had been taken from him in a horrible manner.

McDermott cleared his throat. His wife's hand moved from his forearm to his shoulder. He looked at her as if drawing strength. "She goes on:

I couldn't go through with being a part of terrorism. That's not what my ideas are all about. On the way to the first target, a bank in Oklahoma City, I called the FBI. The other leader of the group threatened me. He said he'd have me killed, Dad. He said he'd come after me and kill me.

McDermott lost all semblance of control, bowing his head and turning at an angle away from most of the cameras. Faith saw tears rolling down the man's cheeks.

"Jesus," said someone in the room with Faith. A man's voice, but she couldn't tell whose. She felt eyes on her.

Suzanne McDermott gently took the papers from her husband's hands and stepped to the microphone. She looked poised and confident. "Let me," she said to her husband, then looked at the cameras. "I'll read you the rest of what the senator wanted to share with you from my stepdaughter's e-mail. She says:

I knew I shouldn't have been with that group, but I really believed we agreed on things. I knew I was guilty of conspiracy to commit terrorism. But I thought I could still stop them if I told someone. I knew the government would want this information. Maybe even you don't know about this, Dad, but there's a part of the government that will give protection and new identities to people who've committed crimes, even terrorism-related crimes, if you have information for them.

"Oh my God," Mark Raines said. Faith had never seen his composure slip before.

I went to them. I asked them to protect me. This government agency is called Department Thirty.

Faith's cell phone began to ring.
Suzanne McDermott kept reading.

A woman named Faith Kelly was assigned to be my case officer. She asked me all kinds of questions and said she'd investigate my information. Then she came back and said she couldn't find any evidence. No evidence! I was all the evidence they should have needed!

Faith felt a chill crawl down her spine. Her phone stopped ringing, then started again.

This Kelly woman told me they couldn't protect me, since my information didn't check out. She just sent me on my way, and here I am, Dad. I'm very, very frightened. These people I was with—I think they'll kill me. I just wanted you to know, in case something happens. I'm sorry, Daddy. I'm sorry I disappointed you so much. I never meant to hurt anyone, and I tried to do the right thing.

Now Suzanne was crying as well. She stepped away from the microphone. Her husband had composed himself and stepped back in front of the cameras.

"My daughter, my only child, wrote this to me a few hours before she was murdered. By the time I checked my e-mail in the morning, she was hanging dead in a tree in Oklahoma City." The glasses went on, then came off again. He pointed them straight toward the cameras. "Department Thirty. Remember that name. You're going to be hearing it more and more, because I'm going to find out what happened. If they could have protected my daughter from these terrorists, and they didn't, because this case officer, this *Faith Kelly*, could find no evidence, and then my daughter was killed . . ." He put the glasses back on and used his index finger to jab the podium. He spoke slowly, precisely. "There will be hell to pay. *Hell to pay.*"

Reporters started shouting questions.

"Faith?" said Deputy Derek Mayfield, the first person who'd befriended her when she was assigned to the Oklahoma City Marshals Service office.

Faith's phone was ringing again. She barely registered that Mayfield and others were talking to her.

Faith watched the screen, even as the cameras pulled back to show a long shot of the Capitol steps, then cut back to the news anchors in Atlanta.

But I couldn't, she thought. *I couldn't protect her. There was nothing to support her story. Nothing!*

Only Sean. Only her brother supported Daryn McDermott's story, and he was gone.

I should have protected her anyway.

She remembered Daryn hanging in the tree.

Faith shook her head and backed away from the TV set. They were all watching her.

"Faith, what can we do to help you?" Raines asked.

Faith shook her head.

"I have to go," she said.

She turned and ran from the office.

She finally anwered her phone when she was alone in her office.

"Go to ground," Yorkton said. "I'm already transferring our funds into emergency accounts. Do you have your own emergency identity in place?"

Every Department Thirty employee was required to have two sets of identity papers, ready for emergencies, that would allow them to travel and move freely without being associated with the department. Faith's primary emergency identity was Kimberly Diamond, with an address in Independence, Missouri.

She nodded numbly. "Yes." She checked the bottom drawer of her filing cabinet. Her small travel bag was there and packed, as it always was.

"Don't go home," Yorkton said. "Leave your office and don't go back. All your case files are on disks, yes?"

"Yes."

"All right, then. Take them with you and go to a hotel. Stay in cell phone contact." Yorkton sighed. "I never thought this day would come. Our existence is now public knowledge, but I may be able to fix it."

"Fix it? How in the hell could you fix it?"

"I'm not sure yet. I don't know Ted McDermott. He's a social issues crusader, hasn't ever served on the Judiciary Committee, so I've never had dealings with him. I'll think of something."

"I don't see how—"

"You don't have to see how. That's *my* job." Yorkton's voice sounded far away. "The attorney general's already called me. The president's already called him. I know the president likes you, Officer Kelly, but I don't know if that's enough. He understands political reality, and the political reality has just changed, quite dramatically."

"What about my cases?"

"Let them know they're all right, they're still secure, and that they will stay that way. They shouldn't be compromised by this. Call them, then go to ground. I'll talk to the other case officers. Where's Simon?"

"He's with Bankston, the new case, in Kansas."

"Call him too. He'll need to go to his emergency identity as well." There was a long pause. "Go to ground," Yorkton said for the third time, then hung up.

"My God," Faith said, still holding the phone. Just a little while ago, she'd kissed Hendler good-bye in her shower. They'd acted like normal people. They'd been sure of their own reality, even if everything about them was shifting. Now not even that was safe.

Faith unlocked the bottom drawer of her desk and took out the envelope that held Kimberly Diamond's life: driver's license, Social Security card, birth certificate, even credit cards. Bank account information, ATM cards. Five thousand dollars in cash. A fresh, untraceable cell phone. A gun.

She thought of Sean, wondered where he was. Wondered if her brother was capable of murder.

No. I refuse to go there.

She grabbed all her things, the travel bag, the Diamond envelope. After a moment's contemplation, she pulled the stuffed fish off the wall and shoved it into her bag. She might never see this office again.

And now, she thought, *Sean and I are both fugitives.*

She ran out of the office and locked the door behind her.

30

"HOLY SHIT," HENDLER MUTTERED.

He and at least twenty others had grouped around the TV in the break room of the FBI's new complex on Memorial Road in far north Oklahoma City. After McDermott said Faith's name, all eyes shifted to Hendler.

When the broadcast was over, most of the others left the room, heading back to their own areas. Hendler stayed behind, sitting at the oval table, staring at the TV, even after he'd turned it off.

Department Thirty had been outed.

Hendler couldn't believe it. It had gone about its mission wrapped in secrecy for so long that it was generally accepted in DOJ that this would always be the case. You just ignored anything about Thirty, did your job, and hoped you didn't cross paths with one of their cases.

McDermott had actually said Faith's name on national television.

After all she's been through already, Hendler thought.

He tried calling her and got voice mail at all three numbers—office, home, and cell. He had to figure that Yorkton was in damage control mode, and had probably sent Faith somewhere. Faith had told him one night a few months ago that she had actually created a new identity for herself, one that she would have to use in case of a departmental security emergency.

He wanted to talk to her, just hear her voice, know that she was okay. Of course he knew Faith handled everything that came her way, but there were times when she wasn't as tough as she wanted everyone to think. He'd seen glimpses—just a few tiny snapshots of her vulnerability—over the last two years. There weren't many, but Hendler was mindful of the fact that he was the only person in the world who got to see them. He carried the knowledge with him, saving it like a child with a weekly allowance.

He felt a presence in the break room, and looked up to see Leo Dorsett, the special agent in charge of the Oklahoma City FBI field office. Dorsett was a good boss, and Hendler liked working for him. He was a superior administrator and generally stayed out of the way and let his agents do their jobs. Hendler had been eternally grateful that Dorsett handled the call to Senator Edward McDermott himself yesterday. Dorsett had felt that in the case of a United States senator, a call from the SAC instead of a field agent might be in order.

"How you doing, Scott?" Dorsett said.

"Okay."

"No, you're not, but be that as it may, I have to say this. You need to stay away from your girlfriend until all this is resolved. After the case is closed, deal with your personal life however you like, but until then, you need to back off."

"Look, Leo—"

Dorsett held up a hand. "You know I don't like internal conflict, and you know I hate dealing with people's personal issues. But this is a professional matter now."

Hendler nodded. "You're right, it is. It's just not something I thought would ever come up."

Dorsett shrugged. "Neither did I, or anyone else. Do I need to move you off the case? Perkins can run it."

"No. I was there, Leo. I saw Daryn McDermott hanging in that tree. I'm on it."

"Okay, good. Keep in contact with that city cop Cain. There's going to be political pressure to make sure we're all talking to each other. We're about to be under a big magnifying glass."

"I understand."

Dorsett left the room. Hendler waited a few more minutes, then went back to his desk. He spent a couple of hours on paperwork, then called Rob Cain.

"Rob, it's Scott Hendler."

"My favorite fed," Cain said.

Hendler heard outdoor sounds in the background. "Where are you?"

"I was just getting ready to call you. There's something you need to see, since we're working together."

"Where?"

"Southeast High School on Shields Boulevard. Meet me in half an hour, in the parking lot as it faces Shields. I'll be next to a dark green Jeep Cherokee."

Hendler had a mental image of the morning he'd met Sean Kelly. He and Faith had been out for a run together, and they'd rounded the corner onto her block and seen a dark green Jeep Cherokee sitting in front of her house. At first, until she saw the driver, Faith had been nervous to the point of reaching for her weapon. Then she'd recognized her brother.

"I'm on my way," Hendler said.

Southeast High School had once been one of Oklahoma City's thriving schools. Then as populations shifted, enrollment dropped off rapidly, to the point that it was actually closed, only to reopen within a few years as a technology-oriented specialty school.

It sat on Shields Boulevard, a few blocks south of the notorious strip of motels. Its sign was blue and white, an *S* and an *E* under the stylized logo of a Spartan, the school's mascot. School was out for the summer, but a few cars were scattered in the parking lot. Hendler pulled into the main gate and immediately saw the Jeep, under a tree at the far south end. He nosed the Toyota over and saw Cain, along with two patrol officers.

Hendler got out of the car and shook hands with Cain. "What's up?"

"Tough day," Cain said, not answering him.

Hendler nodded. "What's this?"

They walked around the back of the Jeep. "School's out, but there's some maintenance going on, so there have been contractors in and out. One of the guys spotted the Jeep sitting over here, but thought it must belong to someone else on the crew and they just wanted to park it over here out of the sun. Couple of days go by, the Jeep hasn't moved. The guy comes over, thinks it might be abandoned or might be a gang car or something."

They'd arrived at the passenger side door, which was standing open. Hendler smelled it before he saw it. Then he saw the dark stain that covered the beige upholstery.

"He said since it had that really strong metallic smell, that he figured the blood was fairly fresh. He called 911."

Hendler looked up and down. "So she was killed in the car and then taken to the tree."

"That's an assumption. I'm still waiting on the autopsy report. There's been a little holdup. I've been trying to light a fire under the ME's office, but all I get is that they want to be certain of something."

Hendler had squatted down at the edge of the open car door, and he turned to look up at Cain. "So they have some doubts?"

"I don't know. We'll see, I guess."

"Anything else here?"

"Oh, we're just getting started. After the lab people got through, we searched the vehicle." They walked to the front of the Jeep. Several plastic bags, all bearing evidence tags, were lined up on the pavement. "Number one: a forty-caliber semiautomatic Glock 23. It was in the glove box."

Hendler looked at the gun, felt it through the plastic. "Nice weapon."

Cain nodded. "And a favorite of some law enforcement agencies and officers." He pointed to the next bag. "Number two: registration and insurance verification card, showing that the vehicle belongs to Sean Michael Kelly of Tucson, Arizona."

Hendler kept his poker face.

"Number three," Cain said. "Arizona license plates, found under the rear seat. As you can see, it has Oklahoma plates on it now. I ran them as soon as we got here, before we found the others. The Oklahoma plates were stolen a couple of weeks ago, from a Mr. Martin Guerrero, who doesn't live far from here. The Arizona plates show registration to Sean Michael Kelly of Tucson, Arizona."

"You'll send the gun for ballistics tests," Hendler said, struggling to keep it together. First Senator McDermott, now this. *Not Faith's brother*, he thought. *Please, let this be a mistake.*

"Yep," Cain said. "I've taken the liberty of doing some checking, first on your friend Faith, and then on Sean, who is her brother, as it turns out. You knew that, didn't you?"

"I knew her brother was named Sean," Hendler said carefully.

"Uh-huh. They grew up in Evanston, Illinois, a suburb of Chicago. Father, Joseph Kelly, captain of detectives, Evanston PD. Mother, Maire Kelly, homemaker. Sean is eighteen months older. He graduated from Illinois with a degree in criminal justice, applied for Federal Law Enforcement Academy in Georgia, got accepted, graduated middle of his class. Joined Customs, assigned to Tucson seven years ago. Several citations for outstanding investigative work. But he's currently on administrative leave pending dismissal, due to excessive consumption of alcohol, leading to reckless endangerment of the lives of officers and civilians. I've ordered his federal personnel records, including fingerprints and DNA sample."

Hendler nodded. He knew it had to be done, but that didn't make it any easier.

"Faith Kelly graduated from Illinois with both bachelor's and master's degrees in criminal justice, top of her class. Second in her own class at the Academy, joined the Marshals Service. But let's back up a second. Even though she's obviously very bright, she graduated high school a year later than she should have. School records for ages thirteen to fourteen are missing. It's as if she was just gone for that year. You know anything about that?"

Hendler shook his head in genuine surprise. He'd never heard Faith mention such a thing, not even once.

"Hmm," Cain said. "Well, anyway, she made up for lost time. The Marshals assigned her to Oklahoma City and she was on a fast track here. Then two years ago, she disappears from the Marshals Service's payroll but is still listed as being employed by the Justice Department." He looked at Hendler. "I guess we know now what all that means, don't we? That must be when she joined DOJ's little Department Twenty."

"Thirty. What's your point?"

"My point, Scott, is that none of this looks very good for your 'special projects' girlfriend and her brother. I'm fairly willing to bet that's Daryn McDermott's blood in there. And what do you say are the odds that gun fired the shot that killed her? We've got

Faith Kelly working for some secret little department that kind of twists around the whole concept of witness protection to where it looks more like terrorist protection—"

"Now wait just a damn minute, Rob—"

"And we've got her alcoholic brother with the victim's blood in his truck."

"You don't know that's Daryn McDermott's blood."

"Not yet I don't. But I will pretty soon. What kind of little game are we playing here, Scott? I know you're honest and a good cop, for a fed, but all bets are off about your girlfriend and her brother."

Hendler waited a moment. "How do you want me to respond to all that? Do I know who killed Daryn? No, I don't, but I want to find out. Did Faith kill her? No, she didn't. Did her brother?" He raised both arms, then dropped them to his sides. "I don't know. God, I hope not."

"Do you know where he is?"

"No."

"Does she?"

"No."

"You're sure about that?"

"Yes, I am. She told me that he took her car and disappeared, and she hasn't heard from him since the night Daryn was murdered."

"What did he do, take her car to use as a getaway after using this one to kill Daryn?"

"Now you're speculating," Hendler said. "There's no evidence of that."

"You're right," Cain admitted. "But speculation often

leads to the trail that takes you to evidence, doesn't it?"

"Look, Rob, I see where all this is pointing. I'm not blind to that, whether you want to believe it or not. And I told Faith so yesterday. Her brother has a problem with booze, and he spent time with Daryn." He sighed. "That's what I know right now."

He remembered driving Sean to the safe house in Edmond. He'd tried to talk to him, but Sean was obviously distraught, hands shaking. He'd muttered a few words about Daryn, but had otherwise said little.

Was Sean obsessed with Daryn? Hendler wondered. Faith hadn't told him anything about the connection between Daryn and her brother. He knew—and now the world knew—that Daryn had gone to Faith for protection, and Faith had found no evidence to warrant her staying under Thirty's protection. But he still didn't know how Sean Kelly fit into all of it.

"Tell me something," Cain said. His tone had softened, as had his posture. "Scott, I can tell how you feel about her. You don't have to say anything. I'm big on body language, and it was clear to me that first time I met her, back at Barry's. I also know you a little bit, and I've seen what a stand-up guy you are. I know this isn't easy for you, thinking that maybe the brother of the woman you love could be a killer."

Hendler looked at him and nodded. He didn't trust himself to speak.

"You know I have three kids, right? My son is ten, my older daughter eight, and my baby girl is three."

"I didn't know the exact ages, but I knew you had three."

"They're the best part of my life, Scott. I would do anything for them."

"If you're saying that Faith or I—"

Cain held up a hand. "No, just listen. What you don't know is that my older daughter isn't really my daughter. She's my niece."

Hendler cocked his head.

"My wife's brother was a batterer. He used to beat his wife almost every day, and after Leah was born, he beat her too. She was a baby, less than two years old, and he was hitting her with his fists, day after day. One day he shoved his wife down a flight of stairs. She hit her head."

"Did it kill her?"

"No, but I wish it had."

"What?"

"She's been in a coma for eight years. She's in a nursing home in Stillwater. Beth's brother went to prison for attempted murder. We sued for custody of Leah, and the judge granted it. A year later, we went a step further and legally adopted her. She's my daughter now. But it doesn't change the fact that her biological father—my own wife's brother—did what he did. There's not a day goes by that I don't wonder how my wife, the best and gentlest and most compassionate person who ever walked on this earth, could be the sister of that monster."

Hendler nodded. "You didn't have to tell me that."

"No, I didn't."

Cain walked away and Hendler heard him talking in low tones with the uniformed officers on the other side of the Jeep.

Hendler waited a moment, looking at the evidence bags: the gun, the registration and insurance papers, the Arizona license plates.

Did you do it, Sean?

And if you did, why?

For God's sake, why?

He thought of Faith. He called her again, got her voice mail again. "Hey, it's me. Call me when you can," he said. "I'm thinking about you. I need to hear that you're okay. Call me, or come by if you're able to. I'm going to work at home for the rest of the day, trying to organize my thoughts on some new evidence that just came in." He waited a moment. "I need to talk to you about this."

He shook hands with Cain again before making his way back to his own car. "Good work on all this. I mean, good police work. Everyone should appreciate the local–federal cooperation."

Cain saw that he was straining to lighten the mood. The detective held his hand in his grip a moment longer than necessary. "You want to talk, off the record, let me know. I mean that."

Hendler looked at him for a long moment. "I know you do." He started walking toward the Toyota, but stopped and turned back to Cain. "Thanks for the perspective, Rob."

Cain nodded. Hendler pulled out of the parking lot. Cain watched him the whole way.

As Hendler turned onto Shields, another car pulled from a side street and dropped into traffic one car length behind him.

31

FAITH'S LAST ACT AS HERSELF—AT LEAST FOR A while—was to return the Focus to the rental agency at Will Rogers World Airport. Then she walked around the corner to a different rental counter and, as Kimberly Diamond, signed out a Chevy Suburban.

Since I'm a new person, I'll rent something that Faith Kelly would never get, she thought as she got into the huge Suburban and drove out of the airport.

And now what?

Yorkton had told her—three times, no less—to go to ground. In order words, stay out of sight. It had been a few hours since Senator McDermott had pronounced his public indictment of Faith and Department Thirty. By now, she suspected the media would have found her house. Her home phone was unlisted, but they had their ways—property tax records, that sort of thing. They would be camped out on her quiet street in The Village. They would be talking to her neighbors. Unlike "Katherine Hall," Faith didn't hang around with her neighbors. They were mostly families with kids, or retired people. She was the only single person on the block. They would tell the reporters about Faith Kelly being polite but standoffish, keeping to herself most of the time, but making sure her lawn was mowed and her house maintained.

The obvious answer was to go to a hotel and simply stay there and do nothing. Let Yorkton go into damage control mode. Forget about all that had happened.

She remembered Daryn—*He'll kill me, you know*—and she remembered Sean, the last time she'd seen him, sprawled drunk on her couch after she'd dropped Daryn off at "Kat's" apartment.

Sober up, she'd told him. *We need to talk.*

Then Daryn was dead and Sean was gone.

How could she forget? She might be using documents that identified her as Kimberly Diamond, but her life and her memory and her mistakes all belonged to Faith Kelly. It was a strange twist on the whole idea of Department Thirty. She'd worked with people to assume new identities, had counseled them on leaving their old lives behind.

And now here she was, in the same position her cases had been.

But it's temporary, she told herself. *Yorkton will work this out.*

Or so she hoped.

Her own cell phone had rung incessantly, and she'd finally turned it off after a while. Driving north on Meridian Avenue from the airport, she finally turned it on again to check the messages. There were calls from her friends Alex Bridge and Nina Reeves, from Chief Deputy Raines, from her old college friend Jennifer Ghezzi in St. Louis, from her father, and from Scott Hendler.

"Faith, what's this all about?" her father said on the message. "You call me and tell me what this means." *Click.*

Hendler's message was from a little more than an hour ago. She listened to it twice. He was being her friend, her lover, and an investigator, all at once.

"Oh, Scott," she said.

She knew she would have to check into a hotel as Kimberly Diamond, sit and do nothing. But that could wait, at least for a while.

I need to hear that you're okay, he'd said.

And Faith realized, with increasing clarity, that she needed him as well. Needed him to just be there, to be normal and sane and even-tempered, even needed his silly word games.

She headed toward Edmond.

Half an hour later, she turned off Danforth Road onto a side street and parked in front of the condominium fourplex where Hendler lived. It was less than a mile from the Edmond safe house. Hendler's Toyota was the only vehicle in the lot. He'd told her that the other three units were all occupied by either young single professionals or couples with no kids, who all worked during the day. There were times when he was working a big case that he would escape here in the afternoon to organize data, write reports, and such. It was much quieter than his desk at the FBI field office. Faith smiled. They'd spent a couple of afternoons here engaged in other, less formal activities as well.

All of the condos were split-level, and Hendler's

faced away from the street. Faith walked through a wide breezeway, turned the corner, and rang his doorbell.

She waited a long moment, then knocked.

The condo had two bedrooms, and Hendler had set up the second one as his computer room. It was farthest from the door, and sometimes when he was working back there he wouldn't hear the knock or the bell the first time, especially if he was wrapped up in whatever he was doing.

Faith waited another minute, then pounded the door with her fist. Even when he was wrapped up in work, it wasn't like him to not answer the door for this long.

"I'm going to work at home for the rest of the day, trying to organize my thoughts on some new evidence that just came in. I need to talk to you about this."

Faith walked very quickly back to the Suburban, where she'd left it in the parking lot beside Hendler's Toyota. She pulled Kimberly Diamond's new Glock out of the glove compartment and, holding it close to her body, jogged through the breezeway and back to the condo.

She and Hendler had given each other keys to their respective homes a few months ago, when they began spending more and more nights together. She found her key ring and put the key in the lock.

Turning it, the key met no resistance. There was no click.

It was already unlocked.

"Oh, shit," she whispered. Hendler *never* left his doors unlocked for any reason.

She pushed the door open and stepped into the room, the gun coming up in her hand.

Nothing in the corners.

Everything looked perfectly normal, the same as it had looked the last time she saw it, the morning after Daryn McDermott died. She and Hendler had left hastily after Rob Cain's call, and she hadn't been back here since.

The living room was done in deep blues and browns, the furniture tasteful but not expensive. Hendler wasn't a neat freak like her brother, but he was certainly a better housekeeper than Faith was. Things were well organized, put away. There was no dust. There were several pictures of windmills and train depots, Hendler's two artistic passions. He'd developed into a fairly talented photographer and had taken several of the photos himself in various places he'd traveled.

Faith took a deep breath and closed the door behind her. "Scott?"

She heard nothing.

"Scott, it's me! Hello!"

The kitchen was empty. The bathroom and Hendler's bedroom—the room they'd made love in so many times—empty. The bed was neatly made.

She found him in the computer room.

His desk chair had been spun around and was facing the wrong direction, away from the desk. The computer monitor was still on, a screen saver of three-dimensional pipes scrawling across it.

Hendler was a couple of steps in front of the chair, toppled toward the far wall. He'd fallen straight to the side, as if he had been kneeling and simply fell over. Blood had pooled under his head, and there were a few splatters on the floor and the wall.

Her gun slipped from her fingers and clattered to the floor. She moved forward tentatively, like a child taking its first halting steps.

Then something broke inside her and she rushed to him. He was on his side, his feet pointing toward her.

"Scott!" she shouted. "Scott, no! Dammit, no, *no, no!*"

The first thing she touched was his arm; then she ran her hand up to his shoulder. There was drying blood on his neck. She saw the wound, one fairly small entry at his temple.

Execution style, was how they described such things in movies.

More blood and tissue. Red, white, gray. She picked his head up. No exit wound on the other side. A small-caliber gun, most likely, the round still lodged in Scott Hendler's brain. Some of his blood had gotten on her hand, a little more on her shirt.

Not this man, she thought. *Not this one. Please.*

From the angle of his body, he'd been on his knees when he was shot. They'd forced him to his knees.

She tried to think, but no thoughts would come. Hendler couldn't be dead. That was all, that was the extent of her mental processes. *He . . . could . . . not . . . be . . . dead.*

She needed him, after all.

Not this man, she thought again.

She held his head for a long time. She wasn't sure how long. Faith blinked over and over, but felt no tears. There was nothing in her, not even grief. Not even anger. There was nothing to feel.

She finally lay his head down and touched his face with her fingertips. He was already starting to cool.

She gently backed away and just stared for a long moment. She'd seen death before, and had even taken a life herself, but this . . . there were no words, no thoughts, that could process it.

Faith tried to think analytically. She moved around the body and touched the office chair. It was still warm. She sat in it, swiveled to face the desk.

She leaned forward and was about to touch the computer keyboard's space bar when she thought, *You're contaminating the crime scene.*

She knew this had to be connected to everything else that had happened. Daryn McDermott, Kat Hall, Sanborn . . . her brother. There was no other explanation.

"Trying to organize my thoughts on some new evidence that just came in," he'd said on the phone message.

His yellow legal pad sat just to the left of the computer. She recognized Hendler's neat printing. She read the notes he'd written himself, and her stomach turned.

Daryn dead in SK Jeep??? SK gun, Cain to ballistics— SK obsessed with Daryn?

SK.

Sean Kelly.

The "new evidence" he'd mentioned—they must have found Sean's Jeep and his gun, with some evidence to suggest that Daryn had actually been murdered there.

"Oh God," Faith said.

She'd defended her brother to Hendler, saying she knew Sean wasn't capable of murder.

Or was he?

Had he committed two murders? Had he been so obsessed with Daryn McDermott that he'd had to kill her, and then murdered Hendler when he began to have suspicions of Sean, with a growing amount of evidence against him?

No. He's my brother.

She turned around and faced Hendler's body. Her throat tightened.

It couldn't be.

Why would Sean kill Hendler, then leave evidence right here, the evidence that implicated Sean in Daryn's murder?

He's my brother.

And he might be a murderer.

The phone rang.

Faith jumped. It was the phone on Hendler's desk, right beside the computer. She looked at the caller ID and recognized the number at the FBI field office.

She listened to it ring four times, then stop as the call went to voice mail. The ringing seemed to jolt her into reality. Faith considered her options. She could call 911 and wait, be a good citizen. But how would Kimberly Diamond of Independence, Missouri, explain that she had a key to FBI Special Agent Scott Hendler's condo? Plus, the odds were that at least someone who responded to the call might know her. Wouldn't work—Faith Kelly had to be out of sight.

She could leave and place an anonymous call. But they would want to know how she knew there was a dead man in the condo. And she couldn't answer questions.

Or she could leave him.

Faith folded her hands together, squeezing them until they hurt. To the extent that she had allowed him to be, Scott Hendler had been there for her whenever she'd needed him, no questions asked. He'd trusted her even when she gave him no reason to do so. He'd gone against his own better judgment at times in order to give her the benefit of the doubt.

She may have loved him, though Faith wasn't sure she knew what that meant. She was certain that he had loved her, and it may have cost him his life.

She squeezed her hands tighter. She bowed her head until her lips touched one of her knuckles. She closed her eyes.

It wouldn't be long before someone found him. One of his FBI colleagues, perhaps. Maybe his parents or his brother would call and be concerned when they couldn't reach him. He'd grown up right here in Edmond, and his parents lived barely two miles away. He had dinner with them every week. Faith had met them—they were good people. They would be utterly devastated. In a very real way, they might never recover from their son's murder.

Yes, he would be found.

And she would be gone. She would pick up her brother's trail. Finding Sean was no longer an exercise in family dynamics.

She bent down and touched Scott's cheek again. "I'm sorry, Sleepy Scott," she said. She felt like she should cry, but she had no tears. She couldn't feel anything at all, not yet. It frightened her to think of what it would be like when she finally did allow herself to feel.

"Not now," she said. She stood up and went into the bathroom. She took a towel out of the linen cabinet and wiped down every surface she had touched.

She would do this investigation her way, and she couldn't have the FBI or the Edmond Police Department or anyone else considering her a suspect while she was doing it. She felt a coldness begin to descend on her.

She pulled off the page of Scott's legal pad that had his notes about Sean on it. She was only buying time—she suspected that others, particularly Rob Cain, had the same information. But she needed a head start. She already had a new identity and clean, untraceable money. That would help.

She took one long look back. "I'm sorry," she said again, and left the condo.

She started the Suburban and let it idle for a moment. She pulled out the Kimberly Diamond cell phone and, in a burst of impulse, called the number on Rob Cain's business card.

When Cain's voice mail greeting came on, she said, "This is Faith. I'm going to fix this, once and for all. If you find out anything—about Daryn or about Scott—let me know. You'll know what that means pretty soon. I—I don't know what else to tell you, Rob. Scott trusted you, and I think I have to trust you. I hope you'll return the favor. Call me at this number if you find out *anything*."

She clicked the end button, put the phone away, and pulled out of the parking lot, back into afternoon traffic on Danforth Road. Everything seemed so normal, just an ordinary suburban street on an ordinary suburban afternoon.

Faith blinked again and again. The tears formed in her eyes, but not a single one fell.

32

EVEN BEFORE SENATOR EDWARD McDERMOTT had finished speaking, the director of Department Thirty had been summoned to the attorney general's office.

Yorkton ran Department Thirty from an unassuming gray stone building in Harrisonburg, Virginia, in the Shenandoah Valley, one hundred miles from Washington. It was close enough to D.C. for easy access, far enough away to be removed from the regular business of government.

The AG was Yorkton's only boss. There were no deputies or associates or assistants in between the two. Each attorney general since the Nixon Administration had functioned in this role, some wanting weekly reports from Department Thirty, some wanting as little contact with it as possible.

The current occupant of the office fell somewhere between the two, and while Yorkton couldn't really say he liked the man—he was a political appointee, after all—he admitted the AG was intelligent, capable, and seemed to be honest. He generally let Yorkton do his job and kept his hands off Department Thirty's internal operations.

The two men sat in the AG's sumptuous office at the

Justice Department with no aides, no secretaries, no in-house lawyers.

"Tell me," the attorney general said. "Is it true?"

"Substantially, yes," Yorkton said.

"What do you mean, 'substantially'? I have no patience with your vague answers. If we're going to control this, I need to know what's real and what's not."

Yorkton nodded. "My case officer—"

"The Kelly woman. She was Art Dorian's, wasn't she?"

"Yes. Very talented young woman. Has a tendency to be volatile at times, but she does the job."

"Yes, I know. So?"

"What Senator McDermott said was true, as far as it goes. His daughter came to us and requested protection—"

"How did she even know about us?" the AG interrupted. "Did you wonder about that?"

Yorkton gritted his teeth, forcing himself to be calm. "Yes, of course I did. That still hasn't been answered. But she came to Officer Kelly, who did the preliminary intake work. She investigated the different aspects of it, the girl's claims that this Coalition for Social Justice was set to initiate further acts of terror at banks across the country, and that its leader, a Franklin Sanborn, had threatened to kill her. As I've already told you in my report, Kelly found nothing. No evidence of any kind to support any part of her story. I sent field officers to the places she specified that these terror cells were hiding. They were all old abandoned buildings. As far as we can tell, Franklin Sanborn doesn't exist."

"So why?" the AG said. "Why does Daryn McDermott want us to protect her if there's no terrorist group and she's not in danger?" He spread his hands apart. "Obviously, there *was* a danger to her. She thought so, to the point that she sent her father—a man with whom she does not get along—this impassioned e-mail message."

"I can't explain it," Yorkton said. "Daryn McDermott has a history of unusual behavior that was designed to either get attention, embarrass her father, or both."

"Oh, so being shot to death and strung up in a tree was an attention-getting ploy? It was to embarrass the senator? Come on, you can do better than that."

Yorkton shrugged. "I don't have an answer. But I trust my officer. If Kelly says there was no evidence, I believe there was no evidence. If we protected every small-time criminal who was afraid of their own associates—"

The attorney general crashed his fist down on the desk. "This was no small-time criminal! This was the daughter of the senior senator from Arizona. Ted McDermott is the point man on the president's social agenda, and his daughter was brutally murdered after she'd asked for Department Thirty to protect her. Now McDermott's on national TV throwing around Thirty's name and your officer's name. We have to put a stop to it. Right now. Do you understand me? Plug this before it gets any worse."

Yorkton drummed his fingers on the arm of the deep leather chair. "Maybe we could convince Senator

McDermott to just back down a bit, until we are able to figure out what's really going on here."

"And how do you aim to do that? The man's daughter was just murdered!"

"What do you know about him, about the senator? He's never been involved in oversight of law enforcement or intelligence, so I've had no dealings with him. Is there anything about him, any information"—Yorkton drew out the word—"that would be useful to us?"

The attorney general leaned back in his own chair, steepling his fingers and looking over them at Yorkton.

"Do you have a dossier?" Yorkton asked.

"I won't answer that. But I do happen to know that the man is actually one of the biggest hypocrites in Washington. And that's saying something, isn't it?"

Yorkton didn't want to debate hypocrisy in the political establishment. "What do you mean?"

"His daughter was renowned for a, shall we say, open sexuality."

"Yes?"

"Let's just say she came by it naturally."

Yorkton waited a moment. "McDermott is firmly in the camp of social conservatism. Am I to assume that his daughter's sexual escapades were not near as embarrassing as revealing his own would be?"

"That's a fair assumption."

The two men looked at each other for a long moment.

"You have the evidence?" Yorkton said.

"It's with my other 'special files' on the legislative branch. I'll make it available to you if you think there's a chance it will work. Otherwise I won't spend the administration's political capital on it."

"I'll see that it works."

"You think you can blackmail a U.S. senator into backing off talking about his own daughter's murder? Even though the girl was out of control, she was still his only child, and what happened to her was horrible."

"Agreed," Yorkton said. "But Department Thirty is not culpable in her death, and Senator McDermott must be persuaded to stop acting as if we are."

"Yes," the Attorney General said. "What about your other cases?"

"All secure," Yorkton said quickly. "Our budget is off the books, and there's no way any of our other cases will be affected."

The attorney general stood up. Yorkton took his cue and started for the door.

When he'd put his hand on the ornate doorknob of the huge wooden door, the attorney general stopped him and said, "You understand that any information you use with McDermott did not come from me."

"Of course I understand. I do know how the game is played." *Far better than you do*, he thought.

"Good. I'll get the evidence to you later today."

Yorkton nodded to him and left the office. In half an hour he was out of Washington and back in the rolling Virginia hills.

Of course, Yorkton hadn't told the attorney general everything. He never did. He only revealed to his superior as much as he needed to know to help Yorkton accomplish what had to be done. Otherwise, there could be trouble. A superior who knew too much of day-to-day operations could be very dangerous, far more dangerous than Senator McDermott or his late daughter.

He hadn't told the AG about Sean Kelly being the one who brought Daryn McDermott to the department. Faith had been forthright with him about her brother's involvement, and in return Yorkton protected his officer.

And her brother as well, he thought as he rolled westward on Interstate 66.

But Yorkton thought he knew Faith Kelly well enough by now to understand how she would react to all of this. He already knew she had concerns about her brother—specifically, Sean Kelly's alcohol addiction. The unspoken words had been there, in both the calls she'd placed to him about this case. Her brother's involvement was a puzzle to her, something she couldn't quite grasp yet.

He'd told her quite emphatically to go to ground, to assume her emergency identity. She would, but if Yorkton knew Faith Kelly like he thought he did, she wouldn't be sitting around in a hotel room waiting for the storm to blow over. She would use the new identity to cover herself as she delved deeper into what had happened. And she wouldn't stop until she had the truth, even if the truth was personally painful for her. Faith Kelly was funny that way.

An irritating quality for Department Thirty, Yorkton thought.

But even Yorkton had to admit that it was occasionally a useful quality to have.

Faith's hands hadn't stopped trembling since she'd left Hendler's condo. She was amazed she'd been able to hold the big Suburban on the road. The way her hands shook reminded her eerily of Sean when he was either too drunk or "not drunk enough."

But her mind was in fast-forward. If Sean had killed both Daryn and Hendler, he didn't have much of a head start. The sickening realization came to her that she was now proceeding as if she knew her brother had killed two people, one of whom was her lover. She wasn't viewing it through a prism of doubt any longer. She knew Sean's frame of mind in the time leading up to Daryn's murder. His behaviors were classic obsession, the "if I can't have her, no one can" syndrome that so often arose in crimes of passion.

But she'd told Hendler that Daryn's killing didn't look like a crime of passion. It was more of a message, a point being made.

Then again, that had been when Hendler was still alive. Before he'd discovered new evidence implicating Sean. Before Faith's entire world had shifted under her feet. Before she'd found Hendler's body, she'd been relatively sure of certain things, even if she inhabited the insane gray world of Department Thirty.

Now she was sure of nothing.

Nothing but the fact that she would find her brother.

And then what, Faith?

She stuffed that thought way down. It led to places she wasn't sure she could go.

Coming from the north, she drove down May Avenue through The Village. When she passed her street, she glanced down the block eastward and counted four news units in front of her house. She grimaced.

She drove two blocks south on May, turned into the residential area, and drove two blocks farther. Then she backtracked north until she was a block north of her house, having given her own block a wide berth.

She parked the Suburban—at least *that* fits in this neighborhood, she thought wryly—exactly one block north of her house, got out, and locked it. She jogged across the street, trying to remember which of the homes on this street had the dog in the backyard. She caught a flash of memory—out for her predawn run one bitter cold winter morning three years ago, she'd been chased through this neighborhood by the man she knew as Dean Yorkton. It was her first exposure to him.

She walked up the driveway to the nearest house. The dog was two houses down, or so she thought. She unlatched the wooden gate and carefully entered the backyard. She knew the family who lived here was named Robertson, the husband was in sales, the wife was an obstetrics nurse, and they had two daughters. They were rarely home, either being at work or on the go with the girls' various activities. There were no cars in the driveway.

She climbed the wooden fence, feeling splinters digging into her hands, then dropped into her own backyard on all fours. Her house had privacy fencing, so even if the news people were standing right at the fence, they wouldn't be able to see her unless they were on stilts. Faith wouldn't have put it past some of them, but she saw no sign that any of them were staking out the backyard.

She stayed in a crouch all the way to the back door, reached up and unlocked it, then crawled inside, just in case they were close to her windows and could feel the movement inside. Moving with agonizing slowness, she crept down the hallway to her bedroom.

Her computer was already on. She logged into her e-mail, then navigated to her "Sean" folder. She'd saved her brother's e-mails over the last few years. There weren't many, so she'd saved what little communication she'd had with him.

If she was going to get inside her brother's head, try to track him, she had to know him better. She had to think like him, to feel the way he felt, to know what he knew. Before the days of Department Thirty, Faith had been a deputy U.S. Marshal, albeit for a short time. But one of the Marshals Service's mandates was tracking fugitives. She'd had a couple of spectacular successes, even helping to apprehend one of the nation's most notorious counterfeiters a couple of years ago, after he'd been at large for more than fifteen years.

She began to read the few short e-mails, committing passages to memory:

. . . *my best buddy here in Tucson, a geeky little guy named A. J. Helms. Reminds me of that guy back in high school, Norm Delton. Remember him?*

. . . *my SAC here, big guy named Weller. You'd appreci-ate him, sister. He's completely no-nonsense . . .*

. . . *moonlight in the desert, down by the border. You can see for miles. Sure ain't Chicago, where all you can see is the next building over . . .*

What did you think of the tiger's eye? Got it in a little town called Arivaca, about 20 mi. from the border. An old hippie couple sells them. I got to see the guy bend the wires around the gem and then put it on a string. "How much?" I ask him. "Three bucks," he says. Three bucks! I'm cheap but not free . . .

. . . *there's this cantina in Sasabe, half a mile from the port of entry. I never go in there unarmed. But the Jack is cheap and the beer is cold and the bartender's wife makes the best flour tortillas you've never tasted. Sure as hell ain't Chicago.*

Faith nodded. Sean had come to really love Arizona, just as she'd adopted Oklahoma. She knew that much. It was a start. He was on the run—he would seek out a place he knew, and Arizona was the most logical choice. He wouldn't go home to Chicago. That would mean dealing with their parents, and in his current state, he wouldn't want to do that.

But would he do something as obvious as returning to Tucson? If Sean had just committed two murders and had deceived his sister—arguably the only person in the world who could help him—would he circle around to the beginning?

The average cop might dismiss it as too obvious. *No criminal would be that stupid,* they'd argue. *That's the first place we'd look.*

But he wasn't just a criminal. He was her brother, and she knew things that the average cop didn't. Given his struggle with alcohol, it seemed almost paradoxical, but she knew Sean would seek out a situation where things were ordered and tidy and he knew where everything was. He would seek the familiar. He always had. As a child, he didn't like family trips because he didn't like being away from familiar sights and sounds.

Over the last seven years, Arizona had become his familiar.

"Yes," Faith said.

She made a few notes, names and places: A. J. Helms, Weller, Arivaca, Sasabe.

She called Southwest Airlines and booked the first flight that would connect to Tucson. Given how much Faith hated flying, that alone was testament to how serious the situation had become. She used Kimberly Diamond's credit card and it went through with no trouble at all. *Good old Yorkton,* she thought.

Her travel bag was already packed and in the Suburban. Her new gun was in it, the Glock that was licensed in Missouri to Kimberly Diamond. She would break it down and put it in her checked baggage. She had the carry permit in her purse, along with her other ID.

She walked back into the living room, glancing at the shattered glass on the floor. She'd meant to clean it up, but as always, other things intervened.

A tide of disgust, anger, and even pity rose in her.

God help you if you did it, Sean. God help both of us.

She took a step, then froze. She looked back. The broken glass was on the hallway side of the bookshelf. Just the other side of it was a book, open and upside down on the floor.

He'd even been messing with her bookshelves. It wasn't like Sean to leave something lying on the floor, though. Faith bent down, then stopped when she saw which book it was.

Her heart stopped.

She stood absolutely still for a moment. She heard the sounds of the news crews outside, people walking around, voices, car sounds.

She turned the book over and read the dust jacket.

"Oh my God," Faith whispered.

She snapped the book closed. No longer thinking about hiding herself from the media, she ran full speed for the back door.

Now Faith knew why she recognized the name of Franklin Sanborn, and it changed everything.

33

SHE ARRIVED IN TUCSON AFTER TEN P.M., AND when she stepped out of the airport terminal, was amazed by both the dryness and warmth of the air. It was only early June, yet the temperature was still in the eighties this late in the evening. Still, the clean, clear air of the high desert felt good in her lungs.

"Kimberly Diamond" rented a car, then a motel room close to the airport, where she spent a fitful night. At nine a.m., she called the Tucson office of Immigration and Customs Enforcement and asked to speak to Special Agent Helms.

"Helms," he said a moment later.

"Agent Helms, my name is Kimberly Diamond. I'm an attorney, and I'm representing Sean Kelly in his termination hearing. I'd like to meet with you for a few minutes today, if you can spare the time."

There was a long pause. "I don't know that I can tell you anything that would help Sean. Everything's in the record."

"Yes, it is, Agent Helms. But I understand Agent Kelly has considered you one of his closest friends in Tucson."

Another pause. "Yes, we're pretty close."

"I'm not interested in facts and figures that are in

the record. I'm interested in a more personal view of Sean Kelly."

"I really don't know that I'm supposed to talk to you. Everything is—"

"—on the record. Yes, we covered that." Faith stopped, knowing how most men reacted to silence from a woman.

Helms cleared his throat. "Maybe a few minutes at lunch."

"Just name the place."

"There's a Mexican restaurant on Oracle, just up the street from the office. Noon, maybe?"

"I'll be there."

"I really don't know if I can help, but Sean . . . well, Sean *needs* something. I've tried to help him before, and . . ." Helms's voice trailed away, and Faith wondered what Helms had been through with her brother.

"We'll talk at noon."

Armed with directions from the desk clerk at the motel, Faith drove the rented Suburban—*might as well be consistent, after all*—north on Oracle Road, one of the main north–south drags in Tucson. She skirted the Miracle Mile, with its diners and motels and 1950s-style "tourist courts," and passed a huge automotive dealership larger than anything she'd seen in Oklahoma. Oracle then branched into a commercial area— at least one indoor shopping mall, numerous strip shopping centers, restaurants.

She found the restaurant on the south end of a shopping center and went in. She glanced around for single men who looked like federal agents. She found him in a corner booth. A. J. Helms was in his midthirties, as tall as Sean but rail thin. He wore glasses and had a lot of gray in his light brown hair. He wore the requisite white shirt and dark suit of a federal agent, but looked uncomfortable in it, as if he were more used to jeans and T-shirts. Faith was wearing jeans herself, with a light blue tank top. She also wore a pair of stylish gray cowboy boots, the first time she'd ever worn them. Hendler had bought them for her as a joke for her birthday last year.

Since you're becoming more of an Okie than I am, he'd said, laughing. It had seemed appropriate to Faith—important, even—to wear them now.

"Agent Helms," she said.

He turned, stood up, and froze.

"You're no lawyer," he said.

Faith shook her head. "No, I'm not."

He studied her. "You're Sean's sister. Faith, isn't it?"

"Sorry for the deception. May I sit down?"

Helms indicated the seat. "He had a picture of you in his cubicle at work. You're in DOJ, right?"

Faith sat down, watching him. He showed no indication that he'd connected her name to Senator Mc-Dermott's statement yesterday. "Yes," she said.

"He's very proud of you. He probably never told you that. Wouldn't be his style."

"No, it wouldn't," Faith said. *Proud?*

"He's an alcoholic, you know."

"I know."

"A few months ago," Helms said, "when he really

started going downhill, Sonny—that's Sonny Weller, our SAC—had him referred for counseling and AA. I even volunteered to take him to the AA meetings. There's a meeting place just a few blocks from here. I dropped him off, I picked him up. I later found out that he'd sneaked out the back after I dropped him in front, then came strolling out the front an hour later when I came back to get him. What he didn't realize was that I checked with the person who ran the meeting, and no one remembered him. It's a small group, and Sean does tend to stand out in a crowd."

Faith smiled. "That he does." The smile faded. "Have you talked to him? I mean, recently."

Helms fidgeted.

"Yesterday? Maybe you picked him up at the airport?"

Helms furrowed his brow. "What are you going to do?"

"I'm his sister. I'm worried about him. I want to talk to him."

"And after that?"

Under the gangly, awkward exterior, A. J. Helms was extraordinarily perceptive, Faith realized. "I'm not sure," Faith said. "So he did get in touch with you yesterday?"

"No."

"He didn't?"

"No, I mean he did get in touch, but it wasn't yesterday."

Faith sat very still.

"Let's see, today's Friday, so it would have been Tuesday. Tuesday night. And he didn't fly in. He said he'd driven all day. He showed up at about ten o'clock that night at my house, driving a little Mazda Miata with Oklahoma plates. He just wanted to crash for a few hours, he said, so I let him. He was still asleep when I got up in the morning. When I got home from work in the afternoon, he was gone."

Faith's mind raced. If Sean was in Arizona two and a half days ago, he couldn't have murdered Scott Hendler in Edmond at midday yesterday. The time frame fit. If he'd left Oklahoma City sometime after Daryn was killed, in the early morning Tuesday, and drove straight through, that could have put him at A. J. Helms's door in Tucson at ten o'clock that night. If he stuck to interstate highways, the drive from Oklahoma City to Tucson was about fifteen hours.

She could almost hear Scott Hendler's voice: *Okay, I'll play devil's advocate here. He could have turned around and driven back. If he left Arizona, say, at noon on Wednesday, he'd be in Oklahoma City early Thursday morning.*

In plenty of time to kill you, Scott, Faith thought, and for a moment her eyes clouded.

But it made no sense. If Sean murdered Daryn, why would he then leave town immediately, drive over a thousand miles, sleep for a few hours, turn around and drive back to commit another murder?

And now Faith knew something she hadn't known until yesterday. The secret of the book. The secret of Franklin Sanborn.

Sean couldn't have killed Hendler.

About Daryn, she was less sure. The issue was much

less clear. Sean may have indeed been led to kill Daryn, fueled by his own obsessions, but also driven by the fact that he had been very carefully and skillfully manipulated.

You bastard, she thought. *You may have manipulated Sean into committing one murder, and set him up for another.*

She had to find her brother, and then they would hunt down the man who had called himself Franklin Sanborn.

"Is there somewhere he would go?" Faith asked. "Here in the area, someplace that was special to him. Somewhere . . . I don't know, that he felt safe. Does that sound strange?"

Helms smiled. "Yes and no. Was he always so anal-retentive? A place for everything and everything in its place. Was he like that as a kid?"

"I guess he was," Faith said. "I don't think you notice such things for what they are when you're a kid. He was always neat, I was always a slob. That's the way we looked at it then."

Helms was nodding. "Cleanest desk in our office. Organized, efficient. Until the bottle started getting the best of him, he was the most efficient agent I'd ever seen." He leaned back against the booth. "There were only a few bars he used to go to. He had certain places he liked to go to drink. He knew what to expect there, places where nothing ever changed."

"One of his e-mails a year or so ago mentioned a cantina in a town called—"

"Sasabe," Helms finished. "Man, what a strange deal

that was. With all the operations we did along the border, he got to like those little border cantinas. Sasabe is really remote. It's the most desolate port of entry along the entire Mexican border. But Sean liked to go to that place anytime we were in the area. I went with him once and had a couple of beers." He shook his head. "Not my kind of place. You felt like someone was going to jump you at any minute and if you didn't have a weapon of some sort you might not make it out of there. But Sean never had any trouble there."

"Can you give me directions?"

"Look, Faith, you don't want to go there. I'm sorry, but with all due respect, the only women who go in those kinds of cantinas are women who are offering their services, if you know what I mean. You could get into real trouble."

"No offense taken. But you don't know me very well, either."

"So I don't." He took a pen from his pocket and grabbed a napkin from the dispenser on the table. He drew a detailed map.

Faith stood to go and thanked Helms.

"Sure," Helms said. "If you find him, tell him he's welcome to crash on my couch anytime. Tell him AJ's concerned about him."

"I will."

"Oh, and Faith?"

Faith had already taken a couple of long steps, and had to turn back to face Helms.

"Good luck with the whole Department Thirty thing. Senator McDermott's a grade-A jerk, and his daughter was really screwed up. Most people in Arizona aren't surprised she wound up getting herself killed. But watch your back. The senator doesn't do anything if he doesn't think it'll benefit him politically."

"You knew, the whole time we sat here and talked."

Helms smiled. "You take care, now."

"I will," Faith said.

Clutching the napkin with the directions to Sasabe, she went back to the Suburban.

Sean didn't kill Scott, she thought.

The thought gave her something to hold on to, something she could grasp. Her brother hadn't killed her lover.

But Hendler was still dead. A gaping hole had still been seared into her life.

But now she knew who had done it—or at least who had seen that it was done—and she knew why. There were still puzzle pieces—mostly about Daryn McDermott—that didn't fit, things about the girl that didn't add up. There was no reason for her to have been a part of it. She shouldn't have had to die.

But I'll find out soon enough.

Directions in hand, Faith drove toward Sasabe and the Mexican border.

34

FAITH HAD NEVER REALLY SPENT TIME ALONG THE Mexican border, and certainly not in such a remote part of the world as Sasabe, Arizona.

It seemed an unforgiving landscape, cactus and sage and hard-baked desert ground. But there were always mountains on the horizon, seemingly unreachable, frowning down at the desert below. In some ways, Faith could see her brother in a place like this. Change would come slowly here, if at all. The desert and the distant mountains would always stand their ground, harsh and inscrutable. Sean would always know what to expect here, at least on the surface.

The cantina was hard to miss. As far as Faith could tell, it was the only place of business in the town of Sasabe. Her Miata, covered in dust, was parked squarely in front of it.

She parked the big Suburban away from the cantina's door so that it couldn't be seen from inside. She strapped her extra-large fanny pack, the one she used when she ran, around her waist. Her gun went inside it. She stepped out of the SUV, the stiff boots crunching gravel.

The cantina's door was propped open with a trash barrel. Faith walked through it and stood for a moment, adjusting to the dim light. She saw the bar, two old men at the far end of it, smoking foul-smelling homemade cigarettes. There was the bartender with the droopy mustache, just drawing a beer.

One table was occupied by two Latino men in their twenties, each with a name across the left breast of his uniform shirt. They wore dark work pants and boots.

Everyone looked at her.

Sean had always been better at languages than she, and Faith suspected that seven years on the border had improved his Spanish, while her own was stuck somewhere in high school.

"Buenos días," she said.

No one spoke.

"Hablo Inglés?"

One of the old smokers snorted out a laugh, but otherwise the place was silent.

Faith walked slowly to the bar, feeling the eyes on her. She'd left her purse in the van—she wasn't *that* crazy, after all—but transferred some money and Kimberly Diamond's driver's license to the front pocket of her jeans. She reached into the pocket, pulled out a hundred-dollar bill, and laid it on the bar.

The bartender spread his hands apart.

Faith placed a second hundred beside the first.

The bartender stared at her, eyes lingering on her breasts. He finally shook his head.

"Don't get greedy," Faith said, "or you won't even get the two hundred."

The bartender looked at her impassively. A voice

from the table said, in lightly accented English, "Don't worry about Juan. We don't get many six-foot-tall redheads in here."

Faith turned to look at the table. "I'm only five ten. Where's the man who drove that gold Miata?"

"I just got here," the guy said. The patch on his shirt read *Bobby* in ornate cursive lettering.

"Me too," said his partner, whose patch read *Ramón*.

"The guy's a redhead, like me," Faith said. "You wouldn't have missed him. He's tall, about six three, broad-shouldered. He was probably drinking like a fish."

Ramón snorted.

"What are you, his sister?" Bobby said, and Ramon snickered.

"Yes," Faith said.

Both men sobered. Bobby had clearly meant the remark as a joke and hadn't expected Faith's direct, matter-of-fact reply.

One of the old smokers said something to the other. Both kept staring at Faith. Faith sensed something there and stared back at them, green eyes digging into their brown ones.

The older of the two, who looked to be in his seventies, had a scraggly white beard and was wearing a brown leather vest over a faded denim shirt. He had a Los Angeles Dodgers baseball cap pushed back on his head.

"Dodgers need a new manager and a pitching staff," she said. "They haven't had shit since Lasorda left." She looked over her shoulder at the table. "Would one of you please translate that for me? There's a hundred in it for you if you do."

Bobby looked at her like she'd lost her mind. "You're crazy."

"Yep," Faith said. "Do it."

Bobby shrugged and spoke rapidly in Spanish to the old man, who looked surprised and then spoke back.

"Señor Vargas says girls shouldn't talk like that," Bobby said. "And he says you don't know baseball. Girls don't know baseball."

Faith smiled. "Tell Señor Vargas that the Dodgers haven't had a real pitcher since Orel Hershiser. See what he thinks of that."

Vargas's eyes grew wide at the mention of the name Hershiser, and he looked at Bobby for the rest. After the translation, Bobby said, "He's testing you. You really don't want to get into this with him, lady. He wants you to tell him Hershiser's record in 1988."

Faith shook her head. "Ask me something hard. Twenty-three and eight. But the postseason was what was amazing. Two complete games in the World Series, one shutout, ERA for the series of one. *Uno.* One point zero zero. Same series where Kirk Gibson hit that famous home run against the A's, coming off the bench when he was injured. *That* was real baseball." She shrugged. "I was ten years old. That was the first year I watched the whole World Series on TV. I'm a Cubs fan, so I always have to cheer for someone else in October. I watched that series with my brother. He was so wrapped up in it that he actually cried when Gibson hit that home run. I'll never forget it."

Bobby translated. Vargas looked at Faith while listening. He never dropped his eyes. When Bobby finished, he took off the Dodgers cap and placed it carefully on the bar. He spoke a few words, slowly, then nodded at Bobby.

"Well, I'll be damned," Bobby said. "Señor Vargas says your brother went for a walk."

"Which way?"

"South, toward the border."

Faith nodded to the old man. "*Gracias, Señor Vargas.*" She turned to go.

"*Señorita,*" the old man said in his throaty voice.

Faith turned back to him.

"Ryne Sandberg," Vargas said, articulating each syllable very carefully. He gave Faith a thumbs-up sign.

"He was great, all right," Faith said.

She pulled a hundred out of her pocket and handed it to Bobby as she passed. "Thanks," she said.

"No problem," Bobby said, watching her as she went out.

Faith walked south from the cantina, through the sharp S-curve in the road, looking at the adobe houses, keeping her eyes open. Three or four brown-skinned children ran across the road and back. One little girl, her hair in a long braid, sat in a hardscrabble front yard, spinning a car's hubcap around and around.

She walked past the sign that pointed to Mexico. The port of entry lay before her, brick and steel and glass in the midst of this sand and adobe. Now most of Sasabe was behind her. The country to her right was wide open, the United States blending into Mexico somewhere out there in the desert.

She heard Sean's voice behind her and to the right. "Sorry about taking your car. It was an emergency, and it was all I had."

Faith stopped and turned very slowly. He was standing in a spot she had just passed, thirty or forty steps off the roadway. She blinked. She'd heard that the desert could play visual tricks on a person.

"Just like that, out of thin air," Faith said. "You were always good at tricks."

Sean was wearing dirty, rumpled khaki pants and a white T-shirt. He hadn't shaved. His eyes were shot through with red. He was holding a gun loosely in one hand, as if he weren't quite sure what to do with it.

"You planning on shooting me?" Faith said.

Sean looked at the gun. He let it drop to the ground.

"There," he said. "Happy now? Above all, you should be happy."

"Sean—"

Sean took a few steps toward her. A car went by on the road next to them, the first one Faith had seen between the cantina and the port of entry.

"Why are you here?" Sean said. "This is one of the stupidest things you've ever done, Faith, coming all the way down here."

"Is it? Why? Tell me why you think so."

Sean put his hands in the pockets of the dirty khakis. "What are you, my fucking therapist now? Wanting to know how I *feel*? Sorry, I'm not buying it, sister."

He walked abreast of her, glanced at her once, and kept walking past. She began to move with him, matching his long strides. Faith imagined how they must look—these two tall people with red hair, striding along in this land where everything seemed to be sand-colored.

"Did you kill her, Sean?"

Sean didn't break stride. "I guess it doesn't matter now whether I did or didn't. Even you believe I did."

"It does matter. That's why I asked the question."

Sean said nothing.

"You were crazy over that girl. You were obsessed. She drew you in, fed your obsession, fed your weakness. Then at some point she rejected you, didn't she?" A thought came to her. "She called you, didn't she? That night, the night I took her back to her apartment. After I'd gone home with Scott, Daryn called you. What happened?"

"Rejection," Sean said. "Just like you rejected her, wouldn't protect her. Is that what you mean?"

Faith flinched but said nothing.

"Good to see you've still got some of that good old Irish Catholic guilt in you," Sean said. "Of course, you didn't think you had to protect her from me, did you?"

"What did she say when she called? What did she tell you?"

"Jesus, you just don't give up. Probably why you're so good in Department Fucking Thirty. You get your teeth into someone and shake them around until they cough up whatever you want. Yeah, she called. Said she wanted me, *needed* me. There was some sex talk. Like you said, she played to my weakness."

"And you went to her."

Sean nodded. "She was a crazy woman. I've never seen anyone make love like that. Though I guess you really couldn't call what we were doing making love. It was fucking, pure and simple. I was so drunk I couldn't keep it up, but she kept at it until I came. Then, a few seconds after she rolled off me, she started slapping me and hitting me and screaming at me to get out."

Faith watched him. To her great surprise, a tear rolled down her brother's cheek, unchecked.

"I mean," Sean said, "I'm not stupid enough to think we were in love or anything like that. It was too raw, too . . . I don't know what the word is, maybe primal? But I thought we had a connection. That's why I tried to see her during that week you had her in the safe house. I just wanted to feel that connection. There at the end, I didn't understand it. It's like . . . it's like she knew she was going to die and wanted me to be blamed for it. Someone somewhere will match up the semen sample from inside her with my DNA, and they'll be after me." He looked sidelong at his sister. "Just like you are."

"They're already after you, Sean." Faith stopped walking. They were so close to the port of entry building that they could hear the air-conditioning unit humming. Mexico was only a few feet away. "They found your Jeep. There was blood in it. They're betting it's Daryn's and are probably running the tests right now. They found your gun. They'll be doing ballistics."

Sean sighed. "And your boyfriend will come after me with a vengeance."

Faith felt as if she'd been punched in the stomach. "No," she said slowly. "He won't."

"Oh, they gave some other Bureau hack the case, then."

"No, Sean. Scott is dead."

Sean whipped his head around.

"Scott was murdered yesterday, shot in the head while he worked on his case notes at his condo." Faith blinked at him. She felt her own tears welling.

"Oh Jesus," Sean said. "And you think I did that, too."

Faith reached out and grabbed his shoulder, spinning his entire body around. "What the hell is the matter with you? Can you think for just one minute about something other than yourself? Are you even capable anymore of considering anything except how it affects *you*? Jesus Christ, Sean." Faith's voice rose steadily. "I *loved* him! I loved him, and he was decent and honest and smart and funny, and he was shot in the head!"

Faith's composure cracked, and the floodgates opened. The tears began to stream down her face.

"I found him!" she shouted at her brother. "I found his body, and I had to leave him. Because of all this, I had to leave him right there, like his body was so much garbage, just to be cleaned up later. He showed me respect and kindness, and, goddammit, love! He showed me love, like no one else ever did. And there he was, lying dead on the floor, and *I left him there!*"

A door opened at the port of entry building, and a

burly Hispanic man in a khaki uniform came out. His holster was unbuttoned, his hand on the butt of his weapon.

He took a few steps toward them, then Sean turned to face him.

"Irish?" the man said. "Sean Kelly?"

"Hey, Mike," Sean said.

"What are you doing down here? I heard you were—"

"It's a long story, Mike. Sorry to disturb the peace. This is just a little family matter. This is my sister."

The guard looked uncomfortable. "Hey, Irish, I need to ask you back off from the port, okay? Do I need to make a phone call here?"

"No, no, I don't think so."

Mike nodded. "You'll be safer back up toward town, Sean."

"Right. Thanks, Mike."

Sean backed a few steps away from the border. Faith followed after a moment. The guard went inside. Faith noticed his hand had never left the butt of his gun.

"Jesus, Faith," Sean said softly. "I didn't—"

"And yes, to answer your question," Faith said, "I thought you'd done it. I thought you killed Daryn out of some kind of booze-induced sexual obsession with her, and I thought you killed Scott because he was getting close to you in the investigation."

Sean lowered his voice to a whisper. "How can you think that of me? I mean, this is me, Faith. Anyone else, yeah. They'd look at the evidence and figure it was pretty conclusive. My car, the blood, the gun, the semen. But how could *you* think that?"

"What have you given me to disprove it? Huh? You've lost your job, you're desperate, out here searching for some senator's daughter. You're drunk all the time, you don't listen to anything I say. You're sick, Sean, and when people are sick they're not the same people anymore. You're not the brother I grew up with."

Sean scuffed the sand at his feet. He was silent for a long moment, then he said, "I didn't kill her, Faith. God as my witness, I didn't kill Daryn and I didn't kill Scott."

"I know you didn't kill Scott. Your friend AJ verified that you were here when Scott was murdered."

Sean nodded. "But you don't believe me about Daryn."

"I don't know what to believe." She looked him in the eye. "But I know this: you've been manipulated, very carefully and very skillfully manipulated into the position you're in. I think Daryn was too, though there are some things about her I still don't understand."

"What do you mean, I was manipulated?"

"Franklin Sanborn."

"But I thought you couldn't find any evidence that he even existed. Hadn't you decided that Daryn and I made him up?"

Faith shrugged. "For a while, I was leaning in that direction. I couldn't find him. No one could. He was a ghost."

Sean looked off into the distance. "That night, the

night Daryn was killed. Sanborn followed me after I left her apartment, after we'd . . . he followed me. He found me passed out in the parking lot of a truck stop. He told me if I hurried, I might catch the real killer. It's like he was taunting me, daring me to go."

"I know who he is," Faith said. "I figured it out when I found that book you pulled out of my shelf at home."

Sean looked at her, the question on his face.

"*The Secret Six* by Edward Renehan. It's about the Civil War."

"Oh, I remember that. I remember thinking, 'Since when is my sister into reading about the Civil War?' "

"I'm not. That book was sent to me."

Sean nodded briskly. "There was an inscription, something about 'until we meet again.' I thought it was strange, but I was wasted so I didn't think anything else about it after that."

"Franklin Sanborn," Faith said. "I know now that he's real, all right. Not by that name, of course. He has more identities than I want to think about, and I'd thought he was gone for good. You see, when I knew him, his name was Isaac Smith."

35

THEY WALKED A FEW STEPS TOWARD SASABE. SEAN stopped at the first yard they came to. It was fenced with barbed wire, and a few chickens wandered through it. "Isaac Smith," he said. "That name doesn't mean anything to me."

Faith sighed. "Do you remember last year, when the chief justice of the Supreme Court resigned?"

"Yeah. Cole, wasn't it? Something about a family crisis. It surprised everyone, because he was relatively young, as Supreme Court justices go."

"Right. Well, there was no family crisis."

Sean leaned on a fence post. "Are you trying to tell me Department Thirty was somehow involved in the resignation of a Supreme Court justice?"

"That's exactly what I'm telling you. This man, this Isaac Smith, was in the middle of it. We think his real name was Mikhail Gerenko."

"Russian?"

"Ukrainian. His father was a Soviet physicist who defected when Mikhail was a boy. They came to this country, but by then the Cold War was essentially over. The boy, Mikhail, wound up bitter and angry. He happened on a new and lucrative line of work that let him vent his own anger and make money at the same time."

"What?"

"His clients would hire him to destroy a person's life. Instead of simply assassinating them with a quick bullet to the head, he would ruin them. Take their lives and twist them around, destroy the things and the people they cared about until their own lives were completely devastated. For example, there was one government lawyer that he was hired to ruin. The man was by all accounts honest in his job, faithful to his wife, good to his children. Who knows what the agenda was that brought him down? But Gerenko, or Smith as he was known by then, seduced the man, made him question his own sexuality, carried on a torrid homosexual affair for six months, then dropped him. He'd convinced the lawyer that he was really gay and should leave his family. The lawyer did, left behind his wife and kids. Then Smith disappeared to leave him twisting in the wind. The lawyer wound up jumping off a bridge and drowning himself in Chesapeake Bay."

Sean whistled. "Nice guy. So how did he get from Gerenko to Smith?"

"Somewhere along the way, Gerenko became obsessed with the American Civil War, and particularly with John Brown."

"Whoa, what? John Brown? You mean like Harper's Ferry? That John Brown?"

"That's the one. Isaac Smith was an alias Brown used when he was preparing for the raid on Harper's Ferry."

"So Gerenko adopted the same alias that Brown did."

Faith nodded. "Yes. But after everything that happened last year, Smith was offered protection by Department Thirty."

"What? You protected this guy?"

"No. *I* didn't protect him. Actually, I wanted to kill him, and almost did. But I was overruled—my boss thought he'd be a 'nice catch' for the department. And so he disappeared into Thirty. A few weeks after the last time I saw him, that book came in the mail."

Sean thought for a long moment, gazing off toward Mexico, avoiding his sister's eyes. "Sounds to me like there's more than one obsession running through this. This Smith was obsessed with you, Faith."

Faith blanched. She'd never quite thought of it in that way. She knew Isaac Smith hated her. Because of the way Faith had done her job, he'd had to stop practicing his "trade," and even though he'd been given yet another new identity and relocated far away from her—she didn't know where—she knew he would carry an anger at her for interrupting his business. Faith thought he was the classic sociopath, the one who believed the rules didn't apply to him.

"You're right," Faith said quietly.

"But I still don't understand how you decided he was Sanborn, and what he has to do with all this. Who's his client, and who is he supposed to be ruining? Daryn, her father, you, me, your friend Scott? What's it all about?"

Faith rubbed her scar. She felt suddenly exhausted. Grief, rage, pain . . . they were working their toll on her.

And that's what he wants, she realized.

It started to become sickeningly clear. Even when she'd seen the book, had figured out why she knew the name of Franklin Sanborn, she still hadn't understood why. She'd still been naïve enough to think that Smith might send her a book from wherever he was now, might write a cryptic notation in it, but that he wouldn't—*couldn't*—do anything else.

Isaac Smith—Franklin Sanborn—was his own client.

And Faith was the target.

He'd wanted to make her his ultimate conquest, to see her life tumbling out of control, destroying the people around her. He'd done his homework—that was Smith's trademark, after all, the painstaking research and detail he put into his "jobs"—and found her brother, and knew of his weakness. He would have learned of her relationship with Hendler, and he already had an idea of how difficult it was for Faith to commit to a relationship, how far she'd come with Scott.

All of this, every bit of it, had been accomplished under the nose of Department Thirty and Director Yorkton. Somehow Smith had found a willing vehicle in Daryn McDermott, though she had no doubt that Daryn had been manipulated as well.

"I should have killed him," Faith said, not realizing she'd spoken aloud.

"Oh?" Sean said.

"On a beach at Galveston, a year ago, I had the chance and the justification. He'd already shot at civilians, and with everything else he'd done, if I'd been a little quicker, none of this would have happened. You, Daryn, Scott . . . it was all an elaborate plan to get at me, somehow. There are still holes in it, but he was after me all this time."

Sean was silent for a long time. "You still didn't tell me about the name Sanborn, about how you figured it out."

"The first time I heard the name, I knew I recognized it, but I didn't know from where. After I saw the book on the floor, I picked it up and looked at it, read the dust jacket. The use of that name was a message to me. Smith *wanted* to me to figure it out, to know who was doing this. Franklin Sanborn was one of the 'Secret Six,' this small group of Northern abolitionists who funded and supported John Brown in the revolt he wanted to start. The real Sanborn was an educator, a professor. He was even a friend of Emerson and Thoreau."

"A professor," Sean said. "He used that cover with the Coalition, too."

"More of Smith's sense of irony." Faith kicked the ground with the toe of her boot. "Son of a bitch! He wanted me to know it was him. He wanted me to see what he was doing to me, that even though he was exiled and relocated, he could get to me. He must have been planning this almost from the moment he went under with the department. *Son of a bitch!*"

Sean moved away from the fence post and looked down at his sister. His eyes had changed. Ever since he'd arrived at her house two weeks ago, Faith had seen little but an alcoholic haze, a dullness, in her brother. Now his blue-green eyes flashed anger.

His voice, when he finally spoke again, was tightly controlled. "So this was all about you?"

"I think so. Yes."

"Think about something, Faith. Just a few minutes ago you accused me of not being able to think of anything except about how it affected me. Turn that around. Why would someone go to these lengths to get to you? Are you that important, Faith?"

Faith stared at him, unable to speak. The words had been swept out of her, as if a desert wind had blown them off toward the distant mountains.

"Are you that big a deal now, just because you're working for Department Thirty? Because you can play around with people's lives and create new people, just because you think it's in the 'national interest,' are you that important? Huh? You've been trying to prove something your entire life. Did you prove it? Did you finally prove you were a big deal? Do you think you'd finally get Joe Kelly's approval?"

"Stop it, Sean."

"Except . . . oh, wait a minute, you can't tell anyone you work for Thirty, so no, Dad can't approve, can he? So maybe all this is in your own mind, Faith. Maybe I'm a boozer, but maybe you're just fucking delusional!"

"Sean, you have to understand. Smith—Sanborn— is a master manipulator. He can—"

"Make people commit murder and not even know why they're doing it? Come on, think, Faith! Think about how idiotic that is!"

"This is what he wants. This is part of what Smith

was trying to do. He's destroying us. He wants me to pay—"

"Oh, bullshit!" Sean shouted. "Spare me your goddamn conspiracy theories! You've lived with that Department Thirty crap for so long that now you're believing it yourself, that it's in your own life. Somehow you've figured that your own brother is a cold-blooded killer." Sean tapped his chest with his fist. "I didn't kill Daryn, obsession or not. I don't care what the fucking evidence says, and I don't care what *you* say. Not anymore."

Faith's cell phone rang.

"Better get that," Sean said, the bitterness thick in his voice. "You know how important you are."

The phone rang again.

Sean turned and walked down the hill, toward the border.

"Sean!" Faith shouted.

Sean kept walking, closer and closer to the port of entry.

Faith took a step, willing her mind to clear. *I can't think, I can't think . . .*

Only a handful of people had the number of the Kimberly Diamond cell phone. Finally, she pulled the phone out of her fanny pack and looked at the caller ID. She didn't recognize the number right away, but it was area code 405. Oklahoma.

Sean drew closer to the border. He was leaving her, leaving everything, walking away.

She knew he would have been defenseless in the face of Isaac Smith's machinations and Daryn McDermott's seductive powers. She'd tried to tell him she understood. Had she actually said the words? Suddenly Faith couldn't remember, and suddenly it seemed very important.

She flipped open the phone, watching her brother grow smaller. "Yes?"

"Faith? It's Rob Cain."

"Yes, Rob?"

"Scott was found dead in his condo last night." A long pause. "But you knew that already, didn't you?"

Faith said nothing.

"Your message," Cain said. "I didn't understand it, until—"

"What do you have?"

"Where are you, Faith?"

Faith was silent for a long moment, then said again, "What do you have?"

"The autopsy results from Daryn McDermott. Now I know why it took so long to get the report. They had to be one hundred percent certain of what they were looking at."

"Yes?"

She listened to him for two minutes, to his crisp, professional explanation. When he finished, her hands were shaking as she put the phone away. The last pieces of the puzzle fell into place.

Ahead of her, Sean stepped across the border and into Mexico.

"No!" she shouted. "Sean!"

Faith broke into a run. As she ran down the hill, she realized she was still carrying a gun in her fanny pack, and she knew that if she carried it into Mexico, she might never see the U.S. again. She had nothing identifying her as an employee of the Department of Justice, nothing to justify carrying a firearm across the border.

Without breaking stride, she unsnapped the fanny pack and flung it to the side of the road.

"Sean, wait!"

Sean was a few steps beyond the border now. On the Mexico side, the road wasn't paved but loose gravel. He was heading up a small hill toward a building that presumably served as the Mexican mirror of the port of entry.

He turned back to look at her. "Go back, Faith! You don't have any jurisdiction over here!"

Faith ran. The door to the building on the American side opened. The guard named Mike stepped out. On the other side of the road, from the booth on the northbound side, a female officer was watching her.

"Hey!" Mike shouted.

"Go back!" Sean said.

American citizens didn't have to show any kind of documentation to enter Mexico. They didn't have to stop, didn't have to answer questions, could simply walk or drive across the border and enter the other country. Faith pounded down the pavement, cursing the stiff boots and wishing she had her Reeboks instead.

A few more steps and she would be there.

"Hold it!" Mike shouted. "I want to talk to you! Hey, woman! Stop!"

Ten more steps. Sean had stopped and was staring

at her in disbelief, as if he couldn't believe his sister was crazy enough to follow him into a foreign country.

Five steps.

She heard Mike unsnapping his holster again.

You can't shoot me, Faith thought absurdly. *I work for Department Thirty.*

Then she realized: *Sean was right. This job has changed me into something I don't even recognize.*

She stepped into Mexico, felt the ground change from blacktop to gravel.

"Are you out of your mind?" Sean said.

Behind them, Faith heard Mike talking on the phone.

"You're going to get us both arrested or killed," Sean said. He was twenty steps away from her.

"You have to come back with me," Faith said.

"No, I don't." Her brother turned away. "Go back, Faith. You and I don't know each other anyway. Tell Mom and Dad something, I don't care what."

"Listen to me, Sean—"

"No, I won't listen to you!" Sean kept walking, right in the middle of the road. No traffic came or went.

At the top of the hill, two Mexican men appeared at the edge of the small white building.

Faith kept running at full speed and tackled her brother around the waist. She squeezed his stomach and felt the air go out of him.

"Shit!" he cried, and rolled over, kicking at her.

Faith held on, sliding down his body, even when his foot connected with her face. Thankfully he was wearing soft-soled shoes.

"Let go! Goddammit, Faith, you're insane! Let go of me!"

"No," Faith breathed. They rolled over. She tasted gravel.

Sean scissored both legs back and forth, finally shaking loose of her grip. He stumbled, but managed to get to his feet. The two Mexican border guards began to hurry toward them.

Faith doubled over. "You have to come back with me."

"To hell with you, Faith, and everything you stand for."

Faith absorbed the words like a slap, shaking her head violently.

"I know what happened, Sean," she said, and surprised herself by how steady her voice had become. "That call . . . I know what happened."

"What the hell are you talking about?"

"I know you didn't murder Daryn McDermott."

The Mexican guards were closing. "*No te muevas!*" one of them shouted. *Don't move!*

Sean went still. "How—"

"This wasn't a murder," Faith said. "Daryn McDermott committed suicide."

36

THE MEXICAN GUARDS SEARCHED THEM AND, FIND-
ing no contraband, escorted them back to the port of
entry, requesting that they leave Mexico for "creating a
public disturbance."

They declared their American citizenship at the border and were admitted back to United States soil. Mike
met them as soon as they'd made their declaration and
walked them into the building. Sean did most of the
talking, assuring Mike it truly was nothing but a family
squabble. Never mind that it had spilled over into another country and created an incident at the border.

"Irish, you don't want to be doing stuff like this,"
Mike said. "I believe you're in enough trouble already."

Sean assured him they were leaving the border now,
and they did. They walked back to the cantina, looking
at Faith's Miata and the huge Suburban next to it.

"You drove that?" Sean said. "You *have* changed."

They followed each other back to Tucson, to the airport, where Faith turned in the Suburban to the rental
agency and they left the Miata in the long-term parking area.

They caught a Southwest flight, traveling as Kimberly Diamond and Michael Sullivan, and settled in.
Sean peppered Faith with questions, but she'd gone to

the place where nothing and no one could reach her.

"Trust me," she said.

She dozed off and on for the entire flight, and Sean drank three beers in rapid succession. He thought she was deeply asleep, but Faith heard him order the beer from the flight attendant. She decided against saying anything about it. They'd said enough to each other.

She thought back to what Rob Cain had told her. It all made a sort of sense now. A convoluted sense, to be sure, but now she knew where the pieces fit together.

And she knew that for all the lives that had been shattered, for all the people who had been destroyed, for the families who had been devastated, it had all been about two people: Isaac Smith and Faith Kelly.

Faith felt her rage, and this time, she wasn't sure she could control it. What frightened her more was the fact that she wasn't sure she wanted to.

They landed in Oklahoma City in the late afternoon. After only one day in the desert, the air of the plains seemed thick and humid to Faith. The sky seemed to be split: over the airport in south Oklahoma City, it was a dazzling blue with few clouds. To the north, it was gray and overcast with storm clouds building.

"Where are we going?" Sean asked as Faith rented another SUV.

"You told me he said the Coalition was going to regroup at Mulhall," Faith said.

"But didn't you already check there? You said the house was empty except for some homeless guy."

"But now I wonder," Faith said. "I think that homeless guy may have been one of Smith's people, one of your Coalition people. I think that somehow Smith hurriedly cleaned out the house so it would look like no one had been there, and left one person there to let him know when I came looking. He would have known I would investigate the house eventually, and he was ready. He was waiting for me."

Sean shook his head. "Now you sound like you're talking to yourself."

"Maybe I am."

"That doesn't make sense, though. He would have known that if you didn't find anything to back up Daryn's and my story about the Coalition's plans after Oklahoma, that you'd reject Daryn from Department Thirty. What was the point of having her request protection, just to be rejected?"

"Oh, it makes perfect sense," Faith said, but offered no more.

With the rush-hour traffic headed north out of the city, it took them nearly an hour to reach the exit for Guthrie. Sean showed Faith the route he had taken when he drove Daryn and Britt there the first time, passing over the Cimarron River and Skeleton Creek into Mulhall.

By the time they passed through the town and found the turn at the north end, the sky was almost black and the wind had begun whistling from the northwest. A few fat drops of rain smacked the windshield. Faith stopped at the foot of the rutted driveway and reached across Sean into the glove compartment.

She took out the fanny pack, the same one she'd retrieved from where she'd dropped it near the border in Sasabe. She unzipped it and checked the load in her Glock. There was no safety on this model. It was ready to fire.

Faith didn't try to hide their approach at all. She didn't leave the SUV down the driveway from the farmhouse. She drove right up to the clearing and parked next to the dark luxury sedan there.

"Bastard," she said, looking at the car.

With Sean beside her, she moved up the steps. She remembered which one creaked, and stepped especially hard on it. She wanted him to hear her. She wanted him to know she was here, and that the game was over.

She hauled open the screen door, the one that had flapped in the wind and startled her the first time she came here.

Nothing would startle her this time.

Faith twisted the doorknob and stepped into the house.

The man sat in an old bentwood rocking chair with a wicker seat. He was rocking back and forth, a book in his hands.

"Bravo," Isaac Smith said. "It actually took you less time than I thought it would. I suspect it was difficult to convince your brother to come back with you. I wasn't betting you'd be able to do that part. I should never underestimate you, should I?"

He looked the same as he always had: a few years older than Faith, completely unassuming, of medium height and build, dressed in a way that would let him blend into the wallpaper. But then, that was the idea. The focus was never to be on Smith himself, but on what he could *do*.

"Sanborn," Sean said.

"Agent Kelly," Smith said. "Or Mr. Sullivan, if you prefer. Please, let's avoid confusion. Your sister knows me best as Isaac Smith. Let's stick with that, shall we?"

"Why?" Sean said. "For Christ's sake, why? Why all this?"

"Your sister knows," Smith said.

Faith slowly drew her gun from behind her back, placing it where Smith could see it. "Like I told you in Arizona, Sean, it was all about Smith and me. Everything that happened, happened so he could do to me what he did to so many others. I deprived him of being able to play his games with others, so he decided he'd play them with me." She shook her head. "Didn't you read the fine print when Yorkton promised you a new life under Department Thirty?"

"Indeed I did. There was all kinds of legalistic nonsense about adhering to the letter and spirit of the law, not breaking the law or conspiring with others to break the law, et cetera, ad nauseum. I remember it well."

"But it didn't apply to you."

Smith shrugged. "This was personal." He smiled, and Faith wanted to take the gun and smash his face in.

"You see, Sean," Faith said, "this man had just pulled off something major, something amazing. He reached back more than a century to an obscure frontier massacre and used it to bring down a Supreme Court justice. He destroyed God only knows how many people along the way. My friend Alex Bridge was very nearly one of them. But I stopped him."

"No, you didn't," Smith said. "The justice still fell, didn't he?"

"And so did you. I should have killed you on those rocks in Galveston Bay, but my boss had other ideas. So you got a new identity and spilled what you knew about your previous jobs. Where did they send you, by the way? Who are you now?"

"Do you think that matters?" Smith said. "You have no idea how many identities I can create for myself. My 'relocation' has been a minor inconvenience. The only loose thread has been you, and now you've been tied up nicely."

"Indiana, was that it?" Faith said, ignoring the jab.

"Evansville. Lovely country, right along the Ohio River. I'm a software trainer named David Corcoran. I've had the flexibility to travel, which was very important in bringing my plans together."

Thunder cracked outside. Faith heard rain blowing against the windows of the old house.

"So it's true," Sean said. He'd begun to circle around to the side of Smith's rocking chair. "You really did all of this to get revenge on my sister."

"Revenge? Oh, don't be simpleminded. Revenge is so banal. No, this was a lesson to be taught."

Sean shook his head. "You prick. What did you do to Daryn? How did you get her tied up in this scheme?"

"That was quite easy, actually," Smith said. "I simply

had to be patient and keep my eyes open. Her agenda was no secret. She'd been very public about it. She wanted to get at her father and score her own political points. She offered herself to The Cause." He spoke the last two words in a grand, mocking tone. He glanced at Faith. "But you know that now, don't you?"

"Faith?" Sean said.

Faith looked at her brother. "Remember what I said, that Daryn had committed suicide? Maybe someone else pulled the trigger, maybe someone else put the rope around her neck and lifted her into that tree, but it was suicide, all right."

"I don't understand," Sean said.

"Daryn was dying," Faith said.

Smith smiled.

"At first I couldn't explain it," Faith said. "I simply thought she was dangerous, maybe sociopathic. Her behavior was so erratic—intellectual and articulate one minute, vulgar and profane the next. Plus the headaches. She had those terrible headaches, and they got worse and worse as time went on. That should have been a giveaway, but then, I wasn't looking for it."

"What are you saying?" Sean demanded.

"Daryn had a glioblastoma multiforme lodged on her frontal lobe."

"A brain tumor," Smith added. "Completely inoperable. She would have been dead in another three months." He spread his hands apart. "So she offered herself for The Cause, to be used in whatever way would serve her agenda the best. She rather liked the idea of being a martyr, instead of dying at twenty-four from some useless cancer. This way, she would die for something 'greater than herself.' Or so she believed."

"I don't believe you," Sean said. "Daryn was willing to let herself be killed so you could get to Faith?"

"Well, of course, Daryn didn't know my true motivations. As far as she knew, I was Franklin Sanborn, professor of communication, and shared her agenda for social and political change. But yes, Agent Kelly, she put her life in my hands. She was about to lose it anyway, and she was already growing weaker. You saw that, didn't you?"

Sean appeared to agonize. He clenched his fists at his sides. "After the bomb, down on Main Street after the car crashed into the wall, you had the gun on Daryn. You said something about a moment of pain, then no more pain at all, and something about how she'd probably enjoy that. I didn't know what you meant."

Smith smiled. "Observant, much like your sister. It must be a family trait."

Thunder cracked again. Faith saw a cloud-to-cloud lightning flash through the side window. The clouds seemed lower, a solid wall of them across the dark sky.

"But I still don't understand," Sean said. "She knew then that you were going to kill her? You'd already set this up. Why go through all of that?"

"From the moment you met Tobias Owens in Sasabe, everything was an illusion, Sean. Nothing you saw or heard or felt or did was real. Any interaction you saw between Daryn and myself was for your benefit, to continue the illusion. Tobias Owens wasn't even real. He, of course, was not Senator McDermott's counsel. He was an ambulance chaser from Phoenix who had no scruples and wanted a fast buck. See where it got him."

"He's right," Faith said. "None of it was real. He used Daryn and you to get to me, to devastate me in every way imaginable. I had to watch my own brother falling apart, and it twisted me to the point that I suspected him of murder. Sean, she very carefully drew you in. You thought you were getting close to her so you could convince her to go home. But she knew who you were all the time. That was the whole point. She even got you to participate in her Coalition."

"But why me?" Sean said. "You couldn't know that I was going to screw up at work and be so desperate that I'd go along with Owens."

"Oh, no," Smith said. "You did that all by yourself. I'd identified you long ago as your sister's biggest weakness. I saw what you were doing to yourself and knew it was only a matter of time until something happened that pushed you over the edge. I just had to hope that Daryn lived long enough to do her part."

"How could you know?"

Smith looked at Sean as if he were a child who didn't comprehend the day's math lesson. "I watched you, of course. Just as I did your parents, at various times. Family ties can almost always be used against a person. You're the living proof of it."

Faith stared at Smith in disbelief. "You believed Sean was *my* biggest weakness?"

"Of course. And in exploiting *his* weakness, I exploited

yours at the same time. It was a simple and beautiful plan, and it worked beyond my wildest expectations."

Sean put his hands to his head, as if it were about to burst. "All of this . . . the attacks on the banks. That whole business with Daryn being angry at you for wanting to use explosives . . . that was staged? I mean, you slapped her. You—"

"It was good theater," Smith said, crossing his legs at the ankle. "Remember, *everything* was staged. The two men who broke into Daryn's apartment while you were there with her? The ones who ran you off the road? The incidents were created to form a bond between the two of you, to put you on the run, to put you in a position to come here, to be dependent on each other."

Faith brought the gun up in her hand. She pointed at Smith with it, coming closer to the rocking chair. "All of it was designed to make Sean—and eventually, me—believe that Daryn McDermott was part of this radical group, but that it had become too radical for her and she wanted out. You'd chosen Sean very carefully, exploited his alcohol weakness, made sure he and Daryn got to be mutually dependent on each other. Then you even went so far as to stage a real attack—one that actually killed innocent people. You thought nothing of killing a two-year-old child in order to dress the stage. Then, after Sean brought me into it and asked for Department Thirty to protect Daryn, you yanked the rug out from under it."

"Erase all evidence," Smith said, sweeping a hand around the room. "Then you would have to cut Daryn loose. Tell her she was rejected. Send her back out into the world, where she was afraid of Franklin Sanborn."

Understanding gradually crept onto Sean's face. "And then kill her. Faith and Department Thirty would get the blame."

"Senator McDermott did a fine job reading his daughter's impassioned letter on national television," Smith said. "There she was, at the eleventh hour, trying to be reconciled to her father, only hours before her death. Now Department Thirty has been taken to the public, and so has its renowned Officer Kelly. McDermott can rant and rave about a federal government department out of control, a department that could have protected his darling daughter from terrorists, but chose not to. *And look what happened to her!* Your department will be dismantled. There will be Congressional hearings, and you'll be the star witness. How's our mutual friend, Director Conway, handling all this, by the way?"

Faith had to think for a moment, that Conway equaled Yorkton. "He can take care of himself, and the department," she said. "You might be surprised."

"It'll take a lot for you and the department to overcome this," Smith said. "But it won't matter to me. I'll be gone. I already have my next identities in place. No more David Corcoran of Evansville, Indiana. I hate to leave Franklin Sanborn behind, though. I wondered when you would make *that* connection."

Faith felt a chill. She had never before felt that she could simply raise her weapon and destroy another human being. The man she had killed two years ago had been purely self-defense. He'd shot at her, and at others, and she'd simply shot back. This was different. Smith was, as far as she could tell, unarmed. She recalled that he usually preferred to stay away from weapons himself, leaving actual violence to his "subcontractors." It would be easy to simply erase him from the face of the earth.

She raised the gun. She took aim at a spot on his chest.

Smith acted as if he didn't have a gun aimed at him from less than five feet away. "But all of this, for all its beauty, wasn't the coup de grace. You watched your brother's destruction, saw a girl that you could have protected be killed, and saw the famous Department Thirty veil of secrecy peeled away on national television. Were you writhing in pain by then, Officer Kelly? I know how tough you can be, or think you can be, so I added an afterthought. It had taken you so long to develop the affair with Special Agent Hendler. It's very hard for you to commit, isn't it? You were never sure, and still he patiently waited for you. He was patient to the end, wasn't he? Waiting for you to show up at his condominium. If you'd come a little sooner, you might have saved him. Don't you think so?"

Faith began to circle the chair. It was the only furniture in the room, the only thing to break up the emptiness. "I will kill you right now," she said. "This isn't about Department Thirty or Daryn or anything else. It's only about you and about me. And you finally pushed too far. When you killed Scott, made him get on his knees and shot him, that was it. You've taken everything I have, and I'm going to return the favor."

Faith heard a low rumbling from outside, growing louder.

"Was he on his knees?" Smith said, following Faith with his eyes. "What a clever touch. Go ahead, shoot me. Send me straight to hell, not that I believe in such a thing. It won't change the fact that your life is gone. You have nowhere to go, nothing to do. Everything you've worked for is in ruins. *Everything*. Killing me won't bring any of it back. It just seals your own fate. So go ahead."

"Wait a minute," Sean said, his voice rising above the storm. "You didn't know he was on his knees? You didn't shoot Hendler? What about Daryn?"

"Oh, no," Smith said. "I didn't assist Daryn in her exit from this life. I avoid bloodshed if at all possible."

"Then if you didn't do it," Sean said, "who did?"

"I did."

Faith and Sean turned at the voice. Britt slowly descended the stairs into the living room.

37

THE TALL GIRL WITH THE STRINGY HAIR AND THE
muscular build came down one step at a time, walking
very slowly, cradling a sawed-off shotgun in her arms.

"I know how to use this," she said. "Don't think I
don't. You." She gestured at Faith. "Drop it or I'll blow
a great big hole in you."

Faith backed away from Smith. "Who are you?"

Britt looked at Sean. "*You* know who I am."

"You were Daryn's friend," Sean said.

"What else?" Britt prodded.

"You loved her."

Britt nodded as if satisfied. "You never did, that's for
sure. After you came along, she wanted you all the
time and she didn't want me so much anymore. She
said it would be that way for a while. I thought it was
all for The Cause."

Faith still hadn't dropped the Glock. "You . . . you
loved Daryn McDermott?"

"I said drop it," Britt said. "You think I'm nothing
but a stupid whore? Well, I'm not. I'm worth more
than any of you. Daryn showed me that I could be
more. Now *drop the gun!*"

Faith bent over and gently put the pistol on the
floor.

"You knew," Sean said. "You knew about the tumor."

Britt nodded. "She already had it when she came to Oklahoma City the first time. The doctors had just told her a couple of weeks before she left on her tour. She told me she'd be coming back, that she'd come back for me, that she had a plan. She told me about Sanborn." She glanced at Sean. "She told me about you, too, that you'd be coming, and what to tell you when you got there."

"When I found you at the motel," Sean said, "you already knew. It was all part of the plan, for you to tell me about Daryn becoming an escort named Kat Hall, and how to find her. Even then—" He looked ill.

"As I told you," Smith said, "everything from the moment you met Owens was part of the illusion. Go ahead, Britt. Tell the rest."

"Daryn asked me . . . when the time came . . . if I would do it for her. She wanted me to."

Sean's hands were shaking badly. "I just remembered something. You told me you wanted to take her pain away. Out there on the deck, the first day we were here."

Britt reached the foot of the stairs. "I did. I took away all her pain. She told me everything she wanted me to do. She told me to listen to Sanborn after she was gone, that listening to him would be just like listening to her."

"So that day downtown," Sean said, "you took my Jeep so you could implicate me in Daryn's murder. I'd left my gun here in the house. You took it, you used it to kill Daryn, and left it along with her bloodstains in the Jeep."

Britt nodded. "Uh-huh. She called me that night, after she'd done you one last time, so your come would be inside her. She wrote her dad a letter, all about The Cause. Then she called me. I took away her pain."

"But why put her in the tree?" Sean said.

"That was to make people pay attention. And they did, didn't they?"

"You put her there yourself?"

Britt nodded with a perverse pride. "Sanborn had already timed the security guard, to see how long he took on his rounds. I had twenty-five minutes. I'd already taken Daryn's pain. She'd kissed me and thanked me before I did it. But I think she was scared too, at the very end. It was one thing to come up with an idea, and another to actually know someone was going to shoot you. But I told her I loved her before I pulled the trigger. I think that helped her. I think she was at peace."

"The tree," Sanborn prompted, as if he were bored.

"Right," Britt said. "I'm strong, and Daryn was a tiny little thing. I put the rope around her neck while we were still in the car, put her over my shoulder, and carried her to the tree. It was the middle of the night— there was no one around, just the guard, and he was on the other side. I lifted Daryn up, let her feet dangle, and wrapped the other end of the rope around the tree. Then I just drove away. I even had seven minutes to spare. I took the Jeep and parked it at Southeast

High School. That's not far from where I work. I knew someone would find it there. Then I walked up the street to the Oasis, back to my regular room."

Smith clapped his hands together. "You've done well, Britt. And we haven't even discussed Special Agent Hendler."

"Oh, he was easy. Just like you told me, I followed him from the place where I left the Jeep, all the way to his place. I waited a few minutes, then knocked on his door. I told him I was a friend of Daryn's, and I knew things. He let me in. I guess he didn't expect me to have a gun, since I'm a girl. People never think I can do things, but I always surprise them. He had me come into his little office room. Before I even went in the door, I pointed my gun at him, told him to get on his knees. He didn't want to, but I told him that if he didn't, we were going to kill his girlfriend next." She looked at Smith. "I came up with that part myself. And then I just shot him. I knew Daryn wanted me to. He was with the FBI . . . he was part of the ruling class."

Faith closed her eyes. Scott Hendler had died on his knees, because he thought that in doing so he might be able to save her. He could have gone for his own gun, could have disarmed Britt, but he was thinking of her. In his last seconds, he was thinking of Faith.

"Very good, Britt," Smith said. "Now let's finish this." He turned to Sean.

The storm roared outside. Somewhere very far away, Faith thought she heard a siren. The rumbling outside increased. It sounded like a freight train, amplified many times over.

"Remember how he betrayed Daryn?" Smith said to Britt. He nodded toward Sean. "He never cared about The Cause, never cared about Daryn or about you. He was in it for money. He came to take Daryn back to her father."

Britt swung the nose of the shotgun toward Sean.

"No!" Faith screamed.

Sean took a step toward the foot of the stairs, where Britt stood. His voice became eerily calm. "If you're going to shoot anyone, Britt, shoot him. He's a user. You heard everything he said. He only did all this to get even with my sister."

The nose of the shotgun drooped a couple of inches.

"That's right," Sean said. "Do you think he cared about your Cause? He was selfish, the whole time. It was all about him and my sister. It was never about you or Daryn or me or any of the other Coalition people. He probably hired them, gave them money to play parts here, just like actors."

Smith smiled and slowly stood from the chair. "Very perceptive. But Daryn trusted me, Britt." He spoke very slowly, very deliberately. "And that means you should trust me. You remember what she said, don't you? Listen to me as if you were listening to her. Shoot him, Britt."

"He's just another man who used you," Sean said. "Just like all your customers, Britt. All he's done was use you, from the beginning. I cared about Daryn. Maybe I didn't understand her, but I cared. I wanted to be with her . . . by the end, that was all that mattered to me, being with her."

Panic and confusion painted Britt's face. The shotgun drooped further. "I don't—"

"Shoot him and be done with it!" Smith shouted, showing the first signs of impatience.

Faith had been moving slowly during the exchange between the other three, inching with her feet toward the Glock on the floor. Outside, the storm had built to a scream.

She went into a dive, her arms outstretched. She got her hands around the pistol.

"Shoot him!" Sean said.

"Britt!" Smith shouted. "Remember what Daryn said!"

Britt screamed, an agonized wail. Faith froze, her eyes locked onto the window. A grayish white funnel-shaped cloud had descended from the sky and was churning up the ground, on a collision course with the house.

Tornado.

The scourge of Oklahoma in spring, they were intense storms with winds stronger than any hurricane, and they struck with much less warning. The cloud looked almost like it was dancing, its tail swaying back and forth. A tree in its path suddenly disappeared. Debris swirled around it and inside it.

"Sean!" Faith screamed.

They all turned. For an instant, Faith saw something cross Smith's face that she never expected to see—uncertainty, *fear*.

Thunder, a lightning flash outside, and the interior lights went out.

There was a scream from the stairs—Britt.

The tornado danced across the plains. A window blew out.

"Is there a basement? A cellar?" Faith yelled at Sean.

"The kitchen!" her brother shouted back.

Each moved in the dark toward where the other had been standing. Faith and Sean found each other, and they clasped hands, just like when they were children and something scared them both. And just like then, Sean led the way, pulling Faith toward the kitchen.

More windows exploded. "Here!" Sean shouted, but couldn't say more because of the deafening din of the storm.

He kicked open a wooden door in the kitchen. It led into blackness. An earthy smell drifted up to them.

Faith glanced up at the kitchen window. The funnel filled her line of vision. She screamed wordlessly.

She caught a glimpse of her brother, half-turned away from her. Then his hand was ripped from hers and she felt herself falling through the doorway. Her foot caught on something. She felt bones snapping, as her foot tried to go a different direction from the rest of her body. After a moment of blinding pain, she was falling again. Then, over the roar of the storm, she heard the boom of the shotgun. She thought she heard Sean's voice one last time, and then everything was dark and silent.

38

FAITH AWOKE SLOWLY, TO THE SMELL OF WET earth all around her. She was lying on her left side, and that entire side of her body was damp. One arm was curled under her. Her hair felt matted. There was no sound whatsoever. She remembered how loud the tornado had been, and the quiet now seemed unnatural, unreal.

She didn't move, waiting for her eyes to adjust. Gradually, objects took shape in the darkness. The kitchen door that Sean had pushed her through seemed to have led down to an unfinished, dirt-floored basement. She saw lumber, paint buckets, cans of food. Surely she must be dreaming—she was in a muddy basement surrounded by cans of green beans and chicken soup.

She sat up. Directly ahead of her was the staircase, except it wasn't a staircase. She began to see that it was a folding wooden ladder. That explained how she'd snagged her foot between the steps—there was an open space between each rung.

Bracing herself with her hands on the muddy floor, she got to her feet. Millions of shards of red-hot broken glass stabbed both her feet. She screamed wordlessly and collapsed again.

She sat on the floor, breathing hard, until the pain receded a bit.

Okay, so one foot is broken. I remember that. And the other one—who knows? But I can't stay down here. I have to find Sean. And what about Smith and the girl, Britt?

She rolled onto hands and knees, trying to keep her weight away from her feet. She grew dizzy and nauseous and collapsed again.

There was a small shaft of light entering the basement from the doorway above. Faith very carefully maneuvered her body so that both feet, still wearing the gray boots Hendler had given her, were in the light. The right one was at an odd angle to the rest of her leg—she'd felt it snap on the way down. The left foot was at yet another angle still. She hadn't felt it break—she must have landed on it and her body's weight twisted it.

Okay, so both feet are broken. Still can't stay down here.

She rolled over again, fighting the tide of nausea. She stayed still until it abated, then crawled a couple of steps, using only her arms and upper body, essentially dragging the lower half of her body behind her.

The pain lanced her again, and tears formed. She struggled against the pain and dragged herself a little farther. More pain, more reflexive tears. She was breathing hard, and she made herself do some breathing exercises, the ones Alex had taught her. In sixty seconds her breath was under control, her mind focused and centered.

She dragged herself to the ladder—the one that had broken one of her feet, she reminded herself. She leaned an arm against it, resting from her trek across the muddy basement floor. Mud caked her arms up to the elbows, and the front of her tank top had the mud completely ground into it.

Now came the hard part—climbing. She'd known people who were rock climbers, who knew all about how to use their upper bodies to pull themselves up. Faith's fitness had always been attuned to the lower half of her body. She took a moment to reflect that she had rarely found her running useful in real life. Fat lot of good all those miles and marathons did her now, with two useless feet dangling at the ends of her legs.

Move your ass, Faith. Get yourself out of this hole. Your brother might need you.

She reached two rungs above her head, wrapped her arms around the wooden ladder, and pulled. Her feet screamed in pain. Faith bit her lip.

One rung at a time.

Her body moved a few inches.

Next rung.

A few inches more.

And so it went. She had no idea how long it took her, rung after excruciating rung of the ladder

By the time she reached the top, there was very little light. Her arms exhausted and aching, she put on one last burst of strength and pulled herself over the top.

She'd heard of the capricious nature of tornadoes, but had never lived through a major one herself. There were famous stories of a tornado making its way down a street, destroying one side completely, flattening everything in its path, while the other side of the street was completely intact, nothing out of place; or about how some tornadoes "skipped" houses, plowing through a neighborhood destroying every other house, leaving the ones in between alone.

What she saw was a microcosm of the stories she'd heard. The kitchen of the old farmhouse was nothing but rubble—two floors worth of rubble. The kitchen sink was upended a few feet away from the opening that led to the basement where she'd been. A toilet wasn't far away, sitting upright but not connected to anything.

There was no wall. The southern wall was simply gone, whisked off the house's foundation. Bricks and lumber were everywhere, housing fixtures no longer recognizable. Faith looked to the left, back toward the living room where she and Sean had found Isaac Smith.

The east wall—the front of the house—was still there and completely intact, standing as if in silent protest against the storm that dared to threaten this place. The north wall, at Faith's back, was standing, but with giant gaping holes. Now that the storm had passed, there was a bit of natural light in the early evening, a tiny bit of sunlight peeking into the ruined house. Faith could see Isaac Smith's rocking chair, sitting upright without a scratch on it, right where it had been.

She cleared her throat. "Sean?" she called. "Sean, are you here?"

Now that she was out of the hole, Faith began to hear sounds. A bit of wind, dripping water, and strangely, birds singing.

Something made a noise to her left, in the direction

of the living room. Faith dragged herself a few feet, but it was even slower going than coming out of the hole, as she had to clear a trail through the debris, using her hands the way a swimmer parts the water ahead. Periodically one of her feet would glance off something—a brick, a piece of lumber—and pain would shoot from her toes all the way up to her neck, stopping her in her tracks.

Still she dragged herself forward. She heard the noise again.

Someone else was alive in here.

Faith blinked against pain and rage, trying to remember the last seconds before she and Sean had clasped hands and he had directed her toward the basement. Britt had been standing on the stairs, aiming the shotgun. Smith was urging her to shoot Sean, Sean had told her to shoot Smith instead, and Faith had dived across the floor for her Glock. Britt had looked confused, doubtful, panicked, as if things weren't as black and white as she'd imagined them to be.

The lights had gone out. They'd found each other and Sean had taken her to the basement door, then practically pushed her through it. He'd turned away from her. She fell. The shotgun roared. The tornado slammed into the house.

Britt had shot *someone.*

Faith's heart began to hammer. "Please, God," she whispered. "Please, please, please."

There was the sound again, someone moving.

Faith dragged herself past the rocking chair, in the direction of the stairs, or at least where the stairs had been. The second floor had collapsed on that side of the house, tons of rubble on the floor. But again, it was surreal in that there were places where Faith could see the actual floor, areas where there was no rubble at all.

Where the stairway should have been, she saw a pair of bare feet sticking out from under some debris. She made her way toward them, her heart still triple-timing.

Dammit, why can't I go any faster?

Who did Britt shoot? Faith thought as she moved, the thoughts torturing her.

"Please," she said again, her voice a rasp.

She froze when she saw the bright red nail polish on the feet.

She pulled herself next to the body and managed to raise herself into a sitting position. Her arms felt nearly as useless as her feet now, from dragging her dead weight all the way through the ruined house.

The lower half of Britt's body was buried in rubble, only her feet visible. Her torso and arms were intact. One hand was still wrapped around the shotgun, her red-nailed hand curled around the trigger. The back of her head was gone, blood and brain tissue sprayed on what was left of the wall behind her. The barrel of the gun was still in her mouth.

"Oh God," Faith muttered. She lowered her head to her hands and wept.

She cried not just for the destruction of this young girl, but for the destruction—in a very different way— of her own brother, of her own family. She wept for the way Daryn McDermott had been used. She'd been a willing vehicle, and it all came down to an elaborate and spectacular suicide for her, but she'd still been used. And she wept for the hole ripped in her own existence by Scott Hendler's murder. Faith cried and cried and cried, becoming oblivious to the external pain, blinded by the pain inside.

"They were cowards," Smith's voice said.

He stepped out of the small closet that had been beside the stairs. The stairs were gone, but the closet enclosure still stood. He'd found the only other safe place in the house. His left arm hung bloodied and limp by his side. His shirt was ripped, a collection of rags. There was blood on his face.

Faith could barely find her voice. "What?" she said.

"Britt and your brother," Smith said, and his voice sounded very far away, as if he were at the bottom of a well. "The stupid girl, she couldn't figure out which one of us to trust, so ultimately she trusted no one, not even herself. A lesson of the streets, I would presume."

"Sean," Faith croaked.

"He turned out to be a coward as well. He turned and ran. He pushed you into the basement, then took a giant leap out the back door. I'm afraid I wasn't able to see what happened to him from there. I suspect he's buried under a few tons of this house, don't you?"

"You . . . *bastard*."

Smith bent over and picked up a brick in his good hand. He started toward Faith.

"Name calling doesn't suit you, Officer Kelly," he said. "It is down to you, and it is down to me now. The way it should be. Can't run, can you?"

Smith took a few more steps. Faith pushed herself away from Britt, but there was nowhere to go. Britt's body and the front wall blocked her on one side and behind, debris on the other. Smith was directly in front of her.

Faith couldn't make herself speak. She began digging at the pile of rubble beside her.

"Think you can tunnel through it in the next five seconds?" Smith taunted. "No, no, no. Never happen."

He knelt beside Faith's legs and dropped his voice to a whisper. "As long as I'm alive, you'll never have peace, Officer Kelly. I've done everything I could to you in this round of the game. Nothing about your life is what it was. And now I'll simply disappear. I'll gather up a few personal belongings and I'll just go away. I already have my identities in place. You know that, don't you? Your friend Yorkton won't find me. No one will find me, because I don't exist. I'm John Brown's Body, remember?"

Faith remembered his DOJ code name, the moniker that had been given to Smith before they unearthed his real identity last year. She nodded, still scrabbling with the debris.

"I win," Smith whispered, raised the brick over his head, and brought it down on Faith's left foot.

Faith screamed in unimaginable agony as the pain rocketed through her. She saw him raise the brick again, saw it coming down toward her right foot.

Mercifully, Faith passed out.

39

FAITH DIDN'T REMEMBER THE ARRIVAL OF THE Logan County Fire and Rescue squad, nor did she remember talking to the sheriff's deputy about the young woman with the back of her head blown off in the ruins of the house. She didn't recall the MedEvac helicopter, or her arrival at the University of Oklahoma Medical Center trauma facility. Incongruous with everything else, she vaguely recalled music, something light and feathery. A flute, perhaps.

When she awoke, she was in a hospital room, and the lights were very bright. She saw IV lines, and both her feet were propped up. She turned her head and saw her friend Alex Bridge sitting beside her bed.

Alex was thirty-one, half Comanche, with the high cheekbones and deep dark eyes common to Native Americans. Her hair was short, dark, and straight, though she'd highlighted it with red and blond streaks. She wore jeans and sandals and a Kerrville Folk Festival T-shirt and held a wooden flute in her hands. Faith could see the tattoo on her upper arm, a crown of thorns intertwined with roses and crosses.

Faith stared at her, as if she weren't quite sure Alex was real. She put out a hand.

Alex clasped her hand, putting her flute aside. "Hey, Faith Siobhan. Man, you Irish redheads are tough."

Faith coughed. She didn't trust her voice.

"Don't," Alex said. "You're going to be okay, but it may be a while before your next marathon."

"Sean?" Faith managed to say.

"He wasn't there. Your brother wasn't there, Faith. They were digging all night. The rescuers dug through tons of debris, they scoured that house and the whole countryside. Your brother's body wasn't found. He may have made it out. While you were delirious, you kept asking for him . . . talking to him."

Faith nodded. "He saved me. Pushed me down into the basement."

Alex squeezed her hand. "They found a girl there, too. Her name was Brittany Ray. She was twenty-one."

Faith closed her eyes. She nodded again.

Alex let go of her hand. Her voice changed. "You mentioned Smith, while you were delirious. Was it . . ."

Faith nodded a third time. Alex had been one of Smith's victims last year. One of the personas he'd adopted for that "job" had been that of Alex's husband. He'd fathered her child, then made her believe he'd been killed. Alex had later confronted him on the beach at Galveston, and Faith had never before or since seen the kind of courage Alex Bridge displayed then, facing down the evil that was Isaac Smith.

Alex lowered her voice. "I thought he was under protection."

Faith held her breath. She remembered Smith—*I win.*

And the bastard had walked away from Mulhall a free man.

"No," Faith whispered.

Alex leaned forward.

A plan formed in Faith's mind.

"I need a computer," she said.

"What?"

"A computer with Internet access. Can you get a laptop?"

"Mine's at home," Alex said, confused.

Faith suddenly looked alarmed. "What time is it? How long have I been here?"

"Ten hours or so. It's nearly seven in the morning."

"Where's Daniel?"

Alex smiled. Daniel was her one-year-old son. Faith had been there when he was born three months premature, and had carried him in her arms to the Neonatal Intensive Care Unit. "Don't worry. He's with my dad. He's fine. But I had to get here. I guess in your delirium, you told them to call me."

"Need that computer. I need it fast."

"Why? They won't let you use a laptop in here."

Faith lay back against the pillow. Her hair felt gritty. "Yes, they will. Smith isn't going to win."

Alex looked at her quizzically, but stood up. "Give me half an hour."

Faith was instantly asleep as soon as Alex left the room, and woke when she returned.

Alex plugged in the laptop while Faith adjusted herself on the bed. A nurse came in, looked at the clock, and said, "What's all this?"

"Business," Faith said, staring at her.

"I'm sorry, Ms. Kelly, but you can't use that in here. It will interfere with—"

Faith had Alex hand her a pen, and she scribbled a phone number on an envelope Alex had had in her purse. She handed the envelope to the nurse.

"What's this?" the nurse said.

"The phone number for a man named Yor—Conway. He'll tell you I have permission to use this laptop right here, right now, for a few minutes."

"I'm sorry, I can't let you—"

"And if you don't like him," Faith continued, "he can put you in touch with the attorney general of the United States. And if that's not good enough, you can speak to the president."

The nurse stared at the envelope with Yorkton's phone number. "I'll need to speak to the nursing supervisor."

"You do that."

Alex shook her head as the nurse left. "You tough Irish redheads."

"Just don't cross us," Faith said.

She logged onto the Internet, then using her high-level passwords, accessed the Department of Justice's massive database. She did a search using "John Brown's Body."

"What are you looking for?" Alex asked.

"The file of the people Smith destroyed before last year. The people whose lives he ruined."

"Why?"

"Do you have any more paper?"

Alex dug in her purse and handed another scrap of paper to her. "You didn't answer my question."

Faith felt suddenly alert, as if she'd been given a direct shot of adrenaline. "Smith broke the law again, so he's not eligible to stay under our protection."

"But won't he just disappear, use another one of his aliases?"

Faith nodded. "That's what he said he'd do. But if I know him like I think I do, he'll go back to where he's been living and pack up his books. Maybe nothing else, but he'll want to keep all his history books, to take them with him into his next identity."

"So? I still don't get it. It's not like you can tell the people he ruined what his new name is."

Text began to scroll across the little screen of the laptop.

"Can you?" Alex said. "Faith?"

Faith began making notes, her impulse telling her to *hurry, hurry.*

"Faith?" Alex said. "You don't have that information."

"He's so damned arrogant," Faith said. "He *told* me his new name, his new occupation, and the city where he lives."

Alex sat back. She waited a long moment, struggling with her own emotions.

"Faith," she said, and the tone made Faith look at her. "If you tell those people, someone's likely to kill him."

Faith's green eyes met Alex's dark brown ones.

"You can't," Alex said.

"Don't tell me you haven't wished him dead a thousand times."

"Yes, I have. That's not the point. You can't . . . you're an officer. And this would . . . I mean, it's not like it's self-defense, like when you chased after him on the beach last year."

Faith thought of Britt and Daryn and Scott . . . and Sean, dead or alive. She thought of Smith's words: *As long as I'm alive, you'll never have peace, Officer Kelly.*

"Yes, it is," Faith said.

EPILOGUE

A week later

THE NEWS CONFERENCE WAS IMPRESSIVE.

Senator Edward McDermott stood once again on the steps of the U.S. Capitol and once again choked back tears as he talked about his daughter.

"Because she felt she couldn't talk to me," McDermott said, "she hid from me the fact that she'd been diagnosed with an inoperable brain tumor. I didn't know until after . . ." McDermott coughed. He sniffed into the microphone. ". . . after the autopsy on her was completed. After I learned this, I was put in touch with Dr. Byron Barth at Johns Hopkins University Medical School, one of the world's leading neurologists. He told me . . . he said that with this disease, as it progressed, Daryn would have exhibited erratic behavior, and she could have experienced delusions, even hallucinations."

McDermott stood silently for a moment, his head down, before going on. "After I spoke to you last, I started looking for this Department Thirty that Daryn mentioned in the letter she wrote me the night she . . ."

McDermott's entire body shook, and he stepped

aside. His wife was nowhere to be seen, but an aide, a slim young Latino in a dark suit, stepped forward to the microphone.

"The senator conducted an investigation, and we could find no evidence that Department Thirty exists. There are no budget appropriations for such an agency, no government facilities, nothing to indicate it ever existed. It was evidently a fantasy created by Daryn's illness. Still, she reached out to her father before she died, and that's given Daryn's father and stepmother great comfort. The senator regrets any difficulty created by his earlier statements, but would like to remind the nation that he did not know of his daughter's illness, or the nature of it."

Faith tuned out the rest. She was at home, her injured feet in casts and propped on the couch. She had both crutches and a walker, but she refused to use the walker. The crutches were much more difficult to manage, but infinitely preferable.

She'd left the hospital after only two days, electing to recuperate at home. Alex looked in on her, as did her friend Nina Reeves, and various acquaintances from the Marshals Service. She had one regret—they'd buried Scott Hendler while she was still in the hospital. Scott's mother had paid her an emotional visit the day after she came home, and the two women had cried together, holding hands in Faith's living room.

At first, Faith had slept all the time. The images didn't pursue her into sleep, which was deep and dreamless. But gradually, she reached the other extreme, where she couldn't sleep at all.

Smith was right about one thing—nothing about her life was the same, and it never would be again.

Her cell phone rang. "Faith Kelly," she said into it.

"Did you still think I did it?" Sean said.

Faith sat up straight. There had been no word from him all this time. His body hadn't been found in Mulhall, and there had been no sign of him anywhere.

Faith's heart pounded. "What?" was all she could think of to say. There was static on the phone line.

"Before Britt admitted it," Sean said. "You still thought I shot Daryn, didn't you? It was suicide, but you believe I pulled the trigger."

Faith was silent a moment. "I don't know, Sean."

"Yes, you do."

"Where are you?"

"Gone. Don't look for me, at least not for a while. Here's a clue, three places I won't be: Arizona, Oklahoma, or Chicago. I leave behind all I know, and see what I can figure out. You know that's hard for me."

"I know. Are you sober?"

"Right now, this minute? Mostly. I feel like shit, though. I may drink later today, or I may not. I'm not sure. Sometimes you take it a day at a time, sometimes an hour at a time . . . and sometimes, sister, you take it one breath at a time."

They were both quiet for a long moment. "You saved my life," Faith said.

Sean let out a rush of breath. "Yeah, Daryn said the same thing to me."

The phone clicked.

The first thing Sean had said came back to her. He'd

wanted to know what she thought of him, if she'd still thought he was a killer. "Oh God," Faith said, bowed her head, and wept.

Two days later

Yorkton visited her on the first day she was back in her office.

She'd tidied up some paperwork, talked to Hal Simon, and received his assurances that Leon Bankston/Benjamin Williams was adjusting well. Simon had seemed very distant.

Yorkton knocked twice on the door, then walked into the office. They looked at each other for a moment. "Something's different in here," the director of Department Thirty said.

"The fish," Faith said. "I haven't put it back up yet."

"Are you going to?"

Faith shrugged. "Want to go for a walk?"

"Is that a joke?"

Faith pointed at the crutches. "I'm getting better with these things."

Neither of them asked where they were going. They walked across the street to the memorial, to the Survivor Tree. Daryn McDermott's blood had been cleaned from the flagstone walkway.

Faith hobbled on the crutches to the curving wall that looked out over the reflecting pool and the 168 empty chairs.

"A lot has happened," Yorkton said, joining her at the wall.

"Yes."

"Had you heard about John Brown's Body? I guess I can tell you the details now. He'd been relocated to Evansville, Indiana, and was living as a software trainer there. A few days ago, a nineteen-year-old boy walked up to him as he unlocked the door to his apartment and shot him dead, point-blank. Emptied six shots into him."

"Really?"

"Really." Yorkton was watching her closely. "The intriguing aspect is that the young man's name was Miles Hayden. His father was one of our friend John Brown's Body's 'targets,' five years ago. George Hayden was the D.C. lawyer who threw himself into Chesapeake Bay after a six-month affair with our man."

"What an irony."

"It is that. How do you suppose that young man knew what his name was, where to find him?"

Faith turned slowly toward him. "There must have been a leak somewhere."

"There must have been."

"Hypothetically, if Smith had broken the law while under departmental protection, he would have disqualified himself from the program."

Yorkton nodded. "Quite true. But hypothetically, that determination would be made by his case officer and, ultimately, by me. I've spoken to his case officer, and Vaughan knew nothing."

"How interesting," Faith said.

"Yes, it is," Yorkton said.

They were quiet for a while. It was mid-June now, a

week away from summer, and the Oklahoma days had become long and hot. Within a few minutes Faith was sweating.

"You got to McDermott," she said.

"It didn't take much convincing. And the irony is that it was true. The young woman's disease *would* have caused delusions and hallucinations. It's interesting, isn't it? The way the truth can be made to serve a lie, and vice versa."

"So it goes. And the media even left my house. Were you behind that too?"

Yorkton smiled. "Not at all. There are eighty-nine women named Faith Kelly in the state of Oklahoma. Twenty-one are here in Oklahoma City. They spent time in front of each of their homes."

Faith reached into her pocket and handed Yorkton a folded sheet of paper.

"What's this?"

"My resignation."

"I trust that's a joke."

"No, it isn't."

Yorkton tapped the folded paper against his pursed lips. "I believe we went through this last year. One doesn't just 'quit' Department Thirty. I understand you've been through quite an ordeal, and—"

"No, you don't understand. *I quit.* That's it, the long and the short of it. I'm not going to do this anymore."

"Look, Officer Kelly—"

"I'm not 'Officer' anymore. That's effective immediately, right now."

"You're not listening. You can't just quit."

"Yes, I can. You can send your goons to follow me if you want to, if they can keep up with me. But I've had enough. I watched almost everything I care about be destroyed in the last few weeks."

"But Smith is gone." Yorkton was beginning to sound desperate. "That should give you some closure."

"Goddammit, it's not about closure!" Faith shouted. Tourists below them on the Memorial turned to look. Faith backed away from the wall a few steps, hobbling on the crutches. "I'm simply not going to do it anymore, and that's that."

They were both quiet for a long time. "No one has ever walked away from the department," Yorkton finally said. "Never."

"First time for everything," Faith said. It was getting harder and harder to keep the bitterness out of her voice.

"We *will* watch you. You know that, don't you?"

Faith shrugged.

"I think you're about to be a very lonely young woman, Faith," Yorkton said.

"I already am," Faith said.

Yorkton tried one more time. "You can*not* just quit Department Thirty."

"Watch me," Faith said, turned the crutches around, and hobbled away.